"WHY DID YOU DO THAT?"

"Do what?" Conor's voice was husky.

"Kiss me." Lizzy closed her eyes and shuddered as he caught her earlobe between his teeth and nibbled.

Finally he raised his head to meet her gaze. "Moon madness," he said, before he bent again to continue his sensual assault.

She felt a shiver of sensation as he nuzzled her neck, kissed her chin. "Moon madness?"

"Aye," he murmured against her skin.

"I don't think——"

"Good. Don't." His head came up quickly, and she could see desire in his blue eyes. The golden glow of the lamplight added shadows to his rugged features.

"Lizzy," he whispered, and she watched his thick eyelashes move as he lowered his gaze to her lips. "What have you done to me?"

She shivered, alarmed, flattered, and most of all confused by these new feelings he stirred. "It's not too late for you to go," she whispered. "You can leave and forget this ever happened."

"Well now, that's where you're wrong, Lizzy lass," he said, his voice husky. "I can't just leave, and I most certainly will not forget this."

Other Zebra Books by Candace McCarthy

IRISH LACE
FIREHEART
WILD INNOCENCE
SWEET POSSESSION
WHITE BEAR'S WOMAN
IRISH LINEN
HEAVEN'S FIRE
SEA MISTRESS
RAPTURE'S BETRAYAL
WARRIOR'S CARESS
SMUGGLER'S WOMAN

With stories in these Zebra collections:

IRISH ENCHANTMENT
BABY IN A BASKET
AFFAIRS OF THE HEART

IRISH ROGUE

CANDACE MCCARTHY

ZEBRA BOOKS
Kensington Publishing Corp.
http://www.kensingtonbooks.com

ZEBRA BOOKS are published by

Kensington Publishing Corp.
850 Third Avenue
New York, NY 10022

All Kensington titles, imprints, and distributed lines are available at special quantity discounts for bulk purchases for sales promotion, premiums, fund-raising, educational or institutional use.

Special book excerpts or customized printings can also be created to fit specific needs. For details, write or phone the office of the Kensington Special Sales Manager: Kensington Publishing Corp., 850 Third Avenue, New York, NY 10022. Attn. Special Sales Department. Phone: 1-800-221-2647.

Zebra and the Z logo Reg. U.S. Pat. & TM Off.

First Printing: December 2001
10 9 8 7 6 5 4 3 2 1

Printed in the United States of America

For Donna Fasano . . .
A true friend and a wonderful writer.
Here's to friendship and brazen brides!
Love you, girl!

PROLOGUE

Baltimore, Maryland, 1844

"Marry me, Elizabeth. You need a father for Jason, and I need a mother for my daughter Emma. You'll not want for anything. You'll have a good life."

Lizzy gazed at John Foley with uncertainty. The older man had become her friend over the last several months. A regular customer at the Bread and Barrel Inn where she worked, he would come in for a meal and a mug of ale, and they would talk. She had learned through the course of time and many conversations that he was a widower who came from Kent County across the Chesapeake. She had suspected that he had initially come to find female companionship and an escape from the loneliness he suffered after his wife's passing two years before. From the way he had spoken of Millicent over time, it had been clear that he hadn't been interested in finding another wife. He had been visiting a woman for the physical comfort she afforded him. And now as a result of that relationship there was a child out of wedlock . . . a child unwanted by her mother.

"John, I . . ." She shook her head. "You're speaking of marriage . . ." After a wary glance at the waiting customers, she got up from the table to return to work. "Why me?"

Those words still lingered in her mind as she hefted heavy ale mugs and brought food to a table.

"Woman! I'm still waitin' for me mug!" one ill-mannered patron shouted from the other side of the room. Lizzy cringed. She was tired of such treatment. Tired of working long hours for little money. Tired of wondering how she would provide herself and Jason with decent food, lodging, and clothing.

"It's right here, Mr. Jones," she said as she came up to the man's table. The customer stank of sour sweat and stale liquor.

Jones scowled as he impatiently grabbed a mug, nearly unseating the filled tray from her hands. "About time," he snarled. "Farley," he called to the manager as the man came out of the back room, "when are ya going to hire a decent girl?"

The innkeeper glared at Lizzy as she flashed him a brief glance while she served the rest of the ale.

"Woman! Can't ya see I've an empty glass! I'll have another!"

Jaw tensing, her anger building, she nodded. "Yes, sir."

The smell of cheap ale and greasy food made her stomach tighten as Lizzy went back to the bar with the empty tray. She filled the requested mug and grabbed two dinners for the couple sitting at the table in the corner.

She swayed a bit as she got a whiff of the poorly prepared and malodorous food on the plates she carried. As she made her way toward the table, a wave of nausea overcame her.

"Lizzy." John Foley's soft voice reached her as she passed by. "Stop on your way back." His smile was a welcome change from the other present, grumbling customers at the Bread and Barrel. "Please. We have to discuss this."

"If I can," she replied. How could she discuss marriage?

As she studied her surroundings and found them depressing, she thought, *How can I not?*

While she delivered the food and drink, she thought of John's tempting offer. John was old enough to be her father. But she had a child to provide for, and John knew and was willing to provide for the boy as if Jason were his own.

Working at the inn was the last thing she had wanted to do, but what other choice did she have before? Now John Foley, a kind man, was offering her a better life. Shouldn't she take it? She wanted to, but marrying him would mean giving up the dream of marrying for love. Could she accept that? Accept John?

As John had asked, she stopped by his table. He gestured for her to sit down. After a quick glance to see that the manager had gone in the back room, she wiped her hands on her apron and sat.

John's fingers surrounded the hand she rested on the tabletop. "Elizabeth," he said quietly. "Beth . . . I'll asking you again to marry me." His smile was gentle. "I'm not ask anything from you but to be a mother for my child."

"But—"

"You can trust me to take care of you."

She knew John was sincere. "I know." Still, what of his needs? Would he expect her to—?

"You'll have your own bedchamber," he said.

She blinked up at him, startled. Had he read her mind?

"You were wondering, weren't you?"

"Yes." Her cheeks burned as she blushed.

"Then, set your mind at ease." He squeezed her hand. "I only ask that you run the household as a wife should." He smiled. "Pretend a mild affection for me in public. And, to be a good mother to Emma and Jason. In return, you'll have a good home, whatever you need for you and the boy, and my undying gratitude that you've agreed to be my wife."

"And that's all?"

His smile reached his eyes. "Aye. I'll not ask you to share my bed. I loved my wife. She was everything to me. The arrangement I'm suggesting allows me to be married for the sake of the children without betraying the love I had—have—for my dear late wife."

What more could she ask?

She fought the tiny notion that again sprang to mind that she would be giving up the hope of true love. "Beth?" He looked at her expectantly.

Her back hurt. Her heart ached. But she had to think of Jason. "Yes, John," she whispered. "I'll marry you."

ONE

"Elizabeth Foley needs our help. Conor, I'd like for ya to go to Milly's Station and get her affairs in order."

"But there is much to be done here on Green Lawns," Conor McDermott said. "I can spare a day perhaps, but—"

Rian Quaid shook his head. "Kathleen and I thought ya would manage the Foley estate for a month, at least."

"A month!" The Irishman glanced from Rian to Kathleen, Rian's wife. "But how will ya manage?" He had been foreman of Green Lawns for a year now. Peterson, the man who had previously been in charge, was getting older and slowing down. The man had been more than happy to hand over the reins to Conor, stepping back to work lighter duties on the plantation.

His employer smiled. "With Peterson and his son Jack's help. Jack has proven to be a fine workman."

"Aye, I know, but—"

"Please, Conor." The soft sound of Kathleen's voice shivered along the Irishman's spine. She approached Conor and touched his arm. "Do it for Lizzy."

He felt a jolt as he stared at her. Why should he do

it for a woman he didn't know? But for the Quaids . . . that was something else.

"Do it for us," she urged, as if she had read his mind. "Since John's death, Lizzy has had a rough time. She knew nothing about the workings of the plantation when her husband was alive. Now when she has the full responsibility of running the farm, her employees have been less than respectful to her and little help. She's had to rid herself of a couple of the workers, but she cannot fire them all."

"Why me?" Conor asked. "Surely, there's someone else to go."

Rian made a face. "Do ya have to ask, friend?" He gestured toward the parlor sofa, then took a seat across from Conor. Kathleen went to her husband's side and perched on the arm of his chair.

"Ye're our best man, Conor McDermott," Kathleen said.

Rian nodded. "There is no one else we'd trust with the task."

Conor grinned. He couldn't help it. How could one not be flattered?

But then his good humor faded as he thought of the coming month, when he would be gone from Green Lawns, gone from the people he regarded as family. And he would be working for Lizzy Foley, the mistress of Milly's Station, helping the brazen young woman who had seduced John Foley for his money, and him old enough to be her father.

The Quaids were good people, too kind to think poorly of anyone. Conor sighed. " 'Tis just for a month, ya say?"

"Aye," Rian and Kathleen said at the same time.

"Put yer mind at rest," Kathleen said. "Yer job will be waiting here for ya when ya return."

"Well, Conor, what do ya say? Will ya go and help our friend Lizzy?"

How could he refuse these two wonderful people?

He would do it, because they had asked it of him.
Conor stood. "Aye," he said quietly. "I'll go."

Kathleen sprang up from the chair arm and across
the distance to give him a hug. "Thank ya!"

Rian shared his wife's gratitude as he rose to join
them. "We appreciate this, Conor." He shook Conor's
hand. "Lizzy Foley is a good friend. It's important to
Kathleen—to us—that her affairs are put in good order."

"We hate the thought of losing ya for a full month,"
Kathleen said. "But we feel it's the only way."

"I may return to visit during the month's time?"

Kathleen frowned. "Of course. Ya must. We insist."

Conor nodded. "I'll get me things together, then."

The wind caught hold of the wet bed linen on the
clothesline and flapped it against Lizzy as she bent
down to retrieve a wet garment. It was a warm spring
day, a perfect day for hanging out the wash, and so
Lizzy had chosen to do the chore herself. She needed
the air and busy work. Mrs. Potts, Milly's Station's
cook and housekeeper, had been cold and silent since
yesterday morning. The housekeeper had apparently
taken exception to the way Lizzy had intervened with
the woman's authority with one of the chambermaids.

It was a pleasure to be outside away from the tension
in the house, away from the memories.

Lizzy thought of her situation and felt a sniggle of
fear. Kathleen said that she and Rian would find a way
to help. She hadn't wanted to confide her fears, but
with Kathleen, it was hard to keep silent. They had
been friends from the first.

She sighed. As promised, the Quaids had arranged
for assistance for her. Help was coming in the form
of Conor McDermott, a foreman from the Quaids' estate. Kathleen had assured her that she could trust Mr.

McDermott, and Lizzy was grateful that the man had agreed to help her.

A strand of blond hair was pulled from her hairpin, and the wind teased it about her face. She brushed it back and attempted to tuck it into place, but it slipped free to tickle and caress her skin. With a chuckle, she pulled out all the pins and allowed her hair loose to fly in the breeze as she went back to her chore. Dragging out a pair of Jason's trousers, she shook them out, then held on tightly as she draped and secured them over the clothesline.

Seeing Jason's garment made her think of the children. She would make this plantation work for the little ones. Her dear husband was gone, but the children lived on. She would do right by them, no matter what it took, even if it meant accepting a stranger's help.

She only hoped that Conor McDermott would treat her with more respect than some of her other employees.

She had seen McDermott, but never spoken to him. Would he be amicable? Brusque?

She reached into the clothes basket for another garment. Picking up one of Emma's gowns, she shook it out and hung it beside Jason's trousers.

The damp garments flapped in the breeze, the sound pleasant to Lizzy as it brought back memories of her childhood and helping her mother with the wash. Those had been good times. She felt a pang in the region of her heart as she remembered her loving parents. Their death had been a terrible loss. Even now, years later, she still missed them.

She grabbed a stocking and dropped it by accident onto the clothes pile. Bending to retrieve it, she felt a sudden stiff breeze rustle her skirts, raising them to show her ankles. She laughed as she straightened, trying to hold down her skirts and keep hold of the stocking at the same time.

And that was how Conor McDermott found her . . .

laughing, battling to secure skirts that the wind struggled to keep free.

The man stopped in his tracks when he heard the feminine laughter and saw the woman near the clothesline. Conor approached her with a smile. She was too busy to notice him as he got within several yards of her.

"Good day to ya, lass!" he called. He heard her gasp as she spun to face him.

"I didn't see you!"

His lips curved as he set down his satchel. "Ya were busy tryin' to take hold of the wind, it seemed."

She responded to his smile with a grin that made his heart thump in his chest. " 'Tis a beautiful day, though, isn't it?"

"Aye," he said. " 'Tis, indeed. May I help ya with that?" He stepped up to assist and quickly grabbed an article of clothing that had become caught up in a gust of wind and torn loose from her hand. He extended the garment to her with a smile that widened into a grin as she looked down and blushed at the realization that he held a pair of lady's bloomers.

"Ya don't want to lose these now, do ya?" he said with amusement.

She shook her head as she averted her gaze.

"Mrs. Foley would be upset with ya, now, if ya did such a thing."

She looked at him, startled. "Is there something I can do for you, Mr. McDermott?"

"Ya know who I am?"

Lizzy smiled, for it was the man's turn to be surprised. The amusement became hers as she realized that he had no idea who she was. "I've seen you before."

"Ye've seen me before, ya say?" His blue gaze became speculative. "Well, I've not seen ya," he said, watching her closely. "I'd have remembered ya, lass, if I'd laid eyes on ya."

Her lips twitched. "Would you now?"

"Aye, that I would." His grin was flirtatious.

"Are you searching for someone?"

"Is the mistress at home?"

"Do you have business with her?"

"Could be that I do."

She smiled. "Mysterious, are you?"

"If ya like me that way."

Her heart thumped hard. She had had no idea that McDermott was such a charmer. "What I like matters not."

"Well, I think it does, lass."

Dangerous, she thought. The man was dangerous. She would have to watch herself with him.

A shout from across the farm field drew the man's gaze to where several workers had congregated together, laughing and joking. McDermott's face hardened. Lizzy, seeing his expression, felt her own annoyance, for she knew that the men weren't earning their pay.

The Irishman turned frosty eyes in her direction. Gone was the charm; in its place was a look of purpose. "Ya said the mistress was about?" he asked her.

Stunned by the change in him, she nodded. He must have sensed her shock, for suddenly he smiled. "I'll have me a look and find her, then. Good day to ya, lass." And he left her standing at the clothesline gaping at him as he retrieved his satchel and started toward the house. He was nearly at the back door when she found her voice and realized that she had to tell him who she was. For a time, she had almost forgotten.

Caught up in the light flirtation with the handsome Irishman, she had once again been Lizzy Hanlin and not Elizabeth Foley, a widow with too many responsibilities and little leisure time. It was her responsibilities that were gnawing at her mind presently as she threw the last of the wash over the clothesline. It was her duties and concerns as mistress of Milly's Station that had her leaving the laundry basket behind and hurrying toward the house.

She heard the argument before she got to the open kitchen doorway.

"I said to you that the mistress isn't here, you upstart," Mrs. Potts shouted angrily.

"And I replied that she is somewhere about," Conor McDermott returned with impatient authority. "She's expecting me."

Lizzy quickly entered as her cook opened her mouth to lambaste the man again. "I'll handle this, Mrs. Potts," she said sharply. "Check on Ruth upstairs," she said, referring to the chambermaid who had been the topic of discussion between the two of them earlier.

The woman flashed her an irritated glance, but at the sound of Ruth's name, she grunted and obeyed.

Feeling a new tension in the man, Lizzy turned to McDermott. "Welcome to Milly's Station, Mr. McDermott. I'm Elizabeth Hanlin Foley."

The sudden chill that entered the man's expression rattled her.

"I'm glad you're here. Kathleen said you'd be the man to assist me. If you'll come with me, I'll show you to your room."

"I'll sleep above the stables." His tone wasn't friendly.

"Fine." A knot formed and hardened in her stomach. "I'll show you the way."

"I can find me way."

She raised her chin, stiffened her spine, and stared at him. "I will show you to your room, Conor McDermott," she said with cold authority.

She turned, unsure whether or not the look he had given her had been a grudging look of respect. She hoped so. She could live without the man's liking as long as she had his respect. She was mistress of Milly's Station, and he was here to help her regain control of the employees, to ensure that the estate ran smoothly and that the books stayed solid and the farm profitable. As long as they managed to discuss these concerns dispassionately, it didn't matter what McDermott thought of her.

Liar, she thought. She had had an earlier enjoyable moment with him. It bothered her that they would share no more. It had been wonderful feeling young and free. It had been a long time since she had been viewed as anything other than the young woman who had seduced John Foley and tricked him into marriage.

She brushed by him on her way out the door without waiting for him. Her heart raced wildly in her breast as she hoped he would follow her.

How would they manage if he didn't respect her authority? She had him pegged as a man who didn't need to yell in order to wield power. He would just have to say a word or give someone a look, and the victim would no doubt jump to his bidding.

Except me, she thought. She would remain immune to him.

As she crossed the yard, she heard his footsteps on the dry dirt behind her, and she sighed inwardly with relief. Whatever the man thought of her, he was wise enough to honor her position.

TWO

"Ya didn't tell me that ya were Elizabeth Foley." McDermott's deep, cold voice came to her from behind as they neared the barn. "Why didn't ya?"

She stiffened, but didn't turn as she reached for the stable door. "I meant to." She couldn't say more. How could she explain that she had been enjoying their flirtation too much? That she had forgotten about their positions, their roles?

He didn't reply as she entered the building ahead of him, and led him toward a set of stairs that rose to the loft above.

"This is the only stable room vacant," she said with apology in her voice. "Tell me what you need to make your stay comfortable, and I shall see that you get it." She faced him, meeting his frosty blue gaze squarely. "I appreciate that you've come, Conor McDermott," she said softly.

He inhaled sharply, then looked away. "I'll have ya a list by morning of the things I need. And ya don't have to worry; it won't be a long list." He shot her a dark glance. "Thank ya for showing me to me room."

She stood a moment to watch him wander about the loft room. "I'll leave you to get settled. Come to the house for supper. We'll be eating at six."

He paused to give her an abrupt nod.

"Good afternoon to you then," she said.

Lizzy felt rebuffed at the man's dismissal of her. Then, with her heart beating rapidly in her breast, she left to return to the day's chores she had set before her.

From the loft window, McDermott watched Elizabeth Foley as she returned to the house. He was annoyed. He had thought he had been talking with a servant only to learn that he had been flirting with the mistress of the manor house.

She was a comely lass. Was it any wonder that John Foley had become enamored of her? But a pretty face could not hide a hard heart . . . a heart that would allow a young woman to take advantage of a much older, kindly man.

He forced her from his mind as he went about unpacking his satchel and settling into his new temporary residence.

Later that evening, he crossed the yard to the house for supper. He smelled a delicious aroma as he knocked on the back door and entered the house at the invitation of a manservant who introduced himself as Jamieson.

"Mrs. Foley is expecting you, Mr. McDermott," Jamieson said. "She's in the dining room and asks that you join her there."

Conor nodded and followed the thin elderly man through the house to the room. He paused near the doorway as Jamieson announced his arrival; then annoyed at the formality, he stood a moment longer and studied the interior.

"Mr. McDermott," she said. "Conor?"

He turned and stared at her. She was more than beautiful; she looked breathtaking. Gone was the carefree laundry maid. In her place was the lady of the manor at Milly's Station, the one he had known only from a distance.

Elizabeth's blond hair had been combed back and secured at her nape. Spiral curls the color of ripened wheat hung at each side of her face, softening the severity of the bun. Her figure was shown to best advantage in a lavender gown that hugged her breasts and fell in full skirts to the floor. Her sleeves reached to just below her elbows, revealing dainty forearms and wrists. An expanse of her soft skin was exposed at the neck and drew his eye to the scooped neckline where he could see the upper swells of lush, feminine mounds.

He caught his breath, fought back the desire, and won.

"Please," she said, gesturing toward a chair. "Be seated."

And it was then that he realized they were not alone. Dragging his gaze from the woman before him, he focused on the two children who sat primly at the dining table.

"Mr. McDermott, this is Jason," she introduced the young boy, who looked to be about ten years old. Jason seemed familiar to him. "And this is Emma."

"I'm six," the little girl said with a smile.

Enchanted, Conor grinned at her, and Emma beamed back.

He sat in the seat designated for him, feeling awkward in the fancy room. Another glance toward little Emma awarded him a lovely smile, and he sat back, relaxed, determined not to allow the mother to affect him.

All was quiet as a young servant girl brought in the evening meal. There was roast chicken, peas, and freshly baked bread with creamy butter.

"You work with the horses at Green Lawns," Jason said as he picked up a piece of bread and spread butter over the slice. "I love Mr. Quaid's horses, especially

Midnight. I think we should raise horses here on Milly's Station."

"Jason!" his mother warned.

Conor raised an eyebrow. Now he recalled where he had seen the boy, in the Green Lawn stables with Thomas, the groom. "It's profitable to raise good horseflesh. Would like to work with the fillies, would ya?"

The boy's eyes glistened. "Yes! Oh, yes! It would be a wonderful thing to do." The joy on his face faded. "But Ma says we don't have the funds or the time."

"Jason Edward!" Lizzy exclaimed, looking embarrassed.

Meeting her gaze, Conor took pity on her. "It's a fine thing to work with the animals, I must admit, but yer mother is right. It takes time and money and is a difficult thing to start."

"But you're here now, and you could do it, couldn't you?" Jason persisted, his expression hopeful.

"Aye, well, I can do it, but I'm here to assist yer mother, not start up a new business, when the old one needs attention."

The chicken was delicious, and Conor enjoyed every bite. But there wasn't enough for a man of his size, and when his supper was done, he was hungry. He would have to arrange for heartier meals if he was to accomplish a good day's work.

And then Mrs. Potts brought in a pie—a large one. When Lizzy made sure that small pieces were cut for the children, but a huge one for him, he thought he might leave the table with his hunger satisfied after all.

The pie was strawberry, topped with cream. The filling was sweet and tasty, and his tongue and stomach appreciated every mouthful he ate.

Conversation over the dinner table was almost non-existent as the four of them enjoyed their dessert with a gusto that spoke of their delight in the meal.

"This pie was the best I've ever had," Conor admitted when he had set his fork on his empty plate.

"Thank you," Lizzy said.

Mrs. Potts entered the room with a dour look as she helped the servant girl retrieve the dessert dishes.

" 'Twas a wonderful supper, Mrs. Potts," Conor told her.

The older woman managed to smile, her pleasure obvious.

"The best part was the pie. 'Tis a treat that will forever hover in me memory as the most tasty confection I've ever enjoyed."

Mrs. Potts's expression dimmed, but she merely nodded as she picked up the last of the dishes and left the room.

Watching her, Lizzy was annoyed. She had made the pie, not Mrs. Potts. But since the woman hadn't seen fit to inform Conor McDermott of the fact, it didn't seem right for Lizzy to tell him herself. Besides, she thought, it didn't matter who had made the pie. It was a pleasure just knowing that the man had enjoyed it.

Dinner had been a nice surprise. After their last conversation when he had all but snubbed her in the barn, she hadn't been sure it had been wise of her to invite him to dine. But the man had to eat, didn't he? And since he had come as a favor to help her, the least she could do was feed the man a simple meal.

She had noted his surprise at seeing the children. What thoughts had gone through his mind when he had first spied them? He had been good with the both of them, kind and patient as they had conversed with him as they ate. He bore the brunt of their childlike curiosity with patience and forbearance, while another man might have been angry at their personal questions and outspoken tongues.

She had tried not to look at him too often during the meal, but found it hard not to study him. Conor McDermott was an impressive man, both in stature and intellect. A large figure, he was a tall, brawny Irishman with broad shoulders and big arms. Add expressive blue eyes, an attractively rugged face, and dark curly hair that invited a woman's touch, and he was impossible to ignore. Next to him, she felt delicate and feminine, and she wasn't a tiny thing by any means.

"Ya haven't finished yer pie," he said, startling her into the realization that she had been staring. There was an odd look in his eyes and the hint of a smile about his lips.

"I—" She looked down to see that she had barely taken a bite. She blinked up at him. "I guess I haven't." She saw that he was eyeing her pie hungrily. "Would you like to eat it? I'm afraid I ate too much else to finish it."

"Can I have it, Ma?" Jason asked.

Lizzy shook her head as she stood and skirted the table to set it before the Irishman. "You've had enough treats today, young man. What of the cookies you had earlier?"

"But—"

"No buts," she said. "Tomorrow is another day, and there will be pie left for the midday meal." She thought then that she should offer Conor a fresh piece rather than the one she had barely touched. She opened her mouth to ask, but then saw that he wasn't bothered by the fact that she had taken one forkful. He was busy enjoying her slice as if he had been awarded a great prize and wanted to savor every moment of enjoying it.

"May I be excused?" little Emma asked.

Lizzy nodded. "You have a chore that needs doing, don't you?"

The girl nodded solemnly as she pushed back her chair. "Jason has to help."

"Jason has his own work to do."

Scowling, Jason asked to be excused, and when his

mother had granted permission, he stood. "Will we see you at breakfast?" the boy asked.

Lizzy sensed a new tension in Conor, but to the man's credit, he handled Jason's question with smiling patience. "I may be working long before ya see the outside of yer eyelids," he told the boy. "I've got me work cut out for me. I appreciate the supper, but I don't expect yer mother to feed me every meal."

"But where will you eat?" Emma asked.

"With the workers—"

"But they eat with their families, except for old John, and you wouldn't want to eat what he cooks." Jason wrinkled his nose. "His pot is black, and his food smells bad," he said softly as if he were relaying a big secret.

"Hmmm. I'd better cook for meself, then."

Jason left to attend whatever task his mother had given him, leaving the Irishman and his mother alone.

Lizzy, who had listened to the conversation with mixed feelings, surprised herself when she said, "Please, we'd be happy for you to eat with us each day."

She felt a jolt when the man focused his deep blue eyes on her.

"I wouldn't want to be any trouble."

She shook her head. "Mr. McDermott. As I said, I appreciate that you're here. It's only right that I feed you, and it will be my pleasure to." She gave him a determined look. "And I'll not take no for an answer."

A spark of amusement lit up his face. "Will there be more treats the likes of this strawberry pie?" He finished the last bite and sighed with pleasure as he put down his fork.

She nodded. "And more."

"I may come to eat when I can."

"There'll be a place set for you."

Finished, he stood. "May I see the books?"

"Of course." Lizzy pushed back a chair and led him

down the hall to the room that her late husband John had used as his study and office. She went to the large mahogany desk that sat in a prominent spot in the room and opened a bottom drawer to pull out a ledger book. "I've gone over these figures and done the best I could to keep them current, but I'm afraid there are notations that John made that I don't understand. And I think there might be another book." She studied the Irishman over the sleek expanse of desk. Her dear friend Kathleen Quaid had assured her that she could trust Conor McDermott with all matters relating to the farm, and she would do so.

"Please feel free to go through John's things," she told him.

He watched her carefully, his blue gaze steady, making her heart skitter. "Thank ya."

Reluctant to leave, she stared back at him, until unnerved by her body's reaction to him, she looked away. "I'll be in the kitchen. If you need anything, please let me know."

Still studying her, he inclined his head.

She left him as he sat behind the huge desk where her husband had once sat, and was aware of the difference in the two men's stature and her reaction to both.

He was in John's study for a long time. She had just heard the hall clock chime the ninth hour when he poked his head into the parlor where she sat doing needlework.

"I'll be going now."

"Will you be here for breakfast?" She saw the struggle in his expression and felt it within herself. "I'm up before the sun, so you'll not have to worry about troubling me from my sleep."

Conor looked at the woman who sat in the pale golden light and tried to harden himself against the allure of her. But a man had to eat, didn't he? And it would be a foolish man not to take advantage of good food when the alternative was to fix it himself.

"If ye're sure 'tis no trouble."

She nodded, and his gaze settled on her pinned hair while he fought the urge to unpin it.

"Then, I'll be here."

She could see him staring at her, and he heard her catch her breath. "Good night, then," she said softly.

"Good night to ya, Mrs. Foley," he said, reminding himself that she was John Foley's widow. He tore his gaze away from her and then let himself out the door.

Lizzy stared at the open archway where Conor McDermott had stood and tried to still her rapidly beating heart. It was going to be a long month if she couldn't learn to control her reaction to him. It had been obvious throughout dinner that while he enjoyed the children he had little regard for her.

He believes what others say of me. And the knowledge made her sad. For while she knew it would be dangerous to become involved with the handsome Irishman, she had hoped for respect if not friendship from him. But he wouldn't respect the woman who had seduced and married John Foley for his money.

THREE

There was only one thing worse than attempting to fight an attraction to a beautiful woman; it was losing the battle in the war upon settling his gaze on Lizzy, who wore a decidedly sleepy look in her lovely brown eyes. Elizabeth Foley was up and fully dressed in a simple calico gown that affected his body more than any ball dress could have done. But the softness in her expression and the tousled hair were what appealed to him the most . . . until he found himself wishing for something that shouldn't be.

So he reminded himself that she was a seductress. A schemer. And he was able to harden his heart against her enough to behave brisk and businesslike as he entered the back door.

"Good morning."

She flashed him a smile over her shoulder. "Good morning. Please, be seated."

She turned back to the stove as he seated himself at a small dining table and took a moment to study his surroundings.

The Foley kitchen was a room for family gatherings as well as for preparing meals. Baskets and fragrant dried herbs hung from the ceiling beams. Fresh-cut spring flowers sat in a vase on the tabletop, where Lizzy had placed table settings for four. He had an impression of white walls, brick hearth, and a wooden floor, all clean and in good repair.

"You're quiet this morning." Drawing his attention back to her, Lizzy Foley smiled at him brightly as she brought him a dish that she had filled at the stove.

" 'Tis up earlier than the sun ye've been to provide such a feast for me." He was surprised to see her blush. "Where is Mrs. Potts?"

"I enjoy cooking." She said it simply and sincerely.

Thoughtful, he narrowed his gaze at her. Not a word about Mrs. Potts. "Ya made the pie."

Her pleased look gave him her answer before she spoke. "I love to bake as well."

He remembered then that Rian Quaid had a fondness for her treats as well as those made for him by Kathleen.

" 'Tis a foolish man who doesn't appreciate such a fine talent in a woman."

"And you're not a fool?" she asked.

He raised an eyebrow. "I'm no one's fool."

And the sudden clipped tone of his response banished the pleasure in her gaze before she spun away to return to the stove.

She filled her plate with less than she had given him. There were eggs, ham, and biscuits. Tension filled the air as she sat down at the table with him.

Conor felt bad. "I'm in a foul mood this mornin'. I'm afraid ye've bore the brunt of it, and I beg yer pardon."

Lizzy paused in the act of scooping up a forkful of eggs and looked at him. "You've a right to your opinion of me. There is no need to apologize."

She had been hurt by his comment, only because it brought home to her how little he liked or respected her. How much he believed in the stories that circulated about her in the village.

"Mrs. Foley," he began.

"I'd appreciate it if you'd call me Elizabeth or Lizzy,

so at least there is a pretense of friendship between us."

"Then, you can't very well call me Mr. McDermott. 'Tis Conor."

She nodded. She had known his given name. She had slipped and called him by that name when he had first appeared for supper the night before.

"Say it," he ordered.

She blinked. "Excuse me?"

"Say me name, and I'll say yers, and we can start the mornin' over."

Lizzy gazed at him, feeling flustered. The man was not acting as she had thought. "Conor," she said quietly.

"I cannot hear ya."

"Conor," she repeated loudly.

His teeth flashed, and the sight of his grin made her heart stop, then start to race. "Aye, 'tis me. And ya'd be Elizabeth Foley, but I shall call ya Lizzy." He held out his hand, wrist up, over the table.

She stared at his palm and found she could hardly breathe. Because he expected it of her and because she sensed the gesture was made in a real willingness to try again, she gave him her hand. His fingers were warm and firm, and callused, and she had never enjoyed a man's handshake such as this.

"Pleased that it is for me to meet ya, Lizzy Foley."

She stared at him, searching for a response, as he held her hand and played havoc with her senses. "Thank you, Conor," she finally managed to say. "I'm glad that you've come. The pleasure of our meeting is mine."

He smiled at her, and she relaxed as she pulled her hand back. She could still feel the warmth of his fingers when she was no longer touching him.

"I thought I would introduce meself to the workers today and see what stage and condition yer crops are in."

She nodded. It was a sound plan.

"Can ya tell me what it is that's been planted?" he asked.

"Our main crop is tobacco, but we've planted corn, flax, and wheat, too."

"Ya export most of yer tobacco?"

"Yes," she said, recalling what little her late husband had told her. "I'm afraid that John handled the business of the plantation." She couldn't help but feel a bit guilty for not learning more, so that she could be prepared in the event he had taken ill. She had never expected John to die so young.

Tears filled her eyes as she thought of him . . . such a kind and gentle man. They hadn't shared a bed, but they had shared affection, a love for each other and the children . . . and a caring for their home.

"Lizzy?" Conor saw the tears in the woman's eyes and was surprised by them. "Are ya all right? Ye're not feelin' ill?"

She blinked them away. "No, I'm fine. Thank you." She met his gaze and managed to smile. "It's still hard to believe he's gone." Her soft voice was filled with sadness.

"Ya cared for him." He didn't know what surprised him more, that she had cared for John Foley or that he believed that she did.

"Yes, I did." Her eyes reflected hurt that he had doubted it. "He was a wonderful, kind man and a good husband."

"Rian Quaid respected him."

Lizzy's expression softened. "Rian Quaid is a good man and a good friend."

Her regard for Rian Quaid almost made him feel jealous of the man. Almost, he thought. For he couldn't be jealous because of Lizzy Foley. He couldn't be.

He pushed back his chair and stood. "I enjoyed breakfast," he said. "Thank ya."

She nodded as she, too, rose. "I'll have the midday meal ready for you as well."

Something inside Conor objected. It wasn't a good idea for him to feel too comfortable in the Foley household. It would be best to stay away from one Mrs. Elizabeth Foley. "I may not make the midday meal. I'll start the morning here at Milly's Station, then I need to head back to Green Lawns for a time before returning this afternoon."

"Then, you will be here for supper?" She seemed hopeful that he would.

The look on her face made all thoughts of avoiding her disappear. "Aye, I'll be here." He smiled. "Especially if ya make another confection for me to enjoy."

Her lips curved upward in response. "Do you like cake as well as pie?"

He nodded.

"Cake it will be, then."

He left her, strolling out of the back door that he had come in through. The last sight of her had her pulling out the ingredients for baking. He couldn't stop the smile that lingered on his lips as he made his way to inspect the land and speak with the field hands.

The children came running down the stairs just as Lizzy put the first cake pan into the oven. Jason burst into the room first.

"Ma," he gasped. "Can I go to Green Lawns today? Mr. Quaid said I could come help Thomas in the stables."

Lizzy looked at him as she wiped her hands on her apron. It amazed her how much the boy loved working with horses. From the nastiest chore of mucking out the stables to brushing the sleek coat of a prized thoroughbred, he enjoyed it all. And thanks to Rian Quaid's patient tutoring of the boy, Jason was in his glory.

"I don't know if it's the best day for you to go."

She went to the stove and began to cook the children breakfast.

"Why not?" Despite his disappointment, there was no whining in Jason's tone. Since John's death, the boy had been a big help to her.

"I may need you to help me make a list of supplies for when old Joe goes to Baltimore."

"If we do that this morning, can I go after the noon meal?"

She spooned some eggs onto Jason's plate, then turned to him with a smile. "How will you get there?"

"I'm old enough to go by myself. I'm almost eleven."

"And I'm a worrier, so you'll have Georgie take you and bring you back."

Jason grinned.

Emma glided into the room then, a graceful child who could at times be a whirlwind of energy. "Good morning, Mother."

Lizzy's lips twitched as she tried to control a smile. "Good morning, Miss Emma." It was clear that little Emma was to play the proper lady today, and so Lizzy would go along with it. "Would you enjoy some eggs and a jelly biscuit this morning, Miss Emma?" she asked, knowing the girl's response.

"Thank you, Mother," the little girl replied. "That would be delightful."

"Sit down, Emma," Jason said.

The child pouted. "Miss Emma."

Lizzy flashed Jason a warning look. "Please," he said softly. "Miss Emma."

Emma nodded. Then with a huge grin, she abandoned her role long enough to bounce into a chair. She sat swinging her legs as Lizzy fixed and brought her breakfast.

"I smell chocolate," Emma said as she raised a fork of eggs toward her mouth.

"You making only a chocolate cake, Ma?" Jason inquired. He preferred vanilla himself.

Lizzy smiled at him as she began to whip up the second batter that Jason preferred. "I'm making vanilla, too."

"Good!" He flashed Emma a satisfied glance.

"I like both," she retorted, sounding smug.

"You were on your best behavior last night at dinner," Lizzy said as she regarded them with a smile. "Thank you."

"When he goes back to Green Lawns, do you think Mr. McDermott will let me help with the horses. Thomas lets me help, but he always tells me not to bother Mr. McDermott. But Mr. McDermott seems nice to me. Do you suppose he'll let me?"

"I don't know, Jason." Lizzy's heart thumped hard within her breast. "He's only just come."

"Yes, but he's only to be here for a time. He'll be going back someday, right?"

She nodded, an odd little ache settling in her chest. "That he will." Why should she care if he left when she barely knew him?

Because during the short time he's been here he's made me feel more like a woman than all the years of my life before now.

The thought remained in her mind through the rest of the morning and past the afternoon until she was feeling a bit jittery as she made supper. Mrs. Potts hadn't bothered to come in this day. The fact that she hadn't alerted her bothered Lizzy, who felt she had little control over the servants.

Well, she wouldn't put up with this behavior any more! Mrs. Potts and she had reached an understanding while her husband John had still been alive. Now it seemed that the woman might be slipping into her old ways, and she didn't have to tolerate it! Surely there were other women looking for work who could help out at the house. If not, she would take care of the kitchen chores herself.

Fortunately, John's manservant, Jamieson, had remained faithful to her. He was kindness in itself, always willing to help out the "missus" as he called her. But Jamieson knew only certain aspects of the running of the house. She couldn't ask him to step in and take over some of Mrs. Potts's responsibilities, could she? Not the cooking, but overseeing the household servants—the small number that they employed?

If he couldn't manage the chore, she thought, she would do so. She was more than capable of handling the house, as long as McDermott was here to help with the running of the farm.

She would learn what she could from McDermott and be well able to do everything with confidence by the time he left Milly's Station.

The house was filled with the smell of beef stew when the time arrived for supper.

Lizzy pulled a pan from the baking hearth and studied the golden brown muffins with satisfaction.

"Jason! Emma! Did you set the table?"

"Yes, Ma." Jason appeared at the archway to the hall, young Emma behind him. "Just like you said."

Lizzy smiled at him. "You're a good little man."

"And so you'll ask Mr. McDermott if I can visit him when he leaves?"

"I will," she said. "But not today. He'll be here awhile so there is no reason to ask him now. If you're good and prove to be helpful to him, I'm sure he won't object."

She hoped she was right. She knew little of Conor McDermott but what Kathleen had told her. But from what her friend had said, he was a good and honorable man.

Could she blame him if he believed the neighbors' gossip? That he thought so little of her that he seemed surprised that she had loved John?

She hadn't given him a time, so she set the meal to keep warm and waited for him to come. When the clock chimed the half hour after six, she wondered if he would show.

She knew he had returned from Green Lawns, for she had seen him out near the stables midafternoon. He had been deep in conversation with Fetts, the groom. Then later he had been in the fields, she knew, for when she was out in the garden earlier she had heard one of the workers complaining about what a taskmaster the new foreman was.

So where was he? Had he changed his mind about coming? Had she cooked all this food for nothing? For she had made enough to feed five men rather than just one, having realized that the last meal she had given him had barely been enough for a man of his size and stature.

And there were the cakes she had baked—two of them. One was vanilla, Jason's favorite, and the other was chocolate with rich chocolate frosting and a raspberry preserve filling.

"Ma, I'm hungry," Jason said. "When is Mr. McDermott coming?"

"I don't know, Jason. I imagine any time now."

"Can I have a muffin?"

"May I," she corrected.

"May I have a muffin?"

"When he gets here."

"What if he doesn't come?"

Her heart thumped. "If he doesn't come by seven, then we'll eat. He may have been held up in a meeting with the men."

"Georgie said that some of the men don't like him," Jason confided, confirming what Lizzy had overheard earlier. "But Georgie does, and so does Mr. Brant. He says that Mr. McDermott has a quiet authority about him. He's not mean-spirited or bossy. He simply sees what must be done and ensures that the job is completed."

Lizzy looked at the boy. "Georgie said that?" It was what she had envisioned the man to be. To have her gut instincts confirmed by a child and a worker told her to trust her instincts. *With the farm,* she thought. *But not the heart.*

And a knock sounded on the door.

"I'll get it!" Jason cried, and Lizzy was only too happy to let him answer it.

She heard Jason greeting Conor McDermott before the tall, brawny Irishman entered the room.

FOUR

"Markins. Brant." Conor nodded at each man. "Where are the others?" He stood in the yard and waited for the workers to gather.

"They're coming," Brant said.

"All but Pherson," Markins added.

"Well, ya find Mr. Pherson and inform him that if he doesn't come, he'll have to find himself new employment."

Markins's eyes widened. "Will do, Mr. McDermott." And the man ran off to do his bidding.

Within minutes everyone had assembled in the yard. It was quitting time, but no one dared to defy the new foreman. Even Pherson had come, reluctantly and unhappily, but he had come nevertheless.

"As ya are all aware, me name is Conor McDermott and I'll be running Milly's Station for a time. Anyone have a problem with that?" His gaze ran across the motley group of ten men and settled on the man Pherson. "Mr. Pherson, how is Mrs. Pherson?" he asked.

The man seemed surprised by McDermott's knowledge of his wife. "She's due any day, sir."

"I thought so. See me after we're done here."

A flash of alarm settled in the man's expression, but he nodded.

"I'm unhappy with the work production here,"

Conor told them. "And I hear that some of ya have been giving the missus a bit of trouble. If I hear of that again, ye'll be gone so fast, ya won't know what to do with yer belongings."

"Brant—Markins—I want a word with each of ya tomorrow mornin'. I've got a few changes in mind for the running of this plantation, and I'll need some capable men to help me deal with them."

"Aye, Mr. McDermott," Brant replied.

"Yes, sir," said the other man.

"Pherson, I understand that yer eldest son has been helping Mr. Fetts in the stables. See that he comes earlier to the stables. The stalls need some extra work. The horses we have may not be of breeding stock, but they provide a service to Milly's Station and its people. Ya must take proper care of them."

Pherson nodded.

"I'll be meeting with each one of ya over the next week. We'll discuss what is expected from ya and what ya can expect from me. Don't get yerself in a worrisome state, for it may be a simple thing for the most of ya."

The sun had set, and twilight had brought a dusty haze to the barn and surrounding outbuildings. "Now, go home to yer wives and families, lads. I'll see ya bright and early in the mornin'."

He dismissed the men, all but Pherson, who came closer, looking wary. "Yer wife is with child, I hear, Mr. Pherson."

"Yes, sir."

"Due any time is she?"

The man nodded.

"Well, I don't mind ya bein' in a hurry to go home to her, just keep me informed, will ya? A man likes to know who's with him and who's not."

Appreciation shimmered in Pherson's eyes. "Yes, sir. I'm sorry, sir. It's just that I've been powerful anxious about the babe. My wife—she's not as young as she used to be."

Conor nodded. "I understand, and of course ya should be near her when ya can. When her time comes, ya tell me, and I'll see what I can do to help."

Pherson's expression held surprise. "Thank you, Mr. McDermott."

"What's yer name, Mr. Pherson."

"Henry, sir."

"Well, Henry, just understand that I'm trying to do a job here, all right?"

The man bobbed his head. "Yes, sir. Thank you again, sir."

"Now go home to yer wife and wish her the best from me."

With a grin, Pherson left.

When the last man left for his home, Conor glanced at the main house and thought not only of the supper that awaited him, but the woman who had prepared it.

He scowled as he headed toward the house. He didn't want to think of her. He didn't want to remember how she had looked outside handling laundry with her hair free and her simple homespun clinging attractively to her womanly figure.

Irritation with himself had him hardening himself to her charms as he knocked on the back door that led to the kitchen.

Then the door was opened by the lad Jason and he saw her standing behind him at the stove, and his annoyance left him. The scent of something delicious reached out to tease his nose. It smelled heavenly, and his stomach grumbled. And he entered the room, eager for the meal and the company.

Conor sat in John Foley's study, poring over the ledger books for the second night in a row. Dinner had been delicious. The beef stew had filled and warmed his belly, and the cake—pieces of both—had been tasty. He didn't remember when he had eaten a meal he had appreciated more.

The day had been a long one. It had started well before light and breakfast when he had heard a mewling sound in the barn. Upon getting up to investigate, he had come across a mother cat giving birth. He had watched fascinated, ready to help should the tired mother need it. When the task was done, the cat had given birth to four: one white, one black, and two calico kittens. And he had been anxious to share the news with the Foley children, but when he had gotten there, they had still been in bed. And the fact that he had been alone with their mother had made him uneasy, and perhaps less than gracious in accepting the meal.

He hoped he had made up for it over dinner, although he still had mixed feelings about coming to the main house to dine. When he had told the children of the kittens, they had been excited, and all of them, he, the children, and their mother, had hurried out to the barn immediately after the main meal to see them. Then, they had gone back to the house for dessert. And once he had gone back, it had seemed somehow wrong not to get some more work done.

So he sat in John Foley's study, behind John Foley's desk, and thought of John Foley's lovely young wife. And it angered him.

He forced himself to concentrate on the numbers, the listings, made in John Foley's hand. He saw the notations for supplies bought in Baltimore, the bushels of wheat he had planted last year during the final months of his life. . . .

"I brought you some tea." Lizzy Foley stepped into the room with a steaming teacup. He looked up. She set the cup on the desk top within his reach.

"Thank ya," he said huskily.

She inclined her head. "Any luck?"

"Yer husband's notes are out of alignment, but clear."

"I see." But she didn't. And she couldn't think straight for being near him. He was a big man, and she could feel the power of him. *Dangerous,* she thought. "If you need anything, I'll be in the parlor," she said as she turned to go.

"Mrs. Foley—"

She paused, turned, and gave him a look.

"Lizzy."

She felt her pulse race. "Yes?"

"Later this week, I'll go over these books with ya," he said. "So ye'll understand."

So he can finish his business and leave, she thought, disappointed. "All right."

"Thank ya for the tea."

"You're welcome."

"I'll be finished in a few minutes, and then I'll be heading back to me room." She watched as he took a sip of tea, and then he returned his attention to the ledger book.

"Fine." She studied his bent head for a moment. "Shall I have breakfast for you in the morning?" she asked. It would mean getting up earlier than usual again, but she didn't mind. She enjoyed cooking for him, enjoyed his company while she ate.

He raised his head and fixed his eyes on her. "If it's not too much trouble."

Her spirits lifted. "No trouble, Mr. McDermott— Conor," she corrected with a smile. "No trouble at all."

The days became a pattern for Lizzy. She rose early to see to McDermott's breakfast. Then by the time he was done, her day's baking was well on its way, and she had the children to feed and the household staff to instruct. Mrs. Potts arrived early one morning after being absent for three days, and Lizzy was not happy to see her. She had thought she couldn't do without the woman's help, but now she knew differently. Her days had been less tense, more enjoyable, even with the extra workload since the woman had gone. Lizzy decided that she would no longer tolerate the woman's contrariness.

"Mrs. Potts," she said by way of greeting after the woman had entered the back door, her face in a scowl that Lizzy had come to know so well.

"Mrs. Foley." The servant's voice was clipped.

"You have not come for three days."

"I was ill."

"You didn't send word."

Mrs. Potts sniffed. "I thought you'd know."

"Well, I didn't, and frankly, during your absence, I've found that I don't need your services anymore."

The cook's eyes narrowed. "You need me. No one else would dare to work for the scheming likes of you."

Lizzy's teeth snapped. "You're fired, Mrs. Potts. I'll have the last of the money owed to you first thing tomorrow. Good day to you."

The woman began to sputter. "You can't fire me. I've worked for John Foley for over ten years!"

"Well, Mrs. Potts, John had told me himself that I could fire you if I'd wanted, and until now, I've put up with your mean-spiritedness because you were a faithful employee to John and I thought I couldn't do without you. But now I know differently. And as I'm the mistress of Milly's Station, I will not put up with you anymore!" Lizzy felt herself begin to tremble . . . not with fear but with anger. "Now, good day to you, Mrs. Potts!"

"You're not the mistress of Milly's Station," the woman snarled, "and you never will be! There was only one mistress, and that was Miss Millicent, whom the master loved dearly! See if you can get along without my services. See if anyone in the village will lift a finger to help you!"

"What's this?" A deep voice boomed from behind them in the back doorway.

Lizzy's breath caught as she saw Conor McDermott. "Just a disagreement between Mrs. Potts and myself."

Conor raised an eyebrow. "Mrs. Potts?"

The woman firmed her mouth, refusing to answer.

"I've fired Mrs. Potts, Mr. McDermott, and she apparently doesn't know how to leave graciously."

The woman in question glanced at Lizzy and Conor, and a speculative gleam entered her gaze. "So that's the way of it," she mumbled.

"Mrs. Potts," Conor said coolly. "I believe that Mrs. Foley wants ya to leave." He gestured toward the exit. "Shall I show ya the door now?"

Stiffening her back, the former housekeeper turned to leave. "I'll be back for my wages tomorrow first thing."

And she left without an answer from Lizzy, who slumped back against the kitchen worktable, exhausted from the exchange.

Conor turned from the door to see Lizzy, her eyes closed, looking worse for the wear. "It was as bad as all that, was it?"

She opened her eyes and nodded. "I don't know why I put up with her all these years. John said I didn't have to; but I knew she was fiercely loyal to John, and so I . . ."

"Took her abuse to please him?"

She managed a smile. "Something like that."

He approached the table where they usually took their breakfast and sat down.

"I've made hotcakes," she said.

He grinned. "Thank ya."

She set out a plate of hotcakes before him. On the table, she placed maple syrup, strawberry jam, butter, and sugar mixed with cinnamon. Conor chose the butter and jam and slathered both over his hotcakes.

Lizzy used butter and syrup and watched him surreptitiously while she ate.

"You're later than usual," she said.

"I had a brief meeting with some of the men."

Frowning, she paused in the act of forking up another bite. "Is anything wrong?"

"If ya are askin' if I'm havin' any trouble, then no. The men and I understand each other."

Sighing with relief, she nodded and began to eat again.

"I had a few ideas I wanted to discuss with them. Some of the fields have been planted with the same crops for too long. I want to rotate them, leave one of the fields go fallow. If you rob the soil of all its plant feed, then you won't have much of a crop."

She smiled sadly. "I'm afraid I've not much of a head for such things. John handled those matters on his own."

"But ya'd like to change that," he said perceptively.

"Yes. Yes, I would. I need to understand everything about Milly's Station. I mustn't ever be made to feel so vulnerable again."

"Understood."

"And will you have the time to teach me?"

He eyed her thoughtfully. "Let me do what needs to be done first, and then I'll show ya what it's about."

Her sigh of relief was audible. "Thank you."

"That's what I'm here for, Mrs. Foley. To help ya."

Mrs. Foley, Lizzy thought. *So it's business, all in all.*

Well, that was fine with her.

FIVE

"Mistress, a Mr. Thompson is here to see you."

"Thank you, Jamieson. Please tell Mr. Thompson that I will be down to see him shortly." Knowing that she could trust the servant to see the guest comfortable in the front parlor, Lizzy finished instructing Ruth on what she wanted done to the second-floor sitting room.

"Ruth, please take down all the curtains here and air them on the clothesline outside. Have young Margaret help you."

"Yes, missus."

"And when you're done, I'd like you to see that all of the upstairs rooms are dusted."

The maid nodded. The fact that Ruth didn't seem threatened by the prospect of all this work surprised Lizzy. Had Mrs. Potts been the cause of trouble with the servants? Lizzy no longer doubted it.

"Missus?"

Lizzy looked at her. "Yes, Ruth?"

"Is it true that you let Mrs. Potts go?"

"Yes. It's true."

Ruth appeared worried. "Was it because of me?"

Lizzy smiled as she patted the maid's arm. "Not at all. Mrs. Potts and I didn't see eye to eye with each other."

The girl seemed relieved. "Forgive me for saying

so, missus, but Mrs. Potts didn't see eye to eye with anyone."

"Then, you'll not miss Mrs. Potts."

The maid gave a light laugh. "No, missus. She's not a fair one. Mrs. Potts . . . well, she's not."

Lizzy smiled. Just as she had thought. Mrs. Potts hadn't been well liked by anyone in the household. Why hadn't she seen that? *Because Mrs. Potts pretended to champion the servants under her.* "I'm glad she won't be missed."

"May I speak my mind?" Ruth asked.

"You may."

"She didn't treat you very well," the girl said. "And despite what I've heard I'm not certain she treated Mr. Foley's late wife well either."

That knowledge stunned Lizzy, for Mrs. Potts had always compared the two of them—Millicent and Lizzy—and had found Lizzy the one lacking. "But she was always speaking highly of Mrs. Millicent."

Ruth shook her head. "She was always making comparisons, missus. Margaret and me. Ann and Jane. One could never satisfy Mrs. Potts."

"And Mr. Foley."

Ruth's smile was sad. "Mr. Foley was too nice a man to see the bad in anyone, especially Mrs. Potts."

"I see." Lizzy's heart felt lighter after hearing the girl's opinion. She hadn't realized it before, but she had found herself lacking in someway because of what Mrs. Potts had said and done over the years she had been there. "Thank you for telling me this."

"You're welcome, missus." Ruth smiled before she went to work. Lizzy watched as the maid pulled over a chair and began to unhook the sitting room curtains. "I'll see that all is taken care of, Mrs. Foley," the girl said.

Lizzy left then to head downstairs where she would confront Mr. Thompson, a business associate of her late husband's.

* * *

"Mr. Thompson."

The man turned from the fireplace to face her as Lizzy entered the room. James Thompson was a tall, thin fellow, well dressed in navy jacket, waistcoat, and trousers. He would probably be considered attractive by many with his dark hair, gray eyes, and charming smile, but there was something about him that bothered Lizzy.

He approached with his hand out. "Mrs. Foley, how are you this day?"

She looked at his hand, but didn't offer her own. "I'm well, thank you. Please sit down." Lizzy sat on a chair near the fireplace, while the man chose a chair directly across from hers. "How can I help you today? If you've come about my late husband's account—"

"No, no," the man assured her smoothly. He flashed her a smile that revealed even, perfect teeth. Why his straight teeth bothered her, Lizzy didn't know. "I've come to see you actually. To see if there is anything I can do to help."

To help? Help with what? "Thank you, but no." Her smile for him was polite. "I have my foreman to assist me."

The man looked nonplussed. "You have help?"

She nodded as she hid her amusement. He had obviously thought she would be eager for his assistance. *He and a lot of other men looking to have a shot at the "lonely widow,"* she thought.

Suddenly, his expression relaxed. "Well, of course you do. I thought my help could be of a different nature."

"A different nature?" she echoed. She didn't care for the gleam in his eyes.

"Yes. I know how difficult it is for a woman to handle the financial side of business," he began.

"I'm managing," she said. "And as I said, I have Mr. McDermott—"

"I could make things easier for you."

He spoke as if he hadn't heard her. Her irritation with him grew. "How so?"

"If you'd allow me to come by and look over your books . . ." He paused, biting his lip as if he were shy. Lizzy wasn't fooled by his act for a second.

She stood. "Thank you for your kind offer, Mr. Thompson."

"James," he urged as he, too, rose from his seat.

"Yes, well, thank you, but I can't take up any of your time."

"Why, certainly you can."

"No," she said firmly, her gaze direct, "I can't."

"Oh, I see." But she could tell that he didn't. He was confused about why she hadn't jumped at the chance for his help.

She turned toward the door. "I appreciate the visit."

"Yes . . ."

"And I'll get back with you on the amount we owe you." She still found it hard to believe that she owed Thompson and Thompson all the money that firm had claimed was due them. "How much did you say that sum was?"

He named a figure that had her insides clenching.

"As I said, I'll have to get back with you about payment." She would have to discuss the matter with Conor. She had learned of the unpaid account only last month, shortly before her friend Kathleen had mentioned having Conor McDermott come to help her.

She had been meaning to bring the matter up with Conor from the first, but there had been so much to do, so much to remember. And Conor and she were getting used to working together in this strange new relationship.

"Ah . . . well . . . fine then." Mention of account payment changed the expression on James Thompson's face. His eyes seemed to focus again, and Lizzy didn't care for his calculating look. "Yes. Well, I'll be back to discuss that account, Mrs. Foley."

"I'll expect it, then." She walked to the door in a silent invitation for him to leave.

Taking his cue, Thompson put his hand on the doorknob. "Next week, Mrs. Foley." His look gave her gooseflesh. She had the feeling that he wasn't interested in money at all . . . but in her.

"Yes, Mr. Thompson. And thank you again for stopping."

When the man had left, she leaned back on the closed door and sighed . . . and was grateful that Thompson was gone. Conor McDermott could handle matters during the man's next visit.

There was something on Elizabeth Foley's mind, and Conor planned to get to the bottom of it.

It was a warm late spring day. The hills in the distance were crested with green, and in the fields, he could see seedlings sprouting up from the rich soil. The men had worked hard and quickly. He was pleased with the progress on Milly's Station, pleased with the changed attitude of the workers and their families.

Each day was a new challenge for Conor. He had made some headway interpreting John Foley's system of record keeping, and he had suggested and was granted full decision-making authority to disperse money for renovations. The barn and other outbuildings needed some work. The main house itself was in good repair, but even he could see that some of the rooms could use better furnishings. He didn't understand the man's reluctance to spend money. Conor had been not only surprised, but also stunned by the wealth of John Foley. But the man had lived modestly, so no one seeing his lifestyle would think him a man of means. Only one person could have—must have—known, and that was his wife Lizzy.

Lizzy had spent enough of the plantation's funds in the months since John's death, hadn't she? Wasn't that the real reason that he had been asked to step in and help? Had the Quaids somehow known and wanted to ensure that Milly's Station thrived and the children and the residents were provided for?

Elizabeth Foley. Every thought, every action, on Milly's Station brought his mind back to her. She had spent money; it was true. But on what? Surely not on the house or her wardrobe? And the children, although well dressed, were not extravagantly clothed. Where had the money gone?

Conor wondered if Lizzy knew the full extent of John's riches. He had found other papers . . . bank records and money that had never been touched. Would she have gone through those funds, those assets, if she had known?

Which brought him back to recalling her odd behavior this morning at breakfast. It had been obvious to him that something had been worrying her; yet, when he had asked, she had denied it. And when he had inquired again later, she had avoided his gaze while she gave the same answer.

What was bothering the lass?

"Conor? Sir?"

McDermott turned and saw Michael Storm, a young man who was always eager to assist in the farm chores. "Yes, Mike, what it is?"

"Pherson said the hole in the rear barn wall is fixed, and he wondered what it is you'd like us to do next."

Conor hid a smile. "Well, that's fine then, lad. You tell Mr. Pherson that he is to go home to his wife for the midday meal and to take his time."

Michael's eyes widened. "I will, sir."

"And you—can ya get away tomorrow? If possible, I'd like ya to make arrangements to head into Balti-

more with me. I'm going for supplies, and I'd like ya
to accompany me."

The young man grinned. "Yes, sir."

Conor cleared his throat.

"I mean Conor, sir. Sorry . . . Conor."

Conor smiled. "We'll leave tomorrow and be gone
overnight."

"I'll be ready."

The Irishman watched the young man head back
toward the barn with a spring in his step, no doubt
ready to tell Pherson that he was dismissed early so
he could spend extra time with his pregnant wife.

Conor glanced up at the morning sky and realized
that in a half hour or so, it would time for him to head
in for a meal as well. For a brief moment, he wondered
what Lizzy was cooking for him this day. Then, with
the clear knowledge that he was looking forward not
only to the meal, but seeing her again, simmering in
his head, he scowled and forced his attention back to
the work at hand. He wouldn't be taken in by Elizabeth
Foley's charms, as lovely and as tempting as they
might be.

Lizzy waited expectantly in the garden for him to
come. She already had the midday meal prepared.
Having done so earlier, she had decided to go outdoors
and work in the soil around her flowers, herbs, and
vegetables while she waited for Conor McDermott to
show.

The sky overhead was a glorious shade of blue. The
sun was a bright yellow orb, and she enjoyed the heat
of it on her skin. She wore a yellow homespun dress
with lace-trimmed sleeves at the elbows and a full
white apron with pockets, where she placed her garden
spade. Earlier that morning, she had plaited her hair
in one long braid, which hung tidily to her shoulder
blades. On the ground, inches from where she knelt,

lay her straw bonnet, protection against the sun that she decided she didn't need.

A few yards away little Emma crouched in the dirt, her hands busy as she helped Lizzy clear away the weeds and turn up the soil. Like Lizzy's, Emma's blond hair was braided, and she wore a garden apron over a blue dress that Lizzy had sewn for Emma in the same style as her own.

"Mother?"

Lizzy smiled at the lovely picture the little girl made. "Yes, Emma?"

"I picked you a flower."

"Thank you, dear," she replied, noting that Emma had picked a weed and not one of the flowering precious herbs that she had planted last year.

"Is Conor coming soon?"

Lizzy's heart thumped an extra beat. "I believe he is." She frowned. "And it's Mr. McDermott."

"He tells everyone to call him 'Conor.' "

"Everyone doesn't include young girls and boys. Like yourself and Jason."

Emma pouted prettily. "I shall ask him at dinner."

"You will not!"

"But, Mother—"

"That wouldn't be proper manners, Miss Emma."

"I think he will let me ask—"

"Ask what?" a deep voice entered the conversation. Catching her breath, Lizzy glanced up to meet Conor McDermott's curious blue gaze. The intent way he watched her made her skin tingle.

"If I can call—"

"Emma!" her mother warned.

"But he asked—"

"Yes, I did," Conor said with some amusement. "Now, what is it ya want to know." His smile was for Lizzy. "I promise I'll not be angry whatever the question."

Lizzy sighed, knowing that Emma would ask, and she would be embarrassed for making an issue of it.

"I called you Conor, and Mother said it wasn't right."

Conor glanced from the mother to the little girl and back again. "Hmmm. Well, yer mother is quite right. It's not proper for a little girl to call a man by his given name—"

Lizzy started to smile.

"But, then, ye're a special young girl, and I'm not just any man; so it's perfectly all right for ya to call me Conor."

Eyes widening, Lizzy blustered. *"Mr. McDermott!"*

"Uh, oh," he said to little Emma. "I think yer mother is angry with me."

"Emma, go up to the house and pull the biscuits I made out of the pantry closet. Mr. McDermott and I will be in shortly to eat."

After nodding, the little girl left to do her mother's bidding.

"Mr. McDer—"

"Don't!"

She blinked. "Don't what?"

"Don't say Mr. McDermott in that tone of voice. Ye've called me Conor before, why stop?"

Her cheeks turned red with anger. "For one thing, Mr. McDermott, little girls don't call adults by their given names, and—"

"Ye're not a little girl." The suggestive way he spoke momentarily silenced her.

"Please," she said through clenched teeth.

He sighed, as if disappointed. "Go on."

She gasped with indignation. "Thank you," she said stiffly.

"My pleasure."

She nodded, only slightly mollified. "For another thing," she continued, "I think it best to keep a distance between us. You'll only be here a short while, and—" She halted. "Why are you shaking your head?"

" 'Tis as if ye've read me mind."

"It is?" she said. Her gaze was drawn to his sensuous mouth.

"Aye."

She hid her disappointment. "Oh, well, then . . . good. Good." She frowned, trying to think, trying to remember what they had been discussing before he had distracted her. She brightened. "Mr. McDermott, I realize that you're only trying to be friendly to my daughter, but I do not believe that allowing her to call you Conor is the right way to teach the child."

"What do you suggest, then?" he asked. "I'd rather not have her call me Mr. McDermott. What else can she call me?"

She raised her chin. "I wouldn't know. That's something you'll have to consider for a time, I imagine."

"And in the meantime? What should she call me until then?"

"Mr.—"

"No," he said.

She studied him in shock. *"No?"*

Hiding his amusement at her reaction, he shook his head. "Emma and Jason shall call me Mack."

"Mack?" He could tell she didn't like that name for the children to use any better than their using Conor.

"Aye," he said with no small sense of satisfaction. He loved to see her riled. Seeing her this way made her seem more vulnerable . . . more appealing.

"I don't—"

"Mack," he insisted.

"No. They should call you Mr. McDermott."

"McDermott, then. Not mister."

She sighed. "All right."

He grinned, because he could tell that she wasn't

happy about it. "Will ya be playing in the garden all day? Or can ya find it in yer heart to feed me?"

Lizzy narrowed her eyes. Was he teasing her? "The meal is ready. You were late, so I thought I'd get some work done out here."

He made a big pretense of studying the rows and patterns of plants. "Very nice."

"Thank you," she said ungraciously, for she was sure now he had been mocking her.

"Ma, is it time to eat yet?" Jason's call drew their attention.

"Yes, we'll be in a moment," Lizzy called back.

"Shall we go, then?" Conor said, holding out his arm.

She stared at his brawny arm foolishly, afraid to take it. The man with his bright blue eyes, dark ringlets, and Irish charm was just too attractive for her peace of mind. He didn't move. He waited with his arm extended until she was forced to take it.

Not that it was a hardship, she thought as her fingers settled on his muscular upper arm. No, it was no hardship to be near the man at all.

And that was what frightened her.

SIX

"You'll be careful, won't you, Mr. McDermott?" Lizzy asked. She stood on the dock, gazing up to where the man stood on the *Millicent,* her late husband's sloop.

The Irishman gave her a look that made her insides tighten. "Aye, Mrs. Foley, of course I will." He glanced up at the masts of the vessel with a satisfied look. "The *Millicent* is a fine craft."

"Yes," she said. She had sailed on the ship often enough when John was alive. Named after his first wife, it was a source of pride for him. And she knew the ship was safe. But what if she encountered the danger of an unexpected storm?

"Ye'll be fine until I get back," McDermott assured her.

"And when will that be?" she said, although she knew.

"Tomorrow afternoon. Is there anythin' I can get for ya?"

She nodded and handed him her list.

He took the list, scanned it, and then gazed at her with a puzzled look. "A length of yellow fabric, some thread, and a few buttons?"

Lizzy frowned. "Is it too much, then?" She held her hand out for the list.

"It's certainly not much. I would have thought ye'd want more from the city."

She shook her head. "It's Emma's birthday in three weeks. I thought I'd make her a new dress."

He smiled. "And if there is no yellow?"

Lizzy considered. She didn't want a homespun gown for the child. She wanted something fancier, something that couldn't be made from flax or spun cotton. "Then, pick out a color that suits her."

"I'll do that."

The captain warned McDermott that they would be leaving shortly.

The Irishman nodded before turning back to Lizzy. "Are ya sure ya don't want to come?"

Heart pounding, she eyed him and the vessel with longing. "I'd love to come, but I can't leave the children." *Or Milly's Station.*

"Perhaps next time we can arrange for the children to come. And I'll ask Rian for someone capable to oversee the plantation in our absence."

Next time, Lizzy thought with pleasure. Would there actually be a next time? The prospect sounded delightful, but she doubted she would ever get to go with him. He wouldn't be at Milly's Station for much longer. She sighed. A trip into Baltimore! She hadn't been back in a long while. The last time had been when John was alive. Since his death, she had been afraid to leave the farm, unsure what she would find upon her return, for her position as John's heir—although legal—seemed tenuous to her at best. Only the Quaids would care if she and the children left Milly's Station and never returned.

"Yes," she said. "I'd like that."

"Conor, we're ready to shove off now," the captain called. "Begging your pardon, missus," he said upon seeing Lizzy.

"Have a good trip, Captain Logan."

Hired recently by McDermott, the man seemed to

know his business and had been respectful whenever he had seen Lizzy.

"Thank you, missus."

Lizzy stepped farther back on the shoreline and watched while the captain and his crew prepared to make way.

"I've left Markins in charge. He'll report to ya later this afternoon and then again in the mornin'. If there is something ya need done, just ask him and he'll see that it's completed."

She nodded and felt her stomach give a lurch as the vessel started to move from shore. Conor McDermott had been a hardworking, respectful employee, yet he was still virtually a stranger. Why was she already feeling the loss of his presence? In a few weeks he would leave, and except for an event or two when she might see him from a distance, he would be gone from her life. Why did that thought bother her?

With young Michael Storm by his side, he waved as the ship sailed away. She waved back, staring longingly, wishing for things that would never be. And the image of his dark curls and vibrant blue eyes stayed with her long after she had returned to the house and gone about her daily chores.

Later that day, Lizzy decided to work in the gardens. She dressed for the task, found her tools, then headed out the front entrance to tackle the flower beds.

"Why, Mrs. Foley, hello!" a man greeted her as she exited the house.

"Mr. Olsen!" Lizzy was surprised and not pleased to see Martin Olsen, a middle-aged man who lived upriver.

"Mrs. Foley, you're looking well this afternoon."

Lizzy eyed the man warily. It had been only hours since Conor's departure had left her feeling at a loss, but the sight of this man woke her from her daze. Mr.

Olsen had come calling several times since John's death, and although he had been respectful, his eagerness to court her made her nervous. It bothered her that he made no secret of his longing to step into her husband's shoes.

"Thank you for the compliment, Mr. Olsen, but I'm not dressed to take company. It's such a lovely day, and I've been working outside."

The man frowned. A rotund little fellow with a balding head and a bulbous nose, he was not much to look at. Worse yet, he had the personality of a fish, and Lizzy wasn't impressed by anything about him. That he thought he could court her and envision himself as her next husband made her shudder. Yes, it was all conjecture on her part. Still, she was sure she was right.

Every time she saw Martin Olsen, he watched her like a vulture stalking his pray. The unholy gleam in his dark eyes stripped past the several layers of fancy dress as if envisioning her naked.

"A woman as lovely as you shouldn't have to lift a finger to tend these grounds." He glanced about the property as if the notion of her working offended him.

"I assure you, Mr. Olsen, that I enjoy the work. I find it relaxing. A woman doesn't like to spend every moment in the kitchen."

The look he shot her agreed, but the nature of the glance had her longing to shoo him away and hug herself.

"I understand, and that's a commendable trait in a female."

Lizzy had to bite her tongue to keep from snarling at him. *A female, indeed,* she thought. *As if we are inferior creatures who must be humored and protected against ourselves.*

"I'm afraid you'll have to excuse me, Mr. Olsen. I've a very busy schedule today."

"Oh?" He looked nonplussed that she was sending

him away. His expression cleared. "Perhaps I can be of assistance."

"No, that won't be necessary. I've Mr. Markins and the others to help me. You've such nice clothing on. I wouldn't want to see any of it dirtied."

He seemed relieved. "You're very thoughtful. I've only just bought these garments a week past. Perhaps I can come to visit another time?"

"Perhaps," she said evasively. "This is a busy plantation; there is much I must do over the next few months."

"Surely, you must take time to visit with friends?"

She blinked. "Why, of course, Mr. Olsen. In fact, I've a visit to the Quaids planned for later this week. Other than that, the rest of my time is not my own."

" 'Tis a pity."

She controlled her irritation. "Yes, well, it's how I like it, Mr. Olsen. So if you don't mind, I'll say good day to you now. Mr. Markins will be waiting for me."

And she left the man standing within yards of the house. Hurrying toward the outbuilding, she attempted to put as much distance as possible between her and Mr. Olsen . . . and wondered what she would do the next time he came.

Tell him the truth, she supposed. But how did one do that without causing trouble or hurt feelings? She would have to think of something. Her eyes gleamed. *Perhaps pretend affection toward another?*

Mr. Thompson and Mr. Olsen weren't the only men with an eye on her and Milly's Station. She would have to do something to discourage the whole lot of them.

The Port of Baltimore was a bustling place with shops lining the cobblestone streets and vendors hawking their wares in loud, singsong voices. Conor strolled along the street, his gaze searching the shops for a dry goods store. Spying what he wanted, he entered the store and studied the bolts of fabric.

"May I help you?" a feminine voice asked.

Conor turned with a smile to face the shopkeeper. "I'm on a mission to buy some yellow cloth."

A startled look had come over the woman as he had turned, followed by a look of appreciation that only slightly dimmed when she heard him speak. "A big man like you?"

"Aye. Something suitable for a young lass."

"Your daughter?"

"A friend's daughter."

"I see." Sensing something hidden in his answer, she turned to study the selection of material, her gaze expertly moving from one roll of cloth to another. "Yellow, you say?"

"Aye."

"Calico? Linen? Satin? Silk?"

He raised his eyebrows, at a loss. "I have no idea."

She gave him a generous smile. "May I suggest the calico, then. It's perfect for a young girl of—"

"Six going on seven."

"Yes, perfect."

"Nay. Not calico."

"Silk? Is this for a garment to match her mother's?"

"I wouldn't know," he said. He considered the bolt of fabric she held. "I'll take it."

"How much do you need?"

He rifled in his pocket and pulled out Lizzy's list. "Three yards. And some matching thread. And five buttons."

The woman nodded and helped him make the proper selection. As he was preparing to pay for the materials, the woman asked, "How about a length of lace? For trimming the sleeves and neckline."

He considered it. "How much do I need?"

She named an amount that seemed reasonable to him.

"Fine. Give me a bit of the lace."

He left shortly afterward with his purchases in hand. Spying Michael, he waved the boy over. "Will ya take this to the boat, lad?" he said when Michael had reached his side.

"Yes, sir—Conor."

"Good lad. When ye're done, would ya like to eat?"

Michael's eyes glistened. "Yes, Conor." He grinned. "I'm starved."

For a brief moment, memory tugged at the darker side of Conor, making his gaze blacken. His vision cleared, and he forced a smile. "Meet me over there in few minutes. I've a stop to make before I can satisfy me hunger."

As Michael headed toward the ship, Conor continued down the street, searching for John Foley's lawyer. He found the building he needed not far from the dry goods store. Entering the front room, he waited until an employee announced him.

"May I help you?" Samuel Tardy, a tidy man in his midfifties, eyed Conor curiously.

"Me name is Conor McDermott, and I've come to speak to ya of John Foley's assets. John Foley of Kent County."

The look in the lawyer's eyes alerted Conor that he knew immediately to whom Conor was referring. "Come into the back office," the man invited.

"I've been hired by Mrs. Foley to manage the estate. There are some discrepancies in Mr. Foley's books, and I've found some papers." Conor went down the list of items he had questioned.

"Can ya tell me where this place is?" he said, pointing to a name on the list.

"Ketterman," Tardy said. "The man's a banker. His office is one block over."

"Is it possible that John Foley had funds at this bank?"

"He did, and as far as I know, still does."

"And why doesn't his widow know about this?"

Tardy blinked, looking surprised by that statement. "Why, I assumed she did."

"Have you ever met Elizabeth Foley, Mr. Tardy?"

"Once, Mr. McDermott."

"And your impression."

"She was a pretty enough thing. Seemed to dote on John. John himself seemed quite taken with Elizabeth."

"And do you think it was his intention that his widow inherit all of his belongings?"

"Yes," he said without hesitation. "He wanted her and the children to be well provided for."

Conor stood. "Thank ya, Mr. Tardy. Ye've been of tremendous help."

The man shook his head. "Don't thank me. I've done nothing to deserve thanks." He rose and followed Conor to the front room. "Please give my regards to Mrs. Foley."

Conor nodded. "I'll tell her." Then he left the building. He spied Michael in the prearranged spot and headed in his direction.

A heavy hammering on the front door caught Lizzy's attention, where she worked on the second floor. She hurried down the stairs just as Jamieson came out of his quarters from the rear end of the house.

"Mrs. Foley! *Mrs. Foley!*" came the cry from the other side of the door.

"I'll get it, mistress." It was obvious that the man-servant hadn't heard the summons until he had come on another errand to the front of the manor house. He looked surprised by the sound.

"Oh, Jamieson, I'm sorry," Lizzy said, spying him. "I didn't realize that you were near."

"Sorry, mistress. Truth is I didn't hear it until just

now." He frowned. "Someone is in a hurry to be noticed."

Lizzy nodded and stood back anxiously as Jamieson opened the door. Had something terrible happened to the *Millicent*? To her crew and Conor?

As the door opened, the Pherson boy burst into the house. "Where is Mrs. Foley?" he gasped.

Frowning, she stepped forward. "Robert?"

The boy looked relieved to see her. "Oh, missus, we need your help. My ma—the baby's coming, and she's having trouble."

Lizzy nodded, her senses kicking into full alert. "Run home to your family. Tell them I'll be right there."

"Yes, missus."

"And, Robert?"

"Yes, missus?"

"Has someone sent for the doctor?"

The boy shook his head.

"Find Mr. Brant. Tell him to go for Doc Albright."

"Yes, missus."

Her heart pounding, Lizzy turned to her manservant. "Jamieson, could you find my medicine pouch? I need to change." She still wore her gardening clothes. Hardly the attire to wear to a birthing.

"Very well, mistress."

Without waiting to see if he left, Lizzy ran upstairs to her bedchamber. Her thoughts awhirl, drawing deep breaths, she worried about what she would find when she arrived at the Pherson residence . . . and whether or not she could help Adda.

As mistress of Milly's Station, it was her duty to administer assistance to the families on the plantation. She knew enough about medicinal herbs to cure a stomachache, salve a wound, and give relief to the pain-ridden. Surely, she would be able to help a mother during a difficult birth.

Fortunately, her gardening gown had buttons up the

front, making it easier for her to undress without help. Lizzy hurriedly exchanged the garment for a clean, similarly styled one. Then she went to find the children to tell them where she was going.

"Ruth," she said as she left her room and saw the chambermaid. "Have you seen Jason and Emma?"

The girl nodded. "They're in the playroom, missus." The playroom was on the third floor, a large attic room that John had converted into the children's play area. Why hadn't she thought they would be there? Probably because it was a lovely day, and the children rarely stayed indoors when the weather was nice.

"I need to leave the house. Mrs. Pherson has gone into labor. Would you mind the children for me?"

Ruth beamed, pleased with the mistress's trust in her. "Why, yes, missus. I'll see that they come to no harm."

Lizzy managed to smile. "Thank you. If you need anything, just ask Jamieson. I'll tell him I'm going and that you're in charge of Jason and Emma."

"Thank you, missus.

After a quick conversation with Jamieson, who handed her the medicine bag, Lizzy ran out of the house and hurried toward the Pherson residence.

SEVEN

"Mrs. Foley!" Pherson answered the door, looking relieved to see her. "Thank goodness!" He stepped back to allow her entry.

"How is Adda, Henry?" Lizzy asked. She stepped inside the house and shut the door.

"She's in a lot of pain." The man seemed beside himself. "I don't know how to help her!"

"Don't worry, Henry. I've got something that may help."

As if on cue, a woman's cry came from the back room. Hearing it, Lizzy hurried toward the bedchamber where Adda Pherson lay.

"Mrs. Pherson," she soothed as she moved quickly to the bedside. She placed her hand on the woman's forehead. "Relax," she urged. "Breathe deeply."

The woman's hair and forehead were damp with sweat. Adda's face contorted with pain as she tried, as instructed, to breathe deeply through a contraction.

"She's been fighting it a long while," a feminine voice said from the back corner of the room.

"Mary." Lizzy was pleased to find Mary Markins, wed to one of her most trusted workers, wetting a cloth in a washbasin. The woman nodded, before she wrung out the fabric and returned to the bed, where she placed it across Adda's brow.

"She's suffering in her back. I suffered so when I had my third."

Lizzy placed a hand on Adda's back and pressed to relieve the pressure.

Adda nodded. " 'Tis true, missus," she whispered weakly, exhaustion taking hold as the pain left her.

"I need to examine you." Lizzy grabbed the woman's hand and squeezed reassuringly. "Will you let me?"

"Aye," the woman gasped. "I'm afraid, missus. This one—he's taking much longer than my others. Something is wrong. I can feel it."

Lizzy gently moved Adda so she could examine the progress of the birth. Adda was right. The babe was taking too long. If she didn't do something to help it along, she was afraid that Adda would lose the strength to give birth to a healthy child. The longer Adda's labor took, the weaker the woman would become and the greater the chance for the unborn child to suffer injury or death.

She had to do something to help the process. She thought quickly of all she had learned. First, she would use warm compresses made of boiled goldenrod root in water for Adda's painful contractions and back cramps. While Mary helped to administer the compresses, she would prepare the root of the painted trillium, which would not only help the pain, but also stop any bleeding in the womb

Adda gave a wild cry as her body tightened in its effort to expel the baby.

"Mary," Lizzy said, "will you help me a moment?"

"Aye." The woman helped Adda into the right position for Lizzy to reexamine her.

Lizzy frowned. Adda should be farther along after hours of intense labor. "You're coming along nicely," she encouraged. "But I'm going to make a compress for your abdomen and then your back . . . for the pain. It should help you have a longer rest between contractions so you can regain some of your strength." Her gaze settled on Mary. "Can you put a kettle of water to heat on the fire?"

Mary nodded and left, and Lizzy began to search through the contents of her satchel for the medicinal herbs she would need.

He had been gone for only a night, but he was anxious to return. He had discovered some interesting information in Baltimore about John Foley and about Milly's Station. And he wasn't sure whether or not Elizabeth Foley knew of it.

He had also conducted some personal business in Baltimore. For over a year, since coming to America, he had been searching for his sister without success. And he had had no luck in locating her this trip either. Several times in the last six months, he had come close to learning of her whereabouts, only to find out that the information he had received had been wrong . . . misleading. Still, he wasn't about to give up the quest.

Conor stood on the bow of the sloop and gazed out over the water. It was a fine day. The sun warmed his skin, and a light breeze teased his hair and ruffled his clothing. Michael Storm was at the wheel, being instructed by Captain Logan. The young man's eagerness to learn made Conor smile. The lad was a good worker, but he was anxious to explore the world, to see and be taught new things. But for now he would stay on Milly's Station, for the young man had good employment. His family needed him—his mother and four siblings. And so he would remain, the boy had told him, until his younger twin brothers were old enough to work.

Conor turned to face the front again and gazed at the land in the distance. Kent County. Milly's Station. Soon, he would be back on the plantation, where he would see Elizabeth Foley again.

It felt like a homecoming.

And he didn't like that.

He had come to America for a purpose, and that was to find the half sister he had only just learned of after his mother's death. He had stayed at Green Lawns longer than he had expected, found he liked it there too much to be in a hurry to leave.

He had known when he had first come to Kent County that he would soon be on his way again . . . and that hadn't changed.

Which was why he should forget Lizzy Foley. His stay at Milly's Station would be even shorter than his time at Green Lawns.

Soon, he would find his sister. Bitterness rose up to choke him, for she had been the sole child of his father's love. The man who had sired him had abandoned mother and son; yet, he had married another and accepted a daughter . . . and Conor had to know why. Why had his father loved one child and not the other? How could he have been so heartless as to cast a helpless woman with child aside?

It was mid morning when Lizzy returned to the main house. Exhausted from the lack of a night's sleep, she climbed the stairs to the second floor.

"Jason! Emma!" she called as she reached the top landing.

"In here!" Jason shouted back.

The children were in the upstairs sitting room. They were playing mumbly peg while Ruth looked on dotingly.

Lizzy entered, and Ruth sprang up from her seat.

"Missus!"

"Ruth. Thank you for watching the children."

The girl smiled. " 'Twas my pleasure, missus."

Jason gave the maid a look. "She beat me four games, Ma."

A smile lifted the corners of Lizzy's mouth. "Four?"

"He lost five," Emma said proudly. "I just beat him."

"That's because I allowed you."

"Did not."

"Did too!"

"Did not!"

"Children!" Lizzy exclaimed. She felt the beginning of a headache, and their arguing didn't help. "Please, it's been a long night, and I don't want to hear this."

Jason immediately apologized, "Sorry, Ma." He eyed her with concern. "How is Mrs. Pherson?"

"She's fine. Tired but fine, and so is her babe. She had a girl."

"A girl!" Emma gasped with pleasure.

"Elizabeth Mary."

"Can I see her?" the little girl asked.

"May I," Lizzy corrected. She nodded. "Not right away, mind you. Later, after Mrs. Pherson and her new daughter have had a chance to rest."

"You look tired, Ma," Jason said.

"I am," she admitted. "So if Jamieson and Ruth will mind you both a little longer, I thought I'd lie down for a nap."

Ruth beamed. "I don't mind at all, missus. Master Jason and I will have a rematch."

"Can I—*may I*—" Emma corrected, "play, too?"

The maid nodded. "Don't worry yourself a bit, missus. All the rooms have been cleaned as you asked. We'll clean the downstairs tomorrow, if you don't mind waiting."

Lizzy gave her a thankful smile. "It can wait." Yawning, she turned to go. "Thank you, Ruth."

"You're welcome, missus. Jason! Let your sister have a turn first!"

Smiling, Lizzy headed to her bedchamber. Once inside, she drew the drapes, then stripped to her shift.

Pulling back the bedclothes, she slipped beneath the blankets and lay down, closing her eyes. She thought of the night, the fear she had experienced when Adda continued to take too long with the birthing. She had been grateful when, after the last dose of trillium she had given Adda, the babe had started to come.

Afterward, she had needed to clean up and dispose of the afterbirth. Mary Markins had returned to her family, and so Lizzy had stayed until she had been certain that the Pherson family had help for the rest of the day. She had fixed Mr. Pherson and the children a meal and sent for Alice Brant to stay with the family. When Alice had arrived, Lizzy had left, too tired to do much more than complete the walk home.

Her last sight of the Pherson family had had her smiling, as they had been happily enjoying their breakfast while Alice had been cooing over the beauty of the new Pherson girl child.

"Take the day off, Mr. Pherson," she had told Henry. "Stay with your wife. We can make do without you today."

"But Mr. McDermott—"

"I'll explain to Mr. McDermott. I'm sure he'll understand and agree that a man needs to be home with his wife when she's just given him a pretty babe."

There had been tears in Henry Pherson's eyes when he had thanked her. And the sight of such emotion moved Lizzy as she had left the house and started back to the manor.

How wonderful it must be to have a child of one's own. She knew the process was a painful one, but every mother she had helped had seemed to forget the hurt once she held her babe within her loving arms.

She loved Jason and Emma as if they were children from her body, but that didn't make her stop from longing to give birth . . . from yearning to experience the pain and joy of bringing another precious life into the world.

As she lay, thinking of the night and the morning that followed, her eyes dropped, and sleep overcame her . . . finally.

Conor returned to the main house to find Lizzy Foley asleep in her bedchamber. He had had no idea that she was in bed when he had sought her out. It was just past noon; how was he to know she would still be sleeping?

He frowned, recalling the early hour during which she usually fixed him breakfast. It wasn't like her to sleep late. Was she sick?

Concerned, he went to her and gently shook her awake.

Lizzy rolled over and blinked, trying to focus, and saw Conor McDermott sitting on the edge of her bed.

"Conor!" Flustered, she started to rise, then gasped as she realized that the covers had fallen. The only thing shielding her soft curves from the Irishman's gaze was a thin white shift. She gasped and tugged up the bedclothes, but not before seeing a flame spark in the Irishman's gaze. "Mr. McDermott," she corrected. "What are you doing here?" Her heart was pounding so hard that she feared he could hear it.

"I'm sorry, but I was afraid ya were ill."

"No, just tired." Her heartbeat resumed a steadier pace. "I've been up all night with Adda Pherson."

"She had the babe?"

"Yes. A little girl."

"And she's all right?"

Taken by his look of concern, she nodded. "She's fine. She has ten perfect fingers and toes."

He seemed to relax as he smiled. "Good. Good. Pherson will be overjoyed."

"He is—" She shifted on the bed, hugging the covers to her tightly. "You're back," she said, then silently scolded herself for stating the obvious.

"I just got in. I came to look for ya, and Jason answered the door. He told me that ya were upstairs." His smile became crooked. "I thought ya'd be instructin' the servants on some daily task. It didn't occur to me that ya'd be in bed."

His voice had thickened, and Lizzy felt a flash of fire as tension sparked in the air between them. "Ya must be exhausted," he said.

She inclined her head as she studied him greedily. He looked wonderful with his blue eyes glistening and alert . . . his dark, wind-tossed hair. There was the scent of the bay and the outdoors about him . . . and a fragrance that she thought must be only his. She liked his scents . . . wouldn't mind enjoying them on a daily basis.

She gasped, horrified by the direction of her thoughts. She averted her gaze as she felt her cheek burn.

"Was it a difficult birth?" His quiet voice drew her gaze to him.

"It was a long one. Adda had already been in labor for some time before I arrived, and that was yesterday afternoon. It was an hour before dawn when she finally gave birth."

"But now mother and child are resting as they should."

Lizzy noted the compassion in Conor's gaze and felt warmth in her chest. "Yes."

She caught her breath at his look of approval. Her whole body was beginning to heat under the Irishman's intent regard.

He shifted closer suddenly and ran a finger across her cheekbone. "Ya need yer sleep," he said huskily.

The warmth of his finger nearly undid her. She loosened her grip on the bedclothes as she felt a yearning.

He sat back abruptly, withdrawing his touch, and Lizzy felt a chill at the loss of his heat. "I'll leave ya now."

She nodded, watching silently as he stood and started to leave. She realized that she didn't want him to go. She didn't want the distance between them. *"Conor!"*

He paused and turned.

She drew in a sharp breath, hoping that he couldn't read her thoughts . . . how much she wanted to be near him. *So much for maintaining my distance,* she thought. "Why did you need to see me?"

His blue eyes studied her with a heat that took her by surprise. Her insides warmed.

"I've got yer yellow fabric." He looked suddenly uncertain, charmingly, boyishly so. "Silk. Will it work, now?"

It wasn't what she had expected to hear. Nodding, she smiled. "Yes, very well."

He looked like a little boy who was excited about successfully completing an assigned task.

"And the buttons?" she asked.

"Aye. I've got the buttons." He grinned. "And a bit of lace . . . for the sleeves and collar," he said. "Me treat."

"Oh, but—"

"I added the lace as a gift to Miss Emma."

She had to smile at his use of Emma's "playing proper" name. His caring and generosity overwhelmed her. "Thank you."

He nodded, stared at her a moment, then turned back toward the door.

"And did you take care of the business you wanted?" she asked. She was reluctant to see him leave. It was wholly improper for a single man to be alone with her in her bedchamber, but she didn't care. Not when the man was Conor McDermott.

"Aye," he said without turning, his voice muffled and thick.

And then he was gone, leaving Lizzy to settle back down in bed. Her heart fluttering, she wondered how she would sleep after such an encounter. Thoughts of Conor whirled in her head as she closed her eyes.

Though she had forgotten she had suffered a full night's loss of sleep, her body hadn't, and so it was only minutes later before she drifted off again with visions of a big, strapping Irishman haunting her dreams.

Conor paused outside Lizzy's door for a moment until the silence inside her room had him continuing down the hall to the stairs. The image of Elizabeth Foley, all tousled and appealing, went with him, and he fought to banish it. Just as he fought the memory of how her skin felt beneath his fingertips.

Desire for her stirred hard and urgent, and he cursed beneath his breath.

He must get over this feeling. Lizzy Foley was not what she seemed. She was a seductress, a temptress; he had to remember that. And while he could enjoy her charms, he wouldn't. It wouldn't be fair to her . . . to the children . . . to himself.

But he couldn't put out her of his mind . . . her delight in the prospect of making her daughter a new dress . . . her sacrifice of a night's sleep to help Adda Pherson deliver her babe safely. And he couldn't forget all the other little generous things he had seen her do. These weren't the actions of a scheming seductress.

Who was Lizzy Foley? Schemer or friend? Selfish or giving?

And the answer that came to him scared him, for he realized that he was beginning to think highly of her. *Too highly.* And he had things to do yet in America. He didn't need a woman to complicate his life . . . a woman who had land and money while he had nothing but bitterness to give.

EIGHT

It was late when Lizzy awakened. There was barely light enough to see in the room. She lay a moment as she struggled from the last remnants of sleep. Then she sat up with a start. "The children!" she gasped. Suddenly, she recalled that McDermott was home and Emma and Jason were safe, and she relaxed. The thought of Conor McDermott made her tingle. Had he really been inside her room?

Yes, she thought. Picturing him, she inhaled sharply. She could still detect a hint of his scent. Smiling, she hugged herself, ready to face the world. *Face him.*

Swinging her legs over the side of the bed, she felt the room spin before it settled down again. She stood then and dressed, donning a fresh shift before slipping on a blue muslin gown.

Lizzy went to the window, pushed aside the drapes, and peered outside. Her bedchamber overlooked the river. It was dusk. There was no sign of the setting sun, nor was there a ripple of current on the water.

She dropped the curtain and headed toward the door. With Mrs. Potts gone for good, someone had to prepare supper. She frowned. She was surprised that Jason and Emma weren't knocking on her door, demanding something to eat.

Someone must have kept them from disturbing her. She smiled as she left the room.

There was no sign of the children as she descended the stairs, but she wasn't worried. They had to be somewhere about. They were probably in the kitchen, playing with one of the new kittens that Conor had discovered in the barn only last week.

As she neared the back of the house, she thought she could detect the scent of cooking. With a frown, she hurried toward the kitchen . . . and was startled to find Conor McDermott alone in the room, near the stove, stirring a simmering pot.

He turned as if sensing her presence. "Good day!" he said cheerfully.

She hurried over to relieve him. "I'm sorry. I didn't mean to sleep so late. You shouldn't have to cook dinner."

He waved her away with the spoon. "Go and sit," he ordered. "Ya needed yer rest, and the cooking of this meal was me own idea." His grin took the sting out of his rejection. She sat as indicated in a chair at the kitchen area dining table where they had shared breakfast.

"Where are Jason and Emma?" she asked, expecting to be told that they were outside or upstairs in the playroom.

He carefully set the spoon down on a plate on the worktable, then joined her at the table. "Ya don't remember?"

She frowned. "Remember what?"

"Kathleen Quaid was here. She offered to take the children back to Green Lawns. I didn't want to disturb ya, but I thought it best if ya were asked."

"You came up to my bedchamber?" she said, aghast.

"Twice," he said with a grin. "Don't ya remember?"

"I remember the first time . . ." She blushed. "At least, I think it was the first time."

He nodded.

"And you came upstairs again?"

His lips twitched. "Nay. I truly didn't want to disturb ya, so I said 'twas all right for them to go. Kathleen is to keep them overnight. I told her that if ya objected that I'd come meself and get them for ya." He rose again and went to the hearth, where he checked on the progress of something he was baking. "Do ya have an objection?"

She should, she knew. The man had taken authority over the children into his own hands. She should be furious, angry. But she sensed that his motives had been good. He had known she was exhausted and worried about the children. And he knew that she trusted Kathleen and wouldn't worry about leaving Emma and Jason in her capable care.

"No. They love to visit the Quaids."

His smile brightened the blue of his eyes. "Jason was excited about going. The boy certainly enjoys horses."

Lizzy's face softened. "Yes, he does. In fact, he wanted me to ask you if—"

"He already asked, and I've already granted. He can come anytime as long as he has yer permission. He's a good boy; it will be a pleasure to teach him what I know."

"You're very kind," she said.

He shook his head. "Kindness has nothing to do with it. I've simply stated a fact. The boy will be a help, and I'm not so foolish as to reject it."

"Nevertheless—" she began, then halted when she saw that her words were embarrassing him. What a puzzle this man was!

He was quiet after that as he finished preparing the meal, and Lizzy was loath to disturb him. She wondered what he was fixing, but then figured that she would learn soon enough when the food was ready to be served. So, she sat, feeling like royalty while a good-looking, virile man did a woman's work and yet appeared at home in her kitchen—and seemed all the more masculine for it.

He would be a good man to keep, she thought. And then she cursed herself for even entertaining the idea.

"Here ya go." He set a plate before her.

She stared at the slice of beef pie, covered with gravy, that had been simmering in the pot, and noted the delicious smell. "This looks wonderful."

He smiled.

"I didn't know you could cook."

He raised an eyebrow. "There is much about me ya don't know." He forked up a piece of pie. "I'm a man of many talents."

"I'm beginning to see that." She caught her breath at his grin.

"I purchased the supplies we need," he began, watching her intently. "And I paid a visit to yer late husband's lawyer."

"You did?" Tension filled the ensuing moment of silence. "Why?"

"I wanted to have some things clarified about John's holdings."

"And?"

"There are a few things I need to go over with ya concerning the plantation."

Lizzy felt her chest tighten. "Now?"

"Nay." He smiled. "And don't look so alarmed. 'Tis not a terrible thing. Ya wanted to learn the ropes, didn't ya."

She nodded.

"Then, smile and eat yer supper. Ye've brought a healthy baby into the world this morning. 'Tis something to be happy about."

His good humor charmed her. Her lips curved.

"That's a lass," he said approvingly.

They ate dinner while chatting companionably; then when they were done, they worked together to clean up.

"I need to go over John's ledger again,"

"All right."

Conor wondered why she had suddenly gone pale.

He headed toward John's study, aware that she followed closely behind. He entered the room and went to the desk. He could sense her in the open doorway. He glanced up questioningly. She seemed to hover uncertainly, as if debating whether to leave or come in.

"Did you want to discuss them this evening?" she asked.

"Nay," he said, and noted her look of relief. He watched as she raised a trembling hand to brush back a lock of golden hair. "Is there something ya need to tell me?" His voice was soft. "Ya seem worried about something."

"The books . . . Milly's Station. Things aren't good, are they?"

Puzzled, he frowned. "Why do ya think that?"

She moved into the room and took a seat in the chair facing the front of the desk. Conor listened with patience, then with growing disbelief as she recounted the visit from James Thompson, who claimed that Milly's Station owed a large sum.

When she was done, she was pale, but looked as if she had unloaded a heavy burden. "I can't imagine why John wouldn't pay the man. I can only think that our financial situation was grave." She stood and moved nervously toward the window within feet of his seat. "And these last months . . . I've made matters worse." She brushed aside the drapes to peer out into the night.

He stared at her with dawning comprehension. "Ya really didn't know about yer husband's business," he said, amazed. She really didn't know the true state of affairs, he realized. He scowled. He didn't want to see her in a different, brighter light. For his own sake, he would rather continue to think of her as the scheming woman who had married John Foley for his riches.

But she hadn't known the extent of John Foley's wealth. And when Conor had first arrived at the plantation, and she had spoken of John, she had talked of him with affection. Had her neighbors—*had he*—misjudged her?

There was a sweetness about her, which couldn't be an act.

Or could it?

He watched her hug herself with her arms as she left the window to approach him and stand by the edge of the desk.

Confused, he stared up at her.

"Mr. McDermott?"

He saw the alarm in her lovely brown gaze and realized that she was frightened. He found himself reaching for her hand. Her skin was soft and smooth, but her hand was like ice. And it wasn't a chilly night.

"I'll check," he said softly. "I don't believe Mr. Thompson is correct that ya owe him money. Except for recent purchases, ya don't owe money to anyone."

"I don't?" She sounded afraid to hope.

"Nay." He heard her sigh, and couldn't stop a grin. "Don't ya worry about Thompson. I'll take care of him."

"Thank you." She turned her hand and squeezed his fingers. Her smile was warm and generous, and it made his insides tighten and his stomach muscles clench.

He nodded as he released her hand. "Let me work on these now," he said huskily. "We'll talk about this tomorrow afternoon."

Her face relaxed. With the concerned look gone, Lizzy thanked him again and left, shutting him alone inside the room.

Conor stared at the closed door and fought the kick

of desire that tightened his gut and hardened his body. Then with a mild curse, he tried banishing the image of blond hair, glistening brown eyes, and full pink lips. But his thoughts only turned to her lovely body instead, and his desire for her only intensified.

And he couldn't forget that except for the elderly Jamieson, a man who was nearly deaf, in the servants' quarters, they were alone in the house.

NINE

After sleeping away half the day, Lizzy was too keyed up to consider going to bed. She went to the kitchen to make some hot chocolate, then took the steaming cup with her into the parlor. If she had been alone with the children in bed, she would have headed upstairs to the sitting room near her bedchamber. But with Conor working so diligently in John's study, she didn't feel the desire, or the need, to retire to the second floor.

Lizzy placed her cup on the sofa table, went to fetch a book of poetry from the bookshelves, then sat on the parlor sofa and began to read. She had reread the same verse four times when she realized that she wasn't concentrating on the book. Her thoughts were with the Irishman in the room down the hall. She sipped her chocolate and stared into space, wondering how she was going to rid herself of this attraction to him.

Thoughts of Conor suddenly made her feel edgy. She set her book aside, rose to her feet, and wandered about the room. She searched for something, anything, to take her mind off her desire for the Irishman.

Spying a statue on a top shelf near the fireplace, she moved to get a closer look. *John,* she thought. She grabbed on to the memory of her marriage as though a lifeline. The statue had been a gift from John for her birthday. Made of porcelain and of Oriental design, the lovely figurine was of a woman with her eyes shut, her head bent, and her hands folded before her.

"She reminded me of you, Beth," John had told her after he had given it to her. "Serene. Beautiful. Peaceful . . . which is how you make me feel." Smiling, he had looked deeply into her eyes and touched her cheek. "Beth, I'll always be thankful that you came to me when you did. You're a blessing in my life. I don't know what I would have done if you'd said no to me."

It was a good memory. She had felt especially close to John that night.

Wanting a closer look at the porcelain lady, Lizzy pulled over a chair and climbed up. She could make out the woman's tiny features, her porcelain-smooth finish . . . the exquisite color and artwork. She stretched high to reach the statue . . . and lost her balance.

He heard a heavy thump, and he sprang from his chair and hurried out of the study.

"Lizzy!"

"I'm all right," she called back breathlessly.

He headed in the direction of her voice and found her in the parlor. She was on the floor, her skirts tangled about her legs, her expression sheepish. Alarmed, he hastened to her side.

"Are ya injured?"

"No."

He stifled the urge to check for her injuries himself. "Are ya certain?" She nodded. "What happened?"

"I was trying to take down that figurine," she said, pointing toward a top shelf near the fireplace.

He reached down and enjoyed the warmth of her fingers as she accepted his assistance. "Why?"

Her face turned a becoming shade of pink. "I wanted to look at it."

He raised an eyebrow. "Look at it," he repeated blankly. He held her hand a moment before releasing it.

"It's a beautiful statue. I wanted to examine it more closely."

"At—" As if on cue, the tall case clock in the foyer chimed the ninth hour. He thought how he should be asleep in his room above the stables and realized that he wasn't in any hurry to go. "Nine o'clock at night?"

She nodded without meeting his gaze. "I know it seems silly, but—" She bit her lip as she righted the chair that she had knocked over. "It doesn't matter why, does it?"

He frowned. She seemed nervous to him. Anxious. "Lizzy, it matters." He wanted to touch her . . . to reach out and take her into his arms.

She looked at him then and gave him a crooked smile that did odd things to his midsection. "I'm restless," she admitted. "It's too quiet here without the children."

Unable to help himself any longer, he extended his hand to touch her hair. She jerked in reaction, but he didn't pull away. Instead, he studied the golden strands he fingered, running the lengths of silk through his hand to the ends before reaching for another section. He heard the increased sound of her breathing.

"What are you doing?" she whispered.

"Admiring yer hair." He shifted the focus of his eyes, and their gazes locked. " 'Tis a warm color. Reminds me of a lazy summer day . . . bright but calming. Something to be appreciated and cherished."

Lizzy stood, trembling, as Conor systematically lifted and caressed one lock of her hair after another. "At—" She paused for effect as he had done earlier. "—nine o'clock in the evening?" She had tried for lightness, but failed. His nearness was having a strange, unwanted effect on her.

"Aye." He released her hair and cupped her face.

"Ye've lovely hair . . . and the most beautiful brown eyes."

She started to sway in his direction. "Conor—"

"Nay, Lizzy. Don't speak. Don't fight this."

"Fight—"

"Shhh," he urged. "I'm trying me damnedest not to touch ya, but I'm havin' a terrible time of it. I've been wanting to do this for days now."

"What?" she asked. Her gaze focused on his mouth. It was a handsome mouth, firm and very masculine . . . a mouth made for a woman to enjoy.

"This—" He bent his head and captured her lips in a kiss that far surpassed anything she had ever imagined. His lips were warm and firm, and they were gentle at first. Then he became more demanding as he deepened the kiss.

Fire and warmth, she thought. Sensation shot through her, making every nerve tingle. Lizzy moaned and leaned into the contact, glorying in the intimacy, in his hard strength and masculine heat.

The deep shaft of desire that accompanied his kiss astonished her. She had been afraid it would be like this. She had feared that it would be this good, and she would be unable to deny him anything.

He lifted his head, and it was a minute before she opened her eyes and caught her breath. She felt a tightening in her chest as she peered up at him. His expression surprised her. She had expected his expression to be unreadable, but it was obvious that he had been as moved by the kiss as she.

Daring to be bold, she reached up to caress his jaw with trembling fingers. His blue eyes burned hotly as he allowed her touch for several seconds. Then he seemed to regain control of his emotions, and his expression cooled. Still, he didn't try to pull away.

Uncertain, Lizzy frowned and dropped her hand. She spun and put a distance of several feet between them. "I didn't mean to disturb you from the study," she said, her voice tight. She halted; then with her back to him, she pretended an interest in straightening her skirts.

"Ye've disturbed me from the first moment I laid me eyes on ya, Lizzy Foley," he said gruffly.

His words startled her. She gasped and faced him . . . and was rewarded with his look of naked desire. She melted inside as she approached him.

Lust burned in his blue gaze, and then the flame was stifled. He looked away. " 'Twould be best if I left," he said. "If there is time, we'll go over the accounts tomorrow."

"Conor—"

His mouth tight, he again focused his eyes on her. "No, Lizzy. 'Twould not be wise. Lock up the door behind me."

She nodded silently. Emotion swirled in her breast, threatening to overwhelm her and make her do something she could regret. She wanted to grab him, to stop him from leaving. She wanted him to take her upstairs.

But she knew he was right. It wouldn't be wise for them to get involved. A relationship between them would only complicate both of their lives.

She followed Conor to the door on wobbly legs and watched helplessly as he settled his hand on the doorknob. He faced her, and she felt the tension between them. They seemed like strangers barely able to be civil to each other. But Lizzy knew they were something more.

"Good night," she said primly.

"Hell." He snatched her into his embrace for one long-lasting kiss that rocked her on her toes, infused her with heat, and left her gasping and wanting more.

He set her away from him. "Good night." Then he left.

Her senses still reeling, Lizzy gaped at the door, giddy with the heady knowledge that he had wanted that kiss as badly as she had needed it.

* * *

As he crossed the yard toward the barn, Conor couldn't get Elizabeth Foley out of his mind. He halted, glanced back at the house, and was startled to see light glowing from a second-story room. *Lizzy's bedchamber,* he thought.

He had a vivid impression of her surroundings from that afternoon, when he had gone to look for her and found her in bed asleep. He drew up a mental image of the room and how she had looked in it.

Done in shades of purple and white, the bedchamber was feminine without being frilly. The coverlet on the bed, from what he had seen, was a purple and white floral pattern. The same fabric made up the drapes that hung at the two windows. The bed was a large four-poster without a canopy and made of cherry. So were the night and washstands and the table near the chair by the window.

He recalled Lizzy lying upon white sheets, her blond hair spread across a white pillow. . . .

The smell of lavender had filled the room and mingled with her own personal sweet scent. He vaguely recalled that the chair was upholstered in light purple . . . and she had a vanity with little on its surface but for a vase of multicolored spring blooms, a single perfume bottle, a hand mirror, and a hairbrush with comb.

He could still taste the sweet flavor of her lips, still smell the clean floral fragrance of her.

She was alone in the house. Except for Jamieson. But the man lived at the back of the manor and was too hard of hearing to detect an explosion at the front part of the house.

Conor fought the urge to return, to knock on her door and shoulder his way in, then take her into his arms and enjoy more than just kisses.

"Conor?" The gruff voice, which had abruptly come

to him from the darkness, jolted him from his thoughts.

Conor hid his agitation well as Henry Pherson stepped out of the shadows and into the moonlight.

"Henry." He frowned. "What are ya doing out here at this time of night?"

"Mrs. Foley . . . she said I wouldn't have to work today. I hope that doesn't set poorly with you."

Conor's expression softened. "Congratulations on yer new daughter."

The man grinned, looking relieved in the moonlight.

"About today—"

Pherson tensed. "Yes?"

"I think it was right for ya to be with yer wife. Ya may take tomorrow off as well. We've got nothing to be done then that couldn't be done by ya the day after."

Disbelief, then gratitude, flashed over the man's features. "Thank you!"

Conor grinned. "Now, don't ya think ya should be at home, tending to yer missus?"

Pherson's lips curved. "She'll be wondering where I've gone."

"Then, get home with ya. And I'll see ya the day after tomorrow."

The man nodded. "Yes, sir. Thank you." Then he wished Conor a good night and left.

With a lingering smile on his face, Conor entered the stables and then halted. He heard the deep sound of snoring coming from the rear room where Fetts, the groom, slept. His smile became a grin.

He continued up the stairs, his thoughts returning to Lizzy, as they had many times since he had come to Milly's Station. His grin faded. She was too deep in his thoughts . . . in the air he breathed and in the world as he knew it. Would he dream of her while he slept?

He fell asleep within minutes of finding his bed. And the dream came immediately. . . .

* * *

"Conor?"

"Yes, Ma?"

"Ya must come in now, Conor, and shed those smelly clothes from ya. Your da will be home soon."

Conor felt a flicker of fear. His father was a terrible man when he was in a temper; and when he learned that Conor had been working the horses for their landlord Richard Payton, he would be furious. But, he thought, they needed the money, for his family, like others in County Roscommon, had recently known hard times. Working the horses for Payton, when the man was willing to pay him, was the right thing to do. He was sure of it.

"Coming, Ma." Conor entered the thatched cottage and went to the back room. There, he shucked off his shirt and trousers, before he hurriedly threw on clean garments.

"Conor!" The bellow came from the front room, the main living space where the family ate and spent their time before bed and when they were not working.

After rolling his dirty clothes into a ball, he shoved them into the corner of the room behind a chair. Conor ran his hands through his hair and hurried to the front room. "Aye, Father."

Donal O'Reilly was a hard man, barely tolerant of his wife and often cruel to his only son. "Did ya get in the peat from Sean Shaunessy's place?"

"Aye." Conscious of hands that weren't as clean as they should be, Conor slipped them into the pockets of his trousers.

Donal's gaze narrowed at his actions. "Why do ya have yer fingers in yer pockets? Having a play with yer cod, lad?"

"Donal!" his wife gasped.

"Shut yer mouth, Katie," he growled at her with a glare. "Did I ask ya to interfere?"

Shaking her head, Katie O'Reilly shrank back. Watching, Conor saw a red haze as anger at the man who had sired him sparked and quickly burned brightly. He was tired of living in fear of his father. And his ma didn't deserve to be treated poorly either. She was a kind and good woman, who loved her husband and son and who tried only to do right by them.

"Ya shouldn't talk to Ma that way."

"What?" Donal turned sharp brown eyes on Conor. "Who do ya think ya are to come between me and me wife."

"I'm her son!" he yelled back. "Yer son!" he shouted, although he hated to admit it.

Donal's face turned a dark shade of purple as his anger reached the same intensity as Conor's. "Ye're no son of mine, ya sorry bastard."

"No!"

Conor heard his mother gasp and saw her turn pale. His heart began to pound.

"Donal, no!" Her features anxious, Katie grabbed her husband's arm, but Donal only shook it off as he continued to glare at Conor.

"Did ya think I'd sire a whelp like ya? Nay! Me own son would be a better man than the bloody likes of ya! Ye're a lad without a da. And I'll not lay claim to such a sorry whelp as yerself any longer."

Could it be true? Was he not O'Reilly's son, but that of another?

"Ma?" Anger warred with hope as he looked to his mother. "Is it true?" He had never truly felt like Donal O'Reilly's son. He had never felt loved as a son should; but then, O'Reilly hadn't treated his wife any better, and Conor knew that in his sorry way Donal loved Katie McDermott.

Her silence was telling. Tension filled the small cottage room as Conor waited for his mother's response.

Katie began to weep. "I'm sorry, Conor," she cried. "But, aye, 'tis true."

He started to go to her. "Ma—"

But Donal apparently didn't like that. He bellowed

loudly to draw attention to himself. "Of course 'tis true. I wouldn't lie!"

"Wouldn't lie!" *Katie surprised them both by coming alive then. For the first time that Conor could remember, his mother stood up defiantly to her husband.*

"Donal O'Reilly! Ye're a liar, ya are!" *Hands on her hips, she stood, her eyes flashing, her back straight, and Conor thought she had never looked more beautiful.* "Ya told me that we'd both be welcome in yer house. Ya told me that ya'd love me son as if he were yer own. Well, ya haven't, and so ya lied, ya did! And now ya hurt both me and me boy, and I'll not put up with it!"

"Katie—"

"Nay, Donal O'Reilly. Ye've had yer say, and now we're finished. Me and me boy will be leaving here. If Conor is not welcome here, then neither am I!"

It was the first time that Conor had ever seen O'Reilly looking pale and ill. "Katie, darlin', I—ye're me wife!"

"I'm the boy's mother is what I am." *Katie's gaze speared her son.* "Come, Conor. Pack up yer belongings. We're leaving. We'll not stay where we aren't wanted and treated right."

"Ye're wanted!" *Donal cried, panic-stricken. All that had happened was that he had had too much to drink, and his tongue had just gotten the best of him. He wanted, needed his family. Even Conor.*

On her way to the back room, Katie spun to face him. Her expression was serene. She had had her say and was at peace with her decision. "No, Donal. We're leaving, and ya can't stop us. Hurt either one of us and ye'll live to regret it."

"Hurt—" *He looked shocked.* "Nay, Katie! Ya know that I wouldn't hurt ya. Not even a single hair on yer lovely head—"

"Oh?" *she said, her blue eyes darkening.* "Then,

*what's this?" She pulled up her dress sleeve to show
dark bruises.*

*Seeing them, Donal gave a hiss of surprise. Furious
at his mother's injuries, Conor made a move toward
the man who had laid a hand on his mother.*

*"Nay! I didn't do that to ya." Donal looked ashen.
"By all that's holy, tell me I didn't do that to ya. I
couldn't!"*

*"As God is me witness, Donal O'Reilly, ya did. Ya
were full of the drink as ya are now—"*

"I can't remember—"

*"Nay." She sighed. "Ya never do." She continued to-
ward the door.*

"Katie!" Donal cried. "I tell ya I can't remember it!"

*She seemed sorry for him as she stopped to address
him one last time. "Well, now ya will," she said quietly.
"For ye'll be alone to think of it. Me boy Conor and
I are leaving. Going where we'll be accepted and safe."*

*His stomach clenching, his fists itching to fight,
Conor followed his mother into the back room to pack
their meager belongings, before they left in the
night. . . .*

*They moved to a village near Strokestown. Times
were tough, and his mother had taken work as a seamstress; but the jobs were few, as the wealthy were pur-
chasing their clothing from England.*

*"Conor?" Katie looked unwell this day. She lay in
bed, her face pale. She had been coughing a lot lately.
Studying her, Conor grew concerned.*

"Yes, Ma."

"I want to tell ya about yer da. Yer real da."

" 'Tis not important."

*"Aye, Conor, 'tis. And I should have told ya about
him years ago, but I thought O'Reilly would be a good
husband and a good father. And I was wrong. I'm so
sorry, son, that I was wrong. 'Twas me own fault that
Donal put ya through hell." Tears filled her eyes, and
seeing them made Conor's throat tighten.*

"Ya real da's name was Maguire. He thought himself a kind man, and I loved him. He cared for me, but not as much as I cared for him. I would have married him. Thought we would. But he married another. She had money, ya see. And so he left me."

Conor scowled. "He left ya when ya were with child?" It stung him that he was a bastard, but not as much as it had upset him to believe he was Donal O'Reilly's son.

"Aye, he did." She grabbed his arm and stroked it.

Katie had a fit of coughing that left her weak, breathless. "Find him," she said. "If something happens to me, find him. He'll help ya."

"I don't need him. I won't take the man's charity!"

"It'd not be charity, don't ya see? Ye're his son. What he has should be yers by right."

Her health worsened over the next few days, until she was feverish and talking wildly. "Married him because he promised to take care of me," she cried. "Said he loved me, but married another."

Conor sat at his mother's bedside, in the dingy room they shared, his heart aching as he bathed Katie's brow and listened to her disjointed sentences. She was confusing O'Reilly and Maguire, he realized.

He felt a surge of anger for Donal O'Reilly and a bitter hatred for Conlan Maguire for leaving his mother at a time when she had needed him.

"Conor!" she cried out. "I had to marry him. He promised to take care of us!"

His heart thundering in his chest as he stared at her, he saw Lizzy's face replace his mother's pale one. "I had to marry John Foley," she cried. "He promised to take care of us . . . me and the children!"

She lay in the place where his mother had lain, looking every bit as pale as Katie. She was moaning and coughing, and every bit as sick. "Help me, Conor! Help me, Conor!"

He reached for her, but her image started to vanish.
"Lizzy!"

"Lizzy!" he cried as he shot upright in bed, awakened by the dream. His blood drumming in his head, he stared into the room, lit by the moonlight that filtered in through the loft's window.

His mind filled with her image, her scent. He shuddered. He couldn't fault her for marrying John Foley, not without faulting his own mother for doing what she had thought was right.

He thought of the children—Emma and Jason. She had done a good job with them. Despite all they had been through, she had raised wonderfully bright and charming children.

Fear clutched at his chest as he sprang up from the bed and started to pace the room.

Lizzy's marriage. She had done it to survive . . . and for the children.

And he understood . . . which scared the hell out of him, for it made it harder to resist her, harder to fight his growing attraction for Elizabeth Hanlin Foley.

And he didn't want to want her. He didn't want to think of her at all, but it was getting damn near impossible to think of anything but Lizzy.

"Nay!"

So, he tried to focus on her life before John. She had birthed two children, hadn't she? And he had heard things about her. She was a wanton creature, tempting to any man, and now she had charmed him.

And he had to forget her . . . even if there was only one hurtful way to do it.

Cursing, he left his room, descended the stairs, and headed back to the house.

TEN

She couldn't sleep. The imprint left on her lips by Conor McDermott's kiss was still warm and tingly. She couldn't get it—or him—out of her mind.

It seemed strange in the house with the children gone and only Jamieson in the servants' quarters. She sat in bed, trying to read, but as she had found earlier, the book—a novel this time—couldn't hold her interest. Her thoughts kept returning to Conor. With an exasperated sigh, she climbed out of bed and slipped on a dressing gown.

Why him? Why couldn't she put him out of her mind? She knew every reason why she shouldn't tangle with him, but all she could think about was how right it felt. . . . *He felt.*

She grabbed an oil lamp and left the room. The golden glow of the lamplight cast an eerie path down the hall to the stairs. The house was still, silent. She could hear her own breathing, feel her heart's rhythmic beat. The floor felt cool against her bare feet. Then she heard a sound. She froze, and her heart raced as she continued to listen. When it remained quiet, she took another step and again heard the noise.

Understanding dawned, and she gave a harsh chuckle. "Fool!" she scolded herself. How could she not recognize the sound of the squeaky floorboard beneath her feet, something she had been hearing for years, since moving to Milly's Station?

Downstairs, in the front parlor, Lizzy lit another lamp, and the combined light brightened the room. She felt restless as she wandered about the parlor, looking, touching things, and reflecting on how her life had changed since she had married John.

She fingered the rim of a porcelain bowl on an end table. She had gone from a tavern maid struggling to raise a child in near poverty to a wife and mother with a good husband and a lovely home with servants.

Milly's Station. It was truly a wonderful estate, but now that John was gone, she had found it difficult finding her place here.

She moved away from the bowl and wandered to the fireplace where she ran her hand across the mantel. Directly above the fireplace was a painted portrait of John, and she regarded it fondly—and with a hint of tears—as she thought of their years together.

When her husband had been alive, she had had his affection. And her time with him had been good . . . but . . .

She recalled the portrait that had hung in the spot where John's now hung . . . the one that had been there when she had first come to Milly's Station. The painting that now hung in an upstairs bedroom, the one that had once belonged to John, was a portrait of Millicent, John's first wife.

Lizzy smiled sadly. During her marriage to John, she had enjoyed his affection, but she had lived in the shadow of his first wife. Millicent had been the heart of John's heart, his true love . . . his chosen mate.

Not that Lizzy regretted marrying him. She couldn't regret their marriage. John Foley had been a good, kind man and provider . . . and he had cared for her more than any other man before him.

Lizzy stepped back to stare into the empty blackened firebox. John was gone, but he had left her with a good home and two children she loved. *More than most women have,* she thought. Then, why did she feel restless and discontented?

She moved back to the sofa and dropped down. With a sigh, she stretched out on the damask seat and crossed her ankles. Wiggling her toes, she studied a bare foot as she considered herself. She was a woman with passable features, she thought.

Conor had said she had beautiful eyes. Did she? She felt an infusion of warmth at the memory.

And she had caught him staring at her mouth. Did he like that, too?

Or was the Irishman just like the rest of the men who had called on her since she had become a widow? Men looking to sample her as if she were a fruit ripe for plucking.

Oh, she knew what people thought of her. Over the years, she had overheard things easily enough. People could be cruel when they didn't know the truth . . . and worse when they did. *Brazen.* They all thought she was a brazen trollop who had captured an innocent old man's fancy.

A trollop? She laughed harshly and out loud. If only they knew how wrong they were, she thought. She was a virgin. Her laughter rang falsely in the night's quiet. Not that they would believe her if she told the truth. People wanted to believe what they wanted.

She thought of the feelings that had been churned up by Conor's kiss, and her body responded at the memory. Could it be true? Was she brazen? For wanting to kiss him again? Touch more of him?

Her skin tingled, and she rose jerkily to her feet. Dear heavens, what was she to do? She had been unsuccessful in her attempt to keep distance between them. She had been so long without a man to hold her in any way; was it any wonder that she couldn't ignore Conor?

Lizzy ran a hand raggedly through her hair. As she

began to pace, she felt herself come alive with her desire for him. Her breasts ached. Her nipples hardened. Her skin burned. She was horrified to experience an unfamiliar ache in her abdomen.

She froze and hugged herself with her arms. What kind of a woman was she that she could feel this way?

She closed her eyes and felt the pinprick of tears.

She *was* wanton. They—neighbors and townspeople—had all been right about her. She was a doxie. A trollop. No decent woman would dare have these feelings.

And she had no idea what to do about them.

Conor saw the light disappear in the upstairs window. Scowling, he halted on his way back to the house.

What was he doing? What madness had inspired him to visit Lizzy Foley in the wee hours of the night?

He had started to turn back when he saw a lamplight flicker in a room downstairs. He stared at the brightness, watching it move through the glass, and was drawn to it.

Cursing, he continued to the house. He might as well be damned for doing as well as for thinking, he reasoned.

Jamieson slept in the back of the house, so he went to the front door. If it was Lizzy who roamed the house, he didn't want to alert the manservant. The conversation he planned to have with Lizzy was for her—and for her alone. There was only one way to get rid of this feeling, and it was to discuss it openly and logically.

A voice inside called him a fool as he hesitated briefly before he climbed the porch steps. Would he be able to keep his hands off her long enough to talk?

As he lifted his hand to knock, the door swung open, startling him . . . and Lizzy Foley stood before him, looking more lovely and tempting in a flowing house gown that promised secret hidden delights. *Ye're worse than a fool.*

"Conor!"

He lowered his arm and stared at her. "Ya saw me coming." He didn't mean for it to sound like an accusation.

"No," she gasped. "I didn't. I couldn't sleep. I thought perhaps a breath of fresh air would help."

He gazed at her a long moment. "Must be the night."

Lizzy nodded, still reeling from the shock of finding Conor on her doorstep. "Must be," she echoed lamely.

The blood thrummed through her veins, making her feel warm. The back of her neck and down her spine felt prickly.

He stood there, studying her with his intense blue gaze. A spark of anger made her lift her chin and her eyes hold steadily to his gaze. She felt herself thoroughly inspected and found wanting. "What did you want?"

His mouth firmed. "We need to talk." He went down a step.

Putting some distance between them, Lizzy decided.

"Did you want to walk?" he asked.

She gazed past him into the moonlight and felt a sudden chill. "No." Against her better judgment, she gestured him inside. "Please. Come in."

He scowled, but entered the house, and as the door shut behind him, Lizzy was aware of increasing tension between them.

"I presume that you've come to discuss the plantation?" she said briskly. "Shall we go into the study?" She started down the hall.

"I've not come about the books." His quiet reply halted her.

Her breath hitched as she slowly faced him. "You haven't?"

"Nay."

Her stomach fluttered. "What have you come to talk about, then?"

"Us."

Nerves skittered across her skin. "Us?"

"Aye." He stepped closer. "Us . . . Our kiss."

She swallowed hard. "You want to discuss our kiss?"

Conor noted that she was nervous and was irritated by it. "Among other things."

"What kind of things?"

He made a sound of impatience. Her beauty, her vulnerability, had him aching to hold her in his arms. And that wouldn't do. "Must we stand in the corridor for our discussion?" he asked, his Irish brogue thickening.

"Oh, no, of course not." Her gaze darted about wildly. "The parlor?"

"Aye," he said. "That will do."

Conor followed her into the room, noting the number of lamps she had lit. As if suddenly aware of the waste of good lamp oil, Lizzy extinguished all the lamps but one. When she faced him again, he thought that it wasn't the wasted oil that concerned her. She had lowered the light to hide her expression.

"Please, sit down." She seemed to hover in the room, as if waiting for him to choose a seat first so that she could pick one the farthest away.

He chose the sofa and snagged her arm before she could move away. He heard her gasp as he steered her onto the seat cushion beside him. And he didn't release her hand.

"Mr. McDermott," she began.

"Conor." He narrowed his gaze. "Ya were calling me Conor. 'Tis no sense changing me name now."

"Conor, it's late." He could feel the pulse jump in her wrist and found he liked his affect on her.

"Aye, 'tis late." He began to rub his fingers across her wrist, pleased when he heard her increasing breathing. "And I wasn't sleeping, and ya weren't sleeping. What does that mean, I wonder?"

"That we were hungry?" she suggested, and then looked embarrassed when he grinned.

"Hunger is a good word for it, I'm thinking."

"I could fix us a bite—" She attempted to rise, but he tugged her back down again.

"Lass, the only thing I'd like to nibble on at this moment is ya."

Lizzy felt a burning heat. "Why did you say that?" Dear heaven, what was he trying to do to her? She had deliberately ignored his reference to hunger, but he seemed intent on making her uncomfortable.

He raised a dark eyebrow. She could see the gleam in his blue eyes, a tiny scar on the right side of his face. Why hadn't she noticed that scar before?

"Because 'tis true," he said. "Since I've had a taste of yer sweet lips, I've found meself wanting another sample."

"Please. Don't!" The warmth in his eyes unnerved her. He was studying her as if he wanted to scoop her onto his lap and devour her . . . and heaven help her, she wanted it . . . wanted him.

"What are ya afraid of, Lizzy? Ye've had a husband. Ye're no stranger to kissing."

Kissing, she thought. Yes, she knew of kissing—a little. But not of the kind and nature as the kissing she had shared with Conor McDermott. And she knew nothing else after kissing. Her relationship with John hadn't been like that.

She felt a flash of heat. The look in the Irishman's eyes promised more than just kissing. She had had little experience with the feelings he has aroused in her . . . of the longings stirred to life by a single look from him.

It wasn't an innocent kiss she feared. It was where that kiss could lead. She had firsthand knowledge of what Conor had called a simple kiss. Nothing about

Conor's kisses could ever be considered simple, for his kisses were like the man himself . . . mysterious . . . complex . . . intensely arousing with the promise of untold delights.

"We shouldn't be discussing this," she said, as she attempted to gain control. Burying those feelings, she raised her chin. "If you've come to make fun of me—"

He seemed startled. "Make fun of ya! Why would ya think that?"

She was horrified to feel tears. "You're like the others. You think that because I'm a widow I'm ready and willing. Well, I'm not." She looked away. "And don't tell me that I've lead you a merry chase, because I haven't. Not intentionally," she whispered.

Conor stared at her bent head and felt his gut wrench. Had he thought she had been teasing him, luring him on for more? Perhaps. But mocking her? Poking fun? *Nay.* At times, he might have teased her with harmless flirtation, but that was before he had tasted her sweetness, found he wanted more from her each time he looked into her eyes, and saw an innocent at odds with what he had heard about her.

Either she was a good role player or he was a fool for starting to believe that she *was* an innocent. But how could that be? She was a widow with two children.

He suddenly realized that her hand was trembling in his grip. Shaken himself, he released her and stood. "I've enjoyed our kisses, and I don't find that a joking matter." He crossed the room to put distance between them.

"I'm not understanding you . . ."

He sighed as he faced her. "Then, let me explain. Our kisses, they may be good"—he met her gaze— "more than good," he admitted. "But I'll not be here long, and ya need someone who can care for ya . . . *and* satisfy yer needs."

"Excuse me?" Lizzy stared at him, aghast. Had he

insulted her? Had he just told her that while he wanted her physically, he didn't like her? She stiffened. *Satisfy my needs!*

She cursed at him as she stood. "Did I say I was looking for another husband?" she said tightly, and was rewarded when she saw his jerk of surprise.

"Nay—"

"Or a lover?" She felt a measure of satisfaction when he seemed at a loss for words. "Then, I can hardly see why you felt the need to come in the middle of the night to tell me this." She stood and walked to the opposite side of the room.

She turned to glare at him. "Did I invite you into my bed? Nor did I ask you to marry me, did I?"

"Nay, but—"

"I expect nothing from you, Conor McDermott. Nothing but that you continue as my foreman until the security of this plantation is assured. If you find that too difficult to manage, if you find yourself too tempted by the sight of me that you can't handle the situation—" Buoyed on by confidence, she continued. "I need to learn how to run this place. Once I've learned what I need to know, you can go back to Green Lawns and take up there where you left off. Surely, you can't possibly think that a few kisses between us changes anything?"

Her heart was thudding hard like a blacksmith's hammer against iron. She hid the fact that she was trembling with anger by straightening the ends of her robe, although she was more than adequately covered.

"Our kisses—our behavior . . . It was probably the result of the full moon. I'm sure you've seen the moon this evening, Mr. McDermott. You could hardly have missed the fact that the moon is full. It's said that people do strange things when there is a full moon."

"Oh?" he said softly. "Is that true?"

She nodded, her anger calming as she saw the reasoning behind her own words—and thought he saw it, too. She tugged aside the window curtain. "Yes. It's true. Some say that the moon on a night like this can drive a person to madness."

"Aye," he agreed.

She relaxed. "Yes. I believe animals rut during the cycle of the full moon." She blushed. Dear Lord, what made her say that? Taken off balance, she rambled on, "It's as if the moon controls their behavior."

She was too caught up in the logic of her theory to notice that he slowly began to approach, too pleased with herself to note the sudden sly gleam that now lit up his blue eyes or the amused sensual tilt of masculine lips. "The light changes their behavior," he echoed.

She nodded. "Yes." She turned toward the window and gestured at the moon. "See? It's beautiful . . . haunting. Is it any wonder that they—we—have been affected by it?"

"Aye, is it any wonder," he murmured.

And she suddenly realized that he was close, too close. Affected by her logic, Lizzy brushed a flicker of uneasiness aside and continued while she watched his approach.

"Look at us," she said. "You and I—neither of us could sleep. Why? Because we had too much sleep last night or several nights before? No, because I know myself that I've slept little—" She gasped, glad that she had lowered the light so that he couldn't see her embarrassment. Surely, he couldn't guess that it was thoughts of him that had made sleeping for her difficult?

"Aye," he said with understanding. "A previous night's sleep has very little to do with our lack of ability to sleep now."

She relaxed. "Yes."

"In fact"—he reached out and caught her about the waist—"it has everythin' to do with me desire to do this."

She inhaled sharply as he snagged her closer to him, so that their bodies came together without space, soft curves against hard.

Heat burst into flame as his strength, his power, surrounded her. She didn't struggle or speak. She couldn't. It felt too good to be in his arms. She shuddered as his gaze dropped to her lips.

"Just as it has everythin' to do with me desire to do this."

He lowered his head and kissed her, a hot mating of mouths that had her head reeling as she clung to his waist.

ELEVEN

His lips were warm and insistent . . . and knew how to evoke intense pleasure. Lizzy leaned into the kiss and felt her body heat.

"Conor," she gasped when he had lifted his head. He transferred his mouth to her neck and began to wreak havoc there.

"Mmm . . ." His lips and tongue did wonderful things to the curve of her neck. She caught her breath and arched her throat, moaning softly as he trailed a pleasurable path to where her pulse raced at its base.

"Why did you do that?"

"Do what?" His voice was husky.

"Kiss me." Then she closed her eyes and shuddered as he caught her earlobe between his teeth and nibbled.

He raised his head up to meet her gaze. "Moon madness," he said, before he bent again to continue his sensual assault.

She felt a shiver of sensation as he nuzzled her neck, kissed her chin. "Moon madness?"

"Aye," he murmured against her skin.

"I don't think—"

"Good. Don't." His head came up quickly, and she could see desire in his blue eyes. The golden glow of the lamplight added shadows and highlights to his rugged features. Mesmerized, she could only hold on to him for dear life.

"Lizzy," he whispered, and she watched his thick eyelashes move as he lowered his gaze to her lips. "What have ya done to me?" He pressed a soft kiss on her nose, her chin.

"What have I—?" She stiffened in his arms. "I've done nothing!"

He smiled at her. "But ya have. Do ya think I make a habit of visiting beautiful women in the wee hours of the night?"

She felt a sharp stab of jealousy. "I don't know what you do."

"This is me first," he said. His tone was gentle, light, and she felt herself relaxing. "Ye've made me do things that I'd never ordinarily consider—"

She gazed up at him with worried eyes. "I didn't do anything."

"Ye're being is doing something, Elizabeth Foley. Ye've a face to tempt any man. A form"—he grinned when she looked away, embarrassed—"a form that makes a man want to put his hands on ya."

And he did just that, cupping her breast through her dressing gown, rubbing the nipple until she moaned softly and pressed into his hand.

"Conor!" The quiver began in her midsection and encompassed every part of her. The feeling was good, but his words still bothered her. "How can you say this?"

His smile was gentle as he touched her cheek. " 'Tis easy, lass. Ye're magic and light. Ye've everything to capture a man's hunger and thirst . . ."

Lizzy shuddered as he caressed her jaw, her neck. She was alarmed. She was flattered. And she was confused by these new feelings he stirred in her. Conor and John were as different as night and day. John had been more friend and father to her. He had never incited her to think that it could be this way between a

woman and a man. While Conor . . . He made her feel
uninhibited . . . alive. It wasn't right for her to feel
this way. Surely, decent women never felt this yearning . . . this burning desire.

She shivered as he found a pleasure point. She struggled to think, to remember why she shouldn't allow
him to continue. "This is wrong," she gasped as he
nipped her neck. Her brain was too fuzzy to conjure
up the reason why. She blinked to clear it.

Emotion flashed across his expression. "Hell, don't
ya think I know it?"

His agreement hurt, but she hid it. "You shouldn't
have come."

He didn't comment.

"It's not too late for you to go," she suggested. "I've
got no power over you. You can leave and forget this
happened."

"Well, now, that's where ye're wrong, Lizzy lass."
His grip tightened about her waist.

"About what?" she gasped, as he trailed kisses along
her throat. Her hands shifted, and she clung to his back,
feeling the muscles bunch beneath the linen fabric of
his shirt.

"I can't just leave." He raised his head and traced
her trembling mouth with his finger, pressing against
the warm flesh, then parting her lips with his thumb.
"And I most certainly will not forget this." He kissed
her, as if he couldn't bear the distance between their
lips.

Lizzy groaned beneath the onslaught and slid her
hands to tangle in the dark hair at his nape. He was
right, she thought dazedly. She would never forget how
he made her feel. She cupped his head, and she struggled to get closer to him. But she didn't feel close
enough. She wanted to fuse his strength into hers . . .
feel every part of him against her . . . over her.

She felt his fingers dip below her night rail, and
her breath stilled with anticipation, then shuddered

with pulsing pleasure as his hand found and cupped her breast.

She didn't want him to go. God help her, but she didn't want him to leave. Strength and heat, she thought, he was all warmth and power. She was vaguely aware that they were moving across the room. She felt the sofa against the back of her legs . . . and it took all of her strength not to slump back against it and pull him with her.

"Don't ask me to leave, Lizzy," he said gruffly.

As if she could, she thought, allowing his magic to wash over her. Her hands slipped between them to explore beneath his shirtfront. She felt herself trembling as she started to sink down. "Conor, why aren't your lips pressed against mine?"

With a deep-throated groan, he pressed her to the sofa, capturing her mouth with his own. He deepened the kiss as he settled his weight against her, surprising her with the deep intimacy and the unexpected delight.

"Lizzy."

His weight felt wonderful. His lips were doing magical things to her . . . and his hands knew all the right places . . . the most pleasurable places to touch. She wanted to plead with him to hurry the process and take her. But she had never done this before, and she was slightly afraid.

Conor had raised up to open her dressing gown, and now his fingers were making quick work of the ribbons of her nightdress. Each brush of his knuckles against her skin had her holding back a whimper.

As her garment parted, allowing air—and Conor's gaze—to touch and caress her heated flesh, Lizzy inhaled sharply. Then, as he watched her while he captured and fondled each throbbing mound, she was unable to control a moan. The shock of the sound had her tensing, even as Conor continued his sensual assault.

Jason and Emma, she thought.

"They're with Kathleen," Conor's deep, husky voice reminded her, and she realized that she had spoken her concerns aloud.

Which left only Jamieson. And he couldn't—wouldn't—hear a thing. . . .

Conor worried the rosy-tipped breast beneath his fingertips, and the warmth of the soft, white curve beckoned. He leisurely cupped a full mound, watching Lizzy's reaction, enjoying the way her eyes darkened, before her lids lowered as her breath whooshed out.

He studied the curve of her shoulder, lowered his mouth to taste the white smoothness, before he began a path toward the fleshy feminine mound that begged to be kissed. As he inched closer and closer toward his goal, he felt anticipation heighten his arousal.

His head hovered over her breast. He bent, placed his lips briefly on the tip, and felt her jerk in reaction.

"Conor, I—" She tried to cover herself with her hands.

Puzzled, he raised up farther to gaze into her eyes. She looked nervous, and if he didn't know otherwise, he could have sworn that she had never been with a man before. But he knew that wasn't so. She had been married and knew the pleasure God had created for male and female. She had been married, and she had given birth to two children.

His fingers tightened into fists on the sofa beside her head. Why should it bother him that she had been with someone other than him? He fought back the pang of jealousy and focused on her. She looked innocent and sweet, and he knew that she wasn't . . . knew that she was his for the taking.

He couldn't do this. He couldn't do this, and he didn't know why. . . .

He cursed and leveled himself off of her. He stood with his back turned, hard with desire, throbbing with need. He heard the sound of fabric.

"Conor?"

He heard the concern in her voice. She touched his shoulder. He tried not to flinch, but her nearness was the last thing he needed. She was a spark, and he felt like dry gunpowder ready to ignite and explode.

"Conor, what's wrong?" Lizzy felt a chill seeping past her gown. She caught the edges of her robe and drew them tightly together.

"Wrong?" He spun, and she gasped . . . until she saw the heat of desire in his expression. "I'll not do something we'll both regret tomorrow," he said.

Was he already regretting what had occurred between them? His words said one thing, but his gaze said another. "I don't understand. Why should we have regrets?" She nearly tripped and said *you* instead of *we*.

"Ye're John Foley's widow."

Cold filtered into her chest. "So?"

"Ya were wife to a wealthy man."

So it was because she was a soiled dove, was it? She wasn't good enough for him. "I see." She turned away. She wouldn't cry!

He grabbed her by the shoulders and turned her to face him. "No. I don't think ya do."

"If you're reminding me that I had a husband, Mr. McDermott," she said, "I'm well aware of it." She studied his ruggedly attractive face and felt her throat tighten. She attempted to pull from his grasp. "I can't change the fact that I married John Foley."

He was silent as he finally released her. "I know that." His voice was quiet.

She could feel her eyes fill. "Good night, Mr. McDermott." Abruptly, she turned away so that he wouldn't see her tears.

Conor stared at her, aching with the desire to hold her, kiss her. It was better if she thought that he cared that she had made love before. He scowled. Hell, yes, it bothered him that she had known other men, but that wasn't the reason he had come to his senses. He had nothing to offer her, while she had everything and more.

He resisted the urge to cup her face, clenching his hands at his sides until his knuckles whitened.

"Good night, Mrs. Foley," he said. He reached for the door and paused. "Will ya be all right?"

She refused to meet his glance. "I'm fine, Mr. McDermott. Now, if you don't mind, it's late, and I'm suddenly feeling tired."

And he left . . . sorry that he had ever come, sad to realize that he would have her only in his dreams.

Lizzy stood at the door, staring until Conor disappeared into the night. She shut the door quietly and leaned back against it, her body throbbing, and her heart breaking in two.

She was a wanton. She felt hot and tingling and wanted desperately to go after the man.

Sniffing back tears, she slowly moved to extinguish all lamps but the one. Then, with her eyes stinging, she picked up the light and climbed the stairs. In her room, she turned off the lamp until the bedchamber was in darkness, but for the faint glow of the moonlit night.

She lay on her bed, her eyes burning, her throat tight, until the thought of never feeling Conor's arms around her again, never again knowing the taste of his lips, overwhelmed her.

And she cried for everything she had lost . . . and for the true extent of what she had sacrificed when she had accepted John Foley's offer of marriage. . . .

TWELVE

"Is Conor helping ya, then?" Kathleen adjusted her baby daughter on her lap. She cooed at little Fiona and bounced the child on her knees.

"He knows what he's about," Lizzy said. She smiled as she watched her friend with the babe. She was in her friend's home at Green Lawns, sharing a pot of tea and the morning. "He's got the men working hard, and they all seem to respect him."

Kathleen arched an eyebrow as she looked at her friend. "But?"

"But what?" Had it been so obvious, that the relationship between Conor and her was a tense one?

"There's something ye're not tellin' me."

Lizzy felt a jolt. "Why do you say that?"

"Elizabeth Foley, we've been friends since the day we met. Don't ya be dodging me question."

She couldn't help but smile. "You read me well."

After rising to set her daughter on the floor with a toy, Kathleen returned to the sofa where Lizzy sat. "Are ya and Conor at odds about something?"

"We get along," Lizzy said cautiously.

"Lizzy!"

She sighed. "I like him well enough, but he doesn't care much for me."

"I don't believe that."

Lizzy met Kathleen's gaze. "It's true. He works well because I've asked him—because you and Rian have asked him to, but he doesn't like me. He thinks I'm . . ." Her eyes drifted from her friend as her voice trailed away. Her glance met Kathleen's when she felt her friend's hand covering her own. "He believes the gossip. He thinks as all the others."

Kathleen frowned. "It doesn't seem like a thing Conor would do." Then her expression changed to one of doubt.

"It's true, isn't it? He's said something to you about me."

Pink rose to stain Kathleen's cheeks. " 'Twas before he left here. He seemed a bit reluctant, but then he agreed." Her mouth firmed. "I don't like to think that he'd believe the gossips."

"Why should he be any different?" Lizzy said. But she had wanted him to be different. Oh, how she had wanted him to like and respect her. And now she knew she had neither from him . . . neither the liking nor the respect. *Lust.* The only thing she knew was that Conor McDermott was physically drawn to her. But, still, his desire had condemned her in his eyes. He blamed her for his weakness, seeing her as some siren who had charmed him into craving something that endangered him.

Kathleen Quaid studied her friend's expression and saw the hurt. Her jaw tightened with irritation. Lizzy was a lovely woman. There was no better friend, no one who was more honest and good than Lizzy Foley. She would have to have a talk with Conor McDermott. *Or have Rian talk to him,* she thought, brightening. Conor would take the scolding much more easily if it came from a man.

"Are you sorry he came to help?" Kathleen asked, watching her friend closely.

"No!" Lizzy's eyes shot to hers, then skittered away. "No," she said more evenly. "He's been a tremendous help. I don't know what I would have done without him."

"Hmmm." Kathleen made no secret of her displeasure with him. "Perhaps he's in need of a sound dressing down."

"No!" Lizzy cried. Kathleen watched with interest as Lizzy struggled for composure. "I mean, if you do, then he'll become angry with me, and where would I be? He hasn't taught me everything I need to know to run Milly's Station."

Kathleen nodded as she watched Lizzy closely. "Aye," she said. "I see what ya mean." Lizzy's barely discernible sigh of relief had her hiding a smile. "Well, then, I'll leave it to ya to disabuse him of the notion."

"Me?" Lizzy gazed at Kathleen as if the woman had gone mad.

"Aye, of course. He thinks ye're a trollop, if I'm reading this correctly."

Feeling miserable, Lizzy could only nod.

"Well, change his mind."

"How can I possibly do that?"

Kathleen smiled. "Ye're a smart young woman. If ya think about it for a time, ye'll know." Her gaze went to her daughter. "No, Fiona! Don't hit the kitty. She'll scratch ya."

It was too late. The little girl had tugged on the cat's tail and earned a swipe of the kitty's paws against the back of her hand. While Kathleen picked up her daughter to scold and then comfort her, Lizzy's mind raced. What did Kathleen expect her to do? How could she possibly convince Conor that she was an innocent?

She opened her mouth to ask. "Kathleen—"

"Good day!" Rian Quaid came in, causing a distraction, and Kathleen and her daughter were engulfed in his arms. After a sound kiss for his wife, Rian spied Lizzy on the sofa and grinned.

"Well, Mrs. Foley, ye're a sight for sore eyes this morning."

Lizzy smiled. "Don't ya be fooling with me, Rian Quaid," she teased back with an Irish accent.

He roared with laughter. "As if I'd get the better of ya," he said with a lingering grin. "Ye've got a wise friend, Kathleen," he said. "A man can't take her on a merry chase, can he?"

Lizzy felt the blood drain from her cheeks.

"Rian," Kathleen scolded.

The man looked nonplussed. "What? What did I say?" He narrowed his gaze as he switched his study from one woman to the other. "Never mind," he decided. "I don't want to know." With his daughter in one arm, he came to Lizzy and picked up her hand. "Ya know I wouldn't do or say anything to hurt ya intentionally." The Irish in his voice had grown thick, a testament to how upset he was that he might have hurt her.

Lizzy's expression softened. "Kathleen, you've got a nice husband." She grinned at her friend.

Kathleen returned the grin as she came up behind him and touched his shoulder. "Don't tell him that," she said in a loud whisper. "He'll be impossible to live with. A man with a swollen head can't think but for the praise ya give him."

Rian released Lizzy's hand to lock eyes with his wife. "Ya love me Kathleen Quaid, and don't ya be saying otherwise."

"Of course I do," she said softly, and leaned to kiss his cheek. Rian turned so that she caught his mouth instead. And after one long, breathless kiss that should have, but didn't embarrass their friend, Kathleen and Rian broke apart.

"Ma!" Jason took that moment to burst into the room. "You've got to come to the stables. Rainbow's had a new foal. Just now! You should see him! He's magnificent."

Lizzy gave him a soft smile. "He is, is he?"

The boy bobbed his head. "Yes, come."

"Perhaps later."

"Your mother is relaxing, Jason," Kathleen said. "Why not head to the kitchen for some cookies?"

"Can I, Ma?"

"May I," she corrected.

He sighed. "May I, then?"

"Of course you may. But don't eat too many." She watched with a smile as Jason ran off, before turning back to her friends.

"He's a good boy," Rian said.

"I know." Little Fiona reached toward her from her father's arms, and obliging, Lizzy took her. She tickled the child's chin, chuckling when the girl giggled, before settling the baby on her hip. "Thank you for keeping him and Emma. I appreciated not having to worry about them."

"How is Mrs. Pherson and her babe?"

Lizzy beamed. She had checked on mother and daughter just that morning before coming. Both were happy and healthy, and doing fine. "They're doing well, thank you."

"Sounds like ya had quite a night." Rian accepted his struggling daughter from Lizzy, who chuckled at the fickleness of a child.

"It was a long time for Adda," Lizzy said.

"And ya, too," Kathleen added. "Conor said—" She narrowed her gaze. "Ya're not angry with him for allowing the children to come?"

Lizzy blinked. "No, of course not. He knew I trust you with the children." She bit her lip. "I'm not angry with him at all." *Hurt,* she thought. *But not angry.* The pain, the longing, went too deep for anger.

Rian glanced from one woman to the other with a blank look. "What's this? Lizzy's angry with Conor?"

"I'm not angry."

He relaxed. "Good. We sent him to help ya. I hate to think that he's caused ya any concern."

"No," she said. "No concern." But she and Kathleen exchanged knowing looks.

Rian left with his red-haired daughter in his arms, leaving the two women alone.

"Ya should talk with Conor," Kathleen urged. "He's a good man."

"Talk with him about what?" Lizzy asked. "I know he's a good man."

"Tell him—"

"Tell him what? That, although I was married for six years, I'm still pure?" She laughed harshly. "As if he'd believe me."

"Make him believe—"

Lizzy raised an eyebrow. "And how do you propose I do that?"

"I don't know." Kathleen frowned in frustration. "There must be some way."

"I'm afraid not. And besides, he's leaving for Baltimore again the latter part of this week. Something about personal business this time."

Kathleen reached for the teapot and held it over Lizzy's cup. After Lizzy waved it away, she poured tea for herself. "Hmmm," she murmured. "That would be the relative."

"Relative?" she echoed. Lizzy was hungry to learn more about the intriguing Irishman.

"Aye. A cousin or some such relative, I think. He hasn't said." She stirred a lump of sugar into her cup. "All I know is what I've learned from Rian. 'Twas the reason he came to America. To find his loved one."

"I see." *Relative?* She had a dying need to learn more about Conor's search, about anything regarding his family and his past.

" 'Tis a shame he's had no luck in locating the lad."

"Yes," Lizzy agreed. "A shame." Her thoughts raced with questions. "What will he do when he finds him? Will he leave here?"

Kathleen set her cup onto its saucer after she had

taken a sip. "I don't know. I believe so, and I don't like to think of it. Rian and Conor . . . Well, they're more than employer and employee. They've become friends."

Days after she returned home to Milly's Station with the children, Lizzy still couldn't put her conversation with Kathleen out of her mind. So Conor was searching for a family member, she thought. How close was he to finding him? Was it true that he would leave after he had completed his search and found his relative?

He had been here for almost three weeks now. The thought of his departure bothered her. She wanted him to stay. There was so much to learn yet, she reasoned. Would Milly's Station continue to run smoothly the way it had since Conor's arrival? Would the workers revert to their former ways and give her a hard time? Would she have learned enough by the time he left that she could handle them or anything that came her way?

She had to speak with Conor. It had been three days since their night encounter, and he hadn't come in for a meal. *He's avoiding me*, she realized.

Well, she still had to learn, didn't she? And he had to see and talk to her in order to teach her. As things stood, she felt he should report to her. After all, she did own Milly's Station.

Happy or not, he would come to supper, she decided. *Tonight.*

She saw that the children were busy before she looked for him. She found Conor in the back forty, working the fields along with the men.

"Mr. McDermott?" she called. "Mr. McDermott!"

Conor tensed as he heard Lizzy's voice. He straightened slowly and turned to face her. He had known that as the foreman he couldn't continue to avoid her.

She came across the field, looking flushed and

sounding breathless as she reached him. "Mr. McDermott," she said.

He nodded. "Mrs. Foley."

"Mr. Markins. Mr. Brant." He watched as she acknowledged both men, and several more, before focusing her attention back on him. "Mr. McDermott, if I may have a moment of your time?"

"It's yer time as well as me own," he replied. She led, and he followed her for a distance.

She paused, and he waited for her to speak. He saw that she had difficulty framing the right words, and became intrigued.

"Mr. McDermott," she began. "I realize that you don't like me, but that's not important." She paused to draw a breath, and he suspected that whether or not he liked her *was* important to her.

"You are my foreman," she continued without waiting for him to comment. "At least for the time being. And as my foreman, I expect you to report to me daily. We've yet to go over the books and discuss other business matters. So given that, I expect you to come to the house this evening. For supper." She seemed to punctuate every word. "After which we will move to the study for a meeting. Is that clear?"

Conor had listened to her with growing fascination and a grudging respect as Lizzy firmly, fearlessly, issued him instructions. He should have been angry that she had adopted such a tone with him, but the sight of her flashing eyes and bright cheeks hit him like a ton of bricks. She was magnificent as she outlined his duties and issued orders. He grinned; he couldn't help it. And he could see that his amusement infuriated her, for her face darkened and her brown eyes snapped with anger.

"Do you find me amusing, Mr. McDermott?"

His resolve to avoid being near her faded away. "Nay, I find you refreshingly delightful."

Lizzy gaped at him. That was the last thing she had

expected him to say. The man had angered her, and laughed at her, and now it seemed he had chosen this time to flirt with her!

She refused to be taken in. Not by his nonsensical comments or his charm. "You will be at the house for supper. Six P.M. sharp."

He nodded, his blue eyes twinkling.

"I don't find this situation funny, Mr. McDermott."

"Now, that's a shame," he said. " 'Tis better to laugh than cry. After the two, what else is there?"

She glared at him, tightening fingers into fists at her sides. "I will see you at six, Mr. McDermott." She made a sound of exasperation as she turned and walked away.

"I'll be there, Mistress Foley. With an appetite," he added.

His last statement continued to linger in her mind after she had gone back to the house, throughout the afternoon, and while she made the last preparations for dinner. His comment about appetite had been too much like an earlier conversation they had shared when they had discussed hunger of a different sort.

She fed the children early with the excuse that the supper with Conor McDermott would be brief so they could get on to business.

"But, Ma, Conor hasn't eaten with us for a long time," Jason protested once he learned that the Irishman was coming, and that he couldn't be here to sit and talk with him.

"Mr. McDermott's last meal with us was less than a week past, Jason. He and I have farm business to discuss. You and Emma are just going to accept that you need to eat early and be done."

"Emma's going to eat, too?" he asked.

Lizzy scolded him with a look. "Didn't I just say that?"

"Can we eat with him tomorrow?" Emma asked. She sat at the table with her doll in her lap, fastening up the buttons on the dress that her mother had made for Lily.

"Yes. Yes! If he comes for supper tomorrow, you shall eat with him."

"And for the noon meal?" Jason asked hopefully.

"Yes, for the noon meal, too."

Somewhat mollified, Jason helped set the table and then sat with his sister to eat in silence.

"Ma," Emma said. "Tell Jason to eat with his mouth closed."

"Jason—"

Jason flashed Emma a look. "Yes, Ma."

Emma's response was to smile at him sweetly.

By the time the children were done and gone and the meal prepared, Lizzy was a bundle of nerves. She had fixed roasted pork, potatoes, and fresh beans, the first of this year's crops. She had made fresh bread and a chocolate pie to complete the meal.

There was one thing left to do, and that was to make the gravy for the meat. She poured some of the drippings into a pan, added a mixture of flour and water and some seasonings. She stirred the gravy while it heated and thickened. So intent was she on the task that when she heard a sound behind her, she gasped and burned her hand. She cried out with pain and cradled her burned hand as she glanced over with a grimace to find Conor McDermott.

THIRTEEN

"Ye're hurt!" Eyes narrowing, Conor hurried to her side and captured her arm to inspect the damage.

She had brushed her fingers across the edge of the hot pot, and they hurt like fire. But, still, she was aware of the gentleness of his touch as he moved her hand to check out her burn. Her skin tingled each time he shifted his fingers.

"I'm fine."

"Aye, I can see that," he mocked. "Sit." He waved her into a chair. "I'll find something to tend that burn."

"But the gravy—"

"Gravy be damned," he growled. Then he sighed. "I'll take the gravy off the fire." He searched for and found a potholder and removed the hot vessel from the flame. "Smells good."

"Pork gravy," she murmured. The burn was throbbing, making it difficult to think clearly. Or was it Conor McDermott's presence that made it difficult to reason?

She sat with aching hand, watching as he removed the pot from the fire, found a cloth, and dampened it with cold water. He brought the cloth to her.

"Thank you." She pressed the fabric to her burn and winced, as the area was tender.

"Do ya have ice?"

She frowned. "Ice?"

"Aye. It will take the sting out of the wound."

"There should be some in the icehouse," she said. "Near the root cellar."

"I'll get it."

"I've got some herbs I could make a paste with," she called to him as he headed toward the back door.

He halted. "Good. But the ice will help ya, too."

Conor left for a piece of ice, and Jason came in as the man left.

"Where's Conor?" he asked.

"McDermott," she corrected without thought, using the name he had offered to the children.

Jason searched the room as if he expected to find the Irishman hidden in a corner. "I thought I heard him."

Lizzy nodded. "You did. He went to the icehouse."

"Why?"

She held up her hand, and the boy clucked disapprovingly. "Would you fetch my medicine satchel?" she asked him.

He nodded and left, no doubt anxious to return to see Conor.

Lizzy sat in the chair, holding the cloth, and eyed the stove helplessly. If she didn't get the meal on the table soon, it would be ruined.

Conor came back as Jason entered the room with Lizzy's satchel. "Hey, McDermott."

The man grinned. "How is me favorite assistant?" He found a towel and wrapped the ice in it.

"Good." The boy glowed. "Why haven't you come to eat with us?"

"Been busy," he said, as he gently took Lizzy's hand and pressed the ice against the singed flesh.

"Oh." Jason watched his actions with interest. "Are you coming tomorrow to eat?"

"Depends," was Conor's answer, "on how busy I get."

"Can I help?"

Lizzy was conscious of the man's touch as he held on to her hand and rubbed the burn with the ice. "Why, I might be able to use your help," Conor answered. He flashed Lizzy a look. "If yer mother doesn't have work for ya to do."

"Ma?" The boy's hopeful look melted Lizzy's heart.

"You're free to help," she told him, and Jason shouted with glee before running off to tell Emma.

"As I've said before, he's a good boy."

Lizzy met Conor's gaze, and they shared smiles. "Yes, he is," she agreed.

As if just aware that he had been holding her hand, Conor released her. "Better?"

She nodded.

"Where is your burn medicine?" he asked.

"Here." She moved the bag with her good hand.

He picked it up and opened the drawstring. "What should I use and how do I fix it?"

"You don't have to—"

"Aye," he said, the blue of his gaze deepening. " 'Twas my fault that ya hurt yerself."

"It was an accident. It wasn't your fault. I was clumsy, is all."

"Ya?" He reached out to caress her cheek. "Not likely."

She inhaled sharply, overpowered by his scent, his quiet strength. "Conor—"

"Aye?"

Her heart thundered. "I've got to put dinner on the table."

"Why don't ya let me serve up dinner while ya decide which medicine ya need."

She agreed, only because she saw that he was determined. As she took the open satchel, she studied him out of the corner of her eye, appreciating the careful way he pulled the meat from the oven and set about slicing it.

She had hoped to keep this dinner and the meeting following businesslike, had hoped to keep her emotions reined and her heart from responding. But already, it seemed a hopeless cause. From the moment she had discovered him in the room, she had been lost. She had been foolish and burned herself. His tender care of her threw all of her good intentions out of the window. How could she ignore what she felt for him when he kept doing nice things? When he was gentle and kind toward her?

With her uninjured hand, she rummaged in her medicine bag and found the dried plant root that was good for preventing infection and soothing burn wounds. She returned the bag to the table.

"Sweet Saint Bridget!"

Conor's cry had her spinning to face him. She saw the grin on his face and felt her stomach flutter with pleasure. He had discovered the chocolate pie and was eyeing it, and now her, with a worshipful look. "Ya don't play fair, Lizzy Foley."

"Pardon?" She frowned. Play? What did he mean by that?

"This." He held up the pie. "The game has just begun, and already ye've won it."

"I don't know of any game, Mr. McDermott."

He replaced the pie where he had found it, on a pantry shelf, and turned to her with a narrowed gaze. "Why such a look? 'Tis just fun that I'm having with ya."

Her look apologetic, she sighed. "I'm sorry. I'm feeling out of sorts. I shouldn't be taking it out on you."

"Ye're entitled." He set a platter of the sliced meat in the center of the table. As he went back for the rest of the food, he accidentally brushed her shoulder, and the brief contact made her pulse race. And her body began to hum.

"No. I'm not entitled," she said softly. "There is no

excuse for rudeness." She rose to help him with the meal.

"Stay where ya are," he urged. "Keep the ice on that burn."

She hesitated and then sat. "Where did you learn about burns?"

He shrugged. "Here or there."

She sighed. Apparently, he didn't want to discuss his past.

When the food was on the table, Conor sat across from her and dished out the meal.

"Everything smells wonderful."

"Thank you."

"Especially that pie."

She grinned.

"Where are the children?"

"You saw Jason. He went upstairs to play. He and Emma ate earlier."

He looked disappointed, and her heart melted.

"Mr. McDermott," she began after they had both eaten quietly for a time.

He glanced up from his dinner and studied her. She felt suddenly tongue-tied. He was so handsome that he stole her breath. She wanted to reach out and finger his dark curls . . . to stroke his cheek . . . his firm jaw. And his mouth . . . She wanted to feel those lips pressed firmly against hers.

She squeezed her fork until her hand cramped. He was beautiful and kind, and she loved everything about him. She felt the blood drain from her face. Dear God, she loved him. She had never been tempted by another man before. Conor McDermott tempted her because she loved him!

Conor frowned. Lizzy had suddenly turned ashen. "Are ya all right?"

She nodded silently and looked down at her plate as she speared a piece of potato.

Concerned, he pushed back his chair, startling her,

and went to her side. "Elizabeth," he murmured. He helped her to rise and placed his hand on her forehead. "Ya feel like ice!" He raised her chin to inspect her face. "And yer eyes are too bright." He slipped his hand about her nape, noting the dampness there. She had left her hair down, and the back of his hand felt like silk as he continued to hold her neck. "Is it the burn?"

She shook her head.

"Are ya feelin' ill, then?"

"No."

His chest burned. "Then, what?"

"It's nothing." She avoided his gaze.

"What's wrong?"

"Nothing," she cried, pulling away. "There is nothing wrong. Please! Don't touch me."

He jerked back, stung.

Lizzy gasped as she glanced up. He looked wounded. It hadn't been her intention to hurt him. She had been protecting herself . . . her heart. She was vulnerable with him. He had made it clear that although he found her physically attractive, he didn't want or like her.

And when he touched her, even a simple touch as he was doing now, it took everything there was in her not to rush into his embrace and beg him to love her.

"I'm sorry," she whispered miserably. "I didn't mean—*Oh!*" She spun away, put distance between them. After she took several calming breaths, she faced him. "I'm fine."

Lizzy felt her stomach turn as he stared at her. He didn't say a word as he continued to study her closely . . . as if he were determined to look through her. She was conscious of the tension in the room, her throbbing burn . . . the scent of pork and bread . . . and chocolate pie. But her awareness was mostly of him. Reaction set in, and she began to tremble.

With a muffled oath, he rushed to her. "For the love

of Mary, ya need to sit down before ya fall." She felt his hands cup her arms as he led her back to her chair. After she was seated, he glanced about as if searching for something. "Do ya have anythin' stronger than a cup of tea?"

"Sherry," she whispered. "In the back of the pantry."

They had both been drinking water—his choice—but now Lizzy agreed that she could use something to steady her. With him so close, it would be difficult to get through the evening. She would need medicinal help if she was to stay near and keep her feelings for him hidden.

She was wholly and hopelessly in love with him.

And he had no respect for her. Thought her a temptress and worse.

She blinked against tears.

Suddenly, he thrust a cup into her good hand. "Drink."

She obeyed, then sputtered and gasped at the foreign taste. He thumped her back lightly until she caught her breath. "This isn't sherry."

"Found this on the top shelf. Figured it would work better."

The fire that had slipped down her throat had heated her belly, and now a pleasant, lethargic warmth spread over her. The feeling made her tingle and feel nice.

"Better?" he asked.

She bobbed her head.

Conor smiled. She certainly appeared better. He could tell by the silly grin that curved her beautiful pink mouth that she had begun to feel the effects of the alcohol.

His gaze dropped to the red mark on her left hand, and he scowled. He should have insisted that she tell him how to prepare that burn medicine. Any wound, no matter how small, could become infected.

"Lizzy." He touched the top of her head, resisted

the urge to comb her hair with his fingers. "Tell me how to fix the medicine for your hand."

She smiled as she looked up, and his fingers enjoyed the texture of her smooth skin as they slipped against her cheek before he removed his hand. "Flax," she said, sounding breathless. "Boil the seeds and wrap them in a cloth."

He felt her gaze as he prepared the medicine as per her instructions at the worktable. He dumped the boiled seeds into a bowl and brought it to the dining table. "Like this?"

She bobbed her head. "Yes," she said. "Looks good."

He arched his eyebrows at her slurred words and then was amused to notice that she had finished all of the brandy and managed to move the bottle closer to pour herself a second helping.

Conor set the bowl on the table, then turned her seat and brought a chair for himself to face her. Then after dumping the seeds into a clean cloth, he gently took her hand and pressed on the poultice.

Such a pretty hand, he thought, turning it slightly to blot the other side. *With long feminine fingers and faint blue lines across the wrist. Feminine. Smooth. Just like the rest of her.*

She wore a forest green gown with lace-edged sleeves which reached to just below the elbows. His hands itched to explore the bare length of arm below her sleeve. He longed to press his mouth to that satin skin and taste it.

As he held the poultice in place, he glanced up and became fascinated with the shape of her mouth. It was pink and perfect with full, symmetrical lips and—he leaned closer and was hit with the scent of lavender—a tiny little mole on the left bottom side near the corner.

He felt an infusion of heat as he recalled kissing that mouth . . . its sweet flavor . . . and he longed for another taste.

His gaze rose to encompass all of her features at once: the small, straight nose, the glistening brown eyes, the soft, tousled blond hair that framed her face. He found himself bending forward to travel the distance to those lovely features . . . that luscious mouth . . . until the obvious scent of brandy on her breath halted him. He cursed and pulled away.

"There," he said huskily. "That should help." Leaving the poultice in place, he picked up the bowl and stood without meeting her gaze. He brought the bowl back to the worktable, then went to the cupboard for another glass. He could use a sample of that brandy.

He could feel her eyes on him as he poured a measure of the amber liquid into the glass. Their gazes locked as he raised the brandy to his lips. He hesitated drinking and held her look unflinchingly. But he felt it more difficult to think, to breathe, when the only thing he wanted to do was to kiss and hold her and carry her upstairs to that bed in her bedchamber.

Conor grimaced, then took all of the brandy in one swallow. He welcomed the burning heat, the brief moment it took his mind off Lizzy and focused it elsewhere. But that moment was all too brief. As the fire settled, he realized that he equated the fire as similar, but not as strong as the one that burned in him for Elizabeth Foley.

He didn't look at her as he set down the glass and poured himself another. This time he sipped from the glass slowly to savor the flavor and the heat.

"Thank you." Lizzy's soft voice made it impossible to avoid her gaze.

He sat down at the end of the table, within feet of her. He watched as she set the flaxseed poultice aside. "Ye're welcome. Are ya feelin' better now?"

"Much." To his amusement, she extended her glass. "May I have more?"

His lips twitched as he filled the tumbler a third full.

"Do you want pie?" she asked.

He couldn't control his grin. "Aye, later."

She slurped a sip of the drink, then eyed him over the glass with raised chin. "Shall we move to the study, then? We need to go over the books."

Conor stood and helped her rise, before following her from the room. Lizzy walked steadily. Perhaps she wasn't as affected by the brandy as he had first thought.

She entered the room that had once been John's office, moved behind the desk, then shoved aside the chair. Standing before the desk, he observed with amusement her head as it disappeared then reappeared into his view. She plunked down a book onto the desk surface.

"Okay," she said, slurring her words slightly. "Let's get to work." With a cry of alarm, she lost her balance, fell backward . . . and hit the floor with a loud *thunk*.

FOURTEEN

One moment she was setting the book on the desk, and the next she was falling. Lizzy hit the floor hard and lay stunned until Conor's voice roused her from her stupor.

"Are ya all right, lass?" He extended his hand toward her, and she grasped it. She felt his strength as he lifted her to her feet. "Lizzy? Are ya hurt?" His concern was obvious as he ran his hands down her arms and over her back.

"I'm fine." She was more embarrassed than hurt.

How could she have been so foolish? The effects of the brandy had taken hold, but she didn't feel intoxicated. Just a little unsteady on her feet.

"Here. Sit down."

She heard the scrape of furniture against wood as he moved a chair closer for her. Lizzy breathed deeply as she sat down. She shouldn't have had that third glass of brandy, she realized.

She had worked at the Bread and Barrel Inn; she had seen how people handled—or didn't handle—their spirits, so she had never before drank anything more than the smallest glass of sherry.

She blushed as she tried to ignore the fact that she had fallen, and opened the ledger book. There were rows of notations and numbers in John's handwriting.

The script blurred for a moment, until she blinked back tears.

Conor McDermott had held little regard for her before this. What must he think of her now? She shuddered at the answer. "Can you explain these to me?" she asked in a low voice.

He didn't immediately answer, and she looked up to find him studying her carefully. When their gazes met, he gave a mild oath before he pulled her from the chair and cradled her face between his hands.

"Are ya certain ye're not injured?" His blue gaze caressed her face. His concern surprised her.

She bobbed her head.

"Ye're crying."

"No, I'm not." Then she ruined her denial by sniffing.

He wiped a teardrop away with his thumb. "Aye, ya are."

"I'm sorry." She stepped away from him.

Conor scowled. "What are ya apologizing for? For crying when ye've hurt yerself?"

"For being a fool and tripping—"

" 'Twas an accident—"

"Because I drank three glasses of brandy!"

His lips twitched. "No harm in that."

Lizzy's heart fluttered as she studied him. He was a head taller than she was, but she felt the direct shock of his shimmering blue eyes. A warm glow began in her midsection and spread outward as the contact held. She saw his gaze drop down to her mouth, and her heart beat harder. She lowered her attention to his lips and willed him to kiss her. Whatever he might think of her, he had kissed her like no other man before, and she had enjoyed it.

Conor stared at her pink mouth and was tempted to take it, to feel her lips soften and part beneath his own. She swayed on her feet, and he cursed and released her.

"Ye'd best sit down again," he suggested. He wanted nothing more than to kiss her senseless, to feel her body pressed against his own, but he resisted the urge.

She looked up as she obeyed, and he almost gave in to the urge to grab her back into his arms. But she was slightly inebriated, and he had a job to do. He needed to finish here at Milly's Station and leave, before he decided he liked it—and her—too much to go.

"There is a list of the seed supplies that yer husband purchased," he said, after he had found the right page. "This is the amount of seed, and this is how much he paid for it. " He bent over the book and ran his finger down the columns as he spoke. "See these entries? There are three listings, because yer husband catalogued more than one year per page." He straightened. "I imagine he kept the accounts together for a comparison."

"That's why it was difficult to understand," she commented. She was conscious of his nearness, was glad when he stepped back and gave her breathing room.

"Aye."

Lizzy was feeling better and more alert. She leaned over the book, her eyes scanning the ledger page. "And this? What is this for?"

Conor came up behind her and leaned over her shoulder to get a closer look. "It's John's catalogue of farm implements and other tools."

She felt his breath against her neck and fought its effect on her. But the soft puffs of air he expelled made her skin shiver with pleasure. "Did he list everything in the house as well?"

He flipped a page, brushing her arm as he did so, causing her pulse rate to jump up a notch. "Aye," he said. His deep voice vibrated along her spine. "See? Here is a list of the furniture in the parlor. And here is the dining room and the study including . . ."

He raised up slightly, and she glanced back, then

wished she hadn't. The impact of his blue eyes was like a thunderbolt to her stormy senses. ". . . every one of his books."

"He was that thorough?" she asked.

"As far as I can tell."

"I'm impressed."

"I am, too," he admitted.

"But you said you had questions?"

He stepped back, moved to a bookshelf, and withdrew a book. "I found this the other day. It's not a novel or farm book or a book of verses. It's a smaller version of an account book."

Lizzy frowned. "What did he use it for?"

"In this, he lists his assets." She saw that he was watching her carefully.

"But you said that he's listed everything here—"

"Items and accounts directly concerning Milly's Station." Conor saw that Lizzy's puzzlement was genuine. He felt a sudden easing of the tension in his neck that had cropped up when they had first started to read the ledger.

"There's more?"

He flipped open the book and found a certain page. "Here." He handed her the open book. "See this?"

She nodded, but didn't seem to know what it meant. He explained. "Yer husband's funds in a certain Baltimore establishment."

"A bank?"

He nodded.

Lizzy looked closer. Her eyes widened as she saw the figure. "No, there must be a mistake. And I thought he had a small account in Chestertown, not Baltimore. John and I lived comfortably, but we weren't rich."

"He was . . . and now ya are."

"No." She looked shaken. *Rich?* Could she actually be wealthy? Why had John hidden this from her?

"Aye." He took back the book and replaced it on

the shelf. "And as for the bank account in Chestertown, I wouldn't know. I haven't found a record of that yet."

"He could have closed out that account," she murmured. She appeared stunned. "I don't know how to handle that much money."

Was she playacting? he wondered. She was supposed to have married because of the man's wealth, wasn't she? And now she was either pretending ignorance or she had truly been an innocent. If she was playacting, he thought, she was very good at it. Even he was convinced.

Lizzy pushed back in her chair and stood. "Is there more?" What other surprises had John left for her? If she had thought she had responsibilities now, the fact of this money's existence had multiplied them tenfold. Hugging herself with her arms, she wandered about the room.

"I don't know," Conor said, and she could feel his gaze on her. " 'Tis possible. I haven't gone through all of the books. I found this one quite by accident. Like ya, I was astonished that a man could do such a thorough inventory of the contents of a house. I wanted to see if he had mistakenly forgotten anything."

Lizzy halted. "In a way, he had," she replied with a wry smile.

When Conor raised an eyebrow in question, she gestured toward the bookshelf. "He apparently hadn't listed that book in his inventory of the study."

"Aye," he agreed with a grin.

Lizzy sighed as she sat in a chair in the corner of the room. "What do I do about . . . everything?"

" 'Tis yer money."

"It's John's."

" 'Twas John's. As his widow, it now belongs to ya. Just as this plantation and everything that John has built here."

"It's a frightening responsibility."

"Not if ya know what ye're doing."

She rose and approached the desk. "But that's it. I don't know—" She leaned against the edge.

"That's why I'm here, remember? To show ya what must be done?"

She held his gaze steadily. "But there's so little time."

"I'll be here for the time it takes."

Her skin warmed as she stared at him. Had he just told her that he would stay for as long as she needed him? She was afraid to believe, afraid to hope. She knew he had to leave. Hadn't he told her? And so had Kathleen. Conor was on a quest, and he would not rest until he found his relative. He had already been here longer than the Quaids expected. And longer than he himself had imagined, she thought.

She reached out to close the ledger. "I appreciate your help." She kept her voice light, casual.

"That's what ye're paying me for."

"Did John list all transactions?" Lizzy asked, remembering James Thompson's visit. "Every one? Even those with the mill and granary?"

Conor frowned thoughtfully a moment; then his expression cleared. "Thompson," he said.

"Yes," she admitted.

"John didn't owe the Thompsons a cent. And neither did ya. Yer husband kept a record of each transaction and had each business associate initial his entry when his accounts were paid."

"So, James Thompson lied to me." Lizzy felt a burn of anger as she straightened away from the desk.

"It would seem so."

"Why?"

Conor gave her a look that warmed her blood. "Why do ya think?" Desire leapt into his eyes, shocking her with its quick intensity.

"No," she murmured. She shook her head as she came around the desk to put away the ledger book.

"Lizzy."

Something in his tone made her skin tingle. "Yes?" She looked up. He had moved from the other side of the desk chair, and now he loomed within two feet of her.

"Are ya really so ignorant of yer power over a man? Ye're a beautiful woman." He narrowed his gaze.

She stiffened. *Power over a man?* "I beg your pardon!"

He shook his head, and she watched with vague awareness as he reached out for her. She felt a jolt as his fingers encircled her arm and tugged to bring her nearer to him.

"Lizzy. The moon isn't full tonight. Shall we test our theory."

"What theory?" she breathed.

"That the moon had instigated our kiss the other night?"

She was suddenly afraid. "I don't think that is necessary."

But Conor didn't agree. He nodded. "I do."

"Conor—"

"Shhh," he soothed her just before he bent his head and captured her lips with his mouth.

The heat started instantly. The spark became a flame and then an inferno that engulfed Lizzy in its fiery burn.

His hands were as skillful as his mouth in making her come alive. His fingers traced her throat, her shoulder, and slipped beneath the upper edge of her green silk bodice.

Lizzy whimpered and surrendered fully to her desire for him. She had been eager to touch him, and now she allowed herself free rein. She thought she would melt into a puddle at his feet when he cupped her breast, then covered the area with his mouth. The moist heat that radiated through fabric made her nipples harden and her breasts throb. She wanted his hands on her. Although she was inexperienced, she knew instinctively that she wanted to explore every inch of him.

"I think you've proven that moon madness is a myth," she said huskily when he lifted his head to study her and tenderly stroke her cheek. It was his tenderness that was her undoing.

"Perhaps," he said. "Perhaps not." He smiled as he traced around each eye, down her nose, and then about her lips with a fingertip. "I should test this again—" He dipped his head.

Lizzy closed her eyes in anticipation of his kiss, felt her lips part in invitation.

She felt the barest brush of his mouth when a loud crackling crash startled the both of them.

Lizzy gasped at the broken window with disbelief, realizing with dawning horror that someone had thrown something through the glass pane. As she reeled from the shock of it, she heard Conor curse, saw him bend over to retrieve what turned out to be a cloth-covered rock.

He unrolled the fabric, and Lizzy saw that there was something written in red on the white fabric. The oath that left Conor's mouth was vicious. She had never before seen him this furious. Scrunching up the note into a ball within his fist, he went to peer out the window.

"What is it?" As she watched him, her stomach burned. "What does it say?"

Conor thought about opening the window to go after him, knowing that if he went to the door, it would be too late to catch sight of him. The shattered glass made it impossible to do either and be successful. So, he turned to Lizzy, tensing, reluctant to show her what was written on the cloth. The tone of the message was hateful, and aimed at Lizzy, the woman he had just kissed and touched and held.

She eyed him with alarm. "Conor?"

He silently, reluctantly, handed her the note. He

watched helpless as she read it, heard her intake of breath, and wished that he had taken a chance with the glass to go after the person who had done this to her.

She started to tremble as she handed him back the note. Conor lifted it to reread it for clues.

"Brazen Lizzy, go home to Baltimore. We don't want your kind in this county."

It looked as if it had been written in blood, which, Conor thought, was in itself an implied threat. The hatred behind the message would have been clear without the red. Lizzy looked ill. He could see that she was unwell from her eyes; he read it in her pallor.

"I—"

He searched quickly, saw a brass bowl on the floor near the fireplace. He grabbed the bowl, and then Lizzy, forcing her to bend over the vessel in time for her to be sick.

FIFTEEN

The next morning Lizzy was embarrassed to recall the previous evening. She had behaved badly, drinking all that brandy and then getting sick in front of Conor.

Breakfast had been a strained affair with Lizzy serving Conor's meal and then disappearing with one excuse and then another so that she could avoid sitting down with him. She knew she couldn't run from him forever. She just needed a few hours, she told herself, to get over last night's humiliation.

Despite the amount she had imbibed, she recalled everything Conor had told her about John's accounts. She was wealthy! How could that be? Oh, she knew she and John had shared a good home, land, a sloop, and a wonderful life, but she had had no idea that John had had other financial assets. And so much!

Lizzy shook her head. She wouldn't have to worry about funds for a while, and if the plantation continued with good crop yields, she would never have to be concerned with money again.

She was relieved that paying the bills wouldn't be a worry, but with the money came an enormous responsibility. If Milly's Station failed and she lost everything, it would be entirely her fault. She had to learn all she could to ensure that didn't happen. There were people who depended on her—the children, the servants, and the workers and their families. That knowledge made her nervous, but she wouldn't allow it to paralyze her with fear.

The children were outside. Emma would be playing with one of the Pherson girls, and Jason would be tagging along somewhere with Conor. The first time she had learned that he had trailed Conor all day, she had scolded Jason. But after Conor had assured her that he didn't mind the boy's company, she had relented and allowed him to go.

The afternoon had Lizzy cutting to make tow trousers for the men. She had already finished Emma's birthday gown, and now she was sewing for the workers. John had bought, and then freed, several black men after a reasonable length of service. After they had been granted their freedom, three of them had elected to stay on and work at Milly's Station. It was for these men that she made the clothes. They lived in the cottages that John had built for all the hired hands.

"Mr. Thompson is here to see you, mistress."

Lizzy frowned. "Jamieson, please tell him I'll be right down." She had just cut out the second set of trousers. She set down the cloth and, with a purposeful stride, headed downstairs. Now that she knew the truth about John's account with Thompson, she intended to dismiss the man's claim of monies due. And she intended to make it clear that he would never again be welcomed on Milly's Station.

Why had he lied and told her she owed him a debt? So that he could be paid twice?

She wished Conor were here. She had proof of the paid account, but it wouldn't hurt to have the Irishman to stand behind her. She had never trusted Thompson, and now she realized that she had good reason.

At the bottom landing, she paused to draw a calming breath. This was her home. She could send the man away if she wanted to. With her heart beating wildly, but maintaining a calm demeanor, she continued toward the parlor.

"Mr. Thompson."

He rose from the sofa. "Mrs. Foley." He smiled. "You are looking fair this afternoon."

She nodded, but stayed just inside the door. Her guest wouldn't be here long, and there was no reason to allow him to think otherwise.

"I suppose you've come about my late husband's account."

"No need to hurry into that matter," he said.

"Well, actually, Mr. Thompson, there is. You see, I'm very busy today, and your visit, I afraid, is a bit of an inconvenience."

He looked taken aback by her frankness. "Oh, I'm terribly sorry." Anger darkened his features briefly, before his expression brightened. "But even you need a break from a day of household chores."

She didn't smile. "I have servants, Mr. Thompson. I've other business that demands my attention this afternoon."

He blinked. "I see."

"Anyway, about that account, I did some research, and it seems that John paid his debt to you and your brother. John kept excellent records. So, you see, Mr. Thompson, I don't owe you anything at all."

The man frowned. "There must be some mistake."

"Yes, and I believe that you have made it."

A spark of anger lit his gray eyes as he approached her. Lizzy had the urge to leave the room. She didn't want the man within three feet of her. "No, Mrs. Foley, you are mistaken."

He held up a piece of parchment that he had withdrawn from his jacket pocket. "Here. See this?" He thrust it out for her inspection. "Ten pounds of oats, fifteen pounds of corn, and twenty pounds of wheat flour."

Lizzy could barely make out the script. "And the date, Mr. Thompson. What is the date?"

He pulled it back to study it. After squinting to see it for several seconds, he pulled out a pair of spectacles and placed them on his nose. "There, that's better." He flashed her a charming smile, then started to read. "I believe it says June 1848. Yes, that's what it says."

"I'm glad you said that, Mr. Thompson." Anger made her tone sharp. "I've got a record of payment made and signed as received by your brother—one Theodore Bernard Thompson. He is your brother, is he not?"

The man narrowed his gaze as he nodded.

"Well, then, it must be correct."

"I know of no such transaction!"

"Did you ask your brother about the account? Or did you simply take it upon yourself to see that I pay it . . . ," she paused for effect, "a second time."

"I'll need proof," he said tightly.

"I have it. It's in the study. If you will wait here, I will fetch it."

"I'll come with you."

"No, Mr. Thompson, I much prefer it if you would wait here." She left the parlor and headed down the hall to the study. She had pulled out the drawer where the book was kept, when she saw that James Thompson had followed her against her wishes.

"Mr. Thompson, I thought I told you—"

He came quickly to the desk, his expression startling her. "Now, Mrs. Foley, is that any way to treat a guest? I thought I'd make it easier for you by coming to you."

Feeling ill at ease, Lizzy set the book on the desk top and flipped open to the right page. Her finger skimmed down the sheet. "Here it is."

"I don't see it," he said as he bent over the front edge of the desk. "No, I can't say I see it. Wait. Let me try it from your side."

To her dismay, he quickly skirted the desk to stand

next to her. He leaned in close as he appeared to give the entry due consideration. "Well, Mrs. Foley, I do see something that suggests that Theodore signed this book, but I can't say I see where it's for this particular transaction of sale."

Lizzy bent to point out the date, and Thompson took that moment to lean forward so that they bumped shoulders.

"So sorry," he apologized, but he didn't move.

Repulsed, she started to back away. "Mr. Thompson—"

The man grabbed her. It happened so fast and she was so surprised that Lizzy didn't see it coming . . . nor did she have time to fight when he first put his mouth to her lips. The cold, wet contact quickly got through to her, and she shrieked; but it came out muffled. She forced her hands between them and shoved.

He had barely come up for air when he tried to kiss her again. She struggled free. "Mr. Thompson!"

"Mrs. Foley, " he said gruffly. "You know you want this. I can see it in your eyes."

"What you see is disgust, Mr. Thompson." She was in a corner with no room to go but past the man who presently was a threat to her. She started to tremble . . . not with fear, but with fury.

He smiled. "You don't mean that."

"I do, Mr. Thompson. First, you came into my home while I was still grieving over my husband's death, and you attempt to make me pay for goods my husband already paid for. Then you assault me."

"Assault!" he interrupted. "There was no assault. I didn't see you fight me the first time I kissed you."

She glared at him with disbelief. "I didn't fight you because you took me by surprise."

His eyes flashed with anger. "There was no surprise. I could read your invitation. I saw it from the first. You wanted it, and I'm happy to oblige you." He lunged for her again. "You enjoy playing hard to get."

She screamed as she hit and kicked him. The scent of him was overpowering. He smelled of sour sweat and some pungent hair grease.

Thompson seemed to enjoy her struggles. Frightened, Lizzy tried to scream louder, for she knew she would have to alert Jamieson or any of the servants on the second floor for help.

The man's hand silenced her. She stomped down on what she thought might be his foot, and was rewarded when he howled and released her.

"You shouldn't have done that," he said. He was livid. His face was bright red, and the veins in his neck stuck out in a shade of dark purple.

"Get out, Mr. Thompson," she said through clenched teeth. "Get out now."

He stared at her, his look suddenly calm. The abrupt change in him gave her chills. "I'll not leave without my due."

"You've already seen that you've been paid for that order—"

His hand went to his neck and undid his tie. That simple act terrified her, for it was totally inappropriate. She moved against the wall, shoving the desk aside as she went, trying to open an avenue of escape. "I'm not interested in money, Mrs. Foley."

Keep him talking, she thought. *Keep him preoccupied while you think of a way to evade him.* "Then, what are you interested in, Mr. Thompson?"

He continued to move closer. "You."

"Me?" She managed to slip between the desk and wall; but the opening was tight, and her skirts were full and hindered the movement. She pushed the desk with her hip and continued to move.

His smile was grim. "Yes, you. I want you. Surely you can give me what you've given all the others . . ."

"Others?" she said. "I don't know what you're talking about."

His face hardened. "Don't lie to me, Mrs. Foley.

I've heard the gossip. What about Charles Nelton and Robert Brockberry? I've heard of their experiences. They've boasted of it at the Rooster and Crow." He named an inn on the road to Chestertown. "They claim you're a skillful lover."

Lizzy felt the blood drain from her face. "I've never been near them. I don't even know who they are."

"Come, come, Mrs. Foley. Don't be so modest. You were able to satisfy old John enough to get him to marry you. Surely you can offer a sample to me."

"No." Her throat was dry, and she had difficulty swallowing. She glared at him, while she forced herself to remain calm.

Suddenly, he made a grab for her, and she shoved the desk with all her might to evade him. Lizzy fell as the piece moved. Thompson took the opportunity and threw himself on top of her where she lay on her side on the floor.

"Get off me!" she shrieked.

He forced her to her back, then groped and nuzzled her neck, and kissed her face at will.

"I said get off!" she cried.

"What's the matter? Can't you handle a real man?"

"Stop!" Her cry became a scream as he squeezed her breast. Sweet heaven of mercy, was she to be violated in her own house? Tears filled her eyes as she tried to fight him, but he had the advantage of weight and freedom of movement while she had none.

"No!" She couldn't breathe. Her world was receding as she struggled beneath his hefty form to draw in air.

Suddenly Thompson's weight was gone, and she felt the air rush into her lungs. She blinked, managed to crawl up to her knees, and saw Conor McDermott throwing Thompson about the study as if the man were a sack of apples. After one final toss by Conor, Thompson fell against a chair, hit his head on that chair, and was rendered unconscious. Conor McDermott stood over him, looking angrier than anyone Lizzy had ever seen.

She stared at him, her heart beating wildly, her world continuing to grow dim.

"Are ya all right?" Conor asked her.

She shook her head as nausea overwhelmed her.

"Are ya going to be sick again?"

I don't know. She wanted to utter the words, but found she couldn't get them out as reaction set in. She bobbed her head instead. She hugged herself as her limbs began to shake.

She heard Conor mutter something harsh beneath his breath, felt his arm encircle her shoulders, then was shocked to feel herself lifted by him. She was vaguely aware of movement as he carried her through the house. She felt the caress of fresh spring air as he brought her outside and into the garden.

He set her on an iron bench. "Still going to be sick?" he asked.

She drew in several deep breaths to control the churning nausea in her stomach. She shook her head. "I don't think so."

She blinked and realized that he was crouched before her, his hands on her knees as he carefully inspected her face. She shuddered as she saw the direction of his gaze, watched it darken with anger as it settled on her neck.

"Ye'll have a bruise."

She gasped as she touched her neck. "It's sore."

He nodded and straightened. "What happened? What were you doing in the study?"

She interpreted his tone as mildly accusatory, and felt stung. She had done nothing wrong, and he wouldn't make her feel as if she had! Lifting her chin, she looked down her nose at him. "Mr. Thompson didn't believe that John had paid that account, so I went to get the book from the desk drawer," she said stiffly. "And against my expressed wishes he followed me."

He stared at her a moment, then seemed to accept her explanation without comment, but his eyes looked fierce. "I'll get ya a glass of water."

She reached out to stop him, grabbed him by the fabric of his trousers, and then blushed, shocked by her boldness. He looked down at her hand, and she quickly released the fabric. Face filled with heat, she studied the ground. "I don't need water," she said quietly.

He didn't move, but he was silent. The moment stretched awkwardly, and Lizzy now wished she had allowed him to fetch the water.

Her stomach was still unsettled. She vowed that she wouldn't be sick, for she wouldn't allow herself to be ill in front of the man ever again.

Finally, she sensed movement, and she looked up. Conor McDermott had walked several paces, and now he came back, locking gazes with her as he approached.

She breathed deeply. "Thank you."

He stilled. "I heard you scream."

"I didn't expect you to come," she managed to choke out as her throat tightened. "I didn't expect anyone to hear me, although I—" Just thinking about the memory made her feel ill again. She jumped up, wanting to escape before she made a fool of herself all over again. She didn't get far before she was bending over and silently cursing her fate.

Conor hurried to Lizzy's side and held her while she heaved her stomach's contents. He fought the urge to rush into the house and use his fists on Thompson until he had the satisfaction of seeing the man bleed.

When he had entered the house and heard Lizzy's scream, his blood had turned to ice. He had experienced trouble discovering her whereabouts until he heard what had sounded like furniture overturning, followed by a second feminine cry.

He had realized then that Lizzy was in the study. When he arrived and saw that she was pinned to the floor by that weasel Thompson, he had felt rage as his vision had gone black, then red. His fury had engulfed every part of him as he grabbed the man and proceeded to pound him.

Conor rubbed Lizzy's back, then helped her straighten and tenderly tucked a strand of golden hair behind her ear. "Better?" he asked.

She nodded, but she wouldn't look at him. He released her and stepped away.

"I'd better get Markins and Brant to see that Mr. Thompson is properly escorted from the premises."

She looked at him. "How can we make him stay away?"

His gut wrenched at the sight of her unshed tears. "I'll see that he understands that he's not welcome on Milly's Station." He said it calmly, but inside he again felt a recurrence of the rage that had clawed at him while the man had his hands on Lizzy.

"Thank you," she said. She glanced down at the mess and hurriedly turned away. "I . . ."

And she suddenly ran, as if she couldn't bear being in his presence, as if she were ashamed of herself. Or him.

"Lizzy!"

But she didn't stop.

He sighed as he fought the urge to go after her. Instead he went to the study, transferring his attention to Thompson. He cursed as he left the room again for help to remove the man's body. Outside, in the yard, he saw the Pherson boy, Robert.

"Lad," he called. "Round up Brant, Markins, and your father. I've got a job for them—and you, too."

"Yes, Conor."

"Tell them to come inside."

Robert nodded, before he ran to do the man's bidding.

Conor turned back to the house and stared at it for a long moment. His first thought was to go to Lizzy, take her into his arms, and hold her until she cried her eyes dry. But he wanted to remove Thompson first, wanted to make sure that the man never again stepped foot on Milly's Station.

He decided to wait for his men in the study. He didn't want to leave Thompson alone in case he awakened. If the man woke up before the others came, he would take great delight in knocking him senseless again.

Thompson was lying where he had left him. Conor bent, checked the man's neck, and found a beating pulse. He scowled. The man had fallen too easily. He hadn't had the satisfaction of blackening his eyes or bloodying his nose.

Next time, he thought. If ever Thompson came within a hundred yards of Lizzy again, he would do more than blacken his eyes or give him a bloody nose. No one would recognize James Thompson after Conor McDermott was through with the man.

SIXTEEN

Conor didn't come to supper that evening, and he left for Baltimore the next morning, so Lizzy didn't have to face him. She was glad. She was mortified over what had happened. First, she had gotten sick twice in his presence, and then he had found her in Thompson's arms. What must he think of her? After that note and the incident with James Thompson, what else could he do but believe all the county gossips?

She sat on the front porch, watching the children at play. She had work to do inside the house, but she didn't care. Her chores would still be there, and the servants were busy. She decided to take time for herself.

"Jason! Stay away from that mud puddle. I just cleaned those trousers," she called. The boy seemed at a loss without Conor, and that worried Lizzy. Her gaze went to her daughter. "Emma, you share your toys with Meg."

She smiled as she watched Emma give her friend Meg Brant her doll. Meg beamed as she stroked the fabric of the doll's dress, before she handed it back to Emma. Lizzy watched her daughter nod at her friend before grinning at her mother. Lizzy grinned back, and as the children continued to play, she closed her eyes for the moment of peace that followed.

A bird twittered in a nearby tree. The June breeze

was warm with the promise of summer, and the sun was bright in a cloudless azure sky. All the crops had been planted. They had sowed corn, cotton, flax, wheat, and oats in the fields, and she had planted a wide array of vegetables in the garden near the house. And Milly's Station had fruit orchards. The apple and peach trees looked green and healthy. Markins had just brought in the first bushel of cherries, and the fruit looked plump and juicy this year. Lizzy realized that she had pies to bake and preserves to make, but she figured they could wait one more day.

It was an altogether nice day, and if Lizzy hadn't had so much on her mind, she would have appreciated it more. But thoughts of Conor kept intruding on her peace, for sometime in the night, she had realized that she loved him. And she couldn't envision a future for them.

Lizzy sighed and tried to ignore the sharp pang near the region of her heart. She had no idea that love could be this painful. Her affection for John had been calm and peaceful. When he had died, she had been devastated, but her loss had been more like that of a daughter who had lost a father, not of a woman who had lost her man.

Not that she hadn't attempted to change things. Two years into the marriage, she had become more than fond of John, and he had seemed enamored of her. It had been the day after her birthday when she decided that perhaps it was time for her to become a real wife to her husband. John had been especially sweet to her the day before when he had given her the lovely porcelain lady statue and told her nice things. John had been everything a woman could want in a husband, but although she shared his name and his home, she didn't have everything. She wasn't a real bride.

Lizzy blushed as she thought of that night. She had been a wife and a mother; but she had still had her virginity, and it had bothered her. She had started to think that somehow this marriage would dissolve if they didn't consummate it, and she had lived in fear that someone else would find out, that then John would feel the need to cast her aside for the loving memory of Millicent.

That evening she had gone into his study to say good night as she usually did, for John often worked late. Warm affection had filled her at the sight of him seated behind his desk with his reading spectacles perched on his nose. He had been writing entries into his ledger book by candlelight. She had moved to the back of his chair and slipped her arms about him.

"Thank you again for my birthday present," she had said.

He patted her arm where it rested against him. "You're a good wife to me, Elizabeth." He set down his pen and captured both arms with his hands so that she stood behind him cradled about his head and neck. He ran his fingers up and down her arms, and his actions felt good. "You deserve better than me, Beth."

She tightened her grip about him. "John, I'm happy to be your wife."

"No, I took advantage of your situation and robbed you of a husband."

"You're my husband."

She heard him sigh. "Am I?"

Frowning, she had released him and slipped to the edge of the desk to face him. "No regrets, John."

His eyes were filled with sorrow, and her heart melted a little more. She leaned forward and caressed his cheek. His mouth curved into a sad smile. "You deserve more, Elizabeth. If I could undo—"

"No," she whispered softly. In a display of affection, she leaned to kiss him, pressing her lips gently against his. The touch of his mouth against her own filled her with longing. She loved this man. Their relationship might not have been filled with romance and passion, but it was a good marriage. The notion popped into her head that perhaps it was time to consummate their relationship. She trusted him, knew he would be gentle with her. She lifted her head and stroked his jaw as she gazed into his eyes.

She gathered up courage to continue. "John—"

Don't tell him. Show him. She brushed her mouth against his lips; then she deepened the kiss, until his hands cupped her head and held her there. There wasn't fire in the exchange, but there was a warm, contented feeling that she liked. He would be gentle, she told herself. It would be all right.

"Beth," he murmured when they broke apart. He seemed startled by the kiss, for theirs had always been quick pecks on the cheeks or a buss on the lips, nothing like the exchange they had just shared.

"It's all right, John." She smiled and leaned to kiss him again. She placed her hand on his chest and felt his heart begin to hammer. "It's all right," she repeated softly. "We're married."

And she kissed him again, pleased when his lips moved beneath her own. He grabbed her head suddenly and deepened the intimacy, opening and invading her mouth with his tongue. Startled, Lizzy stiffened.

"I'm sorry." John looked ashen after he had released her. "I didn't mean to do that." He looked down at the desk, misery in his expression.

Lizzy had been shocked and a bit repulsed by the invasion into her mouth, but one look at his face banished those negative feelings. She just hadn't known, she realized. If she had been prepared, it wouldn't have been so bad; it might even have been pleasant.

"No, no," she said. "I didn't mind." She smiled at him reassuringly. She reached out and lifted his chin so that their gazes met. "I wanted you to kiss me." She felt butterflies in her stomach. "I want . . . more."

John looked down at the dressing gown she wore over her nightclothes, and he raised his fingers as if he wanted to touch her.

"Go ahead," she urged him, but inside she was nervous. He was her husband, and this was his right.

She closed her eyes as she felt him brush against the upper curve of her breast. The touch was light, gentle. It didn't inspire heat, but it wasn't unpleasant. She opened her eyes, then was startled when John's hand completely settled about her breast. She couldn't control the gasp that sprang to her lips, and, she supposed, thinking about it now, he must have realized that she had been innocent of such caresses.

He had smiled at her sadly and carefully removed his hand. "Good night, Beth."

"John—"

He pressed a finger briefly to her lips. "We can't. *I can't*. That wasn't our bargain, remember?"

"Yes, I know, but—" How could she tell him that she had thought their relationship had changed? That she had hoped their marriage would be real? He had given her so much, and she had given him too little. And yesterday he had been so sweet that she had thought, hoped . . .

"Go to bed, Beth."

She had to try one more time. "John, I don't mind, really. I was just surprised. You just have to teach me."

"No." His sharp denial stung. His eyes held regret and apology as he met her gaze, but she could tell he wasn't about to be swayed. "You've forgotten one thing, haven't you." His voice was soft.

"I don't know—" She stopped, felt her cheeks flame. Of course she knew. "Millicent."

"Yes." As if dismissing her, he returned his attention to his ledger.

Humiliated, Lizzy got up from the desk and avoided his glance. "I—ah—I'm sorry," she said hoarsely. "I forgot. I don't know why I did, but—" She hung her head, feeling ashamed.

He caught her hand and squeezed gently before releasing it. "Don't be," he said gently.

But she couldn't look at him. Her humiliation was too great to feel comforted by his words.

"Good night." She barely managed to flash him a forced smile as she turned quickly to leave. "I'll see you in the morning."

"Beth."

She paused in her flight to escape with her hand on the doorknob.

"Someday you'll have what I had with Millicent."

Without facing him, she bobbed her head.

"Someday, when I'm gone, you'll be glad that we never . . ."

She forced her gaze to meet his. After swallowing against a tight throat, she answered. "No, John. I'll be sad, not glad, that I never got to be a real wife."

And with tears in her eyes, she left. Her own husband had rejected her. She would never know his touch. She would never be a true wife to John Foley.

Now, over three years later, Lizzy realized that John had been right. She was glad she and John hadn't shared a bed. She realized that her feelings for Conor were so different than her affection for John. She thought with irony that she was a virgin, but Conor didn't believe it. Not only did he believe that she had slept with her husband, which was fair, but that she had purposely seduced him and got herself with child. Conor thought she had had many lovers, when in fact she had had none. She laughed harshly. Now that she was free, the man she wanted didn't love her; he didn't even respect her.

She had been a virgin wife, and unless she did something drastic or foolish, she would be a virgin widow forever.

The sloop slipped through the water, the wind filling her sails. Conor stood on the deck of the *Millicent*, his gaze on the land ahead.

His trip to Baltimore had been marginally successful. After two and a half years of searching, he felt he was getting close to finding the one he had come to America to find. His half sister. He recalled when he had gone in search of his real father.

He had spent months looking, and when he had located a family by the name of Maguire, it was only to learn that Maguire—his father—had passed away along with his wife.

Conor felt a jolt at the memory of when he had learned the news. He had reached the Maguire home only months after his father's death. His resentment toward the man had driven him on his search, and suddenly there was no man to question. No one to demand answers from.

Neighbors had told him about a daughter—Katie, they had called her—now gone to be with her mother's family. Conor had visited the Maguire grave sites. Standing in the cold with the rain soaking him to the skin, he had stared at the place where his real father lay and was sorry that he had never met him.

Tears had filled his eyes, tears of bitter anger, of pain and loss for a man he had never known but had wanted to so desperately. He had felt empty and lost. He had no family that he knew of. His mother had died and now his father was dead. He would have no answers to his questions. What had Maguire looked like? Why had he left his mother? Why had he married another? Why had he abandoned his son yet accepted his daughter?

He had nearly given up and headed home to Roscommon, where life wasn't any better, but where he thought that Richard Payton might continue to pay him to work his horses. But then he couldn't forget the Maguire child. He had realized that he wouldn't rest until he found her, until he had the answers he sought and the benefit of voicing his bitterness . . . and his anger.

He had traced the Maguire lass to the Dunne family in County Clare. By the time he had arrived at the Dunne estate, the house had been burned, the family gone, and the only thing he could learn from the servants was that Miss Maguire had accompanied her cousin to America to a place somewhere in Maryland. And so Conor had worked until he had just enough passage money for the trip. And he had come to Maryland, wandered the vast land, and wondered how he would find one woman in such a large place.

He didn't find Katie Maguire in Maryland, but he had found the Quaid family, and knew that he had found a trace of home. He had had no luck and no funds, and he had needed work to complete his journey, to continue his search. When he had learned that Rian Quaid and his wife were Irish, he'd felt a homecoming. He had planned to stay only until he had money enough to move on. Friendship and respect had come out of his associations with the Quaids, and the position of authority he had earned made him hesitant to leave. And so he had decided to continue the search from Green Lawns in Kent County, Maryland. If Katie Maguire was still in Maryland, he would find her and soon.

But that was three years past, and he was beginning to feel restless, frustrated with his failure to find her. He was afraid she had died before he could find her.

Would he ever find her? He couldn't, wouldn't, rest until he did. Perhaps it was time he stopped waiting for her to show. Wouldn't it be wise to leave and continue his quest, before his life became too complicated?

He narrowed his gaze to study the shoreline ahead. His life was already complicated. If he didn't leave soon, there would be no hope of untangling himself from Lizzy's life.

Lizzy Foley. She was already a complication in his life. His desire for her, his continued thoughts of her, plagued him night and day, wherever he was, whatever he was doing.

She wasn't what he had thought. The gossips knew little of the woman Elizabeth Foley was. They hadn't mentioned how much she loved her children. That she

was a good mother, and a fair employer, and that she
was lovely and warm and had a good heart.

He wanted her. Hell, he wanted her, and he
shouldn't. If he was wise, he would return to Milly's
Station, tell her that he was done and that there would
be another foreman to help her until she felt comfortable enough to be on her own.

But how could he leave? He recalled the rock that
had been tossed through the study window . . . the
threatening note that had accompanied it, and he worried about Lizzy.

There were other men like James Thompson. Men
out to charm her—to marry her and take everything
she had—because she was young and beautiful and
she had the wealth that so many of them craved.

He would take Lizzy Foley with nothing to her name.
In fact, it would be better if she had none. What was
money, after all? As long as there was clothing and food,
he would be content. He didn't mind working for his
pay. What he craved more than money was a family. He
missed his mother. He sure as the stars never missed
Donal O'Reilly, but he missed what they might have
had as a family if the man had fulfilled his promise and
loved him like the son he had never had.

For the briefest moment, Conor wondered what
Donal was doing, figured that if the man wasn't dead
from the drink yet, he was probably close enough to
it, and so he put him from his mind. Some memories
were better left buried. There was little about his former life that gave him cause to want to remember.

"Conor."

He turned as the vessel's captain reached his side.
"Captain Logan? We're almost home."

The man nodded, his dark eyes riveted on shoreline
and the green hills beyond it. He turned to Conor.
"Have you completed your business successfully?"

Conor sighed. "Nay. I thought that I would have the

information I seek. I paid a man to help me, but he failed."

Logan frowned. "What is it you're looking for."

"Who," Conor said. "And who is a woman."

"A relative?"

"Aye." At the man's questioning look, he explained. "She's me half sister, but we've never met."

"And she's from Ireland?"

"Aye. She came over three years past. 'Tis hard to trace a cold path."

"Do you know the name of the vessel she sailed? Have you tried speaking to her captain?"

"I would, but I've not been able to locate him. Each time I go to Baltimore, I seem to have missed the *Mistress Kate* by a week or a few days."

"Perhaps I can help," Captain Logan suggested.

Interested, Conor met his gaze. "How?"

"Does the *Mistress Kate* still sail into Baltimore?"

The Irishman nodded. "Aye, 'twould seem so."

"What is your sister's name? I'll have friends keep an eye out for her. If she sailed on her, I'll find out for certain. Perhaps I'll learn where she's gone."

"But that was over two years ago—"

"Some captains keep passenger logs. Let's hope that the captain you seek is one of them."

"Maguire." Conor stuck out his hand. "Katie Maguire, and I'd be much obliged if ya'd find out anything ya can."

Logan shook his hand. "You gave me a job when no one else would." He had been down on his luck when McDermott had found him. He had had a bum leg and no prospects. But a man didn't need both of his sea legs to be good ones. "The *Millicent* is a nice craft. It feels good to sail again."

Conor nodded. "Ya handle her well," he said. He knew what it was to seek work and be unsuccessful, just as he was grateful that Rian Quaid had given him a job when no one else would hire an Irishman from

County Roscommon. He figured that every man deserved a chance in life, and after meeting the captain, he felt that Logan deserved it more than most.

SEVENTEEN

The darkened night sky opened up, and the rain began to fall, lightly at first, then as a torrent. Thunder rumbled in the distance. Lightning flashed, briefly illuminating the room, as Lizzy tucked little Emma into bed, before checking on Jason.

Lizzy smiled. Emma had fallen asleep almost as soon as her head had touched the pillow. It had been a busy afternoon. Conor had returned from Baltimore, and the children had been eager to see him. Jason, in particular, had lit up like a bright oil lamp when he had spied the *Millicent* coming in to dock. He had run down to the ramp to meet it, bubbling with questions for Conor as he waited while Conor and the captain secured the vessel.

Following at a distance, Lizzy had watched the easy camaraderie between boy and man as Conor came ashore and ruffled Jason's hair. Emma, who had trailed down with Lizzy, had let go of her mother's hand as soon as Conor had joined Jason. She had run to the pair, unwilling to be excluded in the happy reunion.

When he saw Emma, Conor had beamed a huge grin at her, and she had run into his arms to be lifted high over his head. She had laughed and shrieked as he held her suspended until she begged him to put her down,

which Conor did immediately. Then, of course, Emma
had wanted to enjoy the fun all over again.

As she left Emma's bedchamber for Jason's room,
Lizzy recalled the moment Conor had spotted her,
when they had locked gazes and she had felt a jolt in
her chest. The awkwardness of the moment that she
had expected when she saw him again was nonexistent.
A sensual awareness had hovered between them as
their gazes held during Conor's approach.

She had wanted to jump into his arms and passion-
ately kiss him. She had wanted to hold him, touch him,
and more.

*How can I put him out of my mind when he's so
good with the children?* Lizzy wondered as she shut
the door to Emma's room. *And when he made her feel
so alive?*

He was handsome and kind. He inspired loyalty and
trust. How could she resist all that?

When she entered the next room, she found Jason
half on his side and half on his stomach. His knees
were bent, his arms at an odd angle, but she recognized
the position as one of sleep. She leaned down and
pressed a gentle kiss to his cheek. Rising, she tenderly
brushed back a lock of hair from his brow.

"Good night, Jase," she murmured and turned. And
then froze at the sight of Conor McDermott standing
in the doorway. She raised a finger to her lips, and he
nodded in understanding. Her heart started to pound
as she headed toward the door . . . *and him.*

He moved back to allow her to exit and then fell
into step with her as they went to the stairs.

"I promised Jason and Emma that I'd come up to
say good night," he said.

Lizzy nodded. She wasn't surprised that they had
asked him, but was surprised that he remembered.
"Emma fell asleep as soon as I put her down," she
replied quietly, aware of the intimacy of the two of

them in the darkened hall. "Jason must have, too, for he was asleep when I went in."

"They had a busy day." He paused at the top of the stairs for her to precede him. Their eyes met, and he smiled.

"They were excited to see you again." She paused. "They missed you." *I missed you.*

His blue eyes glowed in the lamplight. "I missed them, too."

Silence followed, thick with meaning . . . with promise. Lizzy swallowed against a suddenly dry throat. "Was your time in Baltimore successful?"

She wanted to ask about this relative for whom he searched, but then she didn't want him to know that she and Kathleen had been discussing him.

"Nay." His frustration showed in his features. "Perhaps I'll have better luck next time."

"And you Irish men believe in luck," she surprised herself by teasing him.

His expression cleared, and his eyes began to twinkle. "And fairies and leprechauns." He gestured for her to go, and she realized with some embarrassment that they were carrying on a conversation on the top step.

"And magic?"

"Of course."

She went down the steps, conscious of him behind her. She had nothing to say. Her skin tingled at his nearness. Her breath felt tight as she imagined his gaze on her, but she could think of nothing to carry on the conversation.

"Don't you believe in magic?" he asked.

A stair squeaked beneath Lizzy's feet. She heard the same noise as Conor's foot found the step while she debated how to answer. What did he expect her to say?

"There's the magic of giving birth," she said. "But then, that's God's miracle more than magic."

"What of fairies?"

She shrugged as she turned on the bottom landing and waited for him.

"No fairies?"

She shook her head.

"No leprechauns?" He reached the end of the stairs.

"Not at Milly's Station." Without discussing it, they moved into the parlor together.

"Then, what other kind of magic is there?"

Lizzy sat on the sofa and waited for him to join her there. "The magic of a child's smile?"

Her response rewarded her with his smile. "Aye. Good thinking."

The storm continued outside, bringing a steady rain and brief flashes of lightning and low rumbles of thunder. Lizzy gazed at the man beside her, aware of the intimacy of being alone with him in the room while the storm played its dance and fury outside, and felt the magical pull that had drawn her to him. She looked away.

"Ye're quiet," he commented.

"Just thinking."

"About what?"

Nervous, unable to confess, she stood. "Would you like something to drink?"

"Tea or brandy?" he asked.

She shrugged. "Either."

"Then, I'll have brandy." His blue eyes regarded her closely. "Will ya join me?"

Memory made her blush. "So that I can get sick on you again?" Was he teasing her or trying to torment her? Either way she wasn't happy.

"Ya didn't get sick on me, and ya had other things to contend with then. A burned hand. An implied threat."

Startled by his understanding, she could only nod. "So you think that I can handle my brandy?"

"I didn't say that." He grinned.

Her lips twitched uncontrollably. "I can handle a glass." After all, she had worked in an inn, where she served it to the customers. She had never imbibed then, it was true. She had seen too many mean drunkards for that.

She moved through the archway and across the hall to the dining room, where she kept several bottles of liquor. "I have port," she called.

"No brandy?" he asked.

"No, there's brandy."

"I'd prefer that, please."

Lizzy drew out two glasses and a bottle from the china cupboard, where she had moved all the liquor, and she brought them with her into the parlor. After placing them on the sofa table, she tried to open the bottle, when she felt the slide of Conor's hands over hers as he came behind her and took over the task. She leaned back against him for a moment with closed eyes. She wished she could always lean against his strength. She moved quickly away back to her seat.

"Here ya are." He handed her a glass with just a small amount of brandy in it.

She studied her glass and then the larger amount he had poured for himself. "You have more than me."

He raised an eyebrow as he sat down beside her. "Thought it best if we don't put it to test . . . yer getting sick. I haven't a spare clean set of clothes."

"Tomorrow is wash day," she said, honing in on the subject of clothes. "If you bring your things over, I'll wash them for you."

And then she was embarrassed that she had begun a discussion about laundering garments.

"Thank ya." He took a sip from his glass, eyeing her over the rim. "But 'tis not necessary. I was only teasing ya. I have a change of clothing."

"Oh." And she was silent as she wondered what to say next. She took her first tiny sip and felt the liquid slide hotly down her throat. The warmth pooled in her belly, and she drank again, this time a bigger swallow.

Conor seemed relaxed as he enjoyed the brandy. She

felt otherwise, until the brandy mellowed her and she was no longer embarrassed by the memory of her behavior or her attraction to the man who sat nearby.

They sipped and enjoyed the muffled sound of the storm companionably and in silence.

"Any problems while I was gone?" Conor's senses went on full alert as he waited for her to answer. Since his departure, he had worried about her, about the rock that had broken her window, about James Thompson and her vulnerability at being a single woman alone in a large house. Yes, the servants stayed at the house, for the most part, but they were a handful of young women and an elderly, partially deaf man. Little defense against a strong-armed, ill-intentioned man.

"No, no problems."

He felt his pulse kick into high gear as he studied her. This evening she wore a gown of violet satin. Her hair had been pulled back and secured with pins, and the severe style, while it emphasized her lovely features with her high cheekbones, long-lashed brown eyes, and bow lips, had him itching to take charge and take out each and every pin. He wanted to comb his fingers through her hair, to cup it in his hand and breathe in her fragrance. He wanted desperately to press his lips to her neck and trail kisses along her throat, then to her breasts, where he would suckle her until she gave a wild cry of pleasure.

Shaken by his thoughts, Conor gulped down his brandy, before rising to pour himself some more. He could feel Lizzy's eyes on him as he carried his glass and the brandy bottle back to the sofa table. Seeing her empty glass, he held up the bottle, but she shook her head. "No thank you. I'm not tempting fate this evening."

"Well, I am," he said gruffly as he poured a good measure of the liquor into his glass. He picked up the glass, held it up to her as if offering her a toast before taking another swallow.

"Conor?"

He raised an eyebrow in question. "Aye?"

"You—" She frowned as she glanced at his glass, then back to him. "Nothing."

They were silent for several lengthy seconds. Conor noticed that the wind had picked up outside, and now he could hear the rain spattering against the house, beating against the glass and hammering on the roof. "Sounds like the storm is getting fierce," he said.

He had attempted to control his desire for her with the brandy and failed. Conor set his glass carefully on the table next to hers.

"Yes," she said, her eyes on his glass. She focused her gaze on him. "Storms can be brutal here in Kent County. I remember the first time I came to Milly's Station, I—"

He grabbed her and kissed her. He couldn't help himself, he thought as he brushed his lips over her surprised mouth. Not when the lights were low and they were sharing the cozy comfort of the room while outside nature wreaked havoc. How could he help it if she was everything female . . . lovely . . . tempting. *Unbelievably sweet,* he thought as he enjoyed the taste of her mouth and tongue. It wasn't only outside that nature had churned up, he realized as he pressed her back against the cushions. Here, inside, he felt the warmth of an increasing whirlwind . . . and he slipped in to enjoy the ride for as long as it lasted.

No one could have been more shocked by a kiss than Lizzy. It had come out of nowhere. One minute they had been talking, and the next, he had captured her lips with that wonderful mouth of his. She wouldn't have been able to utter a protest if she had any, which she didn't. She simply relaxed and floated while his mouth did wondrous things to her, things that made her shudder and moan and cling.

She felt the hard strength of his arms, then the soft brush of the sofa cushions against her back with his weight above her. His scent enveloped her, and she closed her eyes, breathing deeply of him as he explored a moist path along her throat over her shoulder. She shivered as he changed directions and nibbled and kissed and tongued his way across her breast bone . . . the soft upper curves that swelled at the touch and begged to be released for further attention.

She had a hazy image of him tugging off her gown, pulling her to the floor, and doing all kinds of pleasurable things to her, things she couldn't have imagined existed.

She stiffened. *The children!*

In bed, an inner voice reminded her. She shuddered a pleasure-filled sigh mixed with relief as he ran a hand down her arm, then along her side, brushing against her breast on its way to her waist and hip.

And what of the servants? The thought invaded her fuzzy brain. *Upstairs on the third floor.* No, it was Sunday, and they had gone home to be with their families, even Jamieson.

They were alone. *Alone.*

"Lizzy."

She opened her eyes, delighting in his expression, in the flaming brightness of his eyes, and the hard lines of passion in his face. And he wanted her. *Her!*

"Conor, kiss me," she urged.

And he obliged, more thoroughly and more pleasurably than before until she was arching up off the couch in search of more. What that more was she had no idea.

Conor drank deeply from her lips and then buried his face in her hair. Inside his chest, his heart knocked like a woodpecker. Outside the room, the house, the storm had begun to rage, but still its fury wasn't as fierce as the one inside him.

She was soft, responsive, and willing. He rose up to study her and felt his gut wrench at her slumberous gaze. He touched her full feminine mound, cupping the fabric over flesh, and felt the blood rush to fill his cock at her uninhibited response. There was one good thing about a woman who had had other lovers, he thought, and that was that she knew how to enjoy a man—

A wash of jealousy threatened to dampen his desire, but it was quickly ignited again when Lizzy began to nuzzle his chest as she undid the buttons of his shirt.

Good God in heaven, she knew how to touch a man! And he was only human. He wanted her to fondle more of him, just as he wanted to bare and discover every inch of her with his hands, lips, and tongue.

Like nature outside, the storm inside intensified as Lizzy, with his help, tugged off his shirt and threw it aside. Then Conor's fingers made quick work of the buttons of her gown's bodice until he could part fabric to reveal soft linen beneath. Then he tugged aside linen until flesh, full, ripe, and red-tipped, fell free to tease him. But he wasn't teased for long. He quickly cupped a bare breast, worried the nipple, then laved it with his tongue and felt a sharp shaft of pleasure when Lizzy cried out, arched upward, and offered more of herself to him.

Smooth. Hot. Sweet. Wild. She was all this and more, Conor thought as they rolled from the sofa to the floor. Rain fell, lightning flashed, and suddenly there was a loud clap of thunder that had them pulling apart slightly and listening. Lizzy's breasts heaved as she labored for breath. Her body was tingling, buzzing, throbbing for more. She saw Conor raised above her, listening, his face warm in the lamplight. His bright eyes regarded her with sensual fire.

And then she heard the sound that had her falling back to earth quickly, crashing with awareness of where she was and what Conor must think of her for allowing things to go this far.

The sound came again. "Ma!"

Jason.

She struggled to free herself. "Please. It's Jason. He's heard the storm. He'll be frightened."

Conor's eyes were dark as they locked with hers.

"Jason," she said. She didn't really want to go. She wanted to continue, but the storm had stepped in to save her from making a mistake and losing her virginity and all respect. She was an unmarried woman.

In acknowledgment of her request, Conor rolled off her and stood. Lizzy quickly sat up and attempted to put herself to rights—not an easy thing when there were undergarments to contend with and a row of small buttons. How had he unfastened them so easily?

She was vividly aware of Conor shrugging into his shirt as she stood and straightened her skirts. She was only vaguely aware that Emma's cries had joined Jason's.

"I've got to go," she gasped as she hurried toward the door.

"I should go, too." His words halted her in her tracks, and she glanced back. " 'Tis late. I should check on the barn and the animals."

She nodded, disappointed.

He must have sensed it, for he approached and cupped her cheek. "I'll see ya tomorrow, Lizzy." His smile and soft voice eased the fiery burn that had churned in her stomach. "Can you manage the children on yer own?" he asked as they entered the foyer.

"Yes. Thank you for asking."

He frowned, hesitated. "Are ya certain?"

She bobbed her head. Now that she had time to think, she realized that it would be best if he left and did so quickly. Before she made a fool of herself and clung to him while begging him to stay.

"Ma!"

"Coming, Jase!" she called up the stairs. She turned back to Conor. She felt a swell of emotion. Love, she realized. "Be careful." Something hot and thick flowed into the air between them. She fought hard to dismiss it, but couldn't.

"Aye."

And he opened the door and stepped into the fierce night. Worried, she climbed the stairs to comfort the children and think about the man whom she wanted so desperately.

EIGHTEEN

"It's all right," Lizzy murmured to the children. "It's just a thunderstorm." They were in Emma's room, all of them perched on the edge of the bed.

Emma's lip quivered. "It's making a lot of noise."

"I know, sweetie."

"Ma, the lightning can hurt people, can't it?"

She thought quickly for the right answer. "Well, yes, I suppose it can, which is why we must stay indoors."

Lightning flashed, brightening the room. She glanced toward the window just as a huge clap of thunder followed. She worried about Conor crossing the yard to the barn. She couldn't bear it if something bad happened to him.

"How long is this storm going to last?" Jason asked.

Lizzy sighed. "I don't know, Jase. Might be for a few minutes more, or it might be longer."

"I'm tired," Emma complained.

"I know you are, sweet pie. Come here." She extended an arm in invitation. Emma took it gratefully and snuggled against her mother. She lifted the other arm, and Jason hesitated for only a second before he, too, burrowed against Lizzy's side. The storm was awful, worrisome, and loud, but she enjoyed the way the children were nestled in her arms.

The wind picked up its pace, rattling the windows,

throwing rain against the house. She glanced down and saw that although the children were quiet, their eyes were wide with fear. She felt them start at each new rumble from the storm and murmured soothing words to them.

As she sat holding the children, Lizzy wondered if the wind would bring damage to any of the outbuildings on Milly's Station. A fierce gust startled her, and she instinctively gave the children a reassuring squeeze.

"Ma?"

"Yes, Jason?"

"Do you think the animals will be all right?"

"I imagine so."

"What about the horses?"

"They have Conor to take care of them."

The boy sighed. "Oh."

She smiled. It was clear that he trusted the Irishman implicitly.

"Ma?"

"Emma?"

"I'm tired, but I'm afraid."

"It's all right. Why don't you sleep, and I'll watch over you."

"You won't leave?"

"Not until the worst of the storm has passed."

"I think I'll sleep, then," the little girl murmured.

Then a loud thunderclap had them gasping and clinging hard to each other.

After a time, the wind seemed to ease, and the thunder rolled in the far distance, a soft shadow of its former self. The lightning had changed to brief flashes that to Lizzy seemed unthreatening.

The shift in the children's weight alerted her that Emma slept and Jason was either asleep or fast approaching it.

"Jase?"

"Hmmm?"

"The storm has passed. Let's get you to your bed now."

He objected only mildly as she lifted him in her arms and carried him into the next bedchamber. She was glad that she had left a wall sconce lit in the hall earlier. In Jason's room, she set the boy carefully on his mattress, then tucked the bedcovers around him. "Good night, Jason."

" 'Night," he slurred sleepily. Lizzy gazed down at him a moment, noting with a pang how much he had grown in the last few months, aware of a burst of love for him so strong that it brought tears to her eyes.

She left the room quietly and went downstairs to clean up the dishes she and Conor had used in the parlor. The lamp that had lit up the room earlier was still burning. Lizzy picked up the brandy glasses, then felt a lurch in her belly as her gaze fell on the sofa where only a short time ago she and Conor had lain.

A heavy hammering at the front door startled her. Setting the glasses down, she hurried to answer it.

"Conor!"

His blue eyes bright, he was soaked right down to the skin.

"The wind tore away a section of the barn roof," he told her. "I secured the animals in a dry place, but me room . . . 'tis a lost cause."

"Come in. Come in!" Heart pounding, she stepped back, grabbing his arm to jerk him inside as she did so. "Are you all right?" She held tight as she inspected him from dripping head to soaked shoes.

"Aye. Just wet as a duck in foul weather."

"It may be the start of summer, but there is still a chill in the air. You need a hot bath and a dry change of clothes." She led him into the kitchen where she stoked up a fire in the stove and put on bathwater to heat. "Here." She gestured toward a spot near the fire. "Stand there to keep warm." She disappeared into the small storage room off the kitchen.

"How are the children?" he called as he held his hands out to the growing flame.

She came out dragging with her a hip tub, and he hurried to help her. "They were frightened, but now they're asleep." There was a storage chest against the back wall near the door, and from it, she pulled out some towels and a bar of soap. "You'll take one of the rooms upstairs."

As her words sank in, Conor tensed. " 'Tis not necessary. I can bunk with the animals."

"Nonsense!" she exclaimed. Her eyes challenged him. "Afraid?"

He experienced a jolt of surprise. "Nay." He wanted her. He had debated about whether or not he should return to the house and chosen to go back. And he had decided before the storm had made a mess of his quarters. But he had needed to move the animals to a safer place before he could leave the barn.

And now he was here, watching Lizzy as she prepared a bath and fussed over him.

"There are some of John's things yet in the attic," she said as she placed the towels and soap within easy reach of the tub. "I'll run up and find you something that might fit."

He snagged her arm as he started to walk by her. "Lizzy." He could only stare at her. The memory of those last few moments together warmed him, created a tightening in his gut. "Ya don't have to go to all this trouble," he said quietly.

He heard her draw a sharp breath, but she made no attempt to remove his hand. "It's no trouble, Conor."

"Say it again."

She frowned. "What?"

"Me name. The way ya just said it . . . better yet, the way ya said it a short time ago before I left the house."

Her cheeks turned a delightful shade of pink. "Don't—"

"Why not? If the storm hadn't interrupted—"

She shivered and hugged herself. "But it did."

"I can't forget it."

She didn't answer. She went to the stove and checked the water.

He came up close behind her. "Elizabeth."

She twirled, a look of panic on her face. "Please. I can't . . ."

"Can't what?" he said with a scowl. "Can't forget it? Can't think of doing it again?"

"Both," she whispered miserably.

Lizzy was afraid. Only a short while ago, she had been lying on the sofa and all but begging him to take her. She had been shameless, and she feared that she would respond in the same way again if he so much as kissed her. And so she would keep her distance. She loved him, but did he love her? He desired her; it was the only thing she knew for certain.

When the bathwater was ready, Lizzy went to pick up the kettle, but Conor stopped her. "I'll do it," he said. "If ya would find those clothes."

She breathed a sigh of relief as she nodded; then she left. In the attic, she found the trunk where she had stored most of John's belongings after his death. She had left them in his bedchamber for a time, but then each time she had gone in there to see that the chambermaids had cleaned the room right, she would spy John's things and get weepy. He was a good friend and a caring man; she still missed him. But while she dug through the contents of the trunk, it wasn't John she thought about as she pulled out a shirt, eyed the style and size, and then searched for a pair of trousers. Her thoughts revolved around Conor.

After selecting a white linen shirt, a pair of navy trousers, warm stockings, and what looked to be a comfortable pair of shoes, Lizzy headed downstairs to give them to Conor.

"Here," she said as she entered the room. "I found these. They should fit—" She gasped as she halted in her tracks. She must have been in the attic longer than she had thought. Conor McDermott had stripped himself naked and climbed into the bath to wash.

Lizzy swallowed against a dry throat as she moved to put the clothes within Conor's reach. She kept her eyes averted, lest she see more than what was suitable. Still, after she had set down the garments on a nearby chair, she couldn't keep her gaze from straying to that glorious bare male chest, broad shoulders, and muscular arms. She gave a hiss when she saw a scar on his one arm. His modesty and her embarrassment forgotten, she hurried to touch it.

"How did you do this?" she asked. "Does it hurt?" It looked like it had been a nasty wound.

"Accident—or should I say—a 'staged' accident at Green Lawns." His eyes glowed as he placed a wet hand over hers.

For a silent heartbeat, Lizzy stared at him, her breath coming in shallow gasps as the attraction between them sizzled and burned. Her chest tight, she pulled away. She turned to leave. "Your clothes are on the chair," she said without looking back "I'll be in the next room when you're done."

"Elizabeth—"

She stiffened. She heard him sigh.

"Don't go to any bother about the room. Leave me the linens and I'll make the bed meself."

"All the beds are already made." She looked at him then, and wished she hadn't. He was too handsome, too tempting to ignore; and everything inside of her pushed her to go back to him. "Come to the parlor, and then I'll show you to your room." Her gaze slid by, then returned to connect and lock with his.

He gazed back, and his eyes dropped to focus on her mouth. Lizzy felt an infusion of heat that began in her belly and spread outward. Her breasts tingled and longed for his attention. Ashamed, she severed eye contact and left.

She was seated in the Queen Anne's chair not far from the fireplace, working on her needlepoint, when Conor found her after finishing his bath. She didn't know how long it had been since she had left him. It seemed just a short time when he was there in the room with her, looking bigger and more brawny in John's garments than before. The shirt just barely fit him, and Lizzy couldn't look away from the way the fabric stretched tautly over arm, chest, and stomach muscles. His trousers were snug as well, hugging thick thighs and muscular calves and ending at his bare feet.

He held up the hose and shoes. "These will fit," he said, referring to the socks. "I can tell by a glance that these won't." He sat on the sofa and pulled on the hose. "I've emptied the tub and laid my shoes and garments near the stove to dry." He paused and glanced up at her. "I should have asked if ya wanted to bathe before I dumped it."

"No," she said, and tingled at the thought of sliding in the same water that had warmed the big male body of the Irishman before her. "I bathed earlier."

"Good." He smiled as he stood. "Shall I carry these upstairs?"

She nodded as she eyed the shoes in his hand. Her pulse was racing wildly. Her fingers itched to touch, and her body tingled and pulsed wanting his caress. If she didn't take him to his room and leave him soon, she would make a complete fool of herself . . . and she would be sorry for it afterward.

"Follow me," she instructed. She picked up the single glowing lamp and climbed the stairs, aware that he was not far behind her. "You'll find fresh water in the washbasin, and there's a . . ." She felt herself blush, but didn't turn around. "A vessel to relieve yourself is under the bed."

"Convenient," he commented.

"Yes," she agreed.

She turned right instead of left at the top of the stairs.

To the left was her room, the chamber that had once been John's, and Emma's and Jason's rooms. To the right were two guest rooms, which she thought quite comfortable with colorful patchwork quilts on each bed and white-and-blue curtains covering the windows.

She chose the first room in line for Conor. She opened the door, entered the room while holding the lamp up high for him to see, and gestured for him to come in. "I think you'll find the bed comfortable. There are extra blankets in that chest of drawers," she said, gesturing toward a lovely oak dresser. "And if you need another pillow . . ." She stopped, as he was eyeing the bed, which was large enough for a big man . . . even large enough for two.

"Aye, this will do nicely," he said huskily. "Thank ya."

She felt a prick of sensation trail her spine as she nodded. "I'll leave you to find your rest, then," she said, and began to back out of the room. Then she halted. "Here." She approached to hand him the oil lamp. "I can find my way back. I've another in my room. There are matchsticks in the night table."

His fingers brushed hers as he accepted the lamp. "Thank ya again." His blue eyes burned hotly as they roamed her face as if searching.

No, she thought. *Don't think of staying!* She had to leave.

"Good night," she said. And without waiting for his answer, she stepped out of the room and shut the door. As she headed back to her room, she thought of Conor McDermott and wished she had had the courage to linger until he had asked her to stay.

Conor stared at the closed door and called himself all kinds of a fool for allowing her to leave. He had enjoyed her kisses and felt her response to his touch. A woman had never driven him so wild. He was startled by the fact that it was Lizzy Foley who had such a profound effect on him.

So, she was an experienced lover. Was that why he couldn't forget her? Was that why she stole into his thoughts every waking moment and every night that he dreamed?

He respected her. The way she was with her children—her concern for her servants and workers—and the way her one look at him, when he appeared on her doorstep soaked, had triggered the motherly instincts in her.

When it came to Elizabeth Foley, he didn't feel much like a son. He wanted to be her lover, to hold and kiss her, and to make her cry out with passionate abandonment. He longed to see her lose control as she experienced mindless pleasure.

He wanted to do that for her. He wanted to do that for her and much more.

Conor set the oil lamp on the bed table and sat on the bed to test the mattress. The lamplight flickered golden on the wall, creating shadows and tracing patterns of objects in the room. He stared at the fluttering images, envisioning Lizzy's face as he stroked her, then plunged into her, catapulting her into a place of ecstasy . . . and he felt his cock harden.

Cursing, he rose and went to the window. This was a smaller room than Lizzy's, but it was cozy, warm, and dry. He knew he would have been quite comfortable here if he could get out of his mind the fact of her nearby presence down the hall.

He tugged off the borrowed shirt and laid it over the single chair by the window. Turning from the night, he ran his hands over his chest, then cursed, for he thought of Lizzy's hands. Lizzy's touch.

Hell, he wanted her more than air, more than life itself. What was he going to do?

He glared at the closed door, then jerked it open, and strode down the hall to Lizzy's bedchamber.

NINETEEN

Lizzy had undressed and climbed into bed. As she lay back, closing her eyes, her mind was with Conor. She exhaled a shivering sigh. She wanted him. She wanted to lie with him, to give him the gift of her virginity. John had told her the truth when he had said that someday she would find somebody to love and cherish. Only John hadn't told her what to do if she wanted a man who didn't respect her.

Yes, she thought, they had gotten past the point of being strangers to being friends. She recalled their lovemaking downstairs—they had almost become lovers, two bodies joined in harmonic bliss. If she gave in to temptation, what would she have when the relationship was over? A man who loved her? Who wished to take her to wife? No. She would have someone who had wanted only a moment's pleasure before he went on his way again.

But what if she was wrong?

If she offered herself freely, he wouldn't be stealing her virginity. She had been a wife, after all. She should have rid herself of being chaste long ago. She should be a woman who had been thoroughly loved, who knew how to give pleasure as well as receive it. A lover whom no man could ever forget. . . .

"Conor." His name was like a soft prayer on her lips. "If only you knew the truth."

There was one way to make him see that he had been wrong about her, that she wasn't the merry widow who had left a string of lovers behind her. There was only one way to show him that she had saved herself for the man she loved. For him.

She sat up in bed and thought daring things. Like whether or not she should climb out from under the bedcovers, head down the hall, and knock on his bedchamber door. Her breasts throbbed, and she felt a strange sensation in her abdomen.

What if she lay with him, and when her chastity was gone, he thought her shameless for throwing herself at him? What would she do if the man she loved eyed her with contempt—or worse yet, with indifference?

She didn't think she could bear it. In fact, she knew she couldn't, and the remainder of his time here would be worse than horrible. Their relationship would be strained and awkward, and she wouldn't be able to learn a thing about the plantation.

With a sigh, she lay back down and closed her eyes, wishing that things were different. That she and Conor had met under different circumstances . . . that he had no intention of leaving . . . that he wasn't searching for a lost relative.

Thinking of Conor's hands on her, she touched her left breast, feeling the nipple as it hardened beneath her fingertips. She remembered the way Conor had caressed it, kissed it.

The door crashed open. Lizzy gasped and shot upright in bed, clutching the covers to her breasts. Her eyes widened, and her heart took flight as she locked gazes with Conor McDermott.

He came into the room and shut the door. Lizzy felt a thundering within her chest as he approached the bed, his blue eyes hot and bright with desire.

"Lizzy."

"What are you doing here?" she asked shakily.

He reached out a hand, palm up, and without thought, she placed her fingers within his grasp. "I've come to finish what we started earlier."

He pulled her from the bed, and she went willingly, leaving the bedcovers go as she climbed out of bed and stood before him.

"Earlier?" she echoed, but, of course, she knew. Her body swayed forward. Her aching breasts brushed his bare chest, and she couldn't stop her hands from rising to touch him, from stroking his hard muscles and tracing the male nipples . . . and sliding lower to the taut, flat planes of his stomach.

"Trust me," he whispered as he swung her into his arms.

She clung instinctively to his neck. "Yes."

She felt drugged by his magic. She couldn't resist the warm glow in his blue eyes; she didn't want to resist. To her surprise, he didn't place her on her bed. He headed to the door instead, turned the knob, and then kicked the door fully open, before pulling it shut again as he took her from the room. Lizzy felt as light as air and as fragile as glass as he carried her down the hall to his bedchamber.

She felt giddy and alive as they entered the room, and Conor nudged the door closed with his hip. The lamp she had given him earlier sat on the night table, bathing the room in a golden glow. The bedcovers had yet to be turned back. Conor approached the bed with Lizzy in his arms, then allowed her to slip from his embrace, along his length, until she was standing against him.

He kissed her lightly and then again more deeply, before releasing her. He pulled back the blankets. With his gaze boldly assessing her curves, thrilling her, he reached for the hem of her nightdress, tugged it up slowly, his touch sliding, lingering, on her skin as his

callused fingers made the journey until her garment
was gone.

A sudden hot blast of pleasure set her aglow when
he tossed the dress aside and returned to fondle her
breasts with both hands.

"So lovely," he murmured. "Ye're perfect. Soft, but
firm. Beautiful . . ." He bent his head and took a nipple between his lips.

Lizzy gasped and arched against him. She suddenly
felt weak in the knees. As she started to slip downward,
she knew the strength of his grip as he embraced her,
held her steady to endure the pleasure of his greedy
mouth.

"Conor . . ." She knew she shouldn't do this, but
right now she couldn't think of a single reason why.
She could think only of all the reasons why she should.

She inhaled sharply as his head dipped down to her
belly. There, he paused to kiss and caress her quivering
stomach muscles before rising again to recapture a
breast.

Heat sliding against heat. Muscled hardness pressing against feminine softness. The pleasure was mind
numbing for Lizzy. She had never felt such intense
physical enjoyment, and she knew the only one who
could bring it to her was this one man. Conor McDermott, the man she loved.

He rose up, and she murmured a protest until she
saw his hands move to the ties of his breeches. She
sat up, watching him, her body tingling as he removed
the remainder of his clothes.

Then he was back, his body muscular and hard, and
his blue eyes glowing. They slipped under the covers
together, and instantly the heat between them intensified as hands caressed and mouths kissed and explored
sensitive areas.

Lizzy's breath quickened as Conor ran his fingers
over the curve of her shoulder, down her side, brushing
her breast as he explored her. She trembled as he ca-

ressed the line of her waist and the outward slope of her hip.

"Do ya know that ya have the softest skin?" he said thickly.

She opened her eyes, shook her head. "No. I'm no different than any other woman."

"Nay, Lizzy lass, that's where ye're wrong."

She shivered as he proceeded to touch several different parts of her, telling her why each one was special, then kissing the described area.

Lizzy alternately gasped and moaned and whimpered as he made a thorough, delightful catalogue of her features.

"Conor . . . ," she moaned when she thought she would die from the intense sensation.

"Aye, lass?"

"Please . . ."

"What do ya want?" His voice was a sensual growl.

"You," she breathed, panting.

"Who?"

"You," she gasped, as his fingers found and fondled the most private, secret part of her. "Conor McDermott."

"Aye." Satisfied that he consumed her thoughts, Conor raised up and then plunged, entering her with a hard thrust. He frowned when she stiffened and cried out. Shock held him immobile for several seconds. "Lizzy?"

She lay, blinking, tears seeping from beneath lowered lashes.

"Sweet Bridget, Lizzy, why didn't ya tell me?" He cursed, and although it was the hardest thing he had ever done, he started to lift off her.

"No," she gasped, and clung to him tightly.

"But I hurt ya."

"I'm all right." She gazed up at him, her eyes bright, her body tense.

He felt like a monster for taking her like he had.

"Nay," he said, pushing himself up with his hands. "I've caused ya enough pain."

"No, please, Conor," she whispered brokenly. "Don't leave me."

He stared at her, tenderness warring with anger. His expression softened. He lowered himself against her carefully, nuzzling his lips in the curve of her neck. "Lizzy."

"I'm sorry," she apologized, sniffing. "I know I wasn't very good . . ."

Startled, he lifted his head to stare at her. "What nonsense is this!" His fingers were unsteady as he cupped her face. "Lizzy, ye're perfect. Don't ya be saying that ye're not good. Ye're perfect . . . I told ya."

"But—"

" 'Tis me who's at fault."

"Conor, no. I love what you did to me."

He gave her a tender smile. "Lizzy, do ya think that's all there is?"

She blushed. "Isn't it?"

He shook his head. "Nay, lass. We were but getting started." He skimmed his hand down her side, slipped it between them to touch the sensitive area that he had been less than gentle with. "I didn't know," he murmured as he eased his fingers inside her. "I didn't know."

Lizzy had tensed, but now she relaxed and arched into his hand. His touch was doing magic things to her again. Pleasure sparked, then grew. The soreness melted away as sensation took over. Closing her eyes, she moaned softly and allowed the feelings to take over.

"Lizzy, I wish I'd known." He captured her nipple with his lips and suckled.

"Conor!" The intense pleasure was building again . . . climbing . . . Surprised, she could only hold on tight and enjoy the ride.

He threw back the covers, and the air brushed her

skin, pebbling her nipples, chilling her skin until his big hands warmed her.

"Sweet. Innocent," he said hoarsely. "Oh, Lizzy, why didn't ya tell me?"

She gasped as he suckled and kissed her opposite breast. "I didn't think you'd believe me."

He raised his head, his eyes solemn. "I should have known, should have guessed, but I—"

"Believed the gossip," she finished, and then shuddered with pleasure as he dipped to kiss her belly.

"I did, at first," he admitted, punctuating each word with another stomach kiss. "But then . . ."

"Then?" she whispered.

"Ya were everything they said ya weren't. A wonderful mother. A fair employer . . . and ya'd loved ye husband." The last word was accompanied by a frown.

"I can explain." But she was afraid. Would he still think her mercenary for marrying John? For she had married him for the things he could provide for her and Jason.

"Nay," he said. "Not now. We've not finished what we began."

Lizzy stiffened. "Not finished?"

He raised up, and his sweet smile made her stomach flip-flop. "Aye, we've not finished."

"I don't know if I can . . ."

He caught her nipple between his teeth and tugged.

". . . finish," she gasped as her pleasure spiraled.

"Trust me," he asked, his expression sober. "Trust me to show ya."

Did she trust him? *Yes.* Did she expect that it would hurt? *Yes.*

"I trust you."

His beaming smile was reward enough for the pain that she expected to follow. "Aye, Lizzy, that's a good lass."

And he began a slow, sensual assault on her senses. If she had thought the pleasure had been wonderful before, now it was mind startling, earth shattering, as her body tightened with need and the area between her legs grew damp.

"Conor—"

"Hold on, Lizzy. We'll not rush this again."

And she gasped with shock when he held her hips and found her center with his mouth. He kissed her there, as if to apologize for the pain. And then the kiss went farther, and she could feel his tongue and lips. She stiffened slightly and then arched off the bed in rhythmic thrusts as the spiral of pleasure grew and grew.

Bright lights and shooting stars exploded in her brain as her body reached the peak of ecstasy, shuddered, and rode out the storm.

When he was done, she lay in numbed bliss, every part of her sensually awakened and yet lethargic.

Then embarrassment took over as she realized that the gossips had been right. She had behaved like a shameless wanton.

Blushing, she couldn't meet his gaze.

"Lizzy."

"I'm sorry."

He chuckled. "Lizzy. 'Tis not the end of the world. I meant for ya to feel such pleasure." He grabbed her hand, slid it down his belly. "Now we'll share in the pleasure together."

She blinked as he brought her hand to his manhood. It was big and velvety and . . . "Does it hurt?"

" 'Tis a different kind of ache than real pain, Lizzy. It longs for ya. To be inside ya."

She swallowed. "All right."

He smiled. "It will be uncomfortable, but it will not hurt this time. We didn't finish what we started, but if it's done right, ye'll feel the pleasure of what ya just felt."

Was it true? Was it possible to feel that same pleasure when a man was nestled inside you? "Show me."

And he did. When he was done, she knew that God had created Conor McDermott just for her.

Conor got up, turned down the lamp, and returned to her side. He pulled her against him. As she lay with her head on his chest, he stroked her bare shoulder and back.

She had some explaining to do, she realized. She was tired, but they had to talk. "Conor, about John—"

"Sleep," he urged. "We've plenty of time for explanations. We'll talk in the morning."

Conor lay in the darkness, frowning. Why hadn't he known? He should have guessed. She had seemed a contradiction. An innocent widow with children.

Emotion swirled in his breast. If he hadn't realized it before, he did now. He loved Lizzy Foley. And he wanted to marry her, but there were things he needed to contemplate . . . things that stood in the way.

TWENTY

She woke, stretched, and searched the feather mattress for Conor, but he had gone. "Conor?"

Lizzy opened her eyes and realized that she was in her bedchamber. Had it all been a dream? She sat up, saw that she was naked, and knew it had been real. She smiled. Conor had been wonderful. She had never imagined that it could be so pleasurable between a man and woman.

When had Conor carried her to this room? They had slept little. After their first time together, she had dozed for a while in his arms, and then he had awoken her with kisses and tickling touches. And they had made love again . . . and she had learned about pleasing him.

"Ma? Ma!"

Jason. Lizzy stared at the door, clutching the bedcovers to her breasts.

"Don't ya be waking up yer mother now, Jason." Conor's deep tones penetrated the door.

"Conor!" Jason exclaimed. "What are you doing here?"

"I'm spending the night, lad. The wind stole the roof from the barn, and yer mother gave me the room down the hall to sleep in."

"The whole barn!" He sounded in awe.

"Nay, lad. Just part of it. The part over me room."

"You'll be staying with us for a time?"

"Aye, lad."

Lizzy grinned as she heard the boy's shriek of joy. Emma's voice joined in the excitement. Then all was quiet as Conor led the children away.

A smile still on her lips, she lay down, and realized that this was the first morning when she didn't have to get up with Jason and Emma. Conor was there. He would see that they were fed, she realized. And she could linger in the bed, something she had never done before.

Thoughts of Conor brought back memories of the night. Her body tingled as she recalled how thoroughly Conor had made love to her. She had never imagined what one could do with one's mouth and hands.

What happened between them now? Last night he'd made her feel special. Was it just physical between them? It wasn't for her. How did he feel about her? She loved him. Did he care for her as well?

She rested for a few more minutes, and then she got up and dressed, aware as she did so of every pulsating spot on her body that Conor had kissed. Her breasts tingled as she slipped on her chemise. Her belly quivered as she stepped into petticoats and then struggled to fasten her gown.

"Mrs. Foley?" A gentle knock accompanied Ruth's soft words.

Grateful for the help, Lizzy opened the door. "Thank goodness, Ruth. Can you hook up my gown?"

"Yes, missus." Ruth made short work of her dress, then without a word picked up Lizzy's hairbrush. Their gazes met in the vanity mirror as Lizzy sat, and the chambermaid began to untangle Lizzy's long hair.

"Mr. McDermott is staying here now?" Ruth murmured conversationally as she tugged the brush rhythmically through Lizzy's hair.

Lizzy tensed as her eyes met the girl's in the mirror, but there was no censure in Ruth's gaze. She relaxed.

"Yes. Did you see the stables?" When the maid nodded, she asked, "Is the damage bad?"

"Yes, missus. Mr. Fetts has moved his things over to his sister's house. I heard Mr. McDermott tell Mr. Jamieson that he had to move some of the animals to the drying shed so they could have a dry place."

Lizzy nodded. The drying shed was the building on Milly's Station where they hung their tobacco crop to dry. Now it was being used to house a couple of cows, four horses, and a number of chickens. While the shed was a good size, the way it was built wouldn't provide adequate shelter to the animals for long. She imagined that Conor would be working this day to ensure that a repair to the barn roof was executed as quickly as possible.

But she didn't want him to leave. She liked the idea of having him near, and then there might be times, like last night, when they could be together.

If he wanted for them to be together again, she thought with a sigh.

"Thank you, Ruth."

The girl nodded as she replaced the hairbrush. Lizzy outlined for the maid what needed to be done this day; then Ruth left her.

Lizzy stood in the front of the mirror to assess her appearance. Would he still find her beautiful? She recalled the things he had said to her and smiled. He had told her often enough last night. Why did she doubt it now?

Because things can be said in the heat of passion . . .

Because what he thought of her had never before been this important to her.

She stared into the looking glass, pleased with her bright eyes and pink lips . . . lips still slightly swollen from Conor's kisses. She touched her mouth. Had Ruth guessed that she and Conor had become lovers? Would the others suspect?

No. This was their secret—hers and Conor's. No one should guess . . . unless she wasn't careful and made it too obvious.

Lizzy stood back, then pulled at her skirts to ensure that they fell straight. When she was done, she left the room and headed down the stairs. She found Conor and the children in the kitchen, eating the biscuits she had made for the previous evening's supper.

Her gaze met Conor's over the space of the room. When he smiled, his blue eyes darkening with shared memory, Lizzy felt warmth in her chest.

"Are ya hungry?" he asked. He held up a spoon, and she realized that he had set an iron spider on the stove. "I'm cooking eggs."

She smiled as she sat at the table next to the children.

"Is Conor going to stay, Ma?" Jason asked.

Lizzy glanced at the man, saw him nod. "Yes, he is."

"Did the wind really steal the barn roof?" Emma asked.

"Only part of the roof, Miss Emma," Conor said. "The part over me room."

"You're welcome to stay here as long as you want," Lizzy said.

He nodded, and the look he gave her made her tremble.

"Ma, can I go with Conor when he checks the farm?"

"Not this time, Jason," Conor said. "I'll have to see how bad the storm damage is. 'Tis no place for ya."

"*Aw-w* . . . Conor."

"McDermott," Lizzy began, then smiled. "Conor, then. You heard him, Jason. It's too dangerous for you to be about."

"I can't go outside?"

"It'd be best if ya stayed inside this morning, lad. I'll let ya know if 'tis safe to come out."

Jason wasn't happy, but he agreed.

They ate biscuits and eggs; then the children went to the playroom. Lizzy and Conor cleaned up the breakfast mess, their gazes meeting often, their smiles for each other warm.

When they were done, Conor caught Lizzy's hand and dragged her into the parlor. "I've got plenty to do today," he told her as soon as they entered the room.

Lizzy nodded.

"First on me list is to tell ya something." His expression was grave, his smile gone.

Lizzy felt a prickle of alarm. "Yes?"

He picked up her hand and rubbed her wrist. "Lizzy, about last night . . ."

Her heart thumped. "What about last night?" she said quietly.

"It was wonderful. Ya were wonderful. I . . . I never thought anyone could be so giving."

Relieved by his words, she closed her eyes. He caressed her cheek. "You were the giving one," she said softly. She turned her face into his hand, nuzzling against his fingers.

"Nay." His eyes glowed. "When I think of what ya gave me . . ."

Which reminded her that they still had to discuss her late husband. "Conor, about John."

He frowned. "Aye, ye've got something to explain, and I want to hear it, but not yet. There's something more important to discuss. Something concerning the two of us."

His tone made her nervous again. "What is it?"

"Lizzy, the reason I came to America was because I've been searching for me sister. She's somewhere in this country, and I've yet to find her."

She felt a little chill. "I must confess that I heard that you were looking for someone. I knew it was a relative, but . . ." She bit her lip. "A sister?"

He nodded. "Aye. And I've vowed not to rest until I find her."

The chill became ice as Lizzy gazed up at him. "So you'll be on your way again soon," she said.

"It was always me plan to move on. Always me plan to leave Green Lawns and continue me search. I've done a lot of checkin'. 'Twas the reason I went to Baltimore. I've had little luck, but I keep hoping . . ."

"What are you saying—that you have to leave?" She continued quickly, "I know I've no ties on you, Conor McDermott." Her throat tightened, and she felt the threat of tears. "I understood that you were here for only a short time."

His eyes narrowed. "And so ye're telling me to go, is that it?" His tone had become sharp.

"I—" She pulled from his grasp and turned away. "I can't," she whispered as tears filled her eyes.

He caught her by the shoulders and gently turned her to face him. "That's better."

She blinked up at him. "Pardon me?"

"I don't want ya to be sweet and sacrificing, Elizabeth Foley. I want ya to tell me to stay . . . for I've been thinking of ya every moment through the night and especially since I left ya this morning."

"Yes, I noticed you left me," she said. Could it be true? Was he really telling her he wanted to stay?

"Aye. I had to think of the children."

She smiled, and her tears escaped, for she loved this man and loved how considerate he was.

"Ye're crying."

She sniffed, unable to deny it. "Yes."

"But I haven't even told ya what I need to say."

She reached up, wiped her eyes. "What is it?"

He straightened his spine, and she thought he looked nervous. *Conor McDermott anxious?* she wondered.

"Will ya marry me, Lizzy?"

"Marry!" It was the last thing she had expected to hear.

"Aye. I know 'tis sudden."

"Yes."

"But 'tis not like we didn't have something between us."

"Yes."

"And I know I don't have much to offer—"

"Yes—no!" she cried when he stared at her. "I didn't mean yes to that; I meant yes as in 'Yes, I'll marry you.' "

His frown lifted. "Ya will?"

Grinning, she nodded.

"But I've little funds to me name," he said. "And ye've got everything ya need."

"Says you, Conor McDermott," she replied softly. "I don't have *you*. So, don't you be taking back the question, for I've already consented."

She reached up to cup his face. Looking into his eyes, she said clearly and carefully, "I'll wed you, Conor McDermott. Nothing would give me more pleasure than to be your wife."

With a wild whoop of joy, Conor picked her up and spun her in his arms. Lizzy laughed with delight and held on tightly. When he was done spinning her, he kissed her. She felt the fire all the way down to her toes.

"Ye're what?"

"We're getting married," Lizzy said.

Kathleen glanced from Lizzy to Conor and back again. Behind her, her husband Rian stared, and then the two grinned.

"How wonderful!" Kathleen exclaimed.

"Congratulations!" Rian slapped Conor on the back as he pumped his hand.

Kathleen's look became sly. "When did this happen?"

"He asked me yesterday morning," Lizzy told them.

"And she quickly agreed," Conor added. He and Lizzy exchanged looks.

"When is the wedding to be?" Kathleen asked. "We'll have it here. No—" She grinned at the two, who were about to protest, as her husband slipped behind her and hugged her to his side. "We insist."

"Aye," Rian said. "We'd love to do this. Kathleen, she's been wanting to have a party, and what a wonderful occasion to celebrate."

"I don't know—" Lizzy glanced at Conor for his approval.

He smiled at her as he pulled her against him. "We'd like to wed soon. Saturday, I've been thinking."

Lizzy experienced a rush of pleasure that Conor was so eager to marry her.

"Saturday!" Kathleen exclaimed. "There's not enough time to have a party by Saturday!"

It was Tuesday morning, two days after the storm, and there was clean-up work to be done at Green Lawns, for some of the outbuildings had been damaged by the gale force winds.

"Lizzy?" Conor gave her a squeeze. "Whatever ya'd like to do."

"I'd like to marry soon as well, but—John and I—we didn't have a party. I wouldn't mind having a party."

Conor turned to his friends. "Can ya arrange a party by a week from Saturday, then?"

Kathleen smiled. "Aye, it can be done."

"Good. Then Lizzy and I will become man and wife a week from Saturday." He bent his head, and Lizzy was surprised when he kissed her in full view of Kathleen and Rian.

There was warmth in her cheeks when he lifted his head. She could feel the Quaids' eyes on her, and slightly embarrassed, she smiled at them apologetically.

The simple kiss wreaked havoc on her senses. She longed to draw him in for a more intimate meeting of mouths, but she refrained from doing so. She loved Conor, but it wouldn't be proper to be so bold. Some things were better left for the two of them alone.

Kathleen and Rian were grinning at the two of them. Lizzy couldn't help but be overjoyed at their approval and the fact of her and Conor's impending nuptials.

Later, when Conor and Rian had gone off somewhere on the estate, Lizzy followed her friend to Kathleen's bedchamber.

Kathleen opened the door to a large armoire. "Lizzy, I'd like ya to wear me gown," she said, emotion thickening her Irish accent.

"Kathleen . . ." Lizzy was overwhelmed by her friend's generosity as Kathleen withdrew the gown she had worn three years before at her own wedding. "It's lovely."

"I know ya'd rather have one made for ya, but with the wedding less than a fortnight . . ."

Tears filled Lizzy's eyes and beaded on her lashes. "No. There is nothing else I'd rather wear than this."

Her throat had become tight with emotion. She was so happy. She had never imagined that she could be this happy.

John's words came back to her. *You were right, John dear. You told me I'd find a man to love and that I should wait for him.*

Both women were moved by the exchange. Lizzy hugged Kathleen. "Thank you."

When they broke apart, Kathleen took hold of Lizzy's shoulders and held her gaze. "Ya deserve this, Lizzy. Ya deserve to be happy."

"Now, you'll get me crying again."

Kathleen reached into a drawer and handed Lizzy a clean handkerchief. "I can't believe it, but then I guess I shouldn't be surprised. Conor—he's a good man. He'll make ya a fine husband."

"Yes, I know. I think so, too."

"About his search—" Kathleen gestured for her to sit in one of a pair of chairs in the room.

"We discussed it," Lizzy said as she sat. "I know how important it is for him to find his sister."

Kathleen's gaze sharpened. "Sister?"

Lizzy nodded. "Yes. The relative he's seeking is his sister."

"He must care for ya deeply, Lizzy, for Conor has

not been so forthcoming with Rian or me. We knew he was looking, but he kept most of his thoughts private . . . even from Rian. And I'd like to believe they've become more like good friends than employer and employee."

"They are good friends," Lizzy said with a smile. "Conor thinks the world of Rian."

Kathleen smiled. "I'm glad." She sighed. "It's going to seem different without that man under foot."

Lizzy arched her brow at Kathleen's choice of words.

Her friend chuckled. "Oh, 'tis not how it sounds. I mean it in a good way. Whenever I'm out and about, I'd see him with the men, giving an order or laughing and joking with them."

Lizzy nodded. He had been that way with the workers on Milly's Station. "You and Rian . . . Who will you get to replace Conor? I know it's an inconvenience . . ."

"Nonsense. We knew that Conor's time with us was limited. While I must admit that I'd hoped he'd stay, 'tis always been in our minds to find the right person to fill his shoes."

"And did you find someone?" Lizzy asked. It was hard to feel guilty when Conor's permanent absence from Green Lawns meant his permanence in her life, as her husband and lover.

"Aye. Rian has high regard for Robert Chumley, a man he hired on only last year. Apparently, Conor approves."

Lizzy reached across the space between them and covered Kathleen's hand. "I'm sorry. But I can't help but feel happy."

Kathleen looked surprised. "And why shouldn't ya be? Ye're getting married! Ya should be dancing on the roof!"

The friends laughed together at the mental image.

"How do the children feel about Conor?"

Lizzy smiled. "They love him. Jason has been following him about since the day Conor came. Emma thinks the sun rises and sets in him. He recently gave her a pretty carved box for her doll clothes. It was for her birthday, and she had no idea that he would remember it." She smiled at the memory.

It had been only days ago, before Conor's second trip to Baltimore. During the first trip, he had purchased fabric and lace for Lizzy's gift to Emma for her birthday. And then she had learned that he had brought a gift from himself as well. After that thoughtful gesture of caring and kindness to her little girl, Lizzy truly adored him.

"He'll be a good father to the pair," Kathleen said. She paused, and a sparkle came to her green eyes. "And a good father to one of yer own?"

She blushed. "Yes."

"Does he know ye're not the children's mother?"

Lizzy's cheeks turned a darker shade of red. She felt the heat infuse not just her face, but downward past the neck. "I—we—"

Kathleen grinned. "I see."

"You don't think me a . . . wanton?"

"A wan—Lizzy! Ye're a woman, aren't ya? And ya were married for how many years? Almost six was it?"

She nodded.

"Ya were married for nearly six years, and ye've never known what a wonderful gift it can be between a man and wife to show one's love." Kathleen turned her hand, laced her fingers through her friend's. "I told ya ya'd convince him of the truth, didn't I?"

A slow smile touched Lizzy's lips. "Yes, you did."

"And now ye're getting married." Kathleen looked pleased.

"Yes, I am." *I'm getting married!*

TWENTY-ONE

"You look lovely," Kathleen said.

"It's a beautiful gown, Kathleen," Lizzy said. "Thank you."

The gown was made of white Irish lace over lavender silk. Tiny silk roses in lavender and dark purple had been added recently to the neck and to the hem, sparingly, but attached for a splash of color to make the dress Lizzy's own. The garment had long sleeves, puffed out to the elbows and trimmed with lavender silk ribbons entwined in the lace at the wrists. Tiny lavender and white flowers had been woven into the bride's hair.

Fingers shaking, Lizzy pressed her hand to the strand of amethysts encircling her neck. "Do you think Conor will mind that I've chosen to wear these?" She also wore the matching bracelet but left off her amethyst ring.

"Why should he mind?" Kathleen replied. "Because John gave it to ya? The jewelry is yers, Lizzy. And Conor knows that ya were wed. 'Tis yer best that ye're wearing. He'll be glad that ye've done so for him."

Gazing into the cheval mirror in a bedchamber at Green Lawns, Lizzy tried to calm herself. She was nervous. Here she was marrying the man of her dreams, but she was scared. This wedding would be different than the first one. There was more at stake with her relationship with Conor. She loved him desperately and wanted to make him happy, but she feared that something would go wrong to ruin this day.

Since they had become betrothed, there had been no lovemaking between them. Conor and she had agreed that they would wait until after the wedding . . . with the ceremony being less than two weeks from the time of their betrothal.

There were several occasions during the past two weeks when Lizzy had wanted to forget propriety and go to Conor's bed, but she had resisted the urge. It hadn't seemed right, and she didn't want Conor to think her too wanton that she couldn't wait. She didn't want him to think he would be getting a brazen bride.

Lizzy frowned. If Conor had been bothered by the fact that they slept in their own rooms, he didn't show it. And why did that bother her? He was being a gentleman. Hadn't he been thinking of her?

As Kathleen made last-minute adjustments to the bride's hair, Lizzy stared into the mirror.

Did Conor love her as much as she loved him?

He wouldn't have asked her to marry him if he didn't.

"Lizzy, relax," Kathleen told her. "Everything will be fine. All the guests have arrived. Father Joseph's ready, and Rian said that Conor is as nervous as ya are, pacing back and forth all morning."

"Conor's nervous?" she asked, pleased at the thought.

Kathleen smiled. "Aye. He looks fine, though. And he is eager to marry ya, so don't be fretting."

Lizzy sighed, then leaned closer to the looking glass to check her appearance one more time. Her brown eyes seemed over bright; but her complexion was smooth and clear, and her mouth was pink, her cheeks flushed. She couldn't find fault with her hair and dress. "I'm ready."

Outside the manor house, Rian waited for her with

his Dearborn pulled up to the door. "Ya look wonderful, Lizzy," he complimented her.

Her smile wobbled. "Thank you, Rian."

"Are ya ready?" he asked her.

She inclined her head and whispered her reply. "Yes."

He assisted her and then Kathleen inside the wagon. Then he climbed in himself and closed the door.

The ride to the church seemed long to Lizzy, until they arrived, and then it didn't seem that it was long enough.

"Come, Lizzy," Kathleen said soothingly. She reached over from the seat directly across to capture her hand. "Ya love Conor. And ye're getting a fine husband who loves ya."

Lizzy gave her friend's hand an answering squeeze. "Thank you, Kathleen," she said softly. "For everything."

Tears filled Kathleen's eyes as they exchanged smiles. "Be happy, Elizabeth. 'Tis past time that ye're due."

Blinking back tears of her own, Lizzy glanced out the window toward the building. The church was the same one that the Quaids had married in three years before. On that day, it had been Kathleen who had been scared, and Lizzy the one who had calmed her. Now their roles had reversed.

Pushing the window curtains aside, Lizzy peered out into the churchyard. They were marrying in a Catholic ceremony, which was controversial in itself in Kent County, which was mostly Methodist in these times. There were all manners of buggies parked on the grounds. Seeing them filled Lizzy's stomach with butterflies. That so many guests had come was a testament to the amount of respect that Conor had gained in the area since his arrival . . . or to the respect felt for the Quaids, who were giving the party.

The driver, one of Rian Quaid's workers, steered the

conveyance up to the front double doors of the church, and Rian helped Kathleen to alight first, then Lizzy.

Inside the church, Lizzy's gaze fell immediately on her bridegroom waiting for her near Father Joseph at the front of the church. Her pulse picked up its pace as her love for him overwhelmed her.

Conor looked magnificent in a navy frock coat and trousers with white shirt, waistcoat, and cravat. His short Wellington black boots had been polished to a high sheen. Lizzy's gaze slid the length of him, noting his muscular figure and fine form, and she shivered a sigh of pleasure.

The music had not begun yet. As if sensing her presence at the back of the room, he turned and locked gazes with her. Heat warmed Lizzy's cheeks. Conor gave her a slow smile that made her giddy with happiness . . . and caused her heart to sing. How could she doubt this man?

"Ready?"

She nodded without turning and felt Rian Quaid capture her arm.

"Ya look wonderful," he told her.

She flashed him a quick smile before her attention went back to Conor. In the absence of her father, she had asked Rian to escort her down the aisle.

A fiddler began a sweet tune, accompanied by a flutist. As the two musicians played, they were joined by a harpist, whose music swirled about the room in soft, lovely swells.

Her eyes never straying from Conor, she and Rian began their approach. She could hear the music as it swirled about her. She was aware that Rian kept pace with her and that there were people standing on both sides, but her attention remained with the man of her heart.

As she neared the front, she saw Jason, looking dapper in a miniature version of Conor's attire. There was a grin on his little handsome face. She didn't know who had dressed him; but he looked wonderful, and she suspected that it had been Conor.

Emma stood beside her brother, looking like a little lady in her new yellow silk dress, the gown that Lizzy had made for her birthday. She wore her blond hair in ringlets and a crown of tiny yellow and white blossoms. The effect was startling; Emma resembled a fairy princess. Her smile was as wide and as bright as Jason's.

It was a lovely summer day. The sun shone in a cloudless sky; it beamed through the windows, casting its radiance to lighten an otherwise dark church interior. The air temperature both inside and out was comfortable, not hot and sticky, but perfect. As she joined her future husband's side, Lizzy felt loved and bathed in light.

Rian left Lizzy at her groom's side and moved to stand on the opposite side of Conor. Kathleen joined the trio to stand at Lizzy's left, and the priest began the ceremony.

"Do you, Elizabeth Mary Hanlin Foley, take Conor Sean McDermott . . ."

Her gaze locked with Conor's, Lizzy spoke her response eagerly.

Conor did the same, answering each question posed to him without hesitation. His steady calm soothed Lizzy's fears, for she felt he wouldn't be able to answer so easily unless he was certain of their love, of this marriage.

The good Father asked them all to pause and reflect on God's love and work. In those long moments of silence during the ceremony, Lizzy was conscious of the warm strength of Conor's hand gripping her own, of his scent invading her senses . . . and the sound of his even breathing and her own thudding heartbeat in answer.

She was aware that Emma and Jason stood close by, Jason holding Rian's hand, while Emma held Kathleen's, and how good the children were being while she—their "ma"—took a man to husband who was

not their father. That their love for Conor was obvious
and strong made her offer up a little prayer of thanks,
for she felt blessed and loved. Every unhappy moment
in her life up until this point seemed minor in the over-
powering joy of this moment . . . this all-important occasion in her life.

And then the ceremony was over. Conor McDermott
and she were husband and wife. The music played as
they left the church. Outside, she was greeted by well
wishes and for the first time as Mrs. McDermott, and
she felt a funny little jolt in the midsection of her chest.

Conor and she stayed a time to talk with neighbors
and friends, and then soon they were in the Quaids'
Dearborn, being driven away from the crowd at the
church toward the Quaid estate, Green Lawns.

Conor hadn't said a word to her other than the re-
sponses required by the wedding ceremony. Alone in
the vehicle, he finally turned to her, captured her face
between his large hands, and lowered his mouth to her
lips. His kiss was hot and thorough with all the re-
straint of the past two weeks gone. When he lifted his
head, his eyes were bright, and Lizzy was gasping.

"We've done it, Mrs. McDermott," he said with
warmth. "Elizabeth McDermott." He tenderly caressed
her cheek. " 'Tis been too long since I've properly loved
ya. I'm eager to have ya in me bed this night."

Tears filled her eyes as she stroked his jaw, then
traced his mouth with trembling fingers. "I love you,"
she whispered, and felt her world couldn't be more
perfect than it was at this time.

The celebration given by the Quaids for the newly
married couple was spectacular and would be talked
about as a truly amazing event for months, perhaps
years to come. As she and Conor stood in the midst
of the party, Lizzy marveled at the quantities of pre-

pared food and the vast array of wedding gifts that had been set up for display inside the Quaids' dining room.

With the weather perfect, the affair was being held outdoors. Large tables constructed just for this event had been set up on the lawns. Delicious canapés, meat dishes, vegetables, and rich pastries were spread out over each. Everyone had come dressed in his or her finest frock. Many of the folks in attendance were the same people who had spread gossip about her. She was amazed that these same people now seemed to delight in her company.

Happy and in love, it was easy for Lizzy to forgive the gossips. She buried the pain caused by ignorance and focused instead on her new husband and the wonderful life they would have together.

"Hungry?" Conor said as he drew them out of the crowd to wander a bit on their own.

She smiled as she slipped her arm through his and hugged him to her. "A little."

"Meats or sweets?"

Lizzy chuckled as she saw how his gaze had turned to linger on the table of pastries. "Meats first, then sweets," she said with light laughter. "Plenty of sweets."

He joined in the laughter, and they made their way first to the table of main dishes and meat pies, before finding two chairs among the many that had been set out on the lawn for the occasion.

"Ma!" Jason ran up to them, his eyes excited, his mouth smeared with chocolate frosting. Emma was not far behind him, appearing just as excited but clean.

Lizzy exchanged a look of amusement with her new husband. "Hello, Jason. Emma." She smiled. "Been sampling the desserts first, Jase?" she asked.

He bobbed his head. "Aunt Kathleen said I could, 'cause it's a special occasion."

Lizzy nodded, then had to chuckle when Conor made a sound that told her he agreed. She thought it was wonderful that the children had begun to call

Kathleen and Rian aunt and uncle, for they were her closest friends, more like family, and the terms of affection seemed to fit.

"Miss Emma?" It was Conor who addressed the little girl. "Have ya sampled any of those fine treats?"

She hesitated before nodding. "Just one lemon square," she said. "But Ma says it's best to eat the good food first, so I ate meat pie, too."

"Good girl," Lizzy murmured as she threw Conor a teasing look. She laughed when he looked crushed. "Emma, would you do me a favor and get Conor a piece of chocolate cake? He's been longing for a sweet, and I guess it's only fair that he should have it, it being his wedding day."

"My dearest heart," he whispered, then kissed her as Emma left.

Jason remained, watching them, his eyes bright. He gave them a crooked smile. "Are you going to be kissing a lot?"

Conor's lips twitched. "And if we are?" he challenged.

The boy thought about it. "It's all right, I guess. 'Cause it means you love each other."

Lizzy's heart seemed to stop as she waited for Conor's response. When he was silent, she glanced at him to find him studying her with such tenderness and love that the emotion that welled up inside of her stole her breath and made her momentarily speechless.

" 'Tis right ya are, Jason," Conor said.

Lizzy sniffed, squeezed her husband's hand, and then leaned close to kiss him.

"Ma?"

She broke away after only the briefest contact. When she glanced at Jason, he didn't seem bothered by her show of affection for Conor. "Can I go down to the stables? I want to see Midnight."

Lizzy frowned. "Jase, you're wearing your best clothes."

Conor touched her arm, drawing her glance. His gaze asked her if he could handle the boy. Lizzy gave her silent assent.

"Jason, ya may go to the stables only if ya can find Thomas and he agrees to go with ya," he said. "And mind that ya watch where ya walk and don't get dirty."

Jason started to grin; then he seemed to beg Lizzy's permission with a look. "You heard your father," she said.

With a shriek of joy, the boy left them. Conor captured Lizzy's sole attention by grasping her chin and turning her to meet his gaze. His rugged features were unreadable. "Ya referred to me as Jason's father," he said quietly.

Lizzy nodded. Had she done the wrong thing? "Yes, and why not? You've married us."

"Thank ya." Suddenly, his emotions were there for her to witness. She saw gratitude and love, and something more powerful that she couldn't seem to describe for herself. "I want ya."

Her breath slammed in her chest. Desire. Passion. His expression was taut with it. His eyes seemed to glow with it. He wanted her, and it showed.

"I know," she said. And she did now; the knowledge was heady. "I want you, too."

Her response only made his eyes darken before he looked around. "Do ya think they'll miss us if we slip away?"

Her answering laugh was shaky. "Aye, Mr. McDermott," she said in a voice that mimicked his own. "I do."

His mild oath warmed her. Suddenly, she wished the party was over, when she and Conor would be alone, naked . . . kissing . . . caressing . . . pleasing and loving each other.

"How long do ya think this celebration will last?" he asked.

"Only till sundown," she answered brightly. She

would hold the knowledge of his desire close to her, and it would sustain her through the rest of the day till the time when they could be together.

"For the love of—"

"Sweet Bridget?" she finished for him sweetly and with a smile.

"Minx."

"But you want me."

"Aye, lass, that I do."

TWENTY-TWO

The party drew to a close, and Lizzy had to admit that she had enjoyed herself more than any other day. When the last guest had left, Conor helped Lizzy into their shay, then climbed onto the seat next to her.

"Are you sure you don't mind watching the children?" she asked Kathleen.

"I'm certain," her friend said with a smile. "They are always as good as gold. It's a pleasure to have them, and Emma is good with Fiona. She's patient and kind to me babe, and I'm happy to have her." She shifted Fiona from one hip to the other. "Aren't we, Fi?" She grinned at Jason and ruffled the boy's hair. "And Jason here will be content to help Rian run the plantation . . . or Thomas in the stables."

Jason bobbed his head.

"You'll be a good boy?" Lizzy asked.

"Yes, Ma."

"And you'll help Kathleen watch over Emma?" She could see Emma playing in the grass, twirling a wildflower in her hand, before bending to pick another.

He made a face. "Do I have to?"

"Jason."

"Yes, Ma."

Conor grinned at the boy. "Ye ma is nervous about leaving ya, Jason. She'll miss ya."

Jason blushed and looked away, while mumbling something about having to find Uncle Rian.

"Thank ya for the use of yer carriage," Conor said, referring to the vehicle used from the church to the party. Michael Storm had brought over the shay for the Quaids' ride home to Green Lawns. Now the newlyweds were riding it home to Milly's Station.

"It was our pleasure."

"I hate to leave you with the mess," Lizzy said.

"Nonsense," Kathleen assured her. "I've got servants." She smiled. " 'Tis our pleasure to do this for ya." She reached in to squeeze Lizzy's hand. "Ye're a good friend, Lizzy McDermott." She flashed Conor a teasing grin. "And ye'll do, McDermott." It was obvious that she cared a great deal for the both of them.

Soon, Conor and Lizzy were alone, sitting close beneath the raised hood of their vehicle as they headed home to Milly's Station.

The sun had set, but there was still enough light to see. By the time they reached the manor, darkness had descended. A light in the downstairs window welcomed them home.

"I'm sorry we have to stay at Milly's Station," Conor said as he pulled the wagon up to the entrance of the house.

Fetts came out to greet them and waited patiently for them to alight before taking over the care of the horse and carriage.

"I don't care if we go on a wedding trip," Lizzy said after Fetts had left. "It's not important where we are as long as we're together."

Conor's eyes warmed as he studied her. "Aye, I agree. But when there is time, we'll take that wedding trip."

It was time for the spring harvest, and they had decided that they couldn't get away during such a busy time.

As they entered the front door of the manor, they found a light burning in the foyer and another to the left in the parlor. The house was quiet. The servants had prepared for the couple's arrival, then left so that the newlyweds could be alone. Lizzy was never more conscious of the silence and her bridegroom's nearness as Conor closed the door, shutting the world outside.

"Would ya like a glass of sherry?" He moved into the dining room.

Lizzy's lips twitched with good humor and memory as she followed him. She had avoided the drink all day long, but now she felt as though she could enjoy a sip of something. "Brandy," she said with a soft laugh. "I've developed a taste for it."

He chose a bottle of blackberry brandy, made by a neighbor, Mrs. Ways, and given to them recently for a wedding gift, brought back to the house by one of the servants who had come to share in the day's celebration.

Conor uncorked the bottle and poured out a measure of liquid. He handed the glass to her, then poured the same amount for himself.

"To me lovely bride . . . May marriage agree with her. After a time with me, may her beautiful brown eyes continue to sparkle and the smile remain on her sweet lips . . ." He touched his glass gently against hers. "Happy wedding day, Mrs. McDermott."

"Happy wedding day, husband," she replied softly. *Husband,* she thought with joy. It was hard to believe that this big, strapping Irishman was now her husband. He was so handsome that she wanted to just stare at him. His dark hair was curly and short, a style worn by many of the men of the day, but he preferred the shorter sideburns and clean-shaven skin instead of muttonchops and facial hair.

Peering at him over the glass rim approvingly, she sipped slowly from the brandy and swallowed. The drink was sweet and fruity, and it was good; but Lizzy felt she liked the one she had drank previously better. "Alone at last," she murmured.

Conor grinned. "Amen." He grabbed her hand and

tugged her gently up the stairs to the second floor and the master bedroom. The bedchamber had been redone in the past two weeks with her things and his, a delightful combination of feminine and masculine items that blended harmoniously. Millicent's portrait was gone. Lizzy had hung a lovely water scene in its place. And the colors had been changed from the burgundy that John preferred to different shades of blue. *Like Conor's eyes,* she thought with a smile.

After kicking open the door, Conor led her into the room, then stopped to kiss her thoroughly. When he was done, she was breathless as he continued to the bed where he urged her to sit on the edge of the mattress.

Someone had recently and thoughtfully set a lamp to burning low on a table by the window. The room smelled of lamp oil and the fresh flowers that had been arranged in a vase on Lizzy's vanity table.

Conor set down his glass, and then hers, on the table next to the lamp, before he took a seat next to her on the bed. Slipping his arm about her, he held her close.

" 'Twas a wonderful day," he said. He buried his face in her hair and kissed her. "Are ya happy?"

He pulled back, and she met his gaze. "Very."

"Good."

"Conor—"

"Aye?"

"You're not sorry? About the wedding?" She hadn't meant to ask. But despite the good relationship between her and her late husband, there had been times when Lizzy had wondered whether or not John had suffered regrets.

"What!" He seemed shocked by the question, and she felt an infusion of happy warmth. He released her shoulders to frame her face with his hands. "Elizabeth . . . Lizzy. Look at me." And she did. "I married ya because it was me most fervent desire to do so. Believe me when I say I could never regret taking ya to wife."

Tears filled her eyes. "I love you."

His smile was tender. His eyes glowed. "I couldn't have asked for a better wife. Ye're a special woman. Stay happy, and I'll be more than content."

With that said, Conor captured her mouth in a brief kiss that nevertheless rocked her to her toes. Then he turned his loving attention to her neck.

Shuddering with pleasure, Lizzy closed her eyes and allowed her feelings for him free rein.

"Conor," she gasped as he pressed her back to the quilt-covered feather mattress. "Husband . . ."

She had changed from the wedding dress to a traveling gown back at Green Lawns, and now Conor made quick work of her bodice fastenings. Each brush of his knuckles against her skin made her tingle. Each puff of his breath as he worked filled her heart with joy. Fabric parted, revealing silk underneath, and he tenderly, lovingly, removed her gown, kissing the exposed skin as he did so. His fingers undid the ribbons at the neck of her chemise, and he slipped his hand beneath silk to stroke across skin and inched downward, until he cupped a firm, fleshy mound.

Lizzy gasped and arched her breast into his hand, while her hands cradled his head. Fingers tangling in his hair, she held him to her, moaning softly while he tugged off her undergarments, then lavished attention to each breast and nipple . . . and lower to her belly.

"Conor . . ."

"Aye, lass," he whispered as he slid up to kiss her neck. "That's it. Feel me . . . Feel me touching ya." And he dipped down again to stroke and kiss her quivering stomach.

She whimpered as he did so, moaning when he slipped his hand lower to that moist private area that had been made to accept his love. He caressed and fondled her there while he continued to kiss her belly, her breasts, and back to her belly again.

She inhaled sharply as his fingers entered her more deeply, finding her most secret spot of pleasure as he explored with a gentle, then a more urgent hand. His touch sent her swirling in a spiral of ecstasy that had her writhing next to him on the bed. Suddenly, she cried out and climaxed, and she was in a world of bright lights and radiant colors.

She barely had time to catch her breath, when Conor began to work his special magic again . . . and then she felt the glade of warm skin against skin . . . the brush of masculine hardness against feminine softness . . . and she was panting, grasping, and calling out his name.

When he slipped inside of her, she was moist and ready for him. As she sheathed him, she kissed his face, his neck. She caressed his shoulders and back.

Conor began a rhythm of thrust and withdraw that drove her wild with the intensity of physical feeling and the depth of her love for him.

"Yes," she whispered. It was happening again! She held on tight, and then her hands moved as she attempted to caress all of him.

"Aye, lass," he grated. "That's it. Touch me."

And she did, running her fingers over his back, down to his waist. She grabbed his hips and held tight as she added to the rhythm by arching abdomen upward, squeezing her buttocks as if to lock him into her so that the two would be forever joined as one.

The crest of sexual pleasure grew as they kissed deeply, fondled, and whispered love words. And then they were spinning out of control, rocked by the sensation their love brought them until they cleaved together as man and wife. Their bodies joined; their souls meshed in one perfect point of unity.

Afterward they floated back to this world slowly, locked in each other's arms. Conor lay with his head on Lizzy's breast and listened to her heartbeat. His hands continued to move over her satin skin. He couldn't seem to get enough of her, and he knew he wasn't by any means done making love to her for the night.

While they rested, he caught his breath, allowed his own pulse to slow. Then he reached over to turn out the oil lamp. Next, he pulled the quilt to envelop their naked bodies in a warm cocoon. Nestling against her breasts again, Conor became more conscious of her presence . . . the scent of her . . . the sound of her breathing, the silkiness of her hair, and the satin smoothness of each line and curve of her.

"Mrs. Conor McDermott," he said thickly.

She sighed. "Conor McDermott's wife," she answered drowsily. And he smiled, as he was certain he had heard immense satisfaction in her voice.

He shifted under the bedclothes, slid down, and parted her legs until he could gain access to her feminine sweetness. He felt her stiffen when he first touched her. Then as he began to soothe her with his mouth, she was up and flying again. He could feel her shock as she shuddered, heard her wild cries of delight as he quickly sent her over the edge again. His moment came later, after a time when they were both rested again.

As the first hint of dawn brightened the new day, Conor woke his new wife with kisses, then was startled when she pressed him back to the bed and began to work a special blend of magic of her own. Soon, he was the one reeling with mindless pleasure while she took her satisfaction in having her bridegroom pleased.

"I'll be back as soon as I can," Conor said as he got ready to leave her the next day at mid morning. There was still work to be done after the storm, on the acreage that the rain had washed clear. He wanted to see that it was replanted while the season was early enough to successfully sow.

Lizzy stood in the kitchen, wearing only her dressing gown, and rose up to kiss his sensual mouth. She would never get enough of kissing and caressing him, she thought. "I'll be waiting for you," she promised.

Desire darkened the depths of his blue gaze. "What time will the children be back?"

Lizzy smiled. "Wednesday morning," she said, and noted with satisfaction his pleased surprise. They both adored the children, but they wanted more time alone together.

"And the servants?"

"Wednesday afternoon." She chuckled when she saw his shocked delight. "We'll have to manage our own food and clothes," she said, as though he might find the prospect tiresome.

"Hell, we can eat berries and drink brandy or port . . . and as for our clothes"—he reached out to caress her breast through silk—"we won't need any."

She shivered and gasped as he aroused her nipple into a hardened peak. "When did you say you'll be back?" she asked in a strangled voice.

He shifted his hand to the other side. "In an hour," he said, his deep voice thick. "Wait for me upstairs, and I'll bring what we need . . . to keep us full and satisfied."

And with a renewal of that promise on his lips and a flaming look in his blue eyes, Conor slipped from the house and headed toward the fields. He only looked back five times, before he had disappeared behind an outbuilding.

TWENTY-THREE

Despite the fact that Conor had to work for a while each day, the McDermotts shared three glorious days together. Conor would leave for an hour or two to oversee work in the fields each morning, only to return to make love to his wife for the remainder of the day . . . attention that she greatly appreciated.

Between bouts of lovemaking and moments of fulfillment, they ate strawberries and baked goods, which had mysteriously appeared on the back doorstep one morning. They breakfasted on waffles or flapjacks, or eggs—also mysteriously brought to their doorstep one morning with potatoes and cheese.

Happy and in love, they shared times of lazy conversation which often lasted well into the next stirrings of their desire. Lizzy described her childhood, her time at the Bread and Barrel Inn, her parents' death, and the care of Jason, her brother. She told him how the boy had come to regard her as more of a mother than a sister and about her subsequent marriage to John Foley. She had fallen in love with baby Emma instantly, she confessed, and was pleased to be raising such a wonderful child.

Conor told her of his native homeland, a little bit about his childhood—which Lizzy thought must have been an unhappy time—and his desire to find his liv-

ing family. There was much about his former life that
Conor kept silent about, but Lizzy didn't mind, for she
felt he would tell her when he was ready. Each hour
of their marriage, she was more sure of their growing
closeness. And it was only a matter of time before he
would open up and tell her everything.

Wednesday morning, Rian Quaid brought back the
children. When Jason and Emma burst in through the
back door, Conor and Lizzy were dressed and eating
the noon meal at the kitchen dining table. As the children ran excitedly into the room, Lizzy jumped up and
opened her arms. Jason and Emma rushed in to happily
embrace their ma, who hugged them back tightly.

Rian had quietly followed and watched the reunion
with a smile. "They were a fine pair to have," he said.

"Thank you," Lizzy said. "I don't know how to tell
you how much we appreciate your friendship."

Rian grinned. "Ya just did."

"Would you like to eat?" Lizzy had made beef
dodgers—corncakes filled with finely chopped beef.

"I can't stay. Kathleen is expecting me. But thank
ya for asking."

Lizzy thanked Rian again, and then he and Conor
left the house together. Conor returned minutes later
after his friend had left. He sat down in the seat he
had vacated just moments before.

"Conor!" Emma cried. She left her mother's arms
and skirted the table.

Lizzy watched with a sudden pinprick of tears as
her little girl climbed into her new husband's lap. The
child placed her arms about Conor's neck, told him
she missed him, and kissed his cheek soundly.

Conor and Lizzy exchanged pleased grins at the evidence of the child's affection. When Jason moved to
Conor to shake hands, Conor accepted the handshake
with a firm grip, then hugged the boy tightly when
Jason relented and initiated the embrace, apparently

having decided that a handshake wasn't enough between hero and new son.

Later, they gathered as a family for the evening
meal.

"And you should have seen me, Ma. Uncle Rian put
me up on Midnight, and I got to ride in a circle. It
was great. I was so high up, I could see the sky!"

Lizzy flashed Conor a worried glance. Conor, seeing
his wife's concern, spoke to the boy. "Ya were careful
to do what Uncle Rian told ya?"

Jason bobbed his head. "Yes. And he kept his arms
tight about me so I wouldn't fall." He didn't seem to
hear his ma's notable sigh of relief.

Little Miss Emma had had a wonderful time as well.
Aunt Kathleen had allowed her to help with baby
Fiona, and she had also had a tea party with fancy
finger cakes and pandowdy. And she had learned to
make gingersnaps, which came out perfect, as Uncle
Rian said so, and Uncle Rian should know as he ate
at least a half dozen of them.

The children sat down and shared in the food; then
they were off to play with the workers' children, to tell
them of their adventures.

And Conor and Lizzy were alone again. . . . They
grinned as they cleared the table. Life was good. They
were happy and in love. They, with the children, made
a wonderful family.

"Captain Logan," Lizzy greeted the man warmly,
then stepped back while bidding him entry into the
foyer.

Logan smiled back at her. "How are you, Mrs.
Foley?"

"It's Mrs. McDermott." The man had been away for
the past three weeks.

She saw him quickly mask a flicker of surprise.
"Then, it's now your husband I'm seeking," he said.

She nodded, and he seemed pleased. "Congratulations are in order, then."

"Yes. We wed this Saturday past." She led him down the hall toward her husband's study. "Was your time away successful?" she asked conversationally.

"For the most part, aye," he replied. "For the rest, your husband will be the one to determine that."

Curiosity urged her to ask why, but she kept silent. Conor would tell her later, she thought. Unless it was something her husband was unwilling or not ready to share.

Although she was overjoyed with her new marriage, there were still sides of her husband that remained mysterious, and it bothered her that he still felt too uneasy to share all of himself with her. *In time,* she thought as she knocked softly, then opened the door.

Conor looked up, saw his wife at the door, and smiled and held out his arm. Her gaze transmitting silent messages of love, she shook her head slightly, then stepped aside to reveal Logan. "Captain Logan is here to see you."

"Logan!" he exclaimed, his eyes bright. He shoved back his chair as he stood, then came around the desk with his hand outstretched. Seeing that her husband's attention was riveted solely on his visitor, Lizzy slipped away, quietly closing the door behind her.

"Lizzy!" Conor's voice through the door stopped her in her tracks as she started down the hall. She heard the sound of the opening door. He popped his head out. "Come here a moment, would ya?" His expression was solemn as he silently waited for her to come.

She approached the few feet, and he leaned close. "I forgot something."

She frowned and raised an eyebrow.

His features grave, he stepped out into the hall and partially closed the door. Then, while Captain Logan waited in the room behind him, he kissed her soundly and deeply, invading her mouth with his tongue. Then, when she was clinging to him in mindless surrender, he set her back from him. "I don't recall if I'd done that often enough this morning." He grinned.

It was with a lighter step that Lizzy left her husband alone in the study with the captain of the *Millicent*. She was married to a magnificent man, she thought with a grin. Her heart was still singing with love as she went about overseeing the morning household chores.

Conor went back to his seat behind the desk, his thoughts filled with his new wife, his mouth still yearning for the taste of her lips. He waved Logan into the chair in front.

" 'Tis been while since I've seen ya," he said, forcing his attention back to business, which was a hard thing to do when his every thought, his every moment, was filled with visions of Lizzy.

"I delivered the samples of tobacco to Brenner's Mercantile, and then I headed up to Philadelphia."

"Philadelphia?"

"I made several inquiries in Baltimore. I heard that the *Mistress Kate* was docked these days at the Port of Philadelphia. She's apparently having some work done to her."

Conor perked up at the mention of the familiar ship name. "And?"

"I found a mate on the vessel who sailed with her for five years now. After an exchange of coin, Mate Halifax's memory miraculously sharpened. It seems he remembers a pair of Irishwomen. The two of them cousins. One of them a Miss Dunne."

Dunne, he thought. "That's the cousin of me sister," he breathed. "Dunne is a common enough surname in Ireland."

Logan nodded. "Aye, but she was traveling with a woman with the name Maguire."

"Did he know me sister? Did he know where they

went?" It was three years past; what was the likelihood of an old salt tar knowing the details of a passenger's destination. Then again, it was a miracle that the man recalled the two Irish women at all.

"He said that the Dunne woman was picked up by her betrothed there in Baltimore. He knew this because the bloke paid him to heft the lady's trunk off the ship. The other woman—Dunne's cousin—is she your sister?"

"Aye."

"Said that she went off the ship with a man. Some American," he said. "She was clinging to his arm, he said, as if she'd fall if she let him go. He had the impression that they were . . . sweethearts."

In fact, the seaman had described the relationship between Conor's sister and the man with her in terms best left unsaid, as they had been crude and uncomplimentary. Logan figured there was no reason to upset or anger the man who had given him his job.

Conor was silent as he bent slightly to open a drawer. "Drink?" He withdrew a bottle and set it down with a sharp thump onto the desk top. He met Logan's gaze. "Irish whiskey," he said.

Logan shook his head.

"Sorry," Conor said sincerely. "I forgot ya gave it up."

The captain shrugged. "Not entirely. I enjoy a short glass of port on occasion, but never more than one and never on the job."

Conor nodded as he put away the bottle without sampling from it. "So now I know that me sister did come to Baltimore, and that she went off with some strange man." He cursed. "She could bloody well be anywhere."

"Aye, she could," Logan said.

"Did he happen to mention the name of the cousin's betrothed?" He had never learned of the man's name from the people he had spoken with in County Clare, the servants who had once worked for Sean Dunne.

Logan leaned back in his chair. "He did."

Conor felt his heart give a lurch. If he could find the cousin, he would learn the whereabouts of his half sister. Meara Dunne would know where the Maguire lass went.

"Who is he?" he asked, his pulse beginning to beat rapidly.

"Quaid," the captain said. "The woman was betrothed to Mr. Rian Quaid from Green Lawns."

TWENTY-FOUR

Lizzy expected Conor for the midday meal, but he came to her shortly before eleven to tell her that he wouldn't be available to eat.

"I need to go to Green Lawns." His look was grave.

"Is something wrong?" she asked.

He shook his head and managed to smile at her, but she could tell that he was troubled. "I need to speak with Rian," was his only explanation.

She started to say something more, then thought better of it. It hurt her that he wouldn't immediately want to share his concerns.

"Will you be home in time for supper?" she asked.

He seemed surprised by the question. "Aye, of course."

She stifled a relieved sigh, then accepted his brief kiss before he left her. What had Captain Logan said? Should she ask Conor when he returned if he didn't offer her any information?

Her next thought was to find Captain Logan and drill the man for answers herself, but that wouldn't be fair to Conor. Conor was her husband, and she had to trust him, even though his secrecy upset her.

He returned, as promised, by late afternoon. Conor kissed her hello but seemed subdued. Again, she wanted to ask him what was wrong, but she didn't. She could only hope that he would confide in her later.

After supper, he retired to the study to do some bookwork. Worried, Lizzy entered the room after she had put the children to bed and went behind his desk chair to slip her arms about his neck.

"You've been working a long while," she said. She kissed the top of his head, then pulled back to rub his shoulders.

He leaned back against her with a sigh, and encouraged, she massaged his neck.

"Will you be done soon?" she asked.

"Aye." He flipped closed the book and continued to enjoy her touch.

"Is there a problem with finances?"

"Nay." He stood suddenly, grabbed her, then sat and pulled her into his lap. "Nay." He began to nuzzle her neck.

"Conor," she breathed as her pulse raced, her heart pounded. "The children—"

"Didn't ya put them to bed?" He slipped his hand down the neck of her gown, skimming his fingers over soft flesh, dipping farther to flick over her nipple.

She gasped with pleasure. "Yes . . . bed," she murmured.

He raised his head, flashed her a grin. "I want to love ya here. In this room, where I can think of us later."

His brilliant blue eyes glistened. He lifted her up and set her on the desk top, shoving things aside as he did. Then he rose and went to the door. She heard the sound of a click as he turned a key in the lock. She tingled with anticipation.

She turned her head, and their eyes met as he crossed the room. His hands lifted and began to leisurely unbutton his shirt. Lizzy's breathing increased.

She didn't move, but waited for him to come to her instead. When he reached her, his shirt was open, his gaze dark with desire. He stood before her, and she raised her hands to his chest, closing her eyes as she enjoyed touching his warm, hard muscular form.

"Conor," she breathed, and leaned to press her lips to his skin.

He lifted her to her feet and launched a sensual assault on her senses with his kiss. And as she sank back against the desk edge, he changed strategies and slipped his hands under her skirts, up her legs, and higher . . . and she was lost in the magic of Conor's lovemaking. They shut out their surroundings as they found pleasure and satisfaction from one another.

Conor was away from the plantation when Lizzy received the second threat. This one came in the middle of the afternoon when it appeared as a message for her at the back kitchen doorway, carved into a piece of wood. This one terrified her more than the other, for someone had been so bold as to deliver it in pure daylight. The note, this time, had threatened the man she loved.

"Get rid of McDermott, or someone will get rid of him for you."

She began to shake as she reread the message. What madness drove a person to write such a horrible thing? She understood that many of the people in the area didn't care much for her, but why Conor? He was respected by his men and well liked by all. *Not all,* she thought with a shudder.

She wouldn't have found it if she hadn't headed outside to the herb garden to pick thyme for a recipe she had planned to cook.

She felt a cold frisson of alarm. What if Jason or Emma had found it? Worse yet, what if they had spied the person who had delivered it?

She ran upstairs, hid the wood chunk under some garments in a dresser drawer, and then went to check on the children.

Would Emma or Jason be threatened next? Who hated her that much to want to do physical harm to her family?

"Emma! Jason!" She didn't hear them answer. "Emma! Jason!" She began to feel ill as she checked the playroom, didn't find them, then still calling, searched every room on the top floor.

She was panic-stricken by the time she had reached the first floor. She searched the parlor, the dining room, and the study, then went back to the kitchen. "Emma! Jason!"

"Missus?" Jamieson appeared in the doorway to his back room.

She spun to him, wild-eyed and worried.

"I believe young Jason went with the master to Green Lawns. And Miss Emma—didn't you say she could visit the Brants to play with Miss Meg?"

The panic slipped away. "Yes," she said with a forced smile. "Yes, I suppose I did."

The old servant looked concerned. "Is there something amiss, missus?"

She looked away. "No. I couldn't find the children, and so I panicked, I guess." She pretended an interest in the ingredients she had gathered earlier. "I'm sorry."

"There is nothing to apologize for, missus," Jamieson replied. There was a moment of silence, and then he said, "Shall I find the young miss?"

Lizzy released a sharp breath before facing the man-servant. Her smile this time was genuine. "No," she said. "I'll send Margaret to fetch her."

"No trouble, missus," he assured her. "I know where the Brants reside."

She nodded. "All right, then, thank you. I would like Emma home." *Where I can see her.*

While Jamieson left to find and return her daughter, Lizzy quickly threw ingredients into a bowl. As she prepared the supper dish, she felt jittery and slightly nauseous. She desperately wanted Conor and Jason to come home so that she could see for herself that they were unharmed.

Emma returned with Jamieson, and she brought with her little Meg. Lizzy was happy to see her, and she fixed the girls a tea party to keep the two entertained in a place where she could keep a sharp eye on her daughter.

As an hour and then another went by, Lizzy began to worry about Conor and Jason. Where were they? They should have been back home by now, shouldn't they?

By the time father and new son made an appearance, Lizzy was near her wit's end. Worry made her voice sharp when she greeted them as they entered the kitchen joking with each other.

"Where have you been?" she shrieked.

Jason stared at her as if he had never seen her behave this way, which he hadn't.

Conor's expression was unreadable as he halted beside the child to stare at her. "At Green Lawns."

"It's late," she said. She knew she sounded like a shrew, but she had been scared that something dreadful had happened to them.

"Aye, 'tis," Conor said, surprising her. "We're sorry."

Lizzy stared at him a moment; then she started to cry. "I didn't know where you were," she sobbed. "I thought that something had happened to you."

At a nod from Conor, the children slipped from the room and went to change for dinner.

"What's wrong with Ma?" Jason asked Emma.

The little girl shrugged. "I don't know. She's been acting different today. She had Jamieson come to get me, but I didn't mind, 'cause then Meg and I got to have a party with tea cakes and everything."

Downstairs, Conor moved to his wife and took her into his arms. *"Shhh,"* he soothed her. She buried her face in his neck and held tight to his waist. He murmured words of comfort as he stroked her hair.

". . . late." Her words were muffled against his chest, but he could sense the drift of them. "Hurt . . . so scared."

He caught her shoulders and set her slightly back from him. "Lizzy, look at me." She did. "I'm here. Jason is here. We are both home and unharmed." His look was tender. "Why did ya think we wouldn't be?"

"It was a feeling that I had."

"A feeling," he said. His gaze warmed. "Afraid I'll not be around to warm yer bed?" he teased her.

She didn't find it amusing. "Don't say that!" she cried. And she began to shake.

Conor narrowed his gaze as he studied his wife. "What's happened?"

Did he imagine that she had tensed briefly? "I was worried." She bit her lip. "The Brogans."

He pulled her back into his arms. He had just heard the story recently from Markins. Matt Brogan and his family lived on the Olsen estate. Matt Brogan's son hadn't shown up for dinner one night. When he had finally shown up the next morning, he had been wounded and badly beaten. Someone had ambushed the young man as he had made his way home alone from Chestertown. He had gone with a friend, but the friend had chosen to stay the night. Poor Will hadn't had a chance against the thieves who had stolen the recent purchases he had made in town and the poke of change that had been lodged inside the young man's coat pocket.

"I'm not Will Brogan," he said. He kissed her ear . . . her neck. "And Green Lawns isn't so far as Chestertown. Jason and I rode over on Star. I'm a competent rider, and Star can outrun many horses in Kent County."

Lizzy held tight to her husband's waist and took comfort in the sound of his words, his breathing, and the steady thump-thump of his beating heart. Now that she had a chance to calm down, she felt foolish. Conor was a big man, sturdy and strong. He was right. He could take care of himself and Jason.

"I'm sorry for being a screaming fishwife," she said.

He pulled back to cup her face. He lifted her chin with one finger. "Neither a screamer nor a fishwife," he replied softly. "Just a loving wife frightened for the men in her life."

Tears filled her eyes and overflowed. "It was silly." She was surprised now that he wasn't furious with her for doubting his ability to come home safely. She loved him all the more for the fact that he understood.

He smiled. "Perhaps a bit silly." He kissed her nose. "But ya care," he said. He kissed her cheek. "And I like that." He kissed her other cheek, her chin . . . her lips.

She responded instantly as their mouths met, and her fear, love, and need drove her to cling tightly and deepen the kiss. It was Conor who was left gasping when they broke apart.

"Ya make it hard for a man to think of food at the supper hour," he said thickly, thrilling her with his words.

"Jason and Emma are waiting to eat," she reminded him, as moved as he. She fought for control. "But I know of a little place where we can be alone later . . . a room that was aired today with clean sheets and flowers on the windowsill."

"Is there a bed big enough for two?" he asked huskily.

"Aye," she said in the accent of his birth.

" 'Twill be a long supper hour."

"Nay," she said saucily. "I've made chocolate squares for dessert."

He grinned. "Oh, then, 'twill be a long mealtime until the chocolate squares are served," he said, and she shrieked with outrage as she tapped him on the arm playfully.

While her husband went to change, then fetch the children, Lizzy finished the last-minute touches to the meal. Her thoughts were reeling. She wanted to tell her husband about the recent threat; but he had had a lot on his mind lately, and she thought it best to hold off for at least one day, perhaps two.

She didn't want anything else to spoil her day . . . or her night with Conor. She had been scared that something dreadful had happened to him and Jason.

Her husband and son were back unharmed. She needed to celebrate their safe return, not arouse fear and worry in her husband's heart.

TWENTY-FIVE

"Oh, no!" Lizzy scrambled to reach the washbasin, where she promptly threw up her stomach's contents. Conor had left early, and she had awoken only moments before, when she had felt her nausea return.

She had eaten little of her supper the previous evening. She had still been so upset over the threat and her concern for Conor that she hadn't felt in the least bit hungry. *Thank goodness,* she thought now as she eyed the mess she had made with a sigh.

She needed to prepare an herbal tea to relieve the sickness. She hurried to dress, and once downstairs, she rinsed out the washbasin. After she replaced the clean basin in its proper place, she searched through her medicine bag. She chose several herbal leaves that she could blend and steep for a soothing tea.

Later, downstairs, she brewed the tea in the kitchen, then sipped it slowly, while deciding to forgo breakfast.

Jason and Emma joined her minutes later, and she felt slightly better as she fixed them something to eat.

"Missus?" Ruth appeared at the open doorway that connected the kitchen to the rest of the house.

"Good morning, Ruth."

"I'm sorry I'm late. I've been feeling sick this morning."

"Stomach?" she asked.

"Yes, missus."

Lizzy smiled as she waved her to a seat. "Sit down here and I'll make you a cup of chamomile tea. I've felt ill a bit myself this morning."

"Thank you." Ruth sat, and Margaret, the other maid, who shared Ruth's room, came downstairs, looking pasty and ill herself.

"Sit down, Margaret. It seems that all of us have a touch of the stomach sickness this morning."

The girl nodded and sat down.

"Jason. Emma. Run up to your rooms and put away your sleeping garments," Lizzy said. "Then when you're done, go up to the playroom and stay away from the sick."

"Can't I go outside with Conor?"

"Master Conor has left the farm, Master Jason." Jamieson entered the room, looking peaked himself.

"Sit down, Jamieson, and have some tea with chamomile. It will help settle your sickness."

The servant looked surprised that she knew of his illness, but he sat down.

Lizzy heated, then poured each of the servants hot tea. Then she sent them to their rooms to rest. "See how you feel tomorrow," she said.

She felt better as the day wore on, but when Conor didn't appear for the noon meal, she worried. Her manservant had said he had gone to Green Lawns. Why hadn't he told her?

She was hesitant to tell him about the new threat, but she knew she must.

Conor arrived home shortly after one; and Lizzy would have spoken with him then, but he came at the same time as company. The Smithfields from Smithfield Manor stopped in to say hello and to pay their respects to the newly wedded couple.

The Smithfields were delightful people, and Lizzy enjoyed their visit. Although she had sent the servants

away to recuperate from their stomach illness, Lizzy
invited the couple to spend the night, after explaining
about the absent help. Mrs. Smithfield accepted, but
only after insisting that she assist Lizzy in preparing
the meal.

"Will you be breeding horses now?" Mrs. Smithfield asked while they stood side by side at the kitchen
worktable slicing yellow and green squash, the first
crop of the summer, into a large bowl. "Your husband
has the knowledge to make a profit in horseflesh for
Milly's Station."

Lizzy picked up a yellow squash and sliced off the
stem. "It's possible. We've discussed it," she said,
which they had, but only once and briefly before they
were married when Jason had brought the subject up.
They had yet to discuss it as a serious prospect.

She was uncomfortable with the conversation, since
she knew little of Conor's intentions. But it seemed
logical to add the horse business to Milly's Station,
didn't it? Except they would be competing with their
good friend Rian Quaid.

"He's presently busy with other business," she said
carefully. "Perhaps next year."

The woman nodded, seeming satisfied with her answer. "My husband has some of the finest horses in
the state." She pursed her lips. "Much better than the
Jones Farm. Tell Conor to come to my Jacob when
he's in the market for some fine horseflesh."

While the women enjoyed tea together before their
preparations for dinner, Conor took Mr. Smithfield on
a tour of the plantation. When the men came back,
Lizzy and Mrs. Smithfield had sliced the vegetables,
put two loaves of bread into the oven to bake, and had
seasoned and put in two roasted chickens, which Lizzy
had instructed Michael Storm to kill and clean for her.

Mr. Smithfield entered the house through the back
door first. He sniffed the air appreciatively as Conor
came in behind him. "What's that delicious smell?"

"Roasted chicken and fresh bread." Lizzy smiled. "You're staying for supper, and the night, I hope."

Mr. Smithfield looked at his wife, who nodded. "Lizzy's servants are ill," she said. "I'd like to do what I can to help."

Conor's gaze met Lizzy's. "Ruth and the others are sick?"

She nodded, her eyes sliding away to Mrs. Smithfield. "I didn't ask you to stay to make you work."

"I know, dear," the woman said. "But allow me to assist. The pleasure will be mine."

"What's this about Ruth and the others being sick?" Conor asked as the Smithfields left them for the dining room.

"A stomach complaint. I sent them to their rooms to rest, then decided it was best to send them home to recover."

Staying behind to finish with the squash, Lizzy wasn't pleased with her husband's decision to leave the plantation without telling her. But now was not the time to discuss it and his unusual behavior of late.

Conor agreed with her decision about the servants as he came to her side, grabbed a piece of cut-up squash from the pile, and crunched into it with his teeth. He chewed and swallowed, then kissed her on the cheek. "Are ya feeling well?" he said with concern.

"I'm fine," she said, and she was. Her earlier bout with nausea had vanished.

They enjoyed a good meal with pleasant company in the dining room, where the table had been nicely set with their good china and the lighting provided by twin candlesticks placed at each end. Afterward they ate a dessert of bread pudding and retired to the parlor where they enjoyed a game of cards. Lizzy had a good time and was able to forget, for a time, the threats she had received and her worry over her husband's safety and his unrevealed absence from Milly's Station.

Later, when the time arrived for bed, her worries

returned, but she was unable to discuss her concerns when Conor, at the last minute, decided to spend an hour working in his study.

When he told her as they were getting ready to head up the stairs, a chill overcame her. "You're going to work?"

He nodded. "Just for a little while. I'll be up shortly."

The Smithfields had been shown to a guest room and had gone to bed. Lizzy heard the foyer clock strike the half hour as she continued up two steps. She halted before her husband had gone three feet.

"Conor—" She could feel herself start to tremble. Was it already going wrong between them? "Is there something you're not telling me? Have I done something wrong?"

He paused at the hall to glance up to where she eyed him over the banister. His expression softened. "Ye've done nothing, Lizzy. Why would ya think such a thing?"

"You left today," she said. "And you didn't tell me."

He drew a shutter over his expression. "Because there's nothing to tell. I needed to speak with Rian."

"Then, why didn't you tell me you were leaving?" She felt certain, by his look, that there was more he wasn't confiding.

He shrugged. "Because I knew I would be back within a short time"

"I had fixed a meal for you." *Don't cry,* she told herself.

She felt the pinprick of tears and hoped that he couldn't see them in the semidarkness of the one sconce lighting the area.

She heard him sigh. "I apologize, Lizzy. I've had a lot on me mind. I should have told ya."

"Yes," she agreed. He should have told her. *What's on your mind? Why won't you tell me?*

He moved to the stair rail and reached up to place

his hand over her fingers on the banister. "I was wrong," he said. He gave her hand a little squeeze. "I'm sorry." The look in his blue eyes mirrored his apology.

How could she stay angry with him when she loved him so?

"Don't be long," she whispered. She turned her hand to interlock fingers with him. She wanted him desperately, with a passion that was sudden and over-powering.

His expression changed. He must have seen something in her eyes that gave away her thoughts, her desire.

Heat flashed in his blue gaze. "Fifteen minutes," he promised.

Conor kept his word. In exactly fifteen minutes, as the tall case clock downstairs struck the quarter hour, he entered their bedchamber and closed the door. Lizzy had dared to slip into bed naked, and as he approached, she lay on her side, with only a sheet covering her from breasts downward.

She had left a candle burning on the nightstand, and she saw how his glistening gaze settled on her bare shoulders and darkened as it moved lower to where the fabric clung revealingly to her hard-nippled curves.

"You steal my breath," she said as he unbuttoned his shirt. "Come to bed."

" 'Tis me intention." He shrugged out of the garment, and then his hands went to his breeches.

Lizzy watched with heightened anticipation as he undid buttons and ties, and removed the last barrier of cloth from his skin. Her mouth went dry as he stood before her naked.

He was a large man, well endowed, and that he was already passionate and wanting her pushed every thought from her mind but her desire to love him, to feel him against her. She wanted him inside her, to become locked with him in ecstasy with his breath against her neck, his heartbeat thundering in a rapid succession that mirrored her own mind-shattering response.

They loved, and the joining was earth-moving to Lizzy, who lay in her husband's arms afterward, drained and content that Conor was with her, safe and satisfied . . . and drowsy after their lovemaking.

She heard the deep, even sound of his breathing that signaled that he had fallen asleep. And although she felt a sniggle of worry somewhere in the back of her mind, she managed to shove it away as she enjoyed the strength of her husband's body as it warmed her . . . until her eyelashes closed and she slept.

She awoke with a start the next morning and rushed to the washbasin as she had the day before. She felt tears of frustration as she hung her head over the bowl and finished getting sick.

An arm surrounded her shoulders as Conor reached her side. "Ye've got the stomach illness," he said.

She nodded, too embarrassed to speak.

"Come, lass. 'Tis back to bed with ya." He led her back and tucked her in after he saw that she had lain down and was comfortable. "I'll pass yer apologies on to the Smithfields." He smiled as he laid a hand across her forehead. "Ya rest. Is there something I can get ya?"

Her stomach roiled, noisily, and she closed her eyes for a moment. "Tea," she said. And she told him how to fix it for her.

He caressed her cheek as he promised to do so. "I'll be back."

She nodded. He started to leave. "Conor!" He turned. "What about the children?"

"Don't worry about the children," he said.

And so she didn't, for she knew that he cared for them as she did, and she trusted him to see that they would be provided for and watched over for the day.

As she lay in bed, waiting for her stomach to settle a

bit, she couldn't help but think of the last few days. She needed to tell Conor about the note and soon. Today.

He brought the tea up to her, and his concern and thoughtfulness overwhelmed her. As he left her to begin his day, she felt measurably better. She had made too much out of his absence from the plantation, she thought. He would tell her why he was called away. He couldn't confide in her yesterday, not with the Smithfields visiting.

The children didn't come in to disturb her morning, so Lizzy slept for a time. When she woke up some time later—how long she dozed, she didn't know—she heard the children.

She sat up and smiled as she listened to Jason and Emma whispering in the hall outside her door.

"You can't go in, Emma. Ma's sleeping."

"I just want to see her. I won't make a noise."

"You can come in," she called to them. She felt surprisingly well. There were no lingering effects of her illness as she swung her legs off the side of the bed.

She heard the sound of the opening door and looked over with a smile as Jason peeked into the room. "You all right, Ma?"

She nodded. "Come in. Both of you. I feel fine. Thank you."

With a grin, he entered the room, tugging his sister by the hand with him.

"Ma!" Emma looked delighted to see her.

"Have you been good for Conor?" she asked.

Jason bobbed his head. "He's fixing the noon meal." He went to a wall peg and retrieved, without her asking, her dressing gown. "Are you hungry?"

"Yes. Amazingly, I'm starved."

"Good." Conor entered the room then, his handsome look stealing her breath. "Shall I bring ya a bite?"

She shook her head. "I'd like to get dressed and

come down." At his frown, she said, "I feel well enough."

"Jason, go downstairs with your sister and set the table. Emma, you help Jason, all right?" She beamed him a smile and skipped behind her brother as he hurried to obey.

Conor helped her to dress, fawning over her like a mother hen over her baby chick. While Lizzy enjoyed the attention, she was amused by it.

They shared a delicious meal that Conor had fixed for the four of them. He had even included a dessert of cherry cobbler, which he had made that morning while she slept.

The day continued on a good note. Ruth, Margaret, and Jamieson had proclaimed themselves well and were ready to fulfill their household duties again. When they had shown up that morning, Conor had insisted they rest one more day, but all of them wanted to work; so Lizzy gave them a list of chores, and they went off, happy to be back to feeling their former selves.

"I think they've had enough of their families," Conor said in an aside to his wife. "I heard Ruth and Margaret comment that they get more rest here in the manor house. Ruth's brother and sisters are a noisy lot and too disruptive. Jamieson confided that he had a falling out with his sister. Anne, it seemed, thought that Jamieson was faking his illness, and she wanted him to repair a hole in her cottage roof."

Lizzy raised her eyebrows. "And did he?"

Conor grinned. "Nay. He promptly got sick on her kitchen floor instead. Apparently, she believed him then."

She chuckled, imagining the scene.

The afternoon was too nice to spoil it by bringing up difficult subjects for discussion, so Lizzy decided that as long as Conor remained close to the manor house, the topics of the new threat and his secret business at the Quaids' could wait until tomorrow.

That night Conor and she didn't make love, but she felt cherished as she lay in his arms on their feather mattress. She had felt only a twinge or two during the day of nausea, but the bouts didn't last long. They disappeared after she sipped tea or ate something light.

When she awoke the next morning, Conor was gone, but she knew he would be close, downstairs no doubt preparing breakfast for the children. She rose to her feet, felt a sudden wave of nausea, but this time she was able to control the urge to be sick.

It wasn't until after that day that it occurred to her that she hadn't received her courses in well over a month's time. That and given the knowledge that Ruth and the others had gotten over their sicknesses within twenty-four hours made Lizzy realize that she didn't have the same illness. In fact, she wasn't actually sick at all.

Cradling her abdomen, Lizzy smiled. She wasn't certain, but she thought she was with child. Conor's babe. A rush of joy accompanied the seed of hope she felt as she dressed and went about her day.

Please, let it be true. She wanted Conor's babe more than anything in the world. And given his love for Jason and Emma, she thought sure he would be happy about this child.

TWENTY-SIX

"Elizabeth." Conor's firm tone alerted Lizzy that something was wrong. Seriously wrong.

Lizzy stepped into the bedchamber, saw the object in his hand, and was aware when the blood drained from her face. "Conor, I—"

"For God's sake, Lizzy, why didn't ya show me this?" He waved the piece of wood in the air as he approached. "Why should ya keep this from me?"

"I—"

"When?" he growled.

Her mouth went dry, and she tried to swallow. She was afraid to tell him. "A week past." Her voice was barely a whisper.

"A week!" He appeared livid. His face had turned bright red, and his blue eyes were cold with barely suppressed fury. Stung, she looked down, away from his angry stare.

He tossed the wood onto the bed, grabbed her shoulders, and forced her to meet his gaze. "Ye've had this a week," he bit out, "but ya didn't see fit to tell me! Me, yer husband!"

"The time didn't seem right." She winced as he tightened his grip.

"Not once," he spat out. "Not once in seven days?"

She nodded. "I didn't want to worry you." She released a shuddering sigh. "I was worried enough for the both of us. Then I got sick and . . ."

Discovered I was with child. And I had two things to tell for which I couldn't find the right time.

She had meant to tell him about the threat. And she was going to tell him about the babe as soon as she was certain, for she didn't want to disappoint him. This day was the first that she had felt sure enough about her state to tell him the news. In fact, she was to have told him shortly after this moment, after they had finished readying for bed.

She had had a vision of them tucked into bed, her lying in his arms with her head on his chest. She would tell him, and he would be so overjoyed that he would turn her face up for his kiss. Then he would tenderly, thoroughly, show his love for her.

But now that opportunity, that dream, was gone. She couldn't tell him now, not while he was angry, for such joyful news should be given when there was peace and an openness for love.

Instead, she was facing an irate husband, who looked as if he wanted to wring her neck . . . and he would need a long time to forgive her.

"Where did ya find it? I didn't see any evidence of broken glass."

"It didn't come through the window as the last one did."

"So this is only the second one? There were no more ya didn't think to tell me about?"

Tears filled her eyes as she shook her head. "No." She looked away. The anger in her husband's eyes hurt her, more than she had ever expected. She had thought not to tell him in order to spare such a scene. She realized now that she had done worse by not telling him immediately.

"Where did ya find it, Lizzy?" he growled.

"I found it outside the kitchen door one afternoon when I needed thyme from the garden."

"Outside the kit—" Conor broke off, unable to finish. He was more than upset; he was beside himself. Seeing that threat had churned up emotions that made him want to find the culprit and strangle the breath from him.

Why hadn't Lizzy told him about the note? Didn't she realize the impact of such a threat? He wasn't worried for himself; he was concerned for Lizzy. He could watch his own back, but what about his wife's? Didn't she realize what this meant? She had received this during the light of day and right on her doorstep! The man—the mad man—had been close, and she hadn't known it until it was too late.

How could someone so be vile, so evil, that he would threaten a helpless woman?

Sweet St. Bridget! She could have been hurt or worse!

"I want ya to tell me if this ever happens again," he told her. He was furious. He couldn't help it. And he couldn't find it in him to banish her fear. He saw the pain emanating from her face, but ignored it. If she would learn from it, then next time she would confide in him immediately.

"Do ya understand, Lizzy?"

"Yes," she whispered.

"I want Jason and Emma to stay close. We've had someone threaten ya and me. The children may be next."

"Oh, dear heavens, no!"

He saw stark terror on her face. He started to reach for her, then stopped himself. "If ya receive another threat, ye'll not keep it from me."

She flinched at his terse command. "Yes," she cried, her eyes filling with tears.

"Ya didn't trust me."

"No, it's not that!"

He sighed. "I've got work to do," he said, even though only moments before he had come to their room for bed. "If this ever happens again . . . ye're not to hesitate. Do ya hear me?"

He saw her swallow hard as she bobbed her head.

"Good." Though he wondered if she would listen and obey.

"You'll stay near?" she said. "You won't go to Green Lawns?"

"I'll not let someone scare me." But he was frightened. Not for himself, but for Lizzy, his wife.

The days following were strained between Lizzy and her husband. She wanted to tell him about the babe, now that she was certain, but he was always busy about the plantation and rarely came home during the day. She understood that work kept him away, but why couldn't he return just one day to eat the noon meal?

Three days later, as she was preparing supper, Lizzy decided that she would tell her husband tonight that he was going to be a father. She fed the children early, then prepared a special dinner. She set a table in their bedchamber with a floral centerpiece and their best china, and then she waited anxiously for Conor's return.

When he didn't come at his regular hour, Lizzy went outside to look out for him.

" 'Afternoon, Mrs. McDermott." The groom waved to her from outside the stables.

"Good day to you, Mr. Fetts," she called. "Have you seen my husband?"

"He hasn't returned from Green Lawns yet."

Lizzy felt a burning in her stomach. Conor had gone to Green Lawns again, and without telling her!

She hurried inside, asked Ruth and Margaret to watch the children, then ran upstairs to change her clothes. Then she hurried to the stables.

"Mr. Fetts? Would you saddle Lacey May for me?"

The man nodded. "Be careful with her, missus. She's been a bit out of sorts this day."

"I will." She climbed onto the roan mare, then headed out of the yard.

It had been some time since she had ridden, but she felt right at home in the saddle. Lacey May was a sweet-tempered mare, who could be lively when it was asked of her.

Lizzy eyed the afternoon sun and figured she would have plenty of time to get to Green Lawns, then back again, before dusk descended. She was determined to get to the bottom of Conor's continued secret visits to the Quaids'. She kicked the mare's flanks and tried to enjoy the day as she hurried to find her husband.

As the Quaid manor house came into view, Lizzy suddenly felt foolish. What was she doing here? She must be mad to follow her husband across the countryside, even if she was familiar with the journey and her destination was the home of friends.

But she was here, and so she would stop in for a visit. The visit wouldn't be a waste of time, as she had wanted to see Kathleen. She hadn't seen her friend in too long a time, since the wedding.

If Conor was angry with her, she would deal with it. But she trembled at the thought.

She rode toward the barn and handed over the care of Lacey to Thomas, the Quaids' groom.

" 'Tis good to see you again, Mrs. Foley—I mean, McDermott," he said with a red-faced grin.

She managed to smile at him. "Thank you, Thomas. Is Mrs. Quaid at home?"

"Aye, missus. I saw her on the porch just a time ago. She was speaking with your husband."

Her husband, she thought. Conor hadn't come to see Kathleen, she told herself. He had come to see Rian.

Her emotions in turmoil, she murmured thanks to Thomas before heading up to the house. There was a burning in her stomach.

Did Conor come to see Rian or Kathleen?

She didn't have to knock. Henny, the Quaids' housekeeper, stepped outside to air out a small rug and saw her as Lizzy climbed the porch steps.

"Miss Lizzy!" she exclaimed.

Lizzy was genuinely glad to see the woman, who had never been anything but kind to her. Her lips curved as she greeted the older woman. "It's good to see you again, Henny."

A woman of fifty years or so, Henrietta Peterson had a sturdy frame and a stern countenance, but her smile for Lizzy was quick and warm. "Marriage agrees with you."

She had difficulty maintaining her smile. "I hear my husband is about."

"Aye, that he is. He's in the parlor with Mrs. Quaid. I'll announce you."

Lizzy held up her hand. "No need," she said. "If you don't mind, I'll see myself in."

Apparently believing the request appropriate, the housekeeper inclined her head. "I'll put on the tea."

"Thank you, Henny, but no. I've had my fill of tea today." She hesitated. "Is Rian at home?"

"No," Henny said. "He's gone to the Jones Farm." She mentioned the place of a well-known horse breeder in the area. "He's expected to return near suppertime."

Rian isn't home. Her heart began to beat rapidly as Lizzy entered the house while Henny stayed outside to finish beating the rug.

If Rian wasn't home, why had Conor come?

She paused in the foyer, listening. She could hear conversation in the next room. As she approached the voices in the parlor, she recognized the hushed tones of her husband Conor and her friend Kathleen.

"I can hardly believe it!" Kathleen said, clearly shocked at what she had recently learned. "Ye're me brother?"

Conor nodded. He stared at the woman he now knew for certain was his sister and marveled at the rush of feelings he experienced. His feelings upon confronting his half sister for the first time were vastly different than what he had expected. This was his third visit to Green Lawns in a week, and he had finally worked up the courage to talk with her, to confirm his suspicion that Kathleen was in fact his father's treasured daughter. Somehow knowing the person before the truth had made a difference. It was hard to be angry when the woman he was supposed to be angry with was one of the finest, kindest people he had ever known.

He sat on the parlor sofa, feeling big and awkward on the small damask seat. But he realized that his discomfort was lodged in the knowledge of this new relationship with Rian Quaid's wife.

"Are ya certain it's me?" she asked.

His smile was crooked. "Ye're Conlan Maguire's daughter, are ya not? Katie Maguire?"

"Aye," she whispered. "Katie . . . only me father and mother called me that." She blinked back tears. "Oh, and there might have been a servant or two who worked in me uncle's household." She shook her head as if she still couldn't believe it. " 'Tis a miracle! I didn't know I had family other than the Dunnes." She smiled through her tears. "A brother! *You.*"

Now that he had told her, he felt the need to confess everything to her . . . his feelings . . . his hopes . . . his bitter anger toward their father. *And her,* he thought. He had been prepared to hate her for being the only child his father had loved. But now that he knew who she was, he understood. What wasn't to like about Kathleen Maguire Quaid?

Kathleen was studying him intently, thoughtfully. "Ya don't carry the Maguire name."

A muscle ticked along Conor's jawbone. How could he carry the name of a father who had forgotten his son?

"Nay," he said. "Me mother wed another, but he was a terrible husband to her. I've taken on me mother's family name. She was Katie McDermott before she married Donal O'Reilly. I thought he was me father. One day in a fit of drunkenness, me mother's husband told me the truth."

Kathleen's expression softened with compassion. "It must have been an awful shock."

"Nay, in truth, it was a relief to know that the vile man wasn't me father at all." He sighed as he thought back to that time with sadness. "Me mother—she'd put up with a great deal from Donal O'Reilly. She did it for me. To give me a proper home and father, but Donal . . . he didn't hold up his end of the bargain—"

"Bargain?"

"Aye. And that was to accept and treat me like his own son. He couldn't stand the sight of me, ya see. I was another man's whelp, and he couldn't forget that. When he made the unforgivable mistake of informing me of that fact, me mother had had enough, and we left—just the two of us. Donal begged me mother to stay, but she would hear none of it."

"How did ya get by? When did she tell ya about Da?"

Da, Conor thought with a hint of bitterness. He quickly squashed it, for he couldn't be mad at this half sister of his. Kathleen and Rian had shown him only kindness since he had come to Green Lawns. Rian had given him employment, and he had respected him enough to make him foreman when James Peterson no longer wanted the responsibility.

"Me mother . . . It wasn't long before her health failed her, and it was on her deathbed that she told me about me real father . . . Conlan Maguire."

"Da," she said.

"Aye. Your da." His mouth firmed. "I have to confess that I first searched for him because I was angry. He had left me mother with child, and I didn't have the father I wanted. I needed to confront him about that."

"I don't understand this," Kathleen said. "The father I knew would never have abandoned his child." Her smile was sad. "He was a wonderful man, Conor. I'm sorry that ya never had the chance to meet him."

"Aye, I am, too." But only because she had said so. This was his sister, he thought. His own flesh and blood. He wanted to hug her, but he reached out to grip her hand instead. When she instantly turned her fingers to clasp his tightly, he smiled.

Her eyes filled as she squeezed his hand. "Won't Rian be surprised!"

Conor chuckled. "Aye, that he will." He paused. "I'm glad I found ya."

"Me, too," Kathleen whispered as she pulled free from his grasp. Me brother!" She shifted to hug him.

Conor immediately took her into his arms and held her tightly. "Kathleen."

Lizzy stood in the open parlor doorway and gaped at the pair in shock. Heat burned in her stomach as she watched her husband—the man she loved—embracing her closest friend.

Betrayal hit her hard. She couldn't move, could barely think. As Conor and Kathleen broke apart, she slipped to one side so she wouldn't be seen.

"I have a picture of father," Kathleen said. "Would ya like to see it?"

"Later," Conor replied, dismissing the man who had caused him to suffer such bitterness and fury. "I want to talk about ya. I need to know everything about ya."

Listening, Lizzy could imagine Kathleen blushing. *How could they?* An acrid taste filled her mouth as she thought of all the times that Conor had visited Green Lawns. He had told her it was to see Rian, but now she knew the truth. It was to see Kathleen.

She stepped away and walked down the hall, trying to think. Should she confront them? Tell Rian? Wait for Conor to slip up and have to confess?

How could they betray me? Betray Rian?

She heard the two murmuring, and she returned to eavesdrop.

"I still can't believe it!" Kathleen said. "I didn't know I had a brother. Are ya certain that Da knew that ye mother was with child?"

Lizzy's eyes widened. Kathleen was Conor's sister? How could that be? How could the two have known each other for as long as they had with no notion? And if they had known, why had they kept the fact a secret?

Why didn't Conor confide in me?

Relief that the pair were siblings quickly vanished in the wake of the hurt that came because Conor hadn't trusted her enough to tell her. He must have known when he had left this afternoon that Kathleen Quaid was the relative he had searched for over two years. The fact that he hadn't told her, hadn't informed her of this visit, pained her deeply.

He can't love me, she decided. She had thought they had a future together, but now she didn't know. She should have felt glad that there was no other woman—no mistress in Conor's life—but instead she had recognized a flaw in their marriage. *Lack of trust.* He didn't trust her. And now, because of his actions, she knew she couldn't trust him to tell the truth or confide in her.

She listened for several seconds more, then left, more disturbed than ever. She had had an earful before she had gone. It seemed that Conor's father had deserted his mother after a brief affair. Conor had been clearly affected by this, as she heard him tell Kathleen about his initial anger, his bitterness, toward his sire.

What she heard and the little she had already learned about him made her realize that Conor would view situations differently than most men. *Including the situation of marriage. And of responsibility and family.*

Lizzy shivered as she hurried to the stables to retrieve Lacey May. After climbing into the saddle, she kicked the horse into a gallop and headed home.

How long would it take for Conor to tell her about his relationship with Kathleen?

Dear God, she was going to have Conor's child. Was that why he had married her? Had the fact that she had been chaste when he had taken her made him feel that they had to wed?

He had never actually told her he loved her . . . although she had thought . . . *Been fooled!* she realized.

"No!" she cried. Tears blurred her vision during the wild ride home. She kicked the horse into a faster pace and held on for dear life as Lacey May was given her head and pummeled the ground with her hooves. He had wed her because he had felt responsible after lying with her. He had wed her because he had been afraid she might get with child, and he wouldn't repeat the mistakes his father had made.

It was one thing to lie and be merry with an experienced widow with two children and a shady reputation for pleasuring men, but to dally with an innocent was something else. Was that what he thought? Was that why he married her?

She had to admit that they shared a good physical relationship.

Would that be enough? She had already settled for friendship in a marriage. Would sexual thrill alone maintain them for the rest of their earthly lives?

Her eyes were red and her cheeks wet by the time Lizzy reached Milly's Station. As she handed the reins of the horse over to Mr. Fetts, she avoided the man's direct gaze.

"Are ya all right, missus?" He must have seen her tears.

When she looked at him, he was frowning. She forced herself to smile. "I'm fine, Mr. Fetts. I had a good ride across the countryside. It was the wind in my eyes, I suspect."

The groom looked at Lacey May's lathered coat, then glanced back at her. Lizzy blushed, recalling his warning to be careful with the mare.

" 'Tis a nice day in the county," he said, but she saw him scowl as he walked the mare for a time, then to a place where he would wipe off Lacey's sweat before bringing the animal inside.

Lizzy paused as she turned away. The man had seen through her, she realized. He knew something had gone wrong.

She froze. She had told him that it had been the wind that made her tears.

The day was as calm as a sea without ripples.

TWENTY-SEVEN

Conor discovered he was late for home as he prepared to leave Green Lawns. Rian had returned, and he had remained while Kathleen told her husband about their brother and sister relationship. Rian had been startled to learn the truth, but he had been pleased for his wife and for Conor. Conor had declined their offer of supper, promising instead to return soon with Lizzy.

As he climbed onto Star's back, Conor grinned, recalling Rian's reaction to the fact that the two of them were related by marriage.

"Sweet glory be!" he had exclaimed. "This means we're brothers-in-law."

Conor had regarded him with amusement. "It would seem so."

"McDermott . . . Maguire. Who would have thought?"

"I thought Kathleen's name was Dunne." Conor had watched a blush creep up from his half sister's neck as she shot her husband a look.

Rian had smiled. "A long tale, best told another day." And although he had been intrigued by this unknown story, Conor had left, his thoughts on Lizzy and the fact that in his preoccupation with Kathleen, he had left home without telling her. And now he was late.

It was still light as he galloped into the yard between

the stables and the house, then turned over his mount
to the groom.

He stared at the house, noting the absence of cooking smoke. "Is Mrs. McDermott in the house?"

"Yes, Mr. McDermott." Since Conor's marriage to
Lizzy Foley, the groom had insisted on using his
proper title rather than Conor, as before. "She came
back from her ride some time ago and went inside. I
saw her call the children a while back, but I haven't
seen her come out again."

She's angry with me. And with good reason, he
thought. He started toward the house, then paused
when he spied the flower garden. He headed there instead and picked her a bouquet of posies, hoping to
win her favor.

He was anxious to see her. He was late, it was true,
but he had much to tell her. Once she heard it, he was
sure she would forgive him. Wouldn't she be surprised
to learn that her friend Kathleen was her sister-in-law
as well?

Lizzy had seemed sympathetic to his need to find
his sister. She would understand, he told himself.

Wouldn't she?

He came home bearing flowers. What woman could
resist that? *I could,* Lizzy thought.

He had found her in the upstairs sitting room, working diligently on her needlepoint. When she was upset,
she needed to keep busy. But this time the work hadn't
helped. As she made rows of even, neat stitches in the
cloth, she had more time to think . . . about her marriage to Conor and what was wrong.

"Lizzy." He breezed into the room, smiling with a
handful of blooms extended before him. "For ya."

"Thank you," she said, but she didn't get up. She
continued to ply her needle and more quickly. The

stitches now were untidy, but she kept going, although she knew she would have to take them all out.

From the corner of her eye, she saw him set the flowers on the table. She quickly refocused her full attention on the fabric as he approached.

"Elizabeth." He hunkered down before her. "Are ya all right?"

She wouldn't cry. "Yes." Her hands continued to move, pulling needle and thread through embroidery cloth.

He captured her hand and stilled her actions. "Lizzy," he said. "Look at me."

With a controlled sigh, she glanced up. "Yes?"

"I'm late."

"I'm aware of that." Her lips firmed.

"I'm sorry."

"For what, Conor? For coming home late? Or for leaving without telling me in the first place?"

"I—" He released a sharp breath as he let go of her hand. "Both, I guess."

"Fine."

"Ya don't understand."

She didn't answer.

"Lizzy?"

"I don't want to talk with you now, Conor. I'm tired." She paused. She was weary after having a good cry. "If you're hungry, there are biscuits and salted pork in the larder. You may have to reheat the meat."

"I'm not worried about me dinner."

"Good, because I'm not worried about your dinner either." With a scowl, she purposely ignored him as she proceeded to work on her needlepoint.

"Ye're angry," he said.

She didn't reply.

"I didn't mean to upset ya."

Silence.

"Ya obviously don't want to discuss anything with me."

She looked up at him then, her eyes hard. "You are obviously right."

"We'll have to talk eventually."

"Yes, I'm sure we will." *Needle through fabric, pull.* She kept up the motions as if she would allow nothing to ruffle her or to sway her from her task.

"Wouldn't it be best if we did so now?" he asked.

She stared at him. "Take the flowers and put them in some water. *Please.*"

"Damn it, Lizzy!"

She rose up from her chair and threw down her embroidery in a fit of temper. "Don't!" she hissed. "Don't you be cursing at me, Conor McDermott. I may be your wife, but that doesn't mean I have to take your abuse!"

She felt a twinge of regret when she saw him whiten.

"Have I treated ya poorly?" he asked gruffly.

"Have you considered my feelings today or before?"

"Aye, of course I have!"

"Ha!" She bent to pick up her embroidery hoop.

He grabbed her as she straightened. She shrieked. "Let me be, Conor McDermott!"

"Ye're me wife!" He caught her against him, angry and panic-stricken that she wouldn't forgive him.

She struggled. "Conor—"

"Nay, lass," he said huskily, and he kissed her, silencing her with his mouth, trying desperately to make her soften and purr. "Don't be angry with me." And he nuzzled her neck, pleased when she relaxed in his arms and moaned with pleasure.

No, Lizzy thought. *I shouldn't allow this.* This wasn't all there was to a marriage. How could she love him so much when she was doubtful about his regard for her?

But he was doing wonderful things to her . . . kissing her neck . . . her throat. Dear heavens, he was sucking her breast through her gown.

"Conor, no." But her protest was a mild one. She loved him, despite discovering the fault in her marriage. She loved him, and he was the only one who could arouse her to a fever pitch . . . the only one who could bring her such sexual pleasure.

He had unbuttoned her gown and slid it off her shoulder. He placed his mouth to the silken curve. "Aye, Lizzy," he murmured against her skin. He trailed his lips over her left shoulder, while he fondled her right breast.

She felt the soft mound throb as it swelled beneath his fingertips. She ached to be free of her garments . . . to feel his tongue on her nipples, her bare breasts in his hands.

He edged the bodice lower, nibbling his way down as he tugged the chemise aside to reveal her skin. She knew she should object, but her mind became fuzzy as her senses basked in a storm of pleasure.

"The children," she gasped.

"Asleep. I checked on them before I found ya." He nipped the skin over her collarbone, then bent his head to capture a nipple with his teeth. She felt the tug of his nibble, the answering, throbbing pull between her legs. She groaned as he laved the area with his tongue.

"That's it, Lizzy. We were made for each other . . ."

She blinked up at him, saw the clarity in his blue gaze, and suddenly became aware of their surroundings. They were in the sitting room, for goodness sake! What if the children awakened? What if they wandered into this room in need of her?

"The door's locked," he said, as if he had read her mind. He slipped his hand down her belly, but she grabbed it before he could work his magic on her sensitive stomach muscles.

He gazed at her, his eyes warm and caring . . . with

passion for her simmering in his expression. "Lizzy, let me touch ya."

He pulled from her grasp and caressed her belly. His fingers slid over the gown covering the flat surface. His eyes darkened as he gave her a promise of what was to come with his hands. Desire fired her blood, making her pliant.

He shifted his grip, and she could feel him inch them toward the fainting couch. He thrust against her, and she could feel his hard sex pressing against her abdomen as he nuzzled her neck and moved.

Suddenly, they were on the couch, locked in each other's arms, their mouths fused, their tongues intertwining in rhythmic thrusts mirroring the act of joining. Frantic to feel him inside her, Lizzy tugged on Conor's shirt.

Desperate to be inside her, Conor tore at her remaining garments, ripping off buttons and splitting fabric as he bared her to his searching gaze.

They came together like two animals in heat, slamming against one another fiercely, groaning and grunting, all tenderness forgone in their desperate need to mate.

Chests labored. Mouths panted for air. Hands groped, and bodies thrust as the ecstasy built between them and they sought to climb the peak that would send them flying over the edge in mindless surrender.

Lizzy gasped as she was tossed up on a zephyr of passion. She clung to her husband's shoulders, arched her hips, and met Conor thrust for thrust in a bid to attain satisfaction for the both of them.

She flew soaring upward on a stream of physical pleasure that far transcended the worldly plane. She heard Conor's deep-throated moan just seconds before she whimpered during the last final moment of release.

Conor heard Lizzy's cry and followed her quickly to the summit. He held tight as they both shared the ride, and he didn't let go during the slow glide back from heaven.

Lizzy was conscious of Conor's arms about her, could feel the strength of his grip, and she kept her eyes shut to hide her tears.

It had been wonderful. Being with Conor was more than she had ever expected from a husband. If only they could communicate with words as well as they could love in the marriage bed.

She grew cramped beneath his weight. The couch was barely big enough for her, never mind Conor's large form as well. She shifted to alert him, and he moved, rising to his feet to stand naked before her. He was damp-skinned and beautiful . . . her huge Celtic warrior with lust in his blue eyes and his sensual mouth curved with a smile of blatant male satisfaction.

"I've torn yer gown," he said. He didn't sound upset about it.

She glanced toward the floor and the torn garment and felt herself redden from the neck upward. She was shocked that she had behaved with Conor in such a depraved manner. She reached to gather her gown and clutched it to her chest.

"This doesn't change anything," she said. She was angry with herself for surrendering to him without a fight. She had wanted their lovemaking, and it galled her that she would accept him so easily when she knew that he refused to share every inner part of himself.

She could feel the air between them turn chilly.

"Aye, lass, it does."

Lizzy shot him an angered glance. "You still don't trust me. You don't trust me enough to confide in me, do you!"

His jaw clenched as he stared at her. "Trust has nothing to do with it."

"It has everything to do with it!"

His eyes widened with disbelief. "Because I came home late?"

"Because you didn't tell me you were going!"

If she was upset because he didn't tell her of his visit to Green Lawns, then she would certainly be upset to learn about Kathleen and his newly discovered relationship with her. Now wasn't the time to tell her, he decided.

Desire slammed him hard as he studied her. Her hair had come undone, and the loosed silken blond strands hung appealingly about her face and neck. She looked delightfully ruffled and as if she had been thoroughly made love to.

He wanted to take her again. Right now. This very second. He felt blood surge to thicken his staff. Hell, he wanted her, and he was ready so quickly.

Lizzy felt a prickle along her spine as she stared at her husband. Why was he studying her that way?

She was overcome with a blast of intense heat when she looked down and saw his rigid manhood, throbbing and alive, amidst the dark, curly nest of hairs at the junction of his thighs.

Her nipples pebbled as she responded to the fire.

"No!" She jumped up from the couch and, covering herself as best she could with her ruined garments, made her way to the door.

"Don't!" she warned as he made a move toward her. "Don't come near me. I won't—I can't—do this again. *Please!*"

He halted, and something bright vanished from his expression. "I'll not force ya."

She swallowed hard. "I'm going to our bedchamber. Please don't follow me there."

Anger flashed in his blue gaze. "I'll not sleep in a guest room."

"I don't expect you to—"

His mouth curved cynically. "Don't ya?"

She shook her head. She hadn't—really. She hadn't thought that far ahead. Her only thought had been to run to her room and slip into her night garments, protection against his gaze, protection from her own flagrant desires.

"No," she gasped, before she struggled to open the door.

Conor watched as the lock gave beneath her fingers, and then she was fleeing from his presence.

He stared at the recently closed door with his hands clenched at his sides. "Hell and damnation! The woman will drive me mad before I reach me next birthday!"

He dressed and waited several minutes before he went downstairs to the liquor stored in the dining room sideboard. After pulling out a bottle of whiskey and a glass, he poured himself a drink.

TWENTY-EIGHT

"Mr. Olsen!" Startled, Lizzy stared at him with uneasiness. She had come downstairs, unsuspecting, only to learn that Emma had let the man into the house. When she had entered the parlor, she had found him standing by the fireplace, casually inspecting the contents of twin bookcases on each side of the hearth.

"You're looking well, Mrs. Foley."

She stiffened. "You haven't heard?" Memories of Thompson's visit rose up, making her instantly wary of the gentleman before her.

"Heard what?" He had a small wooden box nestled in his arm.

"That I've married again."

Tension filled the room as he studied her. "Married?" he echoed.

She edged toward the sofa table, her gaze searching and quickly finding a brass candlestick that she could use for a weapon if needed. "Yes, I thought you knew. I haven't seen you for a time."

"I've been away," he murmured. "London."

"Oh, you must have enjoyed England."

"It was a profitable trip," he said. Lizzy didn't care to learn about his business.

"I'm sorry, but it's best if you don't come to visit unless it's to speak to my husband—"

"And who may that be?"

"Conor McDermott."

He thought a moment; then his face reddened. "The foreman?"

"He's my husband now, Mr. Olsen." Her hands closed about solid brass. "Now, I don't mean to be rude, but I do have things to do. If you'd like I can get my husband—"

"Lizzy."

She turned with a grateful look to find Conor behind her, in the open doorway that led to the hall. Things between them had been tense since their argument two nights past. But the sight of him made her heart beat faster, for she loved him more than ever . . . despite his inability to trust her, despite the fact he had made no effort since that night to talk to her about Kathleen.

She saw him studying their guest with a narrowed gaze. "Conor," she said. "Mr. Olsen just came to pay his respects. He was in England when we married."

"Yes." Mr. Olsen stepped forward with the wooden box now in his hand. "I've brought Liz—you both a present. It's a music box."

"A music box," Conor said quietly.

The man bobbed his head. "Yes. I thought your missus would enjoy it."

Conor's gaze moved to his wife. "No doubt."

Her body warmed with heat. She turned to Olsen. "Thank you, Mr. Olsen." She accepted the wooden box, lifted the lid, and enjoyed the lively tune that played until she closed it again. She had seen only one of these before, at the Smithfields' home. *Such an expensive gift.* She felt guilty for accepting it. She thought of refusing it, but to do so would be adding insult to injury. She didn't believe he would come calling again.

"I'll take my leave now." With a nervous look at Conor, Olsen edged toward the door. "Congratulations to you, Mr. McDermott. Mrs. McDermott."

Conor stuck out his arm, making the man jump. "Olsen."

Olsen hesitated before shaking Conor's hand. The rotund little man was quick to pull away. "I'll be going now."

"Thank you again, Mr. Olsen." Noting the sweat that glistened on the man's bald head, Lizzy could almost feel sorry for him . . . until she wondered how he would have behaved if Conor hadn't arrived when he did. Olsen had been a nuisance. She was glad to see the last of him.

Conor saw their guest to the door, then returned to the parlor to find his wife clutching a candlestick. He approached her slowly and took the candlestick from her hands. "He's gone."

She nodded,

"Did he do or say anything to frighten ya?" His expression hardened. "Should I be sorry for allowing him to leave without cuffing him in the noggin first?"

She flinched at his vehemence. "No. He was surprised when he'd heard that I'd married again," she said. "But he might have been harmless." He held up the candlestick, and she gave him a lopsided smile. "I kept thinking about Thompson. I wasn't going to be taken by surprise again."

Mention of James Thompson hardened his features. "He didn't—"

"No!" she was quick to assure him. "Mr. Olsen is a different sort. He was persistent in his pursuit of me, but I think you've successfully cured him of that."

He arched an eyebrow. "Disappointed?"

His cold, mocking tone stung. "I'll leave you to your day," she said. She had to rush past him on her way out the door. Her joy in seeing him had vanished. Would they forever be cruel to each other?

She missed seeing his smile . . . missed sharing meals with him when they spoke of everyday occurrences and made each other smile.

"Lizzy." He grabbed her arm as she walked by him. She halted, went rigid. "Yes?"

"How long are we going to act like strangers to each other?"

She turned then, met his gaze. "Disappointed?" She tried to be mocking as he had been, but her response came out quietly instead. And she couldn't hide the pain, the hurt, that she was upset that things weren't right between them.

"We need to talk."

"I know," she whispered.

" 'Tis long past due."

"Yes." She found herself moving toward him, floating almost.

"Ma?"

She drew back, spied her son and little Emma behind him. "Jason!"

The boy was injured. He had a split lip and an eye that was red and quickly swelling as she watched.

"Jason fell off Star," Emma said, her eyes bright with concern.

Lizzy crouched before the young boy. "You fell off the horse?" she asked, trying not to panic.

He nodded, looking woebegone.

"How bad, Jase?" Her voice was soft.

"A little." His mouth quivered as he valiantly tried not to cry.

"Have ya broken anything, lad?" Conor knelt beside Lizzy and turned the boy for his inspection. "Yer arms . . . can ya move them?"

"Yes, sir."

"Jason, come into the kitchen," Lizzy said. "Emma, run upstairs and find my medicine bag."

"Yes, Ma."

She stood and shot Conor a worried glance. Conor nodded as he ushered the boy out of the parlor and into the kitchen, where he lifted Jason up onto the worktable.

"What were ya doing on Star?" Conor asked. Lizzy bathed the child's cut lip, then pressed a cold, wet compress to his eye.

Jason hung his head as Lizzy ruffled through her medicine bag to find the right plant for open wounds and abrasions. From the sight of his torn trousers, Lizzy suspected that the boy's knees were in need of doctoring as well.

"Jason?"

"I wanted to ride him," Jason said, his voice low.

"And how did ya get Mr. Fetts to saddle him for ya?" Conor asked. Lizzy flashed him a glance and saw the deep concern behind the anger in her husband's eyes.

"Mr. Fetts didn't saddle him," he whispered, shame-faced. "I did."

"And the cinch didn't hold, and ya slipped off yer mount."

Jason glanced up, surprised that Conor would have guessed so accurately about the details of his accident. "Yes, sir."

That the boy continued to call Conor sir was a testament to how frightened he was that he would be punished because he knew he had done wrong.

"And how is Star?"

"He's all right," Jason was quick to answer. "Honest."

"Then, 'tis a good thing for ya, young lad, for if ya'd injured the animal with yer carelessness, then ya'd be doing more than mucking out the stables and working the fields for the next two weeks straight."

Startled, Lizzy could only stare at him. "Conor—"

Conor gave her a warning look before he turned back to the boy. Lizzy relented. "Work will start day after tomorrow. Black eye or not, ye've earned the punishment, and ye'll learn from yer mistakes."

"Yes, sir."

"Ya think I'm being too hard on ya, lad?"

To Lizzy's surprise, the boy shook his head. "No, sir. Star could have been hurt; and worse yet, I could have been killed."

Lizzy shuddered at the thought.

"That's right," Conor said approvingly. He ruffled the boy's hair. "Rest up and allow yer mother to doctor ya. And mind what she tells ya to do over the next two days. After that ye're mine." When the boy assured him he would behave, Conor turned to his wife. "Later."

She nodded. She sent him a silent message of apology. She was embarrassed that she had doubted the wisdom of Conor's punishment for Jason, but she had been wrong. Conor had known the right thing to do, the right thing to say. If she could doubt him about this and be wrong, perhaps she was wrong to doubt his love for her.

"Tonight," she promised.

He flashed a genuine smile for the first time in a long while. When he left, Lizzy happily turned her attention to her patient.

"Elizabeth." Conor entered their bedchamber minutes after she had gone upstairs and undressed.

It was late. Lizzy sat in the middle of their bed, the same bed they had slept in, spaced apart, at opposite sides during the last two nights. She didn't shift to her side of the bed as she watched his approach.

One look at his face made her stomach muscles tighten. "What is it?" she said. "What's wrong?"

He held up a sheet of paper. "I found this on me desk just a few minutes ago."

Her fingers tightened on the bedcovers as she felt a sudden chill. "Another threat?"

"Aye." He sat down on the bed and set the note on the nearest night table.

"I want to read it."

"It can wait—"

"No! Please, Conor. Let me see it."

With a sigh he retrieved the parchment and handed it to her without opening it.

She unfolded the paper and quickly scanned it. She felt the blood drain from her face as her heart started to pound with fear. "Why?" She turned eyes filled with fear on her husband. "Who would do this? What do they hope to gain?"

"Excellent questions," he told her quietly as he took the paper from her trembling fingers. He set it carefully out of sight in the night table drawer.

"Any answers?"

He stood silently and stripped, then climbed into bed next to her and pulled her into his arms and against him. "Until this third note, I didn't have a clue, but now . . ."

He felt her tense within his embrace. "You know who?"

Conor stroked her arm in comfort. "Not exactly, but I have a hunch, and as soon as I know for certain, I'll let ya know."

"More secrets?" she said, sounding hurt.

"Nay, Lizzy." He reached out to cup her face, turned it up for a thorough kiss. It had been too long since they had shared physical contact of any kind, too long since that wild joining in the sitting room. This kiss was softer and tender. It enveloped Lizzy in a warm cocoon and made her lean into her husband's strength for further contact.

"No secrets. As soon as I'm sure, I'll tell ya."

"You can't give me a hint?"

"It wouldn't be fair to the suspect to give away false claims."

Lizzy pouted. "But I'm your wife."

His eyes glowed. "Aye, ya are . . . and I'd like to pleasure me wife, not talk about some deviant with her."

"Deviant?" she echoed.

"Lizzy."

She sighed. "I thought we were going to talk."

"We are."

And she was disappointed, for the way he was stroking her arm made her tingle and yearn, throb and burn.

She scrambled away from him, hoping the distance between them would clear her head, douse the flaming passion.

She was bothered by the fact that he seemed willing to release her so quickly—and after his talk of wanting to make love with her.

"I'm with child." She didn't know why she had suddenly blurted it out that way. Perhaps to gauge his reaction?

"A babe?" he said after a lengthy hesitation.

She hadn't known exactly what to expect from him, but it hadn't been this. He didn't appear to be overjoyed by the news, nor did he seem upset. He looked . . . indifferent. Or was it just that she couldn't accurately read him?

"How long?" he asked carefully. "How long have ya known?" He was still reeling from the impact of her news.

Why hadn't he guessed? She had been sick of late. It bothered him that he had been too preoccupied with his quest to find Kathleen that he had ignored all the symptoms.

A baby, he thought. Love bloomed in his heart for the unborn child, the tiny life created with the one woman who had been made especially for him.

"Three weeks," she said.

"Three weeks!" He stared at her in shock. She had known for three weeks and hadn't uttered a word. He said as much.

"You were busy . . . and there were things between us."

"Things?"

She nodded. "Things unsaid." She bit her lip, then rushed on before she lost her nerve. "Did you marry me because you learned I was a virgin? Or because you wanted me as your wife?"

Seconds of silence ticked by between them as she and Conor gazed at each other. "Ya want to know why I married ya."

"Yes," she whispered.

"And ya think I may have married ya because I took ya to bed and learned that ya were pure."

She shuddered a sigh. "Yes."

"Damn it, Lizzy! Did ya really think I'd marry ya just because I'd taken yer innocence?" Guilt gnawed at his conscience, not for his reasons for marrying her—his intentions had been pure—but for his thoughts when he had come to Milly's Station, choosing to believe the gossips rather than keeping his mind free from judgment.

She seemed startled by his vehemence. "Conor, you never said why you married me. Only that you wanted to."

"And that's not enough?"

She shrugged. "You've been so distant these last weeks, working long hours, leaving the farm to visit the Quaids. It hurt that you kept a part of yourself secret from me—"

"I didn't mean to cause ya concern," he told her.

"You didn't tell me about Kathleen."

"Kathleen?" His gaze sharpened. "Ya know about Kathleen?"

"Yes. I—" Now came the hard part when she had to confess that she had followed him to Green Lawns, where she had eavesdropped on their conversation, then fled, distressed to learn things about her husband that she should have known first.

He scooted across the bed, caught her arms, and pulled her closer. "How, Lizzy?" His quiet tone frightened her.

"I . . . I followed you."

"What!" He released her and stared at her as if he didn't care for the sight of her.

"I said I followed you. You weren't home at your usual time, and then I learned where you'd gone, and I . . . was worried."

"About what?"

She didn't immediately answer.

"Lizzy?"

"That you'd married me only because you couldn't have Kathleen."

He gave a short bark of harsh laughter. "Ya thought I wanted Kathleen and chose ya instead, for ya were the only woman who was available?"

She blushed. Put that way her reasoning sounded ridiculous. "Yes."

"And so ya followed me to see."

Tears filled her eyes. "Yes."

He shook his head as he studied her. She looked away, unable to bear his anger. His contempt.

"Lizzy."

She sniffed and made a move to climb out of bed. He caught her hand, stopping her. "No!" she cried. "Let me go!"

"Never," he vowed. He tugged her onto the bed. She tumbled onto her back, and he quickly loomed over her, pinning her to the mattress.

His eyes gleamed as he stared at her lips and pressed his naked length against her figure that was clad only in a thin cotton nightdress.

"Ye're not running from me again, wife."

TWENTY-NINE

"Conor—"

She gasped as he moved against her. He was aroused; she could feel his male heat pressing against her thigh. He cursed softly and eased up on his grip. She started to roll away, but he caught her firmly, forced her back to the bed.

"Nay, Lizzy. Ye'll listen to me and ye'll listen now." He had stretched out fully along her length and pinned her wrists to the bed near her head. "Ya think I don't want the babe?" She blinked up at him. "Well, ye're wrong, lass. I'm eager for the child. *Our* child."

She gazed up at him, disbelieving.

"Don't ya realize that I was startled when ya first told me? I've had so many things on me mind, lass. Being a father was not one of them. I was stunned to hear of it. Stunned, but pleased." His expression softened as his gaze caressed her face.

Could it be true? "Is that the truth?"

"Aye, lass." He released one hand and shifted to place his fingers over her abdomen.

"A babe," he breathed with awe. "A babe made between us. What man wouldn't be happy about it?" His features suddenly darkened as he looked away.

"Your father," she said softly.

He shuddered. " 'Tis true. Me father didn't want

me. Not me or me mother." He looked away thoughtfully. "Although, Kathleen said . . ." He stopped, and his voice trailed off as he returned to lock gazes with her. "Ya were at Green Lawns."

She blushed. "Yes. In the foyer."

"Ya heard everything?"

She shook her head. "Enough to know that Kathleen Quaid is the sister you've been searching for."

His chest heaved as he released a shuddering sigh. "Aye. She is, 'tis true."

A lump lodged in her throat. "Why didn't you tell me?"

"I didn't know—wasn't sure meself until the day when I finally confronted her." He leveled himself off her and slipped to her side. She stayed where she was, for she was interested.

"How did you come to suspect it was she?" Lizzy wanted to know everything about him . . . his past . . . his hopes . . . how finding Kathleen had affected him.

"Logan."

"Captain Logan?" Surprised, she rolled to her side, facing him.

"Aye. Ya know I've been making inquiries in Baltimore. Years before I learned the name of the ship she traveled on, and I knew she came with her cousin, Meara Dunne."

Dunne, she thought. The cousin Kathleen had pretended to be when she was left penniless and alone in a strange new world. The cousin who had refused to marry her betrothed, a man chosen for her by her family. Rian Quaid.

She studied him, conscious of the warmth of his hard male body beside her. He lay on his side, his head propped on his arm, his fingers trailing across her arm.

She shivered at his touch. "You didn't know about Rian?"

He shook his head. "The Dunne family had been burned out by the tenants. I found a former servant, who had moved in with her sister. She told me that Katie Maguire had left Ireland before the fire, gone with her cousin Meara Dunne to Maryland in America."

She gave in to the urge to reach out and run her fingers through his hair. His gaze held hers and warmed. She traced his head to his jaw and down his neck to his shoulder, then across his chest. "Katie?" she asked.

"Aye. That's what some called her. Not the Dunnes, I imagine, but the servants." He gripped her hand as she traced a male nipple. "It was the only name I knew for her until I spoke with Kathleen."

"Katie," Lizzy said, tucking her hand free to continue her exploration. "A lovely name, but I guess I'll always think of her as Kathleen."

" 'Twas me mother's name as well." His eyes closed as she dipped her hand to his stomach, where she enjoyed the flat, taut muscles and found the small indention of his navel with her fingertip. *"Lizzy— "* His look pleaded.

She sighed, but relented and removed her hand. It was true; they needed to continue the conversation before they got lost in the magic of lovemaking. She was pleased to note that he seemed disappointed until she captured his hand that lay above the sheet.

"Tell me more," she urged him.

He turned his hand palm up to lace fingers with her. "I told ya just a wee bit about me childhood."

"The tiniest wee bit," she agreed.

He offered her a smile of apology. She pulled free of his grip to tenderly caress his face. "What I didn't tell ya was that me mother's husband, Donal O'Reilly, was a drunkard. He was a cruel man under the influence, and he had a hard fist when he was angry."

She drew a sharp breath. "He hit you?" Tears stung her eyes for Conor, the young boy.

"Aye. When me mother wasn't looking. But then he raised his hand to her as well, and I wanted to kill him." His features hardened. "I'm not proud of the feeling, but I couldn't help it."

"I understand." She knew that if after she had married him John had proven to be someone other than the kind, gentle man he was, she would have felt the same. Especially if he had dared to lift a finger to Jason.

"When Donal made the ghastly mistake of informing me that I was another man's bastard, we left—me mother and me. We moved to another village where me mother took on work as a seamstress." His eyes glistened as he continued. "But it wasn't long before me mother's health began to suffer. She had worked like an animal trying to support me, and—"

She grabbed his hand in sympathy. "She loved you."

His smile was filled with pain. "Aye, that she did. Much as ya love Jason and Emma, I'm thinkin'."

Yes, she thought, *much in the same way.* "You feel guilty."

"Aye." He rolled onto his back, taking her hand with him, pulling it to rest on his chest. She felt the warmth of his muscled firmness as she watched him stare reflectively at the ceiling. His willingness to share everything made her feel closer to him.

"How can I not feel guilt when I'm the reason me father left her?" he said. "When she had to marry a man not of her choosing for companionship and support? Only, there she missed out again, for she had the misfortune of marrying Donal O'Reilly."

She nestled against him and began to stroke his chest. "It was her choice."

He shot her an angry glance. "Was it?"

She flinched until she realized that his anger was with Donal. "I know you don't want to hear this, but I think Katie did what she thought was best, not for you, but for her. Did you ever stop to think that the story about your father wasn't entirely true? Oh, not that she lied, mind you," she quickly added. "But that the way Katie saw things was not the real way it was?"

Conor's frown was thoughtful. "Kathleen hinted as much," he admitted. "She said the father she knew would never have abandoned his child."

"Perhaps Katie never told him she was expecting."

"Why wouldn't she?"

"Because maybe the relationship between them was one-sided. Maybe your mother loved more than your father." She bit her lip, afraid to ask, but she did anyway. "How did your mother meet your father?"

"At a pub, I think, where she worked."

"Where he lived?"

Conor shrugged.

"What if your father—what was his name?"

"Conlan. Conlan Maguire."

"Hmmm," Lizzy said. "Conlan is a name much like Conor, isn't it?"

He nodded. He had noticed that, too. Had he been named after his father, the man his mother should have hated but hadn't?

Perhaps Lizzy was right . . . for if Maguire had abandoned them both, wouldn't she have been bitter? Wouldn't she have drummed angry hatred into the mind of her little boy? Nay, not if she loved the child . . . *and* the child's father.

"Conor, what if your father was simply a traveler on his way to a different place?" Lizzy went on. "He stops at the pub where your mother works, has a few pints, and makes arrangements to stay the night."

She continued to caress him as she talked, her touch gentle, her voice soft. "What if your mother saw the handsome fellow who was your father and immediately became smitten with him." She raised herself up to grin at him. "If he was anything like you"—she kissed him—"then you can't find fault with your mother, Conor. I found you irresistible from the first."

A slow smile came to his lips. "Ya did?"

"Aye, Conor, me lad," she said thickly. "I did."

They kissed for a long moment, their breaths mingling, their tongues tangling as the intimacy deepened. Lizzy reluctantly broke the contact. They had much to say yet.

Conor eyed her with desire. "Ya would have lain with me if we'd met under similar circumstances?"

"Perhaps," she said. "If I didn't have Jason."

"Aye. And Katie didn't have me at the time."

"Maybe she'd hoped Conlan would fall for her as quickly as she had for him," Lizzy said. "And so she offered herself to him. To show her love."

Conor ran his fingers down his wife's arm. "And feeling mellow by the ale and her attentions, he might have taken her up on it."

"Yes." Shivering with pleasure, she laid her head on his shoulder.

"But that doesn't forgive the fact that he'd left after he'd taken her innocence."

Lizzy hesitated. "But had he?"

Conor sat up, pushing her aside. "Ya think she wasn't a maid?" His tone was sharp, his eyes hard.

"I don't know," she said, her heart pounding. She understood his anger, but it hurt nevertheless. Yet, he needed to hear it. For himself. So he could alleviate the burden of his own guilt. "It's possible, isn't it?"

"Ya worked at an inn, and yet ya were a maid."

Her mouth twisted. "I was married for almost six years, and I was still a maid. A maid with two children."

His lips twitched, and then he couldn't seem to control his grin.

"Point taken," he said, snaking his arm around her. He pulled her down with him as he lay back on the bed. "And a good one." He kissed her and began to roam his hands all over her sensitive body.

Lizzy was instantly enveloped in passionate heat.

"I'm not sorry that I was yer first and only," he admitted as he allowed her to come up for air.

"I'm not either," she murmured, her eyes gleaming. The time for talk had gone. Lizzy wanted more, and she wasn't above initiating the actions that would reel them into the passionate storm.

Their lovemaking was slow and tender, punctuated by frantic moments when they couldn't seem to get enough of each other. They reached the peak, finding their release. Then they lay in each other's arms, content and feeling closer than ever before.

"I love you," Lizzy said drowsily. She waited for a heartbeat to hear the magic words from Conor's lips.

Then she realized that her husband had fallen fast asleep. She wouldn't hear the words she desperately yearned to hear. Not tonight anyway.

Soon, she thought.

She snuggled closer to him, content for now with the progress they had made in sharing secrets. She felt a renewal of hope that their future life together would be a happy one. She sighed and relaxed against him . . . and joined her husband in sleep.

Conor slipped from bed and dressed quickly. After a tender kiss on his wife's cheek, he carefully took the note from the night table drawer and left the room. Once downstairs, he reread the note:

"Brazen Lizzy, you'll never be the true Mistress of Milly's Station."

He scowled as he reread it a second time. The author had slipped up. He—or she—had given away a clue when he—or she—had underlined one word. *Milly.*

How many people in the area had known John's first wife enough to be upset when John had taken another?

How many folks had access to this manor house? His desk?

Whoever had written the threat had known Millicent well, Conor thought. Had been devoted to her while she had been alive. Had been angered when Lizzy, a usurper, had come into the manor and dared to become its new mistress.

Who? How did the note get on his desk? The fact that he had found it there terrified him, for it meant that the person had access to their home . . . to Lizzy and the children.

Last night, it had been late when he had found the note, too late to ask Jamieson if the manservant knew of its existence or how it might have found its way to his desk top.

He headed toward the back of the house, where he crossed the kitchen to the door to Jamieson's room. He raised his hand to knock, rapping the wood twice in quick succession. Within minutes, Jamieson opened the door.

"Master Conor!" The old man blinked as he stepped from his room and shut the door behind him. "Is something amiss?

"Have ya seen this, Jamieson?" Conor held up the piece of parchment.

"A letter, sir?" he asked. "No, I can't say I've seen it before."

"Never?" Conor studied the man intently, trying to find anything in the servant's face that would tell him that Jamieson was lying.

"No, Master Conor. Is it something I should have seen?" Jamieson seemed genuinely puzzled.

"Someone's been sending nasty notes to Mrs. McDermott."

"No, sir! Surely it isn't possible. Missus is a kind and generous lady. Who would do such a thing?"

Conor sighed. "I was hoping ya could tell me."

"Sir, you didn't think that I—" He looked shocked. And hurt.

"Nay, Jamieson. Not really, but I had to ask. I found this one in the house. I was naturally upset when I discovered it."

"Naturally, sir."

Conor went to the kitchen table, and the manservant

followed him. "Do ya have any idea who might hate the missus enough to threaten her?"

"No, sir. No one. The only one who never cared much for the missus was Mrs. Potts. I wouldn't think it'd be her, but . . ."

He nodded. "Who has access to this house and me study?"

"Why, myself, sir. And the other servants—Ruth and Margaret . . ." Jamieson named a few others, none of them whom Conor would consider real suspects.

"Can ya think of anyone who was close to Mr. and Mrs. Foley? And I don't mean me wife. I mean the first Mrs. Foley. Millicent."

"She was well liked," Jamieson said. "But then so is your wife, sir."

"What about Mrs. Potts?"

The man bobbed his head. "Yes, Mistress Millicent was a favorite of Mrs. Potts."

"Has Mrs. Potts been around here lately?"

"Not that I've seen. But you might want to check with the chambermaids, Ruth and Margaret. They'd tell you if they saw her. They didn't like her, you see. If she was anywhere near here, they would know and make sure that Mistress Lizzy knew, too."

"I'll do that, Jamieson," Conor said. "Thank ya."

The man hesitated before leaving. "Is the missus in danger, sir?"

"Aye, I believe so."

The old man's mouth firmed. He remained very loyal to the master and mistress of Milly's Station. "I'll inquire of others within the area, sir."

"Thank ya, Jamieson. That would be of great help to me."

"We'll find the culprit, sir."

"Aye. I'm betting on it."

THIRTY

The peaches were ready on the trees in the orchard. Lizzy dressed that morning with the intention of harvesting the fruit. She was looking forward to the morning's task.

If my husband and Jamieson will allow me to leave the house, she thought with wry humor.

Since that third and last note, she had been literally a prisoner of the manor. Each time she had wanted to step out to work in her flower or vegetable garden, someone had to go with her. If it wasn't Jamieson, it was Conor, or young Michael Storm.

Three days had passed since Conor had discovered the missive on his desk—a fact that disturbed her. It meant that someone who disliked her intensely had access to her home. They were watchful, waiting, but nothing else had happened since that night. There had been no other threats, no notes of any kind. Life had been quiet.

The children had been kept inside as well, until yesterday, when Conor had relented, for Emma and Jason were too full of energy to remain indoors.

"Can't I go out to the stables?" Jason had asked Conor the previous morning.

"I think 'tis best if ya remain inside today."

"But why? It's a nice day. The sun is shining, and it's too hot in the playroom."

"May I see Meg?" Emma had asked after offering her own claim of discontent. "Jason won't play with me and Lily. Meg does."

"Of course, I don't like to play with dolls, Emma," Jason grumbled. "Dolls are for girls." He turned his bright eyes on Conor. "Please, Father."

Calling him Father had done it for Conor. That the boy had accepted him so easily in his life had astonished Conor and moved him beyond words. "Ya must stay near Mr. Fetts, ya hear?"

Jason grew excited. "Yes, Da."

Da. Oh, the boy knew how to get to him, Conor thought, hiding a smile. "Let me talk with Fetts first. To make certain he won't mind ya tagging along behind him."

"You didn't mind me tagging along," Jason reminded him.

"Aye, 'tis true. But then, ye've earned a special place in me heart from the first."

The boy smiled.

"Now, don't ya be thinking ye'll always get yer way," Conor warned.

Jason's smile became a grin. "I wouldn't think of it, Da."

Conor found another way to appease Emma. He invited little Meg to join Emma inside, promising the child that her friend could spend the night.

As Emma beamed at the big Irishman Lizzy had married, Lizzy couldn't help smiling. Conor certainly knew how to handle the children.

She cupped her hand over her belly. He would know how to handle this little one as well, she thought. And she looked forward with pleasure to the time when she could hold Conor's son or daughter.

Lizzy was still waiting for that declaration of love from Conor. She knew he cared for her, but she wanted to hear the words. Still, she would have patience. Where before it was his sister who preoccupied his mind, now it was the recent threat and his concern for her. She knew he would tell her when he was ready . . . and she would be waiting to hear it with tears in her eyes.

"What do ya think ye're doing?" Conor's voice made her turn in the act of dressing.

"I'm going to pick peaches."

"Oh, no, I want ya to stay in the house."

She shook her head. "I'll not allow this person who threatened me to keep me inside and afraid."

"Well, I'm afraid, Lizzy," he said, surprising her. He came to her and caressed her cheek. "Don't ya know how much ya mean to me?"

Now, she thought. *Tell me. Tell me you love me.* "Yes."

His fingers dipped down to her throat where he ran his knuckles along the column from chin to base and back.

"Then, ye'll stay inside because I asked it."

She was disappointed. He had been so close. Would he never say the words?

"I want to pick peaches."

"We've workers for picking peaches."

"It's a glorious August day," she insisted. "I want to pick them myself."

"Lizzy—"

"Please, Conor." She captured his hand, brought it to her lips. Holding his gaze, she kissed each fingertip, one by one.

He groaned. "Ya don't play fair, wife."

"I'm tired of being inside, Conor. I want to step outside and enjoy the air—and not from the open window of our bedchamber." Her husband had been leery of allowing open windows on the first floor ever since he had realized that someone had gotten into his study.

"I don't know—"

"What if I ask Michael to accompany me?"

"Young Michael Storm?"

"Yes. He'll come if I ask."

Conor narrowed his gaze. "No doubt." He caught her hand, held it firmly. "Michael is a comely lad."

Lizzy wrinkled her nose at him. "True," she said saucily. "But he's not as comely or as manly as you."

The sound of her husband's delighted laughter made her grin. She knew she was getting close to having her own way this day. . . .

"May I?"

"I'll accompany ya meself."

She was hoping for such an offer, but she wouldn't let him see. "You will?"

"Aye."

She launched herself into his arms and began to rain kisses over his face. "You're the most wonderful husband. The best lover. The most handsome man!" She continued to praise him between kisses.

"I think I'm looking forward to picking peaches," he said with grin.

Lizzy sighed. She was, too.

The day was glorious. As she plucked another fruit from the tree, Lizzy enjoyed the scent of ripe peaches and being out-of-doors. Conor was nearby, picking fruit and placing them carefully into a bushel basket.

"I think I'll make some peach cobbler for dinner," Lizzy said.

Conor beamed at her. "With sweet cream."

"No other way to eat it."

"I'd like to taste a bit of ya," he said.

She flushed with heat as she quickly looked around. "Conor, please, someone may hear you!"

"No one here but the birds and the wind," he said. He grabbed a piece of fruit and sank his teeth into it. Lizzy watched as he chewed and swallowed, the juice dribbling from his chin.

A mischievous twinkle came to his eyes as he approached. "Wanna bite?"

She shook her head, eyeing the fruit warily as he extended it toward her mouth. He was up to something, she thought with a pleasure tickle, but what, she didn't know. "I'll wait to have one later."

"Aw, come, lass. Just one bite." Suddenly he shoved the fruit against her mouth, smearing her with juice and bits of fresh peach.

She shrieked and shoved him away, laughing as she wiped the juice from her chin and licked the trickle near her mouth.

Lizzy saw his intent and backed away from him, giggling, her hands outstretched to ward off his attack. "No, Conor!"

"Just one bite," he hissed, waving the fruit as he stalked her.

"I'm not hungry."

"Just one taste, then." He paused, wriggled his eyebrows. "Just one lick."

"No." She giggled. "I don't want any. Please, go back to picking peaches. You want cobbler, don't you?"

He froze, and his face looked so comical that she couldn't stop laughing. "Ya'd deny a man his lifeblood?" He put his arm to his head in a dramatic gesture.

"Peach cobbler?" she gasped as she inched back. "Since when is your blood orange?"

"Yellow." He grinned. "A nice peachy yellow."

She screamed and ran as he began to chase her. "Stop! Conor! Stop!"

"I'll get ya me pretty one!"

"No!" she cried as he caught her about the waist and lifted her off the ground. He held her suspended, with her legs dangling and her hair loosened about her shoulders. "Put me down!"

"Only if ye'll taste a bite of me peach. A big bite," he added.

"I will."

"Say it."

"It."

He growled as he shook her.

"All right! I'll take a big bite."

"That's a lass." He lowered her to the ground, allowing her to slide against him. As her toes touched soil, he kissed her, and she was suspended in a different way . . . as desire took hold and lifted her up high.

A loud clearing of someone's throat drew Lizzy's attention. Conor released her, and Lizzy stepped back, embarrassed to have been caught in her husband's arms.

"Ruth!" she said.

The chambermaid appeared troubled. "Missus."

"What's wrong?" She approached the girl.

"There's something Margaret has to say."

"Margaret?" Lizzy frowned. "Where is she?"

"Over here, missus." The girl appeared from her hiding place behind a peach tree.

Lizzy flushed. How long had the girls been there? How much had they seen? "Margaret?" She felt Conor advance from behind her. He touched her arm.

"Margaret," he said, his eyes searching. "What have ya got to say?" He paused. "Is it about the letter?"

She stared at him uneasily. "Yes."

"Is it, Margaret?" Lizzy said with excitement. "You know who put it on Mr. Conor's desk?"

"Yes, missus."

"Who?" Conor demanded.

"I did!" She shrank back with terror.

"You!" Lizzy gasped.

Conor released his wife as he approached the chambermaid. "Who asked ya to place the note, Margaret?" She looked frightened. Conor gentled his tone. "Someone did ask ya to do this?"

"Yes."

"Who?"

The girl sniffed. "I didn't know I was doing something wrong. When she asked me, I thought it was the right thing to do."

"Who is she?"

"My mum."

Conor went rigid. "Yer mother told ya to threaten me wife?"

"No!" the girl cried. "My mum told me to deliver the note. I searched for you and the missus. When I couldn't find you, I put it on your desk." Her eyes filled with tears as she rushed on, "I didn't want to do it! But then Mum assured me that it was only well wishes for your marriage. She said Mrs. Potts told her so herself. She didn't tell me it was from Mrs. Potts until recently. Mrs. Potts was away when you wed, so I didn't think anything of it until Ruth said—"

"Mrs. Potts," Lizzy interrupted.

"Yes, missus."

"Do ya know of the other notes?" Conor demanded. "The rock through the window? The wood on the doorstep? Didn't ya think it strange that Mrs. Potts didn't bring her note herself?"

"She told my mum that she'd left with bad feelings between her and the missus. She said she wanted to make amends." The maid hugged herself with her arms. "I don't know nothing about no wood. Nothing about no rock!"

Ruth stepped forward then. "I saw Bernard Beaker in the yard a while back. I didn't think of it much, for it seemed that he'd just come to visit the men, before he took his leave. He could have left the wood . . ."

Lizzy frowned. Bernard Beaker was a disrespectful worker she had had to dismiss after John's death.

"And the rock tossed through the window?" she asked.

"Probably the same man," Conor said grimly. "But I'll find out."

"Missus?" the maids said jointly. Ruth and Margaret looked as if they expected to be dismissed from their positions.

Lizzy smiled. "Thank you for coming to us with this."

"You're not angry?"

Conor opened his mouth to speak, but Lizzy placed her hand on his arm to stop him. "Not with you," she said. "You've given us the first bit of knowledge in stopping this person."

"I'm sorry I didn't come to you sooner," Margaret said. "But I didn't know it was wrong until today when Jamieson told Ruth that you were looking to find the one who'd delivered it."

After they had assured the girls that their positions were secure, Conor and Lizzy were left alone.

"Do you think that Mrs. Potts means me harm?"

Conor scowled. "If she doesn't, she still intended for ya to fret over her message. Why else would she send such words without a signature?"

"What are we going to do?"

"Ye're going to go inside and make that peach cobbler," he said. "I'm going to find Mrs. Potts and this Beaker fellow and issue a bit of a threat of me own. When I'm done with them both, they'll be mad to consider bothering the woman I love again."

"Conor?" Had he just said he loved her?

His eyes were black with fury. "Get to the house, Lizzy." She wasn't afraid of him. It was Mrs. Potts and Bernard Beaker who had reason to fear him.

She obeyed her husband, for it was the only thing to do now. She could talk with him later, when she would make him repeat and clarify his last words about love.

Lizzy felt her heart soar with happiness. Had he actually said that he loved her?

She grinned. It wasn't a declaration of love, but it was close. Later, she would demand more. She would hear those three important words from his lips, even if she had to wring them from him during the throes of passion. But she would prefer to hear them when he was stone-cold sober.

She returned to the house and with Ruth and Margaret's help began to peel away soft, fuzzy peach skins in readiness to make cobbler.

As she worked, it occurred to her that in confronting Beaker, Conor might be facing someone dangerous. She dropped the knife and froze.

"Missus?" Ruth asked with concern. "You've cut yourself."

Lizzy glanced down and saw blood seeping from a small wound. "It's nothing," she said. She wiped the blood away and went back to work.

How could she be concerned about a little nick on the finger when Conor could be facing a much greater evil?

THIRTY-ONE

The cottage was nestled in the woods, not far from the Sassafras River. Conor learned of its existence from Margaret's mother, Mrs. Rhodes, who had appeared genuinely horrified to learn that Mrs. Potts had lied to her.

"She lives with her sister in the woods near the Joneses' place," the woman had told him.

Conor had been reluctant to go at first, for it would mean that Lizzy and the children would be left alone. But Lizzy had assured him that she had enough servants about her if Bernard Beaker came calling. She could call on Mr. Fetts, Mr. Pherson, Mr. Brant, and Mr. Markins as well.

And so he had decided to go, after speaking with Pherson. The man was grateful to Lizzy and Conor for their understanding about the birth of his last child, and he was a trustworthy fellow. When Conor had asked him to keep an eye on the house, Pherson had been eager to do so.

"Sure, Conor," he had said. "I'd be glad to keep an eye on the missus. If Bernard Beaker steps foot on Milly's Station, I'll know it." He had been shocked and disturbed to learn about the threats. "Give Mrs. Potts a piece of my mind when you see her."

"I will."

As he approached the log house nestled amid some pines, he searched the yard and then the windows for any sign of life. He could smell smoke. He looked up and saw a bit of it swirling up from the chimney. The residents were at home. He only hoped that Mrs. Potts was among them.

As he entered the small clearing, he frightened a flock of chickens from the side of the house. He stiffened when they squawked and carried on, and wondered if a certain someone would note his presence and bolt the door when she recognized who had come.

But when the door remained shut as he came close, he realized that the chickens' noisiness must be a recurring thing.

He rapped on wood twice. Moments later, the door opened. "Mrs. Potts."

The woman looked stunned to see him. "Mr. McDermott."

"I want a word with ya." He stuck out his arm when she attempted to close the door. *"Now."*

She appeared frightened as she relented and allowed him to come in. He checked his surroundings quickly, glad to see that the woman was alone. Her sister and any other family must be out visiting.

"Mr. McDermott, this is hardly appropriate for you to be here."

Conor dug the note out of his trousers' pocket. "I believe this is yers?"

When the woman saw it, she blanched. "I—"

"Ye've got some explaining to do."

She raised her chin as she glared at him. "I've a right to my opinion."

"And I've a right to take ya down to the authorities for threatening me wife."

"Threatening her!" she gasped. "I didn't threaten your wife. I simply gave her a piece of my mind!"

"And this?" Studying her, he drew out the other note with his left hand. "What of this one?"

She shook her head. "I know nothing of that message on cloth, sir. My only missive was that one." She pointed toward the one in his right hand.

"Why should I believe ya?"

She sniffed. "Because I'm a lady—"

Conor's mocking laughter split the air. "Ye're no lady, Mrs. Potts. Now I just have to assure meself that ye're no liar either." He scowled at her as he pointed to a chair. "Sit down, woman."

"Well?" Lizzy eyed her husband's grim countenance, and her stomach started to burn. "Did you find Mrs. Potts?"

"Aye," he said harshly.

"And did she send the note as Margaret said?"

"Aye, she did. But she told me she had no knowledge of the others." His lips firmed. "I'd like to think that she was lying about it, but for some reason, I'm inclined to believe her."

"You do?"

"Aye." He sighed as he pulled the cloth out of his pocket and set it on the kitchen table. "She admitted to sending this." He withdrew the folded paper. "Said 'twas not a threat but an opinion of ya."

Lizzy's face warmed with anger. "Her opinion of me," she said.

Conor looked at his wife and grinned. "Ya look like I felt when she was so bold as to tell me so." He slipped his arm about her, hugged her to his side. "We've got the first culprit, Lizzy lass." His eyes darkened as he released her and touched her cheek. "Now all we have to do is find Bernard Beaker."

Lizzy nodded. "I spoke with Mr. Brant this afternoon." Conor had been gone for hours, and she had been worried. "He said that Beaker often frequents the Rooster and Crow."

A gleam entered his blue gaze, and a slow smile

came to his sensual male lips. "The Rooster and Crow."

"Yes." She caught his hand, squeezed it. "You'll take someone with you?"

"I can handle the man meself—"

"I know," she said softly. "But you'll take someone with you. For me? You know I'll be beside myself with worry if you don't."

His features softened. "Aye for ya, I will."

"Take Mr. Pherson and Mr. Markins." She mentioned two men who were loyal to her and Conor, and who, she thought, would be good and strong in a fight. "And not the Pherson boy, but his father, Henry."

"Two of them!" he said, his eyes widening. She saw a protest forming on his lips.

"Please." She pulled him close, captured his head so she could whisper, "For me." Then she kissed his ear.

"That's the second time ya haven't played a fair game, lass."

"This is no game, husband," she said.

Conor had to agree. "I'll take Pherson and Markins."

After Conor and his men's departure, Lizzy went about her day as if nothing unusual was happening. But, although her outward appearance was calm, inside she was a bundle of nerves. The Rooster and Crow was a tavern near Chestertown, and for all she knew Bernard Beaker could have set up an ambush. The man could have friends, a lot of them, and they could be lying in wait for Conor.

With her maids' help, she tackled the downstairs rooms first. Starting in the kitchen, she then cleaned her way into the dining room and parlor before moving to complete the rest of the lower level. By the time she reached her husband's study, it was evening. She had dismissed the maids for the day, prepared to do this last chamber herself.

As she entered the room, she felt a fluttering beneath her breast. Conor's scent was in the air, male and pleasant. She glanced at his desk, half expecting to see him seated there. But the chair was empty. He was gone, gone to Chestertown, and he wouldn't be back until tomorrow at the earliest.

Her heart fluttered. If nothing happened to him and he came back at all.

Her fingers tightened about her dust cloth as her fears returned to worry her. What if he was harmed? What if Beaker was so full of revenge that he had felt impelled to hurt, or murder, the one man who had given her life new meaning.

She loved her children, and she would protect them with her life; but Conor was there, and she was here. And she couldn't protect him. Couldn't offer her life in exchange for his.

Sweet Lord in heaven, please keep Conor safe.

She could not live without Conor, not live life as anything other than a shell of her present self. He had given her pleasure—taught her what it felt like to be really happy—and now that she had realized that he loved her, she couldn't lose him.

Keep busy, she told herself. Supper was finished, and the dishes had been cleaned and put away. The children were in bed. The house was quiet. Too quiet. The silence made her yearn for the sound of Conor's lilting Irish voice . . . long to hear the deep, husky blend of his words with laughter.

Lizzy decided to start with dusting the bookshelves. There were rows above rows of books: novels, poetry books, farm books, and others.

She pulled over a chair and started on the top shelf. The first book was particularly dusty, and she blew off a thick layer before she wiped it carefully with the cloth. She replaced the tome, then took out another, moving down the shelf to clean each one. She took down the family Bible, a book she had never looked through before, because she knew how the family record entries would read. They would list Millicent Rose Keller Foley as wife next to John Jacob Foley, husband. There would be no mention of Elizabeth Hanlin Foley, as second wife, for it wouldn't be something John would do. Not when he and she had never truly been man and wife in the marriage bed.

She dusted the edges of the book. The Bible, she noted, was the Masonic version. John had been a member of the lodge in Kent County, so seeing the Masonic name and emblem on the spine was no surprise to her. John had been Methodist, and Lizzy had accompanied him to church until she had realized that she was the object of contempt for all eyes. Then she had pleaded with John to let her stay home, and he had relented when he had seen her tears.

The book warmed in her hands as she held it. She knew she shouldn't look at the listing, for she would just experience hurt if she checked to see whether or not her name was included. Then she thought of Emma, and curiosity got the better of her.

Had John included his child out of wedlock, the daughter whom he had loved?

She climbed down from her perch, sat on the chair, and flipped open the Bible. She fanned through the pages until her attention was caught by a small slip of paper tucked inside.

Near the record of John's family, she realized. She picked out the paper, and her eyes scanned the open pages. She saw John's name and Millicent's, as she had expected. Her breath caught with surprise. There was hers . . . with *wife* next to it in John's bold script.

He had entered her name! She stared at it in shock. They had been friends, and had shared affection, but since they had never really—

She bit her lip. They had never consummated their

marriage, but yet John had still considered her his wife enough to record her name in the family Bible.

Tears filled her eyes as she studied the page, for there was another line, another space for Lizzy's husband. For Conor. John had drawn an extra line, as if he had known that his time with her would be short, and she would find another to wed . . . the husband of her heart.

"Oh, John . . . you sweet man."

With trembling hands, she put down the Bible and picked up the paper that had been inside it. She unfolded the sheet and began to read. And her tears fell in earnest.

My dear Beth,

I want you to know that I am healthy and alive as I write this . . . no sad or tearful confession, I make. But rather a clear avowal of my feelings while I am still young enough not to be considered feeble, yet old enough to have known the pleasures that life has brought me.

You are one of these pleasures in my life, Beth. You are by far the greatest, far surpassing all that I have known before. You have been a wonderful wife and a wonderfully caring mother to our Jason and Emma.

Lizzy began to sob as she continued to read.

I had expectations of our marriage, but you, my dear Beth, have far exceeded them. You've been a delight and a treasure, and I am a better man for having married you. . . .

As for our marriage . . . Remember the night you came to me so sweetly? It seemed that I rejected you—but know now that the hardest thing for me to do then was to send you away, to remind you of our agreement. I wanted you. Oh, how I wanted you. But, dear Beth, I'm an old man, and you deserve better.

You deserve the best of husbands, someone who can give you the pleasure meant for a beloved wife. I doubt my ability there, beloved. For although I love you with all of my heart, I'm not a young man anymore. I am less than you should have in the marriage bed . . . and I wanted you to save your sweetness for the one who will follow me—the man—the only man you will truly love. . . .

If you are reading this now, then I probably have departed from this solid earth. Know that I am happy. Rest easy in the knowledge that you were a wife whose offer hadn't been cast aside, but a woman so cherished by her husband that he—this old man—wanted only the best for you.

Take care of my Emma and my Jason. And please, dear Beth, take care of yourself . . . for I love you. And I always have. And I'm afraid I was selfish enough to convince you to wed me without true consideration of how much our marriage would hurt you.

Don't cry, my love. Smile, for you were loved once and will be again . . . for no man could do less than love you once he learns of your sweetness . . . for you are like the sun and the moon and the stars. . . .

> *Your loving and old husband,*
> *John Jacob Foley*

P.S. Check the fourth row of the second bookcase. There you'll find another account book. There should be enough money in the bank to see you and Jason and Emma well for a long time.

Lizzy was sobbing loudly as she finished the note. Dear John! He had loved her and sacrificed everything for her. And she hadn't realized it.

Crying, she folded the piece of paper. She picked up the Bible, opened it, and slipped the paper in the place where she had found it.

"Brazen Lizzy Hanlin." The gruff male voice came from behind her.

Startled, Lizzy spun and dropped the book.

THIRTY-TWO

"Elijah Jones," she breathed. It was the sweaty, malodorous patron who had frequented the Bread and Barrel, where she had once worked, and who had always given her a hard time.

"In the flesh. We finally meet again, and it's about time, too." The man's grin was wicked. "Ya got my messages."

She nodded. "What are you doing here?" But she thought she knew. And the knowledge frightened her. It hadn't been Bernard Beaker who had sent those notes; it had been this man.

He came into the room, looking calm. He approached the desk, rather than where she stood near the bookshelf.

Even so, he was only a few feet away, Lizzy thought. "What do you want with me, Mr. Jones?"

"So polite, Miss Lizzy. Always the lady." He scowled as he propped himself on the edge of Conor's desk. "Ya could never fool me, bitch. Ya thought ya were something, even got John Foley to marry ya; but ye're nothing but a scheming trollop, and now I've come to collect a piece of ya. The same thing ya gave to John Foley and now this field hand, McDermott."

She froze, except for her heart, which was thundering so loudly that she was afraid he could hear it. And it wouldn't do for him to see her fear. "How did you know about my husband?"

"Which one?" he snarled. "The rich one or the Irish bastard?"

Anger brought the blood to her cheeks. "John is dead," she said. "Conor McDermott is my husband, and I don't like you calling him 'bastard.' "

He laughed. "I'll call him what I like. Just as I'll call ya what I like." He pushed himself off the desk, and Lizzy eyed the door, wondering if she could make good her escape before he caught her. She judged the distance between her and the door, and her and him, and she realized that she would never make it . . . unless she found a way to render him senseless first.

Her gaze scanned the room, even as she inched back along the bookcase in the opposite direction of Jones.

"I still don't know why you've come. Why me? Why have you chosen to threaten me? Threaten my family?"

"Because ya denied me," he said. "All those years ago, ya denied me and when I was being so sweet to ya."

"Sweet!" she exclaimed. "The only thing sweet about you is the air I breathe when I'm far away from you!"

He made a sound of anger as he stalked her. She continued to back away, wondering if he would catch her before she could find something to hit him with, wondering if she could scream loud enough to alert anyone inside the house.

But not the children, she prayed. *Don't let it be the children.*

"Perhaps we can discuss this over tea," she suggested, grasping at something. Anything to throw the man off balance.

"Tea!" His laughter was a horrible sound. Just as the air in the room was sick with the stench of his sweat and the cheap ale he had no doubt drank before coming.

"Then, a glass of whiskey perhaps?" she said.

His eyes gleamed. "The good stuff?"

She nodded, pretending to be insulted. "Of course. Would John Foley buy another kind?"

He gave her a nod of assent, then gestured toward the door. "Find it. And be aware that I'll be behind ya, following ya every step of the way . . ."

She bobbed her head and eased slowly toward the doorway, not wanting to make any sudden moves that would endanger her chance for escape. She made it into the hall, conscious of him right behind her. The odor of him was so vile that she was afraid she would have to vomit.

"Where is it?" he asked harshly.

"In the sideboard. In the dining room."

"Go ahead, then. And move carefully."

Again, she nodded. She tread down the hall toward the dining room, touching her belly as she did so, praying that she would get out of this with herself alive and her unborn baby unharmed.

Oh, Conor. Come home quickly. Bernard didn't do it. This man did. . . .

"What?" He grabbed her arm, frightening her, making her cry out. "What did ya say?"

"Nothing!" She started to shake her head, but he grabbed her hair and pulled.

"Bitch!"

"Please. I'm only trying to get you whiskey," she reminded him. *Don't cry. Don't panic. Don't faint, or he'll take advantage and have his way with you.*

He released her enough so that she could inch slowly across the floor, for he kept a grip on her hair. If she tried to escape or hurry in any way, the tug to her head would make her scalp burn.

She paused outside the dining room and raised a pointing arm. "In there," she said. "The whiskey is in there."

And so were her good silver candlesticks. And silverware, including forks and knives.

As he shoved her aside, she wondered how she could get to any of them and whether or not she could successfully defend herself against him.

"Get it," he ordered.

She went to the sideboard, opened a door, and pulled out a bottle of fine Irish whiskey given to Conor from Rian Quaid. She had never even had a chance to talk to Kathleen about the discovered fact that they were sisters by marriage.

She took out a glass next.

"Now pour it."

She did so and extended it to him. The man stared at the amber-tinted liquid.

"Drink it," he commanded.

She gasped. "I don't think—"

"Drink it!"

She placed the glass to her lips and sipped.

Jones grinned. "All of it—and quickly!"

She took the rest of the liquor in one swallow, then proceeded to choke and cough as the fiery liquid burned a path down her throat to her belly.

"Now pour me a glass."

She was still gasping as she reached into the sideboard compartment for a second glass.

"No, don't bother with another glass," Jones said. "Use the same one."

She stared at him a moment, feeling slightly light-headed. Not from the whiskey, she thought, but from her difficulty to breathe. She would pour it into the same glass, but she would be damned if she would take another sip after he had drunk from it.

She tipped out his whiskey, then gave him the glass.

Elijah Jones tilted back his head and took in the fiery liquid in one quick gulp. When he was done, he held out the empty glass to her. "More."

"I don't think—"

"More!"

She obeyed, and was grateful when he took the

filled glass and drank it himself. Maybe if she got him so intoxicated that he couldn't see . . . Maybe then she could get free.

She held up the bottle to pour him another. She didn't know if he saw something in her gaze that gave away her thoughts, but suddenly, he slammed the glass down on the tabletop and reached out, grabbing her, so that she shrieked and dropped the whiskey bottle.

Then he was kissing her mouth hotly, and she was fighting to be free.

"No!" The bellow came before Lizzy was knocked to the ground. She blinked when Jones's weight didn't immediately press her down, and saw that Conor had returned and he was dragging Jones by the throat through the dining room doorway. She scrambled to her feet and followed in time to see Conor jerk Jones out the front door.

"Vermin!" Conor shouted as he threw the man into the dirt yard. "Stand up and fight like a man, so I can beat the living crap out of ya!"

Lizzy had never seen her husband this enraged. She watched without interfering as Jones crawled to his feet.

"McDermott!" he spat.

"Come and get me—"

"Jones. Elijah Jones. Remember that name. It's the last one ye'll hear before ya die."

In full moonlight, Conor and Jones began to circle like two wary combatants, ready to claim a life.

Jones threw the first punch, but Conor quickly reciprocated. The two men tussled to the ground, pummeling each other with their fists, rolling across grass and dry dirt.

The noise drove Mr. Fetts from his room in the barn; he carried an oil lamp so he could see. Michael Storm, who had moved into Conor's old room above the stables, came outdoors shortly afterward. Lizzy saw both men and was relieved to see that help would be there for Conor should he need it.

But Conor didn't need it, she realized. He was doing a good and thorough job of beating Elijah Jones to a pulp, until Mr. Fetts caught his arm and stopped the fight. Jones, with his face and head bloody, lay on the ground, unconscious.

"Conor—you've won, son," Fetts said quietly, when Conor turned to him. The glow from the lamp showed the fierce light of battle still gleamed in Conor's eyes.

Conor's face began to clear. "Lizzy?" he rasped.

"Here," she said. She hurried to his side to hug him. Closing his eyes, he held her while the others stood by—all but Jones—including the servants who had exited the house, having heard the disturbance.

"Are ya well, lass?" Conor whispered.

Lizzy bobbed her head against his shoulder. "I'm fine."

She shivered as she thought what might have happened if Conor hadn't again arrived in time to rescue her. "I was scared."

"And so ya should have been."

She pulled back to gaze up at him, saw his bruised and battered face, and cried out as she reached up to tenderly trace an open wound on the right side of his face.

He winced, and she quickly drew her fingers away.

He caught her hand and held it to his mouth instead. His swollen and cut mouth.

She began to cry. Conor held and rocked her until her tears subsided.

"What shall we do with him?" Michael asked.

Irish blue eyes flashed with the light of murder. "Tie him up. Lock him in the tack room until the authorities come for him."

Michael nodded, and then with Fetts and Jamieson's help, he tied up Jones and then lifted to carry him across the yard to the barn.

After sending the others to bed, Conor took his tearful wife back inside the house. He brought her to his study, where he sat in his desk chair with her across his lap.

He held her quietly while she recovered from her tears. Then he reached into a desk drawer and drew out the same bottle of whiskey he had brought out when Logan had come to him with news of the *Mistress Kate*. He put it back that day without sampling it, and he had hadn't touched it since. But he thought he deserved a good belt, now that it was over and he had found the man who had meant to harm his wife.

Holding Lizzy with one arm, he used his other hand to uncork the whiskey. He started to reach into the drawer for a glass, then changed his mind and took a swig directly from the bottle.

He grimaced as the substance burned past sore lips. Then he sighed as the whiskey traveled down his throat to warm his belly. He went to set the bottle down when he lifted it for another taste instead. Lizzy shifted in his arms, making it impossible for him to drink, so he put the bottle down. He cupped her face when she lifted her chin to gaze up at him.

"Conor," she whispered. She looked as if she would cry again.

"Don't," he said. He couldn't bear it when she cried. He blamed himself for her fright. He should have been home with Lizzy. He should have sent someone else to find Beaker and—

His face burned as he remembered how he had punched the man before Beaker had so much as turned around to see who had come to speak with him. When he had learned his mistake, his quick, violent act hadn't set well with him.

Satisfaction had only come later when he had plowed his fist into Jones's face, felt the crunch as his knuckles connected with tissue and bone.

"Conor," she said. Tears filled her eyes again as she

touched his face. "You're hurt." She started to get up. "Let me doctor it for you."

"No, stay where ya are. It can wait." His throat clogged with emotion. He could have lost this woman tonight. He could have lost everything that had meaning in his life. "But this can't . . ."

She looked at him, settling back against him, obviously happy to obey.

He kissed her. "Lizzy, I love ya."

"Conor?" she gasped, her eyes filling.

"Now, don't ya be crying, or ye'll have me doing the same."

She blinked up at him, trying valiantly to fight the urge to cry. "You said it," she said in a voice that quavered. "You told me you loved me."

He frowned. "Of course I love you."

"But you said it!" she breathed. Joy glistened in her beautiful brown eyes. "You said it."

"Lizzy—"

"Say it again. *Please.* I've longed to heard those words from you."

"I've said it before—"

She placed her finger to his lips. "No. You haven't."

"Ah, Lizzy . . . lass, I'm sorry. I've said it so often in me thoughts that I was sure I'd said it to ya as well."

He closed his eyes as he kissed her forehead. "Lizzy . . ."

"I love you, Conor."

He shuddered, moved by her words. "I know."

"I'll always love you."

He pulled back, smiling into her eyes. "And I'll always love ya, wife."

She grinned and snuggled into his arms again, burrowing into his warmth, inhaling his scent. She was glad to be home in her husband's arms, where she belonged.

"What's this?"

Suddenly, she felt Conor stiffen. She pulled back

frowning and saw the direction of his gaze. She stared at the Bible where she had dropped it on the floor when Jones had surprised her earlier that night. The Bible and John's note.

"It's John's Bible. I found it today when I was cleaning."

Her throat tightened as she climbed out of Conor's lap and went to retrieve the book. She returned to her husband's lap.

She felt Conor's blue gaze on her as she flipped open the book, pulled out the folded paper, and handed it to him.

"We weren't the only ones with secrets," she said. Tears spilled over to trail her cheeks as she recalled John's words to her.

With a frown, Conor took the note, unfolded it, and began to read.

When he was done, he looked at her, and she was surprised to see tears in her husband's blue eyes as well.

"And we're not the only ones who've loved," he said.

EPILOGUE

Summer 1859, Milly's Station

The day was warm, and the McDermott family was outside in the yard with their good friends Rian and Kathleen Quaid and the Quaid children: Fiona, Conlan, and young Frederick. It was a perfect day for a barbecue. Earlier that morning, in the wee hours, Conor had put a pig to roasting, and the two families with their hired help had plans to share the meal out-of-doors.

The McDermott children were there as well. Jason and Emma sat on the porch next to their parents while the younger siblings—Shannon, Nicholas, Alexander, and Joshua—were playing a game of croquet with Conlan Quaid.

Little Frederick Quaid was too young to be off and running about the yard, so he sat on his mother's lap, sucking on his thumb. Holding him, Kathleen watched her other son as he shared laughter and gasped with outrage when Nicholas and Alexander McDermott cheated for the win.

Jason got up from his chair and went down onto the grass yard. Still seated beside their mother, Emma followed him with her eyes.

"Jason enjoys the younger ones," Kathleen commented with a smile as she watched the lad lift Alexander, then Joshua, and twirl each of them in turn.

"He'll make some young woman a fine husband," Lizzy said. Beside her, Emma couldn't take her eyes off Jason, and she caught Emma's blush as she continued to watch Jason from beneath lowered eyelashes.

Lizzy pretended that she hadn't noticed Emma's interest as she reached for her husband's hand across the distance between their chairs.

"The children have grown up so quickly," she said.

Conor, whose sharp gaze followed Jason's every move, nodded. "Aye, Jason is a man already. Soon, he'll be leaving us."

And she could tell how much it bothered him to lose the son he adored, the young boy who had worked his way into Conor's heart at the tender age of eleven.

Jason had been a big help with the horses on the farm, and now his expertise had landed him a position in the military.

Neither she nor Conor could bear the thought that their son—Lizzy's little brother actually—might someday find himself in the midst of a battleground. Lizzy prayed every day that Jason would remain safe, that he would never have to witness the fighting.

"Emma will be following close behind," Rian said suddenly. "Soon, she'll be of an age to marry." He smiled as the young woman met his glance. "And such a lovely woman to capture and break young men's hearts."

"Only one man," she said softly. "Only one broken heart." And in a quiet voice heard only by her mother, "Mine."

A bird twittered from a nearby branch. The wind ruffled the tops of the trees, and a bee droned in flight as it hovered about a honeysuckle blossom.

Lizzy sniffed the fresh air and detected the scent of well-cooked pork. Her gaze met Conor's.

"Meat's done," they said in unison. Then, they laughed together.

Still smiling, Lizzy rose. "I'll bring out the plates and silverware."

Emma jumped up behind her. "I'll carry out the food."

"I'll help." Kathleen started to shift baby Frederick to her husband's lap.

"No, Kathleen. Stay," Lizzy said. "If we need help, I'll call Shannon to assist us."

Kathleen had just recuperated from the fever. Her family and friends had been frightened until they had finally learned that she was on the mend.

"Fred looks too comfortable in his mama's lap," Lizzy said. "I'd hate for you to disturb him."

Kathleen smiled as she brushed the hair off her baby's forehead. "All right."

Rian stood, then leaned down to kiss his wife. "Before I help Conor, I'll tell Fiona to head to the kitchen," he told her.

Fiona had wandered down the porch only moments before to watch Jason as he finished with Alexander and Nicholas and to join in the game of croquet.

Later, after the Quaids had left for home and the rest of the family had retired for the night, Conor entered their bedchamber and caught Lizzy in the act of undressing.

"Ye're a fine sight for this man's tired eyes," he said as he approached.

"Conor!" she gasped. "I didn't hear you come in."

She didn't bother to cover her nakedness, for he had seen her many times during their ten years of marriage.

And he would enjoy catching her this way, he thought, for the next fifty years or longer. She was still firm lines and soft, feminine curves, with a body to make a man burn.

He felt himself harden as he gazed at her and

crossed the room. As the blood pumped through his system, he no longer felt in the least bit tired.

She dropped her night garment and met him halfway across the floor. She raised herself for his kiss.

The kiss was hot and passionate. Conor's hand found his wife's buttocks. He pulled her close until his hard sex nestled between her soft thighs and she whimpered . . . the soft, sexual sound that drove him wild whenever he heard it.

He set her down, releasing her, and she swayed on her feet. "Ya haven't changed, Lizzy. Not one bit in ten years."

Her smile was wry. "I've had four children, Conor."

"Ya haven't changed, Lizzy," he insisted, his eyes glowing. "Ye'll never change, for ye'll always be mine. Me Lizzy . . . me lass . . . me wife."

His expression was bright as he touched her hair. His gaze followed the path of his hand as it traced the length of the long golden strands, past her neck, her shoulders, down her back, and up front across her breasts.

"Gold silk," he murmured, bringing a lock of it to his nose and lips. "I love ya, Lizzy. I'll always love ya."

Lizzy's eyes filled with tears. "I love you, Conor McDermott," she whispered brokenly. "And I'll never tire of hearing ya tell it to me."

ABOUT THE AUTHOR

Candace McCarthy lives in Delaware with her husband Kevin of twenty-seven years and has a grown married son. She has written sixteen books for Kensington Publishing. Her works include FIREHEART, IRISH LINEN, and HEAVEN'S FIRE, and the tales of two sisters—SWEET POSSESSION and WILD INNOCENCE. And, of course, there is the book that preceded this one—IRISH LACE.

Candace has won numerous awards for her work. She was extremely pleased to have received the National Readers' Choice Award for her book WHITE BEAR'S WOMAN. She loves to read and garden, and she enjoys music and doing crafts. It was her enjoyment of romance novels that prompted her to first put pen to paper. IRISH ROGUE is her eighteenth book.

You may write to her at P.O. Box 58, Magnolia, Delaware 19962. Candace enjoys hearing from her readers. Check out her web site at:

http://www.candacemccarthy.com